SHARPE'S RIFLES

BERNARD CORNWELL was born in London and raised in Essex, and now lives mainly in the USA, with his wife. In addition to the hugely successful Sharpe novels, Bernard Cornwell is the author of the highly praised Starbuck Chronicles, the acclaimed Warlord trilogy, and the recent bestsellers *Harlequin* and *Gallows Thief*.

For more information, visit:
www.bernardcornwell.net

D1335116

BERNARD CORNWELL

Sharpe's Rifles

Richard Sharpe and the
French Invasion of Galicia,
January 1809

HarperCollins*Publishers*

This edition produced for The Book People Ltd,
Hall Wood Avenue, Haydock, St Helens. WA11 9UL

HarperCollins*Publishers*
77–85 Fulham Palace Road,
Hammersmith, London W6 8JB

www.harpercollins.co.uk

This paperback edition 1994
1

Previously published in paperback by Fontana 1989
Reprinted five times

First published in Great Britain by
Collins 1988

Copyright © Riflemans Productions Ltd 1988

ISBN-13: 978-0-00-787074-5

Set in Postscript Linotype Baskerville

Typeset by Rowland Phototypesetting Ltd,
Bury St Edmunds, Suffolk

Printed in Great Britain by
Clays Ltd, St Ives plc

For Carolyn Ryan

FOREWORD

This was the first 'prequel' I wrote for the Sharpe series, something I had sworn not to do. My original intention was to let the stories run smoothly (for me, if not for Sharpe) from the battle of Talavera in 1809 to Waterloo in 1815. But then, in 1987, some splendid television producers wondered whether I could not provide them with a new story with which to begin *their* series. This was not quite as quixotic a request as I thought, for it turned out that one of the investors in the television series was a Spanish company and the producers, quite rightly, wanted a story in which a Spaniard played a prominent part. Their request was also a reproof to me, for the Sharpe novels tend to give the impression that the French were defeated in Spain solely by the British army, but that army, while its achievements were magnificent, could never have won without the aid of Spanish and Portuguese forces and, of course, the guerrillas.

So, duly reproved, I buckled down to it and wrote *Sharpe's Rifles*, which became the first of Carlton Television's programmes. The story is set in 1809, a few months before *Sharpe's Eagle*, at a time when British fortunes in the Peninsula were at their lowest. A small expeditionary army had been sent to Spain under the command of Sir John Moore who attempted to sever the French supply lines. The French, initially led by

Napoleon himself, turned on him in fury and Moore, vastly outnumbered, was forced to retreat through the Galician mountains. That was the famous, or infamous, retreat to Corunna, a three-week march through mountainous country in ghastly weather. Many units lost cohesion, but somehow the half-starved, half-frozen rearguard protected the army until it reached the port of Corunna where, to give his men time to embark on the ships that would take them safe home to England, Moore offered battle. The battle was won, but at the cost of Moore's own life, and so the army, after a terrible ordeal, was saved.

I was sorely tempted to let Sharpe retreat with Moore all the way to Corunna, for it is a dramatic passage of military history, but that would have dictated that, after the battle, he must have taken ship to England and made it most unlikely that he could have returned to the Peninsula in time to play his part in the battle of Talavera. So instead of fighting at Corunna Sharpe joined the smaller number of British soldiers who split off from the main retreat and withdrew into Portugal. In truth Sharpe gets lost during Moore's retreat, and he stays lost for the rest of the war because he never does rejoin his beloved 95th Rifles. This is a pity, for a fine series of novels could be written about the exploits of a rifle company in Wellington's wars, but if I had attached Sharpe to a genuine unit like the 95th then I would have been limited to describing only those actions in which the 95th fought. The Rifles were not at Talavera, and I wanted him there, and so I attached him to a fictional redcoat regiment. This was a most unlikely circumstance; indeed I doubt it ever happened, but poor Sharpe is doomed to the whims of his creator and, to give him the flexibility to be at every possible siege and battle, it was necessary to make him a loose cannon. It is in this book that he breaks free.

This is also the book in which Sharpe meets the man destined to be his closest friend: Patrick Harper. Some readers have been tempted to see a symmetry in their names which can be conflated as Sharper, but that was never my intention. I named Sharpe after the English rugby player, Richard Sharp, and Harper was given the name and characteristics of a friend of mine from Belfast. He is a good man to have at one's side in a fight, as Sharpe is about to discover.

PROLOGUE

The prize was a strongbox.

A Spanish Major was struggling to save the box, while a chasseur Colonel of Napoleon's Imperial Guard had been ordered to capture it. The Frenchman had been unleashed to the task; told that he could destroy or kill whatever or whoever tried to obstruct him.

The strongbox itself was a chest made of a wood so old that it appeared as black and shiny as coal. The wood was bound with two iron bands that, though pitted with ancient rust, were still strong. The old chest was two feet long, eighteen inches wide, and as many inches high. It was locked with two hasps that were fastened with brass padlocks. The joint between the humped lid and the chest was sealed with red seals, some of them so old that they were now little more than wisps of wax imbedded in the grain of the ancient wood. An oilcloth had been sewn around the strong box to protect it from the weather, or rather to protect the fate of Spain that lay hidden inside.

On the second day of 1809 the chasseur Colonel almost captured the strongbox. He had been given a Regiment of French Dragoons and those horsemen caught up with the Spaniards close to the city of Leon. The Spaniards only escaped by climbing into the high mountains where they were forced to abandon their horses, for no horse could climb the steep, ice-slicked tracks where Major Blas Vivar sought refuge.

It was winter, the worst winter in Spanish memory, and the very worst time to be in the northern Spanish mountains, but the French had given Major Vivar no choice. Napoleon's armies had taken Madrid in December, and Blas Vivar had fled with the strongbox just one hour before the enemy horsemen had entered the capital. He had ridden with one hundred and ten Cazadores; the mounted 'hunters' who carried a straight-bladed sword and a short-barrelled carbine. But the hunters had become the hunted as, in a nightmare journey across Spain, Vivar had twisted and turned to avoid his French pursuers. He had hoped to find safety in General Romana's northern army, but, only two days before the Dragoons forced them into the hills, Romana was defeated. Vivar was alone now, stranded in the mountains, with just ninety of his men left. The others had died.

They had died for the strongbox which the survivors carried through a frozen countryside. Snow thickened in the passes. When there was a thaw it only came in the form of rain; a pelting, relentless rain that turned the mountain paths into mud which froze hard in the long nights. Frostbite decimated the Cazadores. In the worst of the cold the survivors sheltered in caves or in high deserted farmsteads.

On one such day, when the wind drove a bitter snow-fall from the west, Vivar's men hunched in the miserable shelter of a narrow gully high on a mountain's crest. Blas Vivar himself lay at the gully's rim and stared into the valley through a long-barrelled telescope. He stared at the enemy.

Brown cloaks hid the pale green coats of the French Dragoons. These Frenchmen had followed Vivar every

12

mile of his bitter journey but, while he struggled in the highlands, they rode in the valleys where there were roads, bridges, and shelter. On some days the weather would stop the French and Vivar would dare to hope that he had lost them, but whenever the snow eased for a few hours, the dreaded shapes would always appear again. Now, lying in the shivering wind, Vivar could see the enemy horsemen unsaddling in a small village that lay in the valley's bottom. The French would have fires and food in the village, their horses would have shelter and hay, while his men sobbed because of the cold which lashed the mountainside.

'Are they there?' Vivar's second in command, Lieutenant Davila, climbed up from the gully.

'They're there.'

'The chasseur?'

'Yes.' Vivar was staring directly at two horsemen in the village street. One was the chasseur Colonel of the Imperial Guard, gaudy in his scarlet pelisse, dark green overalls and colback, a round hat made of thick black fur.

The other wore no uniform; instead he was dressed in a black, tight-waisted riding coat above white boots. Vivar feared the black-coated horseman more than he feared the chasseur, for it was he who guided the Dragoons' pursuit. The black-coated man knew where Blas Vivar was heading, he knew where he could be stopped, and he knew the power of the object that was hidden in the ironbound box.

Lieutenant Davila crouched in the snow next to Vivar. Neither man looked like a soldier any more. They were swathed in cloaks made from common sacking. Their faces, boots, and hands were wrapped in rags. Yet, beneath their makeshift cloaks they wore the scarlet uniforms of a Cazador elite company, and they were

13

each as hard and efficient as any man who struggled in the French wars.

Davila borrowed Vivar's glass and stared into the valley. Driven snow blurred the view, but he could see the splash of the scarlet pelisse hanging from the chasseur's right shoulder. 'Why doesn't he wear a cloak?' he grumbled.

'He's showing how tough he is,' Vivar said curtly.

Davila shifted the glass to see yet more Dragoons coming to the village. Some of the Frenchmen led limping horses. All carried swords and carbines. 'I thought we'd lost them,' he said sadly.

'We'll only lose them when we bury the last one.' Vivar slid down from the skyline. He had a face hardened by sun and wind, a pugnacious face, but saved from coarseness by the dark eyes that could spark with humour and understanding. Now, watching his men shiver in the narrow gully, those eyes were rimmed with red. 'How much food is left?'

'Enough for two days.'

'If I did not know better,' Vivar's voice was scarcely audible above the wind's noise, 'I would think God had abandoned Spain.'

Lieutenant Davila said nothing. A gust of wind snatched snow from the crest and whirled it in a glittering billow above their heads. The French, he thought bitterly, would be stealing food, firewood, and women in the valley. Children would be screaming. The men in the village would be tortured to reveal whether or not they had seen a tattered band of Cazadores carrying a strongbox. They would truthfully deny any such sighting, but the French would kill them just the same and the man in the black coat and white boots would watch without a flicker of emotion crossing his face. Davila closed his eyes. He had not known what it was to hate

14

until this war had begun, and now he did not know if he would ever root the hate out of his soul.

'We'll separate,' Vivar said suddenly.

'Don Blas?' Davila, his thoughts elsewhere, had misheard.

'I shall take the strongbox and eighty men,' Vivar spoke slowly, 'and you will wait here with the other men. When we're gone, and when the French are gone, you will go south. You will not move until you are sure the valley is empty. That chasseur is clever, and he may already have guessed what I am thinking. So wait, Diego! Wait till you are certain, then wait another day. Do you understand?'

'I understand.'

Vivar, despite his agonizing tiredness and the cold that leached into his very bones, found some enthusiasm to invest his words with hope. 'Go to Orense, Diego, and see if there are any of our men left. Tell them I need them! Tell them I need horses and men. Take those men and horses to Santiago, and if I'm not there, ride east till you find me.'

Davila nodded. There was an obvious question to ask, but he could not bring himself to speak.

Vivar understood anyway. 'If the French have captured the strongbox,' he said bleakly, 'then you will know. They will trumpet their capture across Spain, Diego, and you will know because the war will be lost.'

Davila shivered beneath his ragged cloaks. 'If you go west, Don Blas, you may find the British?'

Vivar spat to show his opinion of the British army.

'They would help you?' Davila insisted.

'Would you trust the English with what is in the strongbox?'

Davila considered his answer, then shrugged. 'No.'

Vivar eased himself to the crest once more and stared

down at the village. 'Perhaps those devils will meet the British. Then one pack of barbarians can kill the other.' He shuddered with the cold. 'If I had enough men, Diego, I would fill hell with the souls of those Frenchmen. But I do not have the men. So fetch them for me!'

'I will try, Don Blas.' It was as much of a promise as Davila dared offer, for no Spaniard could feel hopeful in these early days of 1809. The Spanish King was a prisoner in France, and the brother of the French Emperor had been enthroned in Madrid. The armies of Spain, which had shown such fine defiance the previous year, had been crushed by Napoleon, and the British army, sent to help them, was being chased ignominiously towards the sea. All that was left to Spain were fragments of its broken armies, the defiance of its proud people, and the strongbox.

The next morning, Vivar's men carried the strongbox to the west. Lieutenant Davila watched as the French Dragoons saddled their horses and abandoned a village that had been plundered and from which the smoke rose into a cold sky. The Dragoons might not know where Blas Vivar was, but the man in the black coat and white boots knew precisely where the Major was going, and so the French forced their horses to the west. Davila waited a full day; then, in a downpour of rain that turned the snow to slush and the paths to thick mud, he went south.

The hunters and the hunted were moving again, inching their intricate paths across a wintry land, and the hunted were seeking the miracle that might yet save Spain and snatch a glorious victory from defeat.

CHAPTER 1

More than a hundred men were abandoned in the village. There was nothing to be done for them. They were drunk. A score of women stayed with them. They were drunk too.

Not just drunk, but insensible. The men had broken into a tavern's storeroom and found great barrels of last year's vintage with which they had diluted their misery. Now, in a bleak dawn, they lay about the village like the victims of a plague.

The drunks were redcoats. They had joined the British army because of crime or desperation, and because the army gave them a third of a pint of rum a day. Last night they had found heaven in a miserable tavern in a miserable Spanish town on a miserable flint road that led to the sea. They had got drunk, so now they would be left to the mercy of the French.

A tall Lieutenant in the green jacket of the 95th Rifles moved among the bodies which lay in the stable yard of the plundered tavern. His interest was not in the stupefied drunks, but in some wooden crates that had been jettisoned from an ox-drawn waggon to make space for wounded and frost-bitten men. The crates, like so much else that the army was now too weak to carry, would have been left for the pursuing French, except that the Lieutenant had discovered that they contained rifle ammunition. He was rescuing it. He had already filled the packs and pouches of his Battalion with as many of the precious cartridges as the Riflemen could carry; now he and one Rifleman crammed yet more into the panniers of the Battalion's last mule.

Rifleman Cooper finished the job then stared at the remaining crates. 'What do we do with them, sir?'

'Burn it all.'

'Bloody hell!' Cooper gave a brief laugh, then gestured at the drunks in the yard. 'You'll bleedin' kill 'em!'

'If we don't, the French will.' The Lieutenant had a slash of a scar on his left cheek that gave him a broodingly savage face. 'You want the French to start killing us with our own gunpowder?'

Cooper did not much care what the French did. At this moment he cared about a drunken girl who lay in the yard's corner. 'Pity to kill her, sir. She's a nice little thing.'

'Leave her for the French.'

Cooper stooped to pull open the girl's bodice to reveal her breasts. She stirred in the cold air, but did not waken. Her hair was stained with vomit, her dress with wine, yet she was a pretty girl. She was perhaps fifteen or sixteen years old, she had married a soldier and followed him to the wars. Now she was drunk and the French would have her. 'Wake up!' he said.

'Leave her!' All the same the Lieutenant could not resist crossing the yard to look down at the girl's nakedness. 'Stupid bitch,' he said sourly.

A Major appeared in the yard's entrance. 'Quartermaster?'

The Lieutenant turned. 'Sir?'

The Major had a small wiry moustache and a malevolent expression. 'When you've finished undressing women, Quartermaster, perhaps you'd be good enough to join the rest of us?'

'I was going to burn these crates first, sir.'

'Bugger the crates, Quartermaster. Just hurry up!'

'Yes, sir.'

'Unless you'd prefer to stay here? I doubt the army would miss you?'

The Lieutenant did not reply. Six months ago, when he had joined this Battalion, no officer would have spoken thus in front of the men, but the retreat had jaded tempers and brought hidden antagonisms to the surface. Men who would normally have treated each other with wary respect or even a forced cordiality, now snapped like rabid dogs. And Major Warren Dunnett hated the Quartermaster. It was a livid, irrational and consuming hatred, and the Quartermaster's annoying response was to ignore it. That, and his air of competence, could provoke Major Dunnett into a livid anger. 'Who in Christ's holy name does he think he is?' he exploded to Captain Murray outside the tavern. 'Does he think the whole bloody army will wait for him?'

'He's just doing his job, isn't he?' John Murray was a mild and fair man.

'He's not doing his job. He's gaping at some whore's tits.' Dunnett spat. 'I didn't bloody want him in this Battalion, and I still don't bloody want him in the Battalion. The Colonel only took him as a favour to Willie Lawford. What the hell is this bloody army coming to? He's a jumped-up sergeant, Johnny! He isn't even a real officer! And in the Rifles, too!'

Murray suspected that Dunnett was jealous of the Quartermaster. It was a rare thing for a man to join Britain's army as a private soldier and to rise into the officers' mess. The Quartermaster had done that. He had carried a musket in the red-coated ranks, become a Sergeant, then, as a reward for an act of suicidal

19

bravery on a battlefield, he had been made into an officer. The other officers were wary of the new Lieutenant's past, fearing that his competence in battle would show up their own inexperience. They need not have worried, for the Colonel had kept the new Lieutenant from the battle-line by making him into the Battalion's Quartermaster; an appointment based on the principle that any man who had served in the ranks and as a Sergeant would know every trick of the Quartermaster's criminal trade.

Abandoning both the drunks and the remaining ammunition to the French, the Quartermaster emerged from the tavern yard. It began to rain; a sleet-cold rain that spat from the east onto the three hundred Riflemen who waited in the village street. These Riflemen were the army's rearguard; a rearguard dressed in rags like a mockery of soldiers, or like some monstrous army of beggars. Men and officers alike were draped and bundled in whatever scraps of cloth they had begged or stolen on the march, the soles of their boots held in place by knotted twine. Their unshaven faces were wrapped with filthy scarves against the bitter wind. Their eyes were red-rimmed and vacant, their cheeks were sunken, and their eyebrows whitened by frost. Some men had lost their shakos and wore peasant hats with floppy brims. They looked a beaten, ragtag unit, but they were still Riflemen and every Baker rifle had an oiled lock and, gripped in its doghead, a sharp-edged flint.

Major Dunnett, who commanded this half Battalion, marched them westwards. They had been marching since Christmas Eve, and now it was a week into January. Always west away from the victorious French whose overwhelming numbers were swamping Spain, and every day of the march was a torture of cold and hunger and pain. In some Battalions all discipline had disappeared and the paths of such units were littered with the bodies of men who had given up hope. Some of the dead were women; the wives who had been permitted to travel with the army to Spain. Others were children. The survivors were now so hardened to horror that they could trudge past the frozen body of a child and feel nothing.

Yet if the army had been broken on the rack of ice-storms and a frozen wind that cut like a chasseur's sabre, there were still some men who marched in good formation and who, when ordered, turned to keep the French pursuit at bay. Those were the hard men, the good men; the Guards and the Light Infantry, the elite of Sir John Moore's army that had marched into the centre of Spain to cut off Napoleon's supply roads. They had marched expecting victory, but the Emperor had turned on them with a savage speed and over-whelming numbers, so now this small British army retreated towards the ships that would take them home.

Dunnett's three hundred Riflemen seemed alone in a frozen wilderness. Somewhere ahead of them was the bulk of the retreating army, and somewhere behind were the pursuing French, but the Riflemen's world was the pack of the man in front, the sleet, their tiredness, and the pain of bellies cramped by hunger.

An hour from the village they reached a stream crossed by a stone bridge. British cavalry waited there with news that some artillery was floundering on a slope two miles ahead. The cavalry's commander suggested that Dunnett's Rifles wait by the bridge. 'Give us time to help the gunners to the ridge, then we'll come back for you.'

'How long?' Dunnett asked testily.

'An hour? No longer.'

The Riflemen waited. They had done this a score of

times in the last two weeks, and doubtless they would do it a score of times again. They were the sting in the army's tail. If they were lucky this day no Frenchman would bother them, but the probability was that, sometime in the next hour, the enemy vanguard would appear. That vanguard would be cavalry on tired horses. The French would make a token attack, the Riflemen would fire a couple of volleys; then, because neither side had an advantage, the French would let the greenjackets trudge on. It was soldiering; boring, cold, dispiriting, and one or two Riflemen and one or two Frenchmen would die because of it.

The Riflemen formed in companies to bar the road west of the bridge. They shivered and stared east. Sergeants paced behind their ranks. The officers, all of whom had lost their horses to the cold, stood in front of their companies. No one spoke. Perhaps some of the men dreamed of the Navy's ships that were supposed to be waiting for them at the end of this long road, but more likely their thoughts were of nothing but cold and hunger.

The Lieutenant who had been made into the Battalion's Quartermaster wandered aimlessly onto the stone bridge and stared into the stinging sleet. He was now the closest man to the enemy, twenty paces ahead of the greenjacketed line, and that piqued Major Warren Dunnett who saw an unspoken arrogance in the Lieutenant's chosen position. 'Bugger him.' Dunnett crossed to Captain Murray's side.

'He's harmless.' Murray spoke with his customary mildness.

'He's a jumped-up bloody nothing.'

Murray smiled. 'He's a damned efficient Quartermaster, Warren. When did your men last have so much ammunition?'

22

'His job is to arrange my bed for tonight, not loiter here in the hope of proving how well he can fight. Look at him!' Dunnett, like a man with an itching sore that he could not stop scratching, stared at the Quartermaster. 'He thinks he's still in the ranks, doesn't he? Once a peasant, always one, that's what I say. Why's he carrying a rifle?'

'I really couldn't say.'

The rifle was the Quartermaster's eccentricity, and an unfitting one, for a Quartermaster needed lists and ink and quills and tally-sticks, not a weapon. He needed to be able to forage for food or ferret out shelters in apparently overcrowded billets. He needed a nose to smell out rotten beef, scales to weigh ration flour, and stubbornness to resist the depredations of other Quartermasters. He did not need weapons, yet the new Lieutenant always carried a rifle as well as his regulation sabre. The two weapons seemed to be a statement of intent; that he wanted to fight rather than be a Quartermaster, yet to most of the greenjackets the weapons were a rather pathetic pretension carried by a man who, whatever his past, was now nothing more than an ageing Lieutenant.

Dunnett stamped his cold feet on the road. 'I'll send the flank companies back first, Johnny. You can cover.'

'Yes, sir. Do we wait for our horse?'

'Bugger the cavalry.' Dunnett offered the infantry-man's automatic scorn of the mounted arm. 'I'm waiting five more minutes. It can't take this long to clear some bloody guns off the road. Do you see anything, Quartermaster?' The question was asked mockingly.

'No, sir.' The Lieutenant took off his shako and pushed a hand through hair that was long, black, and made greasy by days of campaigning. His greatcoat hung open and he wore neither scarf nor gloves. Either he could not afford them, or else he was boasting that he was too tough to need such comforts. That arrogance made Dunnett wish that the new Lieutenant, so eager for a fight, would be cut down by the enemy horsemen.

Except there were no enemy horsemen in sight. Perhaps the rain and the wind and the God-damned bloody cold had driven the French to shelter in the last village. Or perhaps the drunken women had proved too irresistible a lure. Whichever it was, there were no Frenchmen in sight, just sleet and low clouds driven to turmoil by a freshening wind.

Major Dunnett swore nervously. The four companies seemed alone in a wilderness of rain and frost, four companies of forgotten soldiers in a lost war, and Dunnett made up his mind that he could wait no longer. 'We're going.'

Whistles blew. The two flank companies turned and, like the walking dead, shambled up the road. The two centre companies stayed at the bridge under Captain Murray's command. In five minutes or so, when the flank companies had stopped to provide cover, it would be Murray's turn to withdraw.

The Riflemen liked Captain John Murray. He was a proper gentleman, they said, and it was a fly bastard who could fool him; but if you were straight with him, then the Captain would treat you fair. Murray had a thin and humorous face, quick to smile and swift with a jest. It was because of officers like him that these Riflemen could still shoulder arms and march with an echo of the *élan* they had learned on the parade ground at Shorncliffe.

'Sir!' It was the Quartermaster who still stood on the bridge and drew Murray's attention to the east where a figure moved in the sleet. 'One of ours,' he called after a moment.

The single figure, staggering and weaving, was a red-coat. He had no musket, no shako, nor boots. His naked feet left bloodstains on the road's flint bed.

'That'll learn him,' Captain Murray said. 'You see, lads, the perils of drink?'

It was not much of a joke, merely the imitation of a preacher who had once lectured the Battalion against the evils of liquor, but it made the Riflemen smile. Their lips might be cracked and bloody with the cold, but a smile was still better than despair.

The redcoat, one of the drunks abandoned in the last village, seemed to flap a feeble hand towards the rearguard. Some instinct had awoken and driven him onto the road and kept him travelling westwards towards safety. He stumbled past the flensed and frozen carcass of a horse, then tried to run.

''Ware cavalry!' the new Lieutenant shouted.

'Rifles,' Captain Murray called, 'present!'

Rags were snatched from rifle locks. Men's hands, though numb with the cold, moved quickly.

Because, in the white mist of sleet and ice, there were other shapes. Horsemen.

The shapes were grotesque apparitions in the grey rain. Dark shapes. Scabbards, cloaks, plumes and car-bine holsters made the ragged outlines of French cavalry. Dragoons.

'Steady, lads, steady!' Captain Murray's voice was calm. The new Lieutenant had gone to the company's left flank where his mule was hobbled.

The redcoat twisted off the road, jumped a frozen ditch, then screamed like a pig in a slaughteryard. A Dragoon had caught the man, and the long straight sword sliced down to open his face from brow to chin. Blood speckled the frosted earth. Another horseman, riding from the other flank, hissed his steel blade to

25

cut into the fugitive's scalp. The drunken redcoat fell
to his knees, crying, and the Dragoons rode over him
and spurred towards the two companies which barred
the road. The small stream would be no obstacle to
their charge.

'*Serrez! Serrez!*' The French word of command came
clear to the Riflemen. It meant 'close up!' The Dragoons bunched, booted knee to booted knee, and the
new Lieutenant had time to see the odd pigtails which
framed their faces before Captain Murray shouted the
order to fire.

Perhaps eighty of the rifles fired. The rest were too
damp, but eighty bullets, at less than a hundred yards,
shattered the single squadron into a maelstrom of
floundering horses, falling men, and panic. The scream
of a dying horse flayed the cold day.

'Reload!'

Sergeant Williams was on the right flank of Murray's
company. He seized one of the damp rifles which had
not fired, scooped the wet sludge from its pan, and
loaded it with dry powder from his horn. 'Pick your
targets! Fire as you will!'

The new Lieutenant peered through the dirty grey
smoke to find an enemy officer. He saw a horseman
shouting at the broken cavalry. He aimed, and the rifle
bruised his shoulder as he fired. He thought he saw
the Frenchman fall, but could not be sure. A riderless
horse galloped away from the road with blood dripping
from its saddle-cloth.

More rifles fired. Their flames spat two feet clear of
the muzzles. The French had scattered, using the sleet
as a screen to blur the Riflemen's aim. Their first
charge, designed only to discover what quality of rearguard faced them, had failed, and now they were content to harass the greenjackets from a distance.

The two companies that had retreated westwards under Dunnett had formed now. A whistle blew, telling Murray that he could safely fall back. The French beyond the bridge opened a ragged and inaccurate fire with their short-barrelled carbines. They fired from the saddle, making it even less likely that their bullets would find a mark.

'Retire!' Murray shouted.

A few rifles spat a last time, then the men turned and scrambled up the road. They forgot their hunger and desperate tiredness; fear gave them speed, and they ran towards the two formed companies who could hold another French charge at bay. For the next few minutes it would be a cat and mouse game between tired cavalry and cold Riflemen, until either the French abandoned the effort, or British cavalry arrived to drive the enemy away.

Rifleman Cooper cut the hobble of the Quartermaster's mule and dragged the recalcitrant beast up the road. Murray gave the mule a cut on its backside with his heavy sword, making it leap forward. 'Why don't you let it go?' he shouted at the Lieutenant.

'Because I damn well need it.' The Lieutenant ordered Cooper to take the mule off the road and up the northern hillside to clear the field of fire for Dunnett's two companies. The greenjackets were trained to the skirmish line, to the loose chain of men who took shelter and sniped at the enemy, but on this retreat the men in green formed ranks as tight as the redcoats and used their rifles for volley fire.

'Form! Form!' Sergeant Williams was shouting at Murray's company. The French advanced gingerly to the bridge. There were perhaps a hundred of them, a vanguard mounted on horses that looked desperately tired and weak. No horse should have been campaigning in this weather and on these bitter mountain roads, but the Emperor had launched these Frenchmen to finish off the British army and so the horses would be whipped to death if that meant victory. Their hooves were wrapped in rags to give purchase on slippery roads.

'Rifles! Fix swords!' Dunnett shouted. The long sword-bayonets were tugged from scabbards and clipped onto the muzzles of the loaded rifles. The command was probably unnecessary. The French did not look as though they would try another charge, but fixed swords was the rule for when facing cavalry, so Dunnett ordered it.

The Lieutenant loaded his rifle. Captain Murray wiped moisture from the blade of his Heavy Cavalry sword which, like the Lieutenant's rifle, was an eccentricity. Rifle officers were expected to wear a light curved sabre, but Murray preferred the straight-bladed trooper's sword that could crush a man's skull with its weight alone.

The enemy Dragoons dismounted. They left their horses al the bridge and formed a skirmish line that spread either side of the road. 'They don't want to play,' Murray said chidingly, then he twisted round in hope of a glimpse of the British cavalry. There was none.

'Fall back by companies!' Major Dunnett shouted. 'Johnny! Take your two back!'

'Fifty paces, go!' Murray's two companies, accompanied by the Quartermaster and his mule, stumbled back the fifty yards and formed a new line across the road. 'Front rank kneel!' Murray shouted.

'We're always running away.' The speaker was Rifleman Harper. He was a huge man, an Irish giant in a small-statured army, and a troublemaker. He had a broad, flat face with sandy eyebrows that now were whitened by frozen sleet. 'Why don't we go down there and choke the bastards to death. They must have bloody food in those bloody packs.' He twisted round to stare westwards. 'And where the hell's our bloody cavalry?'

'Shut up! Face front!' It was the Quartermaster who snapped the order.

Harper gave him a lingering look, full of insolence and disdain, then turned back to watch Major Dunnett's companies withdraw. The Dragoons were dull shapes in the middle distance. Sometimes a carbine fired and the wind snatched at a smear of grey smoke. A greenjacket was hit in the leg and swore at the enemy.

The new Lieutenant guessed it was now about two hours before midday. This fighting retreat should be over by early afternoon, after which he would have to hurry ahead to find some cattleshed or church where the men could spend the night. He hoped a commissary officer would appear with a sack of flour that, mixed with water and roasted over a fire of cowdung, would have to suffice as supper and breakfast. With luck a dead horse would provide meat. In the morning, the men would wake with stomach cramps. They would again form ranks; they would march, then they would turn to fight of these same Dragoons.

Dragoons who now seemed happy to let the Riflemen slip away. 'They're not very eager today,' the Lieutenant grumbled.

'They're dreaming of home,' Murray said wistfully. 'Of chicken and garlic in a pot, good red wine, and a plump girl in bed. Who wants to die in a miserable place like this if that's waiting for you?'

'We'll retire by column of half companies!' Dunnett, convinced that the enemy would not risk closing the gap, planned to turn his back on them and simply march away. 'Captain Murray? Your men first, if you please.'

But before Murray could give an order, the new Lieutenant's voice called in urgent warning, ''Ware cavalry behind!'

'They're ours, you fool!' Dunnett's distaste for the Quartermaster could not be disguised.

'Oh, Christ!' Murray had turned to look up the road along which the four companies must retreat. 'Rear rank! About turn! Major Dunnett! They're crapauds!'

God alone knew how, but a new enemy had appeared behind. There was no time to wonder where they had come from, only to turn and face the three fresh squadrons of Dragoons. The French cavalry rode with open cloaks which revealed their pink-faced green coats. They carried drawn swords. They were led, curiously, by a chasseur; an officer in the red coat, scarlet pelisse and black fur hat of the Emperor's Imperial Guard. Alongside him, mounted on a big roan, was an equally strange figure; a man dressed in a black riding coat and boots that were gleaming white.

Dunnett gaped at the new enemy. Riflemen frantically reloaded empty weapons. The Quartermaster knelt, braced his rifle by looping its sling about his left elbow, and fired at the chasseur.

He missed. Rifleman Harper jeered.

A trumpet sounded from the enemy. There was death in its shrill note.

The chasseur's sabre was raised. Beside him the man in the civilian coat drew a long slim sword. The cavalry broke into the trot and the new Lieutenant could hear the hooves on the frozen ground. The Regiment of Dragoons still rode in squadrons that could be distinguished by the colour of their horses. The first squadron was on black horses, the second on bays, and the third on chestnuts; it was an arrangement common in peacetime, but rare in battle that swiftly diluted the pattern with remounts. The trumpeters were on greys, as were the three men who carried the guidons on their long staffs. The small flags were bright against the low clouds. The Dragoons' long swords were even brighter, like blades of pale ice.

Major Dunnett realized his Riflemen were in danger of annihilation. 'Rally square! Rally! Rally!'

The greenjackets contracted into the rally square; a clumsy formation whereby men crowded together for protection against cavalry. Any man who found himself in the front rank knelt and jammed his rifle butt into the turf so that his sword-bayonet's blade could be held rigid. Others reloaded their rifles, skinning their frozen knuckles on the sword-bayonets' long blades as they rammed the charges home. Rifleman Cooper and his mule sheltered in the middle of the square.

The chestnut squadron wheeled from the rear of the French charge, drew carbines, and dismounted. The other two squadrons spurred into the canter. They were still a hundred paces away and would not rowel their horses to the gallop till they were very close to their target.

'Fire!' Dunnett shouted.

Those Riflemen who had reloaded fired.

A dozen saddles were emptied. The Riflemen jostled each other, shaking themselves into ranks so that the rally square became a real square from which every rifle could fire. There were three ranks of them now, each plumed with bayonets.

'Fire!' More rifles spat, more cavalry fell, then the chasseur officer, instead of pressing the charge home, wheeled his horse away and the two squadrons sheered off to unmask the dismounted men who now opened fire with their carbines. The first Dragoons, the company which had waited by the bridge, closed on the square's eastern face.

The rally square made a perfect target for the dismounted Dragoons. If the Riflemen shook themselves into line to sweep the makeshift infantry away, then the mounted cavalry would spur their horses back into motion and the greenjackets would become mincemeat. The chasseur Colonel, the Lieutenant thought, was a clever bastard; a clever French bastard who would kill some good Riflemen this day.

Those Riflemen began to fall. The centre of the square soon became a charnel house of wounded men, of blood, screams and hopeless prayer. The rain was stinging harder, wetting the rifle pans, but enough black powder fired to spit bullets at the enemy who, crouched in the grass, made small and elusive targets.

The two mounted squadrons had wheeled away to the west, and now reformed. They would charge along the line of the road, and the frozen steel of their heavy straight swords would burn like fire when it cut home. Except, so long as the Riflemen stayed together, and so long as their unbroken ranks bristled with the pale blades, the horsemen could not hurt them. But the enemy carbines were taking a fearful toll. And when enough Riflemen had fallen the cavalry charge would split the weakened square with the ease of a sword shattering a rotten apple.

Dunnett knew it, and he looked for salvation. He saw it in the low cloud which misted the hillside just two hundred yards to the north. If the greenjackets could climb into the obscuring shroud of those clouds, they would be safe. He hesitated over the decision. A Sergeant fell back into the square, killed clean by a ball through his brain. A Rifleman screamed as a bullet struck his lower belly. Another, shot in the foot, checked his sob of pain as he methodically reloaded his weapon.

Dunnett glanced up the hill at the cloud's refuge. He stroked his small bristly moustache that was beaded with rain, then made his decision. 'Uphill! Uphill! Keep ranks!'

The square inched uphill. The wounded screamed as they were carried. French bullets still thumped home and the greenjacket formation became ragged as men stopped to return the fire or help the casualties. Their progress was desperately slow, too slow for Major Dunnett's frayed nerves. 'Break and run! Break and run!'

'No!' The new Lieutenant shouted the countermand, but he was ignored. Dunnett's order was given, and now it was a race. If the greenjackets could reach cover before the cavalry could reach them then they would live, but if the chasseur officer had judged his distance right, then he would win.

The red-coated chasseur had judged very well indeed.

The greenjackets ran, but over the sound of their hoarse breath and the pounding of their boots came the swelling thunder of the hooves.

A man turned and saw the bared teeth of a horse. He heard a sword hissing above the sound of the trumpet. The Rifleman screamed.

Then came chaos and slaughter.

The horsemen split the greenjackets apart then wheeled to the killing. The great swords chopped and speared. The new Lieutenant had a glimpse of a man with pigtails swinging beneath his helmet's rim. He twisted aside and felt the wind of the Dragoon's sword on his face. Another horseman rode at him, but he swung his rifle by its muzzle to crack the horse over the mouth. The horse screamed, reared, and the

Lieutenant ran on. He was shouting for men to close on him, but the greenjackets were scattered and running for their lives. The Battalion's mule bolted eastwards and Cooper, stubbornly trying to save his belongings which were strapped to the beast's panniers, was killed by a sword stroke.

Major Dunnett was ridden down to the turf. A seventeen-year-old Lieutenant was caught by two Dragoons. The first blinded him with a slashing backstroke, the second stabbed into his chest. Still the horsemen came. Their horses stank with saddlesores because they had been ridden too hard, but they had been trained to this work. A Rifleman's cheek was flensed from his face and his mouth bubbled with blood and saliva. The French grunted as they hacked. This was a cavalryman's paradise; broken infantry and firm ground.

The new Lieutenant still shouted as he climbed. 'Rifles! To me! To me! To me!' The chasseur must have heard him, for he turned his big black horse and spurred towards the Englishman.

The Lieutenant saw him coming, slung his empty rifle, and drew his sabre. 'Come on, you bastard!'

The chasseur held his own sabre in his right hand and, to make his killing cut easy, directed his horse to the left of the Rifleman. The Lieutenant waited to swing his curved blade at the horse's mouth. The cut would stop its charge dead, making it rear and twist away. He had seen off more horsemen than he could remember with such a stroke. The skill lay in the timing, and the Lieutenant hoped that the horse's panicked evasion would shake the rider loose. He wanted that clever chasseur dead.

A touch of the Frenchman's spurs seemed to make the horse lunge forward for the killing stroke and the Lieutenant swung his sabre and saw he had been fooled.

34

The horse checked and swerved in a manoeuvre which spoke of hours of patient training. The sabre hissed in empty space. The chasseur was not right-handed but left, and he had changed hands as his horse broke to the right. His blade glittered as it swept down, aimed at the Rifleman's neck.

The Lieutenant had been fooled. He had swung early and into nothing, and he was off balance. The chasseur, knowing this Englishman was dead, was planning his next kill even before his sabre stroke went home. He had killed more men than he could remember with this simple trick. Now he would add a Rifle officer to all the Austrians, Prussians, Russians, and Spaniards who had not been skilful enough.

But the chasseur's sabre did not cut home. With a speed that was astonishing, the Rifleman managed to recover his blade into the parry. The sabres met with a clash that jarred both men's arms. The Lieutenant's four-guinea blade shattered, but not before it had taken the force from the Frenchman's slashing cut.

The momentum of the chasseur's horse took him past the Englishman. The Frenchman turned back, astonished by the parry, and saw him turning to run uphill. For a second he was tempted to follow, but there were other, easier, targets down the hill. He spurred away.

The Lieutenant threw away his broken sabre and scrambled towards the low cloud. 'Rifles! Rifles!' Men heard and closed on him. They scrambled uphill together and made a large enough group to deter the enemy. The Dragoons went for individuals, the men most easily killed, and they took pleasure in thus avenging all the horsemen who had been put down by rifle bullets, all the Frenchmen who had jerked and bled their lives away on the long pursuit, and all the jeers that the Riflemen had sent through the biting air in the last bitter weeks.

Captain Murray joined the new Lieutenant. 'Out-foxed us, by God!' He sounded surprised.

The small group of Riflemen reached safety short of the clouds, up where the litter of rocks made the ground too uneven for the Dragoons to follow. There Murray stopped his men and stared, appalled, at the carnage beneath.

The Dragoons rode among the dead and the defeated. Riflemen with slashed faces reeled among them, others lay motionless until grasping hands turned the dead bodies and began ripping at pouches and pockets. The Quartermaster watched as Major Dunnett was pulled to his feet and his uniform searched for plunder. Dunnett was lucky. He was alive and a pris-oner. One Rifleman ran downhill, still trying to escape, and the man in the black coat and white boots rode after him and, with a chilling skill, chopped down once.

'Bastards.' Murray, knowing there was no more fight-ing to do, sheathed his Heavy Cavalry sword. 'God-damned bloody crapaud bastards!'

Fifty Riflemen, survivors from all four companies, had been saved from the rout. Sergeant Williams was with them, as was Rifleman Harper. Some of the men were bleeding. A Sergeant was trying to staunch a terrible slash in his shoulder. A youngster was white-lipped and shaking. Murray and the new Lieutenant were the only officers to have escaped the massacre.

'We'll work our way east,' Murray said calmly. 'Maybe we can reach the army after dark.'

A morose swearword sounded from the big Irishman and the two officers glanced down the valley to see the British cavalry at last appear in the drizzle. The chasseur saw them at the same time, and the French trumpet called the Dragoons into order. The British, seeing the enemy's preparedness, and finding no sign of infantry, withdrew.

The Riflemen on the cloud's edge jeered at their retreating cavalry. Murray whipped round. 'Silence!'

But the jeer had drawn the attention of the dismounted Dragoons on the slope below, and they believed the mocking sound had been aimed at them. Some of them seized carbines, others took up fallen rifles, and they fired a ragged volley at the small group of survivors.

The bullets hissed and whiplashed past the greenjackets. The ragged volley missed, except for one fatal bullet that ricocheted from a rock into Captain Murray's side. The force of the bullet spun him round and threw him face down onto the hillside. His left hand scrabbled at the thin turf while his right groped in the blood at his waist.

'Go on! Leave me!' His voice was scarcely more than a whisper.

Rifleman Harper jumped down the slope and plucked Murray into his huge arms. The Captain sighed a terrible moan of pain as he was lifted. Below him the French were scrambling uphill, eager to complete their victory by taking these last Riflemen prisoner.

'Follow me!' The Lieutenant led the small group into the clouds. The French fired again, and the bullets flickered past, but the Riflemen were lost in the whiteness now. For the moment, at least, they were safe.

The Lieutenant found a hollow among the rocks that offered some shelter from the cold. The wounded were laid there while picquets were set to guard its perimeter. Murray had gone as white as cartridge paper. 'I didn't think they could beat us, Dick.'

'I don't understand where they came from.' The

Lieutenant's scarred face, Murray thought, made him look like an execution. 'They didn't get past us. They couldn't!'

'They must have done.' Murray sighed, then gestured to Rifleman Harper who, with a gentleness that seemed odd in a man so big, first unstrapped the Captain's sword belt, then unpeeled his clothes from the wound. It was clear that Harper knew his business, and so the Lieutenant went to peer down the fogged hillside for a sight of the enemy. He could neither see nor hear anything. The Dragoons evidently thought the band of survivors too small to worry about. The fifty Riflemen had become the flotsam of war, mere splinters hacked from a sinking endeavour, and if the French had known that the fugitives were led by a Quartermaster, they might have been even more contemptuous.

But the Quartermaster had first fought the French fifteen years before, and he had been fighting ever since. The stranded Riflemen might call him the new Lieutenant, and they might invest the word 'new' with all the scorn of old soldiers, but that was because they did not know their man. They thought of him as nothing more than a jumped-up Sergeant, and they were wrong. He was a soldier, and his name was Richard Sharpe.

CHAPTER 2

In the night, Lieutenant Sharpe took a patrol westwards along the high crest. He had hoped to determine whether the French held the place where the road crossed the ridge, but in the freezing darkness and among the jumble of rocks, he lost his bearings and grudgingly went back to the hollow where the Riflemen sheltered.

The cloud lifted before dawn, letting the first wan light reveal the main body of the French pursuit in the valley which lay to the south. The enemy cavalry was already gone to the west, and Sharpe stared down at Marshal Soult's infantry which marched in dogged pursuit of Sir John Moore's army.

'We're bloody cut off.' Sergeant Williams offered his pessimistic assessment to Sharpe who, instead of replying, went to squat beside the wounded men. Captain Murray slept fitfully, shivering beneath a half-dozen greatcoats. The Sergeant who had been slashed across the neck and shoulders had died in the night. Sharpe covered the man's face with a shako.

'He's a jumped-up bit of nothing.' Williams stared malevolently at Lieutenant Sharpe's back. 'He ain't an officer, Harps. Not a real one.'

Rifleman Harper was sharpening his sword-bayonet, doing the job with the obsessive concentration of a man who knows his life depends on his weapons.

'Not a proper officer,' Williams went on. 'Not a gentleman. Just a jumped-up Sergeant, isn't he?'

'That's all.' Harper looked at the Lieutenant, seeing the scars on the officer's face and the hard line of his jaw.

'If he thinks he's giving me orders, he's a bugger. He ain't no better than I am, is he?'

Harper's reply was a grunt, and not the agreement which would have given the Sergeant the encouragement he wanted. Williams waited for Harper's support, but the Irishman merely squinted along the edge of his bayonet, then carefully sheathed the long blade.

Williams spat. 'Put a bloody sash and sword on them and they think they're God Almighty. He's not a real Rifle, just a bloody Quartermaster, Harps!'

'Nothing else,' Harper agreed.

'Bloody jumped-up storekeeper, ain't he?'

Sharpe turned quickly and Williams, even though it was impossible, felt that he had been overheard. The Lieutenant's eyes were hard as flint. 'Sergeant Williams!'

'Sir.' Williams, despite his assertion of disobedience, stepped dutifully towards Lieutenant Sharpe.

'Shelter.' Sharpe pointed down into the northern valley where, far beneath them and slowly being revealed by a shredding mist, a stone farmstead could be seen. 'Get the wounded down there.'

Williams hissed a dubious breath between yellowed teeth. 'I dunno as how they should be moved, sir. The Captain's . . .'

'I said get the wounded down there, Sergeant.' Sharpe had stepped away, but now turned back. 'I didn't ask for a debate on the God-damned matter. Move.'

It took the best part of the morning, but they succeeded in carrying the wounded down to the derelict farm. The dryest building was a stone barn, built on rock pillars that were meant to keep vermin at bay, and with a roof surmounted by crosses so that, from a distance, it looked like a small crude church. The ruined house and byres yielded damp and fungus-ridden timbers that, split and shredded with cartridge powder, were coaxed into a fire that slowly warmed the wounded men. Rifleman Hagman, a toothless, middle-aged Cheshireman, went to hunt for food, while the Lieutenant put picquets on the goat tracks that led east and west.

'Captain Murray's in a poorly way, sir.' Sergeant Williams cornered Sharpe when the Lieutenant returned to the barn. 'He needs a surgeon, sir.'

'Hardly possible, is it?'

'Unless we . . . that is . . .' The Sergeant, a squat, red-faced man, could not say what was in his mind.

'Unless we surrender to the French?' Sharpe asked acidly.

Williams looked into the Lieutenant's eyes. They were curious eyes, almost reptilian in their present coldness. The Sergeant found a truculence to brace his argument. 'At least the crapauds have got surgeons, sir.'

'In one hour,' Sharpe's voice implied that he had not even heard Williams's words, 'I'll inspect every man's rifle. Make sure they're ready.'

Williams stared belligerently at the officer, but could not summon the courage necessary for disobedience. He nodded curtly and turned away.

Captain Murray was propped against a pile of packs inside the barn. He offered Sharpe a feeble smile. 'What will you do?'

'Sergeant Williams thinks I should take you to a French surgeon.'

Murray grimaced. 'I asked what you wanted to do.'

Sharpe sat beside the Captain. 'Rejoin.'

Murray nodded. He was cradling a mug of tea, a precious gift from one of the Riflemen who had hoarded the leaves in the bottom of his ammunition pouch. 'You can leave me here.'

'I can't . . .'

'I'm dying.' Murray made a deprecatory shrug to show that he wanted no sympathy. His wound was not bleeding overmuch, but the Captain's belly was swelling blue to show that there was bleeding inside. He nodded towards the other three badly wounded men, all of them with great sword cuts on their faces or chests. 'Leave them too. Where will you go? The coast?'

Sharpe shook his head. 'We'll never catch the army now.'

'Probably not.' Murray closed his eyes.

Sharpe waited. It had started to rain again and a leak in the stone roof dripped insistently into the fire. He was thinking of his options. The most inviting choice was to attempt to follow Sir John Moore's army, but they were retreating so fast, and the French now controlled the road that Sharpe must take, and thus he knew he must resist that temptation for it would only lead into captivity. Instead he must go south. Sir John had marched from Lisbon, and a few troops had been left to protect the Portuguese capital, and perhaps that garrison still existed and Sharpe could find it. 'How far is Lisbon?' he asked Murray.

The Captain opened his eyes and shrugged. 'God knows. Four? Five hundred miles?' He flinched from a stab of pain. 'It's probably nearer six hundred on these roads. D'you think we've still got troops there?'

'We can at least find a ship.'

'If the French don't get there first. What about Vigo?'

42

'The French are more likely to be there than Lisbon.'

'True.' The Light Division had been sent to Vigo on a more southerly road. Only a few light troops, like these Riflemen, had been retained to protect Sir John Moore's retreat. 'Maybe Lisbon would be best.' Murray looked past Sharpe and saw how the men were brushing and oiling their rifle locks. He sighed. 'Don't be too hard on them.'

'I'm not.' Sharpe was instantly defensive.

Murray's face flickered with a smile. 'Were you ever commanded by an officer from the ranks?'

Sharpe, smelling criticism, bridled for an instant, then realized that Murray was trying to be helpful. 'No, sir, never.'

'The men don't like it. Stupid, really. They believe officers are born, not made.' Murray paused to take a breath that made him shudder with pain. He saw Sharpe about to enjoin him to silence, but shook his head. 'I haven't got much time. I might as well use what there is. Do you think I'm being damnably rude?'

'No, sir.'

Murray paused to sip at his tea. 'They're good lads.'

'Yes.'

'But they have an odd sense of what's proper. They expect officers to be different, you see. They want them to be privileged. Officers are men who choose to fight, they aren't forced to it by poverty. Do you understand that?'

'Yes.'

'They think you're really one of them; one of the damned, and they want their officers to be touched by something more than that.' Murray shook his head sadly. 'It isn't very good advice, is it?'

'It's very good,' Sharpe lied.

The wind sighed at the corners of the stone barn and

43

flickered the flames of the small fire. Murray smiled sadly. 'Let me think of some more practical advice for you. Something that will get you to Lisbon.' He frowned for an instant, then turned his red-rimmed eyes to Sharpe. 'Get Patrick Harper on your side.'

Sharpe turned to glance at the men who were crowded at the barn's far end. The big Irishman seemed to sense that his name had been mentioned for he offered Sharpe a hostile glance.

'He's a troublemaker, but the men listen to him. I tried to make him a Chosen Man once,' Murray instinctively used the Rifle's old term for a Corporal, 'but he wouldn't have it. He'd make a good Sergeant. Hell! Even a good officer if he could read, but he won't have any of it. But the men listen to him. He's got Sergeant Williams under his thumb.'

'I can manage Harper.' Sharpe said the words with a false conviction. In the short time that he had been with this Battalion, Sharpe had often noticed the Irishman, and he had seen for himself the truth of Captain Murray's assertion that he was a natural leader. Men crowded to Harper's campfire, partly to relish his stories, and partly because they wanted his approval. To the officers he liked the Irishman offered a humorous allegiance, while to those he disliked he offered nothing but scorn. And there was something very intimidating about Rifleman Harper; not just because of his size, but because of his air of knowing self-reliance.

'I've no doubt Harper thinks he can manage you. He's a hard man,' Murray paused, then smiled, 'but he's filled with sentimentality.'

'So he has a weakness,' Sharpe said harshly.

'Is that a weakness?' Murray shrugged. 'I doubt it. But now you'll think I'm weak. When I'm dead, you see,' and again he had to shake his head to stop Sharpe

44

interjecting, 'when I'm dead,' he repeated, 'I want you take my sword. I'll tell Williams you're to have it.'

Sharpe looked at the Heavy Cavalry sword that was propped in its metal scabbard against the wall. It looked an awkward and clumsy weapon, but Sharpe could not make any such objection to the gift now. 'Thank you.' He said it awkwardly. He was not used to receiving personal favours, nor had he learned to be gracious in accepting them.

'It isn't much of a sword,' Murray said, 'but it'll replace the one you lost. And if the men see you carrying it . . .' he was unable to finish the sentence.

'They'll think I'm a real officer?' The words betrayed Sharpe's resentment.

'They'll think I liked you,' Murray spoke in gentle correction, 'and that will help.'

Sharpe, reproved by the tone in the dying man's voice, again muttered his thanks.

Murray shrugged. 'I watched you yesterday. You're good in a fight, aren't you?'

'For a Quartermaster?'

Murray ignored the self-pity. 'You've seen a lot of battles?'

'Yes.'

'That wasn't very tactful of you,' Murray smiled, 'new Lieutenants aren't supposed to be more experienced than their seniors.' The Captain looked up at the broken roof. 'Bloody silly place to die, isn't it?'

'I'm going to keep you alive.'

'I suspect you can do many things, Lieutenant Sharpe, but you're not a miracle worker.'

Murray slept after that. All the Riflemen rested that day. The rain was insistent and, in mid-afternoon, turned to a heavy, wet snow which, by nightfall, was settling on the shoulders of the closest hills. Hagman

45

had snared two rabbits, thin fare, but something to flavour the few beans and scraps of bread that the men had hoarded in their knapsacks. There were no cooking cauldrons, but the men used tin mugs as saucepans.

Sharpe left the barn at dusk and went to the cold shelter of the ruined farmhouse to watch the night fall. It was not much of a house, merely four broken stone walls that had once held up a timber and sod roof. One door faced east, another west, and from the eastern door Sharpe could see far down a valley that now whirled and bellied with snow. Once, when the driving snow was lifted by the wind, he thought he saw the grey smear of smoke at the valley's end; evidence, perhaps, of a tiny village where they could find shelter, then the snow blanketed the view again. He shivered, and it seemed impossible that this was Spain.

Footsteps made him turn. Rifleman Harper ducked under the western door of the small house, saw Sharpe, and checked. He waved a hand at some fallen roof beams that were embedded in stones and turf. 'Timber, sir,' he explained his errand, 'for the fire.'

'Carry on.' Sharpe watched as the Irishman took hold of the rotted timbers and snapped them clear of their obstructions. Harper seemed to resent being watched, for he straightened up and stared at the Lieutenant. 'So what are we doing, sir?'

For a second Sharpe took offence at the surly tone, then realized that Harper was only asking what every man in the company wanted to know. 'We're going home.'

'You mean England?'

'I mean back to the army.' Sharpe suddenly wished he faced this journey alone, unencumbered by resentful men. 'We'll have to go south. To Lisbon.'

Harper crossed to the doorway where he stooped to stare eastwards. 'I didn't think you meant Donegal.'

'Is that where you come from?'

'Aye.' Harper watched the snow settle in the darkening valley. 'Donegal looks something like this, so it does. Only this is a better land.'

'Better?' Sharpe was surprised. He was also obscurely pleased that the big man had deigned to have this conversation which made him suddenly more likeable. 'Better?' Sharpe had to ask again.

'The English never ruled here. Did they, sir?' The insolence was back. Harper, standing, stared down at the sitting Sharpe and there was nothing but scorn in his voice. 'This is unsoiled country, so it is.'

Sharpe knew he had been lured into the question which had released this man's derision. 'I thought you were fetching timber.'

'I was.'

'Then fetch it and go.'

Later, after he had visited the shivering picquets, Sharpe went back to the barn and sat by the wall where he listened to the low voices of the men who gathered about Rifleman Harper. They laughed softly, letting Sharpe know that he was excluded from the company of soldiers, even of the damned. He was alone.

Murray died in the night. He did it without noise or fuss, just sliding decorously into death.

'The lads want to bury him.' Williams said it as though he expected Sharpe to disapprove.

Sharpe was standing in the barn's doorway. 'Of course.'

'He said to give you this.' Williams held out the big sword.

It was an awkward moment and Sharpe was aware of the men's gaze as he took the cumbersome weapon. 'Thank you, Sergeant.'

47

'He always said it was better than a sabre in a fight, sir,' Williams said. 'Puts the fear of God into the bloody Frogs, it does. Right butcher's blade, it is.'

'I'm sure.'

The moment of intimacy, forged by the gift of the sword, seemed to give Williams confidence. 'We were talking last night, sir.'

'We?'

'Me and the lads.'

'And?' Sharpe jumped from the barn's raised doorway into a world made dazzling by new snow. The whole valley glittered under a pale sun that was threatened by thickening clouds.

The Sergeant followed him. 'They're not going, sir. Not going south.' His tone was respectful, but very firm.

Sharpe walked away from the barn. His boots squeaked in the fresh snow. They also let in damp because, like the boots of the men he was supposed to command, they were torn, gaping, and barely held together with rags and twine; hardly the footwear of a privileged officer whom these frightened Riflemen would follow through the valley of the shadow of death. 'And who made that decision, Sergeant?'

'We all did, sir.'

'Since when, Sergeant, has this army been a . . .' Sharpe paused, trying to remember the word he had once heard at a mess dinner. 'A democracy?'

Williams had never heard the word. 'A what, sir?'

Sharpe could not explain what it meant, so tried a different approach. 'Since when did Sergeants outrank Lieutenants?'

'It isn't that, sir.' Williams was embarrassed.

'Then what is it?'

The Sergeant hesitated, but he was being watched by men who clustered in the barn's gaping entrance, and

48

under their critical gaze he found courage and volubility. 'It's madness, sir. That's what it is. We can't go south in this weather! We'll starve! And we don't even know if there's still a garrison at Lisbon.'

'That's true, we don't.'

'So we'll go north, sir.' Williams said it confidingly, as though he did Sharpe a great favour by the suggestion. 'There are ports up there, sir, and we'll find a boat. I mean the Navy's still off the coast, sir. They'll find us.'

'How do you know the Navy's there?'

Williams shrugged modestly. 'It isn't me who knows, sir.'

'Harper?' Sharpe guessed.

'Harps! Lord no, sir. He's just a bog-Paddy, isn't he? He wouldn't know nothing, sir. No, it's Rifleman Tongue, sir. He's a clever man. He can read. It was the drink that did him in, sir, you see. Only the drink. But he's an educated man, sir, and he told us, see, how the Navy's off the coast, sir, and how we can go north and find a boat.' Williams, encouraged by Sharpe's silence, gestured towards the steep northern hills. 'It can't be far, sir, not to the coast. Maybe three days? Four?'

Sharpe walked a few paces further from the barn. The snow was about four inches thick, though it had drifted into deeper tracts where the ground was hollowed. It was not too deep for marching, which was all Sharpe cared about this morning. The clouds were beginning to mist the sun as Sharpe glanced into the Sergeant's face. 'Has it occurred to you, Sergeant, that the French are invading this country from the north and east?'

'Are they, sir?'

'And that if we go north, we're likely to march straight into them? Or is that what you want? You were quite ready to surrender yesterday.'

49

'We might have to be a bit clever, sir. Dodge about a bit.' Williams made the matter of avoiding the French sound like a child's game of hide and seek.

Sharpe raised his voice so that every man could hear him. 'We're going south, Sergeant. We'll head down this valley today and find shelter tonight. After that we turn south. We leave in one hour.'

'Sir . . .'

'One hour, Sergeant! So if you wish to dig a grave for Captain Murray, start now. And if you wish to disobey me, Sergeant Williams, then make the grave large enough for yourself as well. Do you understand me?'

Williams paused, wanting to offer defiance, but he quailed before Sharpe's gaze. There was a moment of tension when authority trembled in the balance, then he nodded acceptance. 'Yes, sir.'

'Then get on with it.'

Sharpe turned away. He was shaking inside. He had sounded calm enough giving Williams his parting orders, but he was not at all certain those orders would be obeyed. These men had no habit of obeying Lieutenant Sharpe. They were cold, far from home, surrounded by the enemy, and convinced that a journey north would take them to safety far faster than a journey to the south. They knew their own army had been outmanoeuvred and driven into retreat, and they had seen the remnants of the Spanish armies that had been similarly broken and scattered. The French spread victorious across the land, and these Riflemen were bereft and frightened.

Sharpe was also frightened. These men could call the bluff of his tenuous authority with a terrifying ease. Worse, if they perceived him as a threat to their survival, then he could only expect a blade in the back. His name would be recorded as an officer who had died in the débâcle of Sir John Moore's retreat, or perhaps his death would not even be noticed by anyone for he had no family. He was not even sure he had friends any more, for when a man was lifted from the ranks into the officers' mess he left his friends far behind.

Sharpe supposed he should turn back to impose his will on the makeshift company, but he was too shaken, and unwilling to face their resentment. He persuaded himself that he had a useful task to perform in the ruined farmhouse where, with a horrid feeling that he evaded his real duty, he took out his telescope.

Lieutenant Richard Sharpe was not a wealthy man. His uniform was no better than those of the men he led, except that his threadbare officer's trousers had silver buttons down their seams. His boots were as ragged, his rations as poor, and his weapons as battered as any of the other Riflemen's equipment. Yet he possessed one object of value and beauty.

It was the telescope; a beautiful instrument made by Matthew Burge in London and presented to Sergeant Richard Sharpe by General Sir Arthur Wellesley. There was a brass plate recording the date of the battle in India where Sharpe, a redcoat then, had saved the General's life. That act had also brought a battlefield commission and, staring through the glass, he now resented that commission. It had made him a man apart, an enemy to his own kind. There had been a time when men crowded about Richard Sharpe's campfire, and sought Richard Sharpe's approval, but no longer.

Sharpe gazed down the valley to where, in the dusk's snowstorm, he thought he had seen the grey smear of smoke from a village's fires. Now, through the finely ground lenses, he saw the stone buildings and small high arch of a church's bell tower. So there was a village just a few hours' march away and, however poor, it would have some hoarded food; grain and beans would be buried in wax-sealed pots and hams hanging in chimneys. The thought of food was suddenly poignant and overwhelming.

He edged the telescope right, scanning the glaring brilliance of the snow. A tree hung with icicles skidded across the lens. A sudden movement made Sharpe stop the slewing glass, but it was only a raven flapping black against a white hillside. Behind the raven a churned line of footsteps showed where men had slithered down the hill into dead ground.

Sharpe stared. The tracks were fresh. Why had the picquets not raised an alarm? He moved the glass to look at the shallow trench in the snow that marked the line of the goat track and he saw that the picquets were gone. He swore silently. The men were already in mutiny. God damn them! He slammed the tubes of the spyglass shut, stood, and turned.

He turned to see Rifleman Harper standing in the hovel's western doorway. He must have approached with a catlike stealth, for Sharpe had heard nothing. 'We're not going south,' the Irishman said flatly. He seemed somewhat startled that Sharpe had moved so suddenly but his voice was implacable.

'I don't give a damn what you think. Just get out and get ready.'

'No.'

Sharpe laid the telescope on his haversack that he had placed with his new sword and battered rifle on the window-sill of the ruined house. There was a choice now. He could reason and cajole, persuade and plead, or he could exercise the authority of his rank. He was too cold and too hungry to adopt the laborious course, and so he fell back on rank. 'You're under arrest, Rifleman.'

Harper ignored the words. 'We're not going, sir, and that's that.'

'Sergeant Williams!' Sharpe shouted through the door of the hovel that faced towards the barn. The Riflemen stood in an arc about the shallow grave they had scooped in the snow. They watched, and their stillness was evidence that Harper was their emissary and spokesman this morning. Williams did not move.

'Sergeant Williams!'

'He's not coming,' Harper said. 'It's very simple, sir. We're not going south. We'll go north to the coast. We talked about it, so we did, and that's where we're going. You can come or stay. It's all the same to us.'

Sharpe stood very still, disguising the fear that pricked his skin cold and churned in his hungry belly. If he went north then he tacitly agreed with this mutiny, he accepted it, and with that acceptance he lost every shred of his authority. Yet if he insisted on going south he was inviting his own murder. 'We're going south.'

'You don't understand, sir.'

'Oh, I do. I understand very well. You've decided to go north, but you're scared to death that I might go south on my own and reach the Lisbon garrison. Then I report you for disobedience and mutiny. They'll stand you by your own grave, Harper, and shoot you.'

'You'll never make it to the south, sir.'

'What you mean, Harper, is that you've been sent here to make sure I don't survive. A dead officer can't betray a mutiny, isn't that right?'

Sharpe could see from the Irishman's expression that his words had been accurate. Harper shifted uneasily. He was a huge man, four inches taller than Sharpe's six feet, and with a broad body that betrayed a massive strength. Doubtless the other Riflemen were content to let Harper do their dirty work, and perhaps only he had the guts to do it. Or perhaps his nation's hatred of the English would make this murder into a pleasure.

'Well?' Sharpe insisted. 'Am I right?'

Harper licked his lips, then put his hand to the brass hilt of his bayonet. 'You can come with us, sir.'

Sharpe let the silence drag out, then, as though surrendering to the inevitable, he nodded wearily. 'I don't seem to have much choice, do I?'

'No, sir.' Harper's voice betrayed relief that he would not have to kill the officer.

'Bring those things.' Sharpe nodded at his haversack and weapons.

Harper, somewhat astonished to receive the peremptory order, nevertheless bent over to pick up the haversack. He was still bending when he saw he had been tricked. Harper began to twist away but, before he could protect himself, Sharpe had kicked him in the belly. It was a massive kick, thumping deep into the hard flesh, and Sharpe followed it with a two-handed blow that slammed down onto the back of Harper's neck.

Sharpe was amazed that the Irishman could even stand. Another man would have been winded and stunned, but not him. He shook his head like a cornered boar, staggered backwards, then succeeded in straightening himself to receive Sharpe's next blows. The officer's right fist slammed into the big man's belly, then his left followed.

It was like hitting teak, but the blows hurt Harper. Not enough. The Irishman grunted, then lurched forward. Sharpe ducked, hit again, then his head seemed to explode like a cannon firing as a huge fist slammed into the side of his skull. He butted his head forward and felt it smash on the other man's face, then his arms and chest were being hugged in a great, rib-cracking embrace.

54

Sharpe raised his right foot and raked his heel down Harper's shin. It must have hurt, but the grip did not lessen and Sharpe had no weapon left but his teeth. He bit the Irishman's cheek, clamping his teeth down, tasting the blood, and the pain was enough to force Harper to release his huge embrace to hit at the officer's head.

Sharpe was faster. He had grown up in a rookery where he had learned every trick of cheating and brutality. He punched Harper's throat, then slammed a boot into his groin. Any other man would have been blubbing by now, shrivelling away from the pain, but Harper just seemed to shudder, then bored in again with his overwhelming strength.

'Bastard.' Sharpe hissed the word, ducked, feinted, then threw himself backwards so that he bounced off the blackened stone wall and used the momentum of his recoil to drive his bunched fists into the other man's belly. Harper's head came forward, and Sharpe butted again; then, through the whirl of lights that seared across his vision, he brought his fists backwards and forwards across the Irishman's face.

Harper would not back down. He punched back, and drew blood from Sharpe's nose and lips, then drove him reeling backwards. Sharpe slipped on snow, tripped on the floor's rubble, and fell. He saw the massive boot coming, and twisted clear. He came up from the floor, snarling through blood, and grabbed Harper's crossbelt. The Irishman was himself off balance now and Sharpe turned him, swung him, then let go. Harper spun away, staggered, and fell against the wall. A stone gouged blood down his left cheek.

Sharpe was hurting. His ribs were tender, his head spinning, and his face bloody. He saw the other greenjackets edging closer to where the two men fought. Their faces showed disbelief, and Sharpe knew that not one of them would intervene to help Harper. The big Irishman had been delegated to do this job, and would be left alone to finish it.

Harper spat, stared at Sharpe through a mask of blood, then heaved himself to his feet. He found his bayonet and drew it.

'Use that, you Irish bastard, and I'll kill you.'

Harper said nothing, and there was something very terrifying in his silence.

'Bastard,' Sharpe said again. He glanced towards his new sword, but the Irishman had edged round to bar that salvation.

Harper stepped forward, coming slowly, the sword-bayonet held like a fighter's knife. He lunged with it once, sending Sharpe to one side, then lunged again, quick and hard, hoping to catch the officer off balance.

Sharpe, expecting the second lunge, avoided it. He saw the flicker of astonishment on the big man's face. Harper was good, he was younger than Sharpe, but he had not fought a man with Sharpe's quickness. Nor had he been hurt so much in a long time, and the flicker of surprise turned to pain as Sharpe's fists slapped at his eyes. Harper slashed with the bayonet, using it now to drive his attacker away, and Sharpe let the blade come at him. He felt it slice at his forearm, he ignored it, and rammed the heel of his hand forward to break the Irishman's nose. He clawed at Harper's eyes, trying to hook them out of his skull. The Irishman wrenched away and Sharpe pushed him off balance again. Fire seared at his arm, the fire of warm blood drawn by steel, but the pain went as Harper fell.

Sharpe followed fast. He kicked once, twice, crunching his boot into the big man's ribs, then he seized the bayonet, cutting his fingers, and stamped his heel onto

Harper's wrist. The weapon came away. Sharpe reversed it. He was panting now, his breath misting in the frigid air. Blood dripped from his hand to run down the blade. There was more blood on the snow which had drifted through the hovel's broken roof and gaping doors.

The Irishman saw his death above him. He rolled, then jerked back towards Sharpe with a stone in his hand. He lunged with the stone, smashing it onto the point of the descending blade and the shock of it numbed Sharpe's arm. He had never fought such power, never. He tried to drive the weapon down again, but Harper had heaved up and Sharpe cried aloud as the rock thumped into his belly. He fell onto the wall behind, his hand still numb where it held the bayonet.

He saw that Harper's face had changed. Until that moment the big Irishman had seemed as dispassionate as a butcher, but now there was a berserker look on his face. It was the face of a man goaded into battle-fury, and Sharpe understood that till now Harper had been reluctantly doing a necessary job that had suddenly become a passion. The Irishman spoke for the first time since the fight had begun, but in Gaelic, a language Sharpe had never understood. He only understood that the words were an insult that would be the threnody of his death as Harper used the stone to crush his skull.

'Come on, you bastard.' Sharpe was trying to massage life back into his numbed arm. 'You Irish scum. You bog-Paddy bloody bastard. Come on!'

Harper peeled bloody lips back from bloody teeth. He screamed a challenge, charged, and Sharpe used the chasseur's trick. He switched the blade from his right to his left hand and screamed his own challenge. He lunged.

Then the world exploded.

A noise like the thunder of doom crashed in Sharpe's ear, and a flash of flame seared close to his face with a sudden warmth. He flinched, then heard the whip-crack of a bullet ricocheting from the hovel's wall.

Sharpe thought one of the other Riflemen had at last summoned up the courage to help Harper. Desperate as a cornered animal, he twisted snarling from the foul smell of the gunpowder smoke, then saw that the Irishman was as astonished as himself. The stone still grasped in his massive fist, Harper was staring at a newcomer who stood in the east-facing door.

'I thought you were here to fight the French?' The voice was amused, mocking, superior. 'Or do the British have nothing better to do than squabble like rats?'

The speaker was a cavalry officer in the scarlet uniform of the Spanish Cazadores, or rather the remnants of such a uniform for it was so torn and shabby that it might have been a beggar's rags. The gold braid which edged the man's yellow collar was tarnished and the chain-slings of his sword were rusted. The black boots that reached midway up his thighs were ripped. A sacking cloak hung from his shoulders. His men, who had made the tracks in the snow and who now formed a rough cordon to the east of the farmhouse, were in a similar condition, but Sharpe noted, with a soldier's eye, that all these Spanish cavalrymen had retained their swords and carbines. The officer held a short-barrelled and smoking pistol that he lowered to his side.

'Who the devil are you?' Still holding the bayonet, Sharpe was ready to lunge. He was indeed like a cornered rat; bloody, salivating, and vicious.

'My name is Major Blas Vivar.' Vivar was a man of middle height with a tough face. He looked, as did his men, as though he had been through hell in the last days, yet he was not so exhausted that his voice did not betray derision for what he had just witnessed. 'Who are you?'

Sharpe had to spit blood before he could answer. 'Lieutenant Richard Sharpe of the 95th. The Rifles,' he added.

'And him?' Vivar looked at Harper.

'He's under arrest,' Sharpe said. He threw down the sword-bayonet and pushed Harper in the chest. 'Out! Out!' He pushed him through the hovel's door, out to where the other greenjackets waited in the snow. 'Sergeant Williams!'

'Sir?' Williams stared with awe at their bloodied faces. 'Sir?'

'Rifleman Harper is under close arrest.' Sharpe shoved Harper a last time, tumbling him into the snow, then turned back to the Spaniard's mocking gaze.

'You seem to be in trouble, Lieutenant?' Vivar's derision was made worse by the amusement in his voice.

The shame of the situation galled Sharpe, just as the Spaniard's tone stung him. 'It's none of your business.'

'Sir,' Major Vivar chided him.

'None of your bloody business, sir.'

Vivar shrugged. 'This is Spain, Lieutenant. What happens here is more my business than yours, I think?' His English was excellent, and spoken with a cold courtesy that made Sharpe feel mulish.

But the Englishman could not help his mulishness. 'All we want to do,' Sharpe smeared blood from his mouth onto his dark green sleeve, 'is get out of your damned country.'

There was a hint of renewed anger in the Spaniard's eyes. 'I think I shall be glad to see you gone, Lieutenant. So perhaps I'd better help you leave?'

Sharpe, for better or worse, had found an ally.

CHAPTER 3

'Defeat,' Blas Vivar said, 'destroys discipline. You teach an army to march, to fight, to obey orders.' Each virtue was stressed by a downward slash of the razor which spattered soapy water onto the kitchen floor. 'But,' he shrugged, 'defeat brings ruin.'

Sharpe knew that the Spaniard was trying to find excuses for the disgraceful exhibition at the ruined farmstead. That was kind of him, but Sharpe was in no mood for kindness and he could find nothing to say in reply.

'And that farmhouse is unlucky.' Vivar turned back to the mirror fragment which he had propped on the window-ledge. 'It always has been. In my grandfather's time there was a murder there. Over a woman, naturally. And in my father's time there was a suicide.' He made the sign of the cross with the razor, then carefully shaved the angle of his jaw. 'It's haunted, Lieutenant. At night you can see ghosts there. It is a bad place. You are lucky I found you. You want to use this razor?'

'I have my own.'

Vivar dried his blade and stowed it, with the mirror, in its leather case. Then he watched pensively as Sharpe spooned up the beans and pigs' ears that the village priest had provided as supper. 'Do you think,' Vivar asked softly, 'that, after your skirmish, the Dragoons followed your army?'

'I didn't see.'

'Let us hope they did.' Vivar ladled some of the mixture onto his own plate. 'Perhaps they think I've joined the British retreat, yes?'

'Perhaps.' Sharpe wondered why Vivar was so interested in the French Dragoons who had been led by a red-coated chasseur and a black-coated civilian. He had eagerly questioned Sharpe about every detail of the fight by the bridge, but what most interested the Spaniard was which direction the enemy horsemen had taken after the fight, to which enquiry Sharpe could only offer his supposition that the Dragoons had ridden in pursuit of Sir John Moore's army.

'If you're right, Lieutenant,' Vivar raised a mug of wine in an ironic toast, 'then that is the best news I've had in two weeks.'

'Why were they pursuing you?'

'They weren't pursuing me,' Vivar said. 'They're pursuing anyone in uniform, anyone. They just happened to catch my scent a few days ago. I want to be sure they're not waiting in the next valley.' Vivar explained to Sharpe that he had been travelling westwards but, forced into the highlands, he had lost all his horses and a good number of his men. He had been driven down to this small village by his desperate need for food and shelter.

That food had been willingly given. As the soldiers entered the small settlement Sharpe had noted how glad the villagers were to see Major Blas Vivar. Some of the men even tried to kiss the Major's hand, while the village priest, hurrying from his house, had ordered the women to heat up their ovens and uncover their winter stores. The soldiers, both Spanish and British, had been warmly welcomed. 'My father,' Vivar now explained to Sharpe, 'was a lord in these mountains.'

'Does that mean you're a lord?'

'I am the younger son. My brother is the Count now.'
Vivar crossed himself at this mention of his brother, a
sign which Sharpe took to denote respect. 'I am an
hidalgo, of course,' he went on, 'so these people call me
Don Blas.'

Sharpe shrugged. '*Hidalgo?*'

Vivar politely disguised his surprise at Sharpe's ignorance. 'An *hidalgo*, Lieutenant, is a man who can trace
his blood back to the old Christians of Spain. Pure
blood, you understand, without a taint of Moor or Jew
in it. I am *hidalgo*.' He said it with a simple pride which
made the claim all the more impressive. 'And your
father? He is a lord, too?'

'I don't know who my father is, or was.'

'You don't know . . .' Vivar's initial reaction was curiosity, then the implication of bastardy made him drop
the subject. It was clear that Sharpe had fallen even
lower in the Spaniard's opinion. The Major glanced
out of the window, judging the day's dying. 'So what
will you do now, Lieutenant?'

'I'm going south. To Lisbon.'

'To take a ship home?'

Sharpe ignored the hint of scorn which suggested he
was running away from the fight. 'To take a ship home,'
he confirmed.

'You have a map?'

'No.'

Vivar broke a piece of bread to mop up the gravy.
'You will find there are no roads south in these
mountains.'

'None?'

'None passable in winter, and certainly not in this
winter. You will have to go east to Astorga, or west to
the sea, before you will find a southern road open.'

'The French are to the east?'

'The French are everywhere.' Vivar leaned back and stared at Sharpe. 'I'm going west. Do you wish to join me?'

Sharpe knew that his chances of surviving in this strange land were slim. He had no map, spoke no Spanish, and had only the haziest notion of Spanish geography, yet at the same time Sharpe had no desire to ally himself with this aristocratic Spaniard who had witnessed his disgrace. There could be no more damning indictment of an officer's failure of command than to be discovered brawling with one of his own men, and that sense of shame made him hesitate.

'Or are you tempted to surrender?' Vivar asked harshly.

'Never.' Sharpe's answer was equally harsh.

His tone, so unexpectedly firm, made the Spaniard smile. Then Vivar glanced out of the window again. 'We leave in an hour, Lieutenant. Tonight we cross the high road, and that must be done in darkness.' He looked back at the Englishman. 'Do you put yourself under my command?'

And Sharpe, who really had no choices left, agreed.

What was so very galling to Sharpe was that his Riflemen immediately accepted Vivar's leadership. That dusk, parading in the trampled snow in front of the tiny church, the greenjackets listened to the Spaniard's explanation. It was foolish, Vivar said, to try to go north, for the enemy was marching to secure the coastal harbours. To attempt to rejoin the retreating British army was equally foolish, for it meant dogging the French footsteps and the enemy would simply turn and snap them up as prisoners. Their best course lay south, but first it would be necessary to march westwards. Sharpe

63

watched the Riflemen's faces and for a second he hated them as they nodded their willing comprehension.

So tonight, Vivar said, they must cross the road on which the main French army advanced. He doubted if the road was garrisoned, but the Riflemen must be ready for a brief fight. He knew they would fight well. Were they not the vaunted British greencoats? He was proud to fight beside them. Sharpe saw the Riflemen grin. He also saw how Vivar had the easy manner of a born officer and for a second Sharpe hated the Spaniard too.

Rifleman Harper was missing from the ranks. The Irishman was under arrest and, by Sharpe's orders, his wrists were first bound together then tied by a length of rope to the tail of a mule which the Major had commandeered from one of the villagers. The mule was carrying a great square chest that was wrapped in oilcloth and guarded by four of Vivar's Spaniards who also, by default, acted as guards over the prisoner.

'He's an Irishman?' Vivar asked Sharpe.

'Yes.'

'I like the Irish. What will you do with him?'

'I don't know.' Sharpe would have liked to have shot Harper there and then, but that would have turned the other Riflemen's dislike into pure hatred. Besides, to circumvent the army's careful disciplinary process and shoot him out of hand would have been to demonstrate a disdain of authority as great as that which had earned Harper punishment in the first place.

'Wouldn't we march faster if he was untied?' Vivar asked.

'And encourage him to desert to the French?'

'The discipline of your men is your own affair,' Vivar said delicately, thus intimating that he thought Sharpe had mishandled the whole business.

64

Sharpe pretended to ignore his disapproval. He knew the Spaniard despised him, for so far Vivar had seen nothing but incompetence from Sharpe, and it was an incompetence made worse by comparison with his own easy authority. Vivar had not just rescued the British soldiers from their precarious refuge in the old farm, but from their officer as well, and every Rifleman in the makeshift Company knew it.

Sharpe stood alone as the troops formed into companies for the march. The Spaniards would lead, then would come the mule with its box-shaped burden, and the Riflemen would bring up the rear. Sharpe knew he should say something to his men, that he should encourage them or inspect their equipment, do anything which would assert his authority, but he could not face their mocking eyes and so he stayed apart from them.

Major Vivar, apparently oblivious to Sharpe's misery, crossed to the village priest and knelt in the snow for a benediction. Afterwards he accepted a small object from the priest, but what it was Sharpe could not tell.

It was a bitter night. The thin snowfall had stopped at dusk and gradually the clouds cleared in the eastern sky to reveal a brightness of cold stars. A fitful wind whipped the fallen snow into airy and fantastic shapes that curled and glinted above the path on which the men trudged like doomed animals. Their faces were wrapped with rags against the pitiless cold and their packs chafed their shoulders raw, yet Major Vivar seemed imbued with an inexhaustible energy. He roamed up and down the column, encouraging men in Spanish and English, telling them they were the best soldiers in the world. His enthusiasm was infectious forcing a grudging admiration from Richard Sharpe who saw how the scarlet-uniformed cavalrymen almost worshipped their officer.

'They're Galicians.' Vivar gestured at his Cazadores.

'Local men?' Sharpe asked.

'The best in Spain.' His pride was obvious. 'They mock us in Madrid, Lieutenant. They say we Galicians are country fools, but I'd rather lead one country fool into battle than ten men from the city.'

'I come from a city.' Sharpe's voice was surly.

Vivar laughed, but said nothing.

At midnight they crossed the road which led to the sea and saw evidence that the French had already passed. The road's muddy surface had been ridged high by the guns, then frozen hard. On either verge white mounds showed where corpses had been left unburied. No enemy was in sight, no town or village lights showed in the valley, the soldiers were alone in an immensity of white cold.

An hour later they came to a river. Small bare oaks grew thick on its banks. Vivar scouted eastwards until he found a place where the freezing water ran shallow across gravel and between rocks that offered some kind of footing for the tired men but, before he would allow a single man to try the crossing, he took a small phial from his pouch. He uncorked it, then sprinkled some liquid into the river. 'Safe now.'

'Safe?' Sharpe was intrigued.

'Holy water, Lieutenant. The priest in the village gave it to me.' Vivar seemed to think the explanation sufficient, but Sharpe demanded to know more.

'*Xanes*, of course,' the Spaniard said, then turned and ordered his Sergeant to lead the way.

'*Xanes*?' Sharpe stumbled over the odd word.

'Water spirits.' Vivar was entirely serious. 'They live in every stream, Lieutenant, and can be mischievous. If we did not scare them away, they might lead us astray.'

'Ghosts?' Sharpe could not hide his astonishment.

'No. A ghost, Lieutenant, is a creature that cannot escape from the earth. A ghost is a soul in torment, someone who lived and offended the Holy Sacraments. A *xana* was never human. A *xana* is,' he shrugged, 'a creature? Like an otter, or a water rat. Just something that lives in the stream. You must have them in England, surely?'

'Not that I know of.'

Vivar looked appalled, then crossed himself. 'Will you go now?'

Sharpe crossed the fast-flowing stream, safe from malicious sprites, and watched as his Riflemen followed. They avoided looking at him. Sergeant Williams, who carried the pack of a wounded man, stepped into deeper water rather than scramble up the bank where the officer stood.

The mule was prodded across the stream and Sharpe noticed with what care the soldiers guarded the oilcloth-covered chest. He supposed it contained Major Vivar's clothes and belongings. Harper, still tied to the pack-mule, spat towards him, a gesture Sharpe chose to ignore.

'Now we climb,' Vivar said with a note of satisfaction, as if the coming hardship was to be welcomed.

They climbed. They struggled up a steeply rising valley where the rocks were glossed by ice and the trees dripped snow onto their heads. The wind rose and the sky clouded again.

It began to sleet. The wind howled about their muffled ears. Men were sobbing with the misery and effort, but somehow Vivar kept them moving. 'Upwards! Upwards! Where the cavalry can't go, eh? Go on! Higher! Let's join the angels! What's the matter with you, Marcos? Your father would have danced up this slope when he was twice your age! You want the

Englishmen to think a Spaniard has no strength? Shame on you! Climb!'

By dawn they had reached a saddle in the hills. Vivar led the exhausted men to a cave that was hidden by ice-sheathed laurels. 'I shot a bear here,' he told Sharpe proudly. 'I was twelve, and my father sent me out alone to kill a bear.' He snapped off a branch and tossed it towards the men who were building a fire. 'That was twenty years ago.' He spoke with a kind of wonder that so much time had passed.

Sharpe noted that Vivar was exactly his own age but, coming from the nobility was already a Major, while Sharpe came from the gutter and only an extraordinary stroke of fate had made him into a Lieutenant. He doubted if he would ever see another promotion, nor, seeing how badly he had handled these greenjackets, did he think he deserved one.

Vivar watched as the chest was fetched from the mule's back and placed in the cave-mouth. He sat beside it, with a protective arm over its humped surface, and Sharpe saw that there was almost a reverence in the way he treated the box. Surely, Sharpe thought, no man, having endured the frozen hell that Vivar had been through, would take such care to protect a chest if it only contained clothes? 'What's in it?' Sharpe asked.

'Just papers.' Vivar stared out at the creeping dawn. 'Modern war generates papers, yes?'

It was not a question that demanded an answer, but rather a comment to discourage further questions. Sharpe asked none.

Vivar took off his cocked hat and carefully removed a half-smoked cigar that was stored inside its sweatband. He gave an apologetic shrug that he had no cigar to offer Sharpe, then struck a flame from his tinder box.

The pungent smell of tobacco teased Sharpe's nostrils. 'I saved it,' Vivar said, 'till I was close to home.'

'Very close?'

Vivar waved the cigar in a gesture that encompassed the whole view. 'My father was lord of all this land.'

'Will we go to your house?'

'I hope to see you safe on your southern road first.'

Sharpe, piqued by the curiosity the poor have about the lordly rich, felt oddly disappointed. 'Is it a large house?'

'Which house?' Vivar asked drily. 'There are three, all of them large. One is an abandoned castle, one is in the city of Orense, and one is in the country. They all belong to my brother, but Tomas has never loved Galicia. He prefers to live where there are kings and courtiers so, on his sufferance, I can call the houses mine.'

'Lucky you,' Sharpe said sourly.

'To live in a great house?' Vivar shook his head. 'Your house may be more humble, Lieutenant, but at least you can call it your own. Mine is in a country taken by the French.' He stared at Rifleman Harper who, still tied to the mule's tail, hunched in the wet snow. 'Just as his is in a country taken by the English.'

The bitterness of the accusation surprised Sharpe who, beginning to admire the Spaniard, was disconcerted to hear such sudden hostility. Perhaps Vivar himself thought he had spoken too harshly, for he offered Sharpe a rueful shrug. 'You have to understand that my wife's mother was Irish. Her family settled here to escape your persecution.'

'Is that how you learned English?'

'That, and from good tutors.' Vivar drew on the cigar. A slip of snow, loosened by the fire in the cave, slid from the lip of rock. 'My father believed that we should speak the language of the enemy.' He spoke with a wry amusement. 'It seems strange that you and I should now be fighting on the same side, does it not? I was raised to believe that the English are heathenish barbarians, enemies of God and the true faith, and now I must convince myself that you are our friends.'

'At least we have the same enemies,' Sharpe said.

'Perhaps that is a more accurate description,' he agreed.

The two officers sat in an awkward silence. The smoke from Vivar's cigar whirled above the snow to disappear in the misting dawn. Sharpe, feeling the silence hang heavy between them, asked if the Major's wife was waiting in one of the three houses.

Vivar paused before answering, and when he did so his voice was as bleak as the country they watched. 'My wife died seven years ago. I was on garrison duty in Florida, and the yellow fever took her.'

Like most men to whom such a revelation is vouchsafed, Sharpe had not the first idea how to respond. 'I'm sorry,' he said clumsily.

'She died,' Vivar went on relentlessly, 'as did both of my small children. I had hoped my son would come back here to kill his first bear, as I did, but God willed it otherwise.' There was another silence, even more awkward than the first. 'And you, Lieutenant? Are you married?'

'I can't afford to marry.'

'Then find a wealthy woman,' Vivar said with a grim earnestness.

'No wealthy woman would have me,' Sharpe said, then, seeing the puzzlement on the Spaniard's face, he explained. 'I wasn't born to the right family, Major. My mother was a whore. What you call a *puta*.'

'I know the word, Lieutenant.' Vivar's tone was level,

but it could not disguise his distaste. 'I'm not sure I believe you,' he said finally.

Sharpe was angered by the imputation of dishonesty. 'Why the hell should I care what you believe?'

'I don't suppose you should.' Vivar carefully wrapped and stored the remains of his cigar, then leaned back against the chest. 'You watch now, Lieutenant, and I'll sleep for an hour.' He tipped the hat over his eyes and Sharpe saw the bedraggled sprig of rosemary that was pinned to its crown. All Vivar's men wore the rosemary, and Sharpe supposed it was some regimental tradition.

Below them the Irishman stirred. Sharpe hoped that the cold was slicing to the very marrow of Harper's bones. He hoped the Irishman's broken nose, hidden beneath a snow-whitened scarf, was hurting like the devil. Harper, as if sensing these malevolent thoughts, turned to stare at the officer and the look in his eyes, beneath their frosted brows, told Sharpe that so long as Harper lived, and so long as nights were dark, he should beware.

Two hours after dawn the sleet turned to a persistent rain that cut runnels in the snow, dripped from trees, and transformed the bright world into a grey and dirty place of cold misery. The strongbox was put back on the mule and the sentries posted on its flanks. Harper, who had finally been allowed into the cave's shelter, was tied once more to the animal's tail.

Their route lay downhill. They followed a streambed which tumbled to the bottom of a valley so huge that it dwarfed the hundred soldiers into insignificant dark scraps. In front of them was an even wider, deeper valley which lay athwart the first. It was an immense space of wind and sleet. 'We cross that valley,' Vivar explained, 'climb those far hills, then we drop down to

71

the pilgrim way. That will lead you west to the coast road.'

First, though, the two officers used their telescopes to search the wide valley. No horsemen stirred there, indeed no living thing broke the grey monotony of its landscape. 'What's the pilgrim way?' Sharpe asked.

'The road to Santiago de Compostela. You've heard of it?'

'Never.'

Vivar was clearly annoyed by the Englishman's ignorance. 'You've heard of St James?'

'I suppose so.'

'He was an apostle, Lieutenant, and he is buried at Santiago de Compostela. Santiago is his name. He is Spain's patron saint, and in the old days thousands upon thousands of Christians visited his shrine. Not just Spaniards, but the devout of all Christendom.'

'In the old days?' Sharpe asked.

'A few still visit, but the world is not what it used to be. The devil stalks abroad, Lieutenant.'

They waded a stream and Sharpe noted how this time Vivar took no precautions against the water spirits. He asked why and the Spaniard explained that the *xanes* were only troublesome at night.

Sharpe scoffed at the assertion. 'I've crossed a thousand streams at night and never been troubled.'

'How would you know? Perhaps you've taken a thousand wrong turnings! You're like a blind man describing colour!'

Sharpe heard the anger in the Spaniard's voice, but he would not back down. 'Perhaps you're only troubled if you believe in the spirits. I don't.'

Vivar spat left and right to ward off evil. 'Do you know what Voltaire called the English?'

Sharpe had not even heard of Voltaire, but a man

72

raised from the ranks to the officers' mess becomes adept at hiding his ignorance. 'I'm sure he admired us.'

Vivar sneered at his reply. 'He said the English are a people without God. I think it is true. Do you believe in God, Lieutenant?'

Sharpe heard the intensity in the question, but could not match it with any responding interest. 'I never think about it.'

'You don't think about it?' Vivar was horrified.

Sharpe bridled. 'Why the hell should I?'

'Because without God there is nothing. Nothing, nothing, nothing!' The Spaniard's sudden passion was furious. 'Nothing!' He shouted the word again, astonishing the tired men who twisted to see what had prompted such an outburst.

The two officers walked in embarrassed silence, breaking a virgin field of snow with their boots. The snow was pitted by rain and turning yellow where it thawed into ditches. A village lay two miles to their right, but Vivar was hurrying now and was unwilling to turn aside. They pushed through a brake of trees and Sharpe wondered why the Spaniard had not thought it necessary to throw picquets ahead of the marching men, but he assumed Vivar must be certain that no Frenchmen had yet penetrated this far from the main roads. He did not like to mention it, for the atmosphere was strained enough between them.

They crossed the wider valley and began to climb again. Vivar was using tracks he had known since childhood, tracks that climbed from the frozen fields to a treacherous mountain road which zigzagged perilously up the steep slope. They passed a wayside shrine where Vivar crossed himself. His men followed his example, as did the Irishmen among his greenjackets. There were fifteen of them; fifteen troublemakers who would hate Sharpe because of Rifleman Harper.

Sergeant Williams must have had much the same thoughts, for he caught up with Sharpe and, with a sheepish expression, fell into step with him. 'It wasn't Harps's fault, sir.'

'What wasn't?'

'What happened yesterday, sir.'

Sharpe knew the Sergeant was trying to make peace, but his embarrassment at his loss of dignity made his response harsh. 'You mean you were all agreed?'

'Yes, sir.'

'You all agreed to murder an officer?'

Williams flinched from the accusation. 'It wasn't like that, sir.'

'Don't tell me what it was like, you bastard! If you were all agreed, Sergeant, then you all deserve a flogging, even if none of you had the guts to help Harper.'

Williams did not like the charge of cowardice. 'Harps insisted on doing it alone, sir. He said it should be a fair fight or none at all.'

Sharpe was too angry to be affected by this curious revelation of a mutineer's honour. 'You want me to weep for him?' He knew he had handled these men wrongly, utterly wrongly, but he did not know how else he could have behaved. Perhaps Captain Murray had been right. Perhaps officers were born to it, perhaps you needed privileged birth to have Vivar's easy authority, and Sharpe's resentment made him snap at the greenjackets who shambled past him on the wet road. 'Stop straggling! You're bloody soldiers, not prinking choirboys. Pick your bloody feet up! Move it!'

They moved. One of the greenjackets muttered a word of command and the rest fell into step, shouldered arms, and began to march as only the Light Infan-

74

try could march. They were showing the Lieutenant that they were still the best. They were showing their derision for him by displaying their skill and Major Vivar's good humour was restored by the arrogant demonstration. He watched the greenjackets scatter his own men aside, then called for them to slow down and resume their place at the rear of the column. He was still laughing when Sharpe caught up with him.

'You sounded like a Sergeant, Lieutenant,' Vivar said.

'I was a Sergeant once. I was the best God-damned bloody Sergeant in the God-damned bloody army.'

The Spaniard was astonished. 'You were a Sergeant?'

'Do you think the son of a whore would be allowed to join as an officer? I was a Sergeant, and a private before that.'

Vivar stared at the Englishman as though he had suddenly sprouted horns. 'I didn't know your army promoted from the ranks?' Whatever anger he had felt with Sharpe an hour or so before evaporated into a fascinated curiosity.

'It's rare. But men like me don't become real officers, Major. It's a reward, you see, for being a fool. For being stupidly brave. And then they make us into Drillmasters or Quartermasters. They think we can manage those tasks. We're not given fighting commands.' Sharpe's bitterness was rank in the cold morning, and he supposed he was making the self-pitying confession because it explained his failures to this competent Spanish officer. 'They think we all take to drink, and perhaps we do. Who wants to be an officer, anyway?'

But Vivar was not interested in Sharpe's misery. 'So you've seen much fighting?'

'In India. And in Portugal last year.'

Vivar's opinion of Sharpe was changing. Till now he had seen the Englishman as an ageing, unsuccessful

Lieutenant who had failed to either buy or win promotion. Now he saw that Sharpe's promotion had been extraordinary, far beyond the dreams of a common man. 'Do you like battle?'

It seemed an odd question to Sharpe, but he answered it as best he could. 'I have no other skill.'

'Then I think you will make a good officer, Lieutenant. There'll be much fighting before Napoleon is sent down to roast in hell.'

They climbed another mile, until the slope flattened out and the troops trudged between immense rocks that loomed above the road. Vivar, his friendliness restored, told Sharpe that a battle had been fought in this high place where the eagles nested. The Moors had used this same road and the Christian archers had ambushed them from the rocks on either side. 'We drove them back and made the very road stink with their blood.' Vivar stared at the towering bluffs as if the stone still echoed with the screams of dying pagans. 'That must be nearly nine hundred years ago.' He spoke as if it were yesterday, and he himself had carried a sword to the fight. 'Each year the villagers celebrate a Mass to remember the event.'

'There's a village here?'

'A mile beyond the gorge. We can rest there.'

Sharpe saw what a magnificent site the canyon made for an ambush. The Christian forces, hidden in the high rocks, would have had an eagle's view of the road and the Moors, climbing to the gorge, would have been watched every step of the way to the killing arrows. 'And how do you know the French aren't waiting for us?' Emboldened by Vivar's renewed affability, he raised the question which had worried him earlier. 'We've got no picquets.'

'Because the French won't have reached this far into

Spain,' Vivar said confidently, 'and if they had, then the villagers would have sent warning down all the roads, and even if the warnings missed us, we'd smell the French horses.' The French, always careless of their cavalry horses, drove them until their saddle and crupper sores could be smelt half a mile away. 'One day,' Vivar added cheerfully, 'the French will flog their last horse to death and we'll ride over that loathsome country.' The thought gave him a renewed energy and he turned towards the marching men. 'Not far before you can rest!'

At which point, from above the gorge where the Moors had been ambushed, and in front of Sharpe where the road led down towards the pilgrim way, the French opened fire.

CHAPTER 4

Sharpe saw Vivar dive to the right side of the road, and threw himself to the left. The big, unfamiliar sword at Sharpe's hip clanged on a rock, then the rifle was at his shoulder and he tore away the scrap of rag that kept rain from the gunpowder in the rifle's pan. A French bullet gouged wet snow two inches to his right, another slapped with a vicious crack into the stone face above him. A man screamed behind him.

Dragoons. God-damned bloody Dragoons. Green coats and pink facings. No horses. Dismounted Dragoons with short carbines. Sharpe, recovering from his astonishment at the ambush, tried to make sense of the chaos of fear and noise that had erupted in the winter's cold. He saw puffs of grey smoke, dirty as the thawing snow, in an arc about his front. The French had thrown a low barricade of stones across the road about sixty paces from the canyon's mouth. It was long range for the French carbines, but that did not matter. The dismounted Dragoons who lined the peaks of the immense and sheer cliffs either side of the gorge were the men doing the damage.

Sharpe rolled onto his back. A bullet cracked into the snow where his head had been a second before. He could see the Dragoons standing on the lips of the chasm, firing down into the deathtrap of the road where, nine hundred years before, the Moors had been slaughtered.

78

Vivar's men had scattered. They crouched at the base of the rocks and fired upwards. Vivar was shouting at them, calling for them to form a line, to advance. He was planning to charge the men who barred the road. Instinctively Sharpe knew that the French had foreseen that move, which was why they had not made their barricade in the gorge, but beyond it. They wanted to lure the ambushed out into the plateau, and there could only be one reason for that. The French had cavalry waiting, cavalry with long straight swords that would butcher unprotected infantry.

Even as that realization struck him, Sharpe also realized that he was acting like a Rifleman, not like an officer. He had taken shelter, he was looking for a target, and he did not know what his men were doing back in the gorge. Not that he had any desire to go back into that trap of rock and bullets, but such was an officer's duty and so he picked himself up and ran.

He shouldered through the assembling Spaniards, saw that the mule lay kicking and bleeding, then was aware of a buzzing and cracking about his ears. The carbine bullets were spitting down into the gorge, ricocheting wildly, filling the air with a tangle of death. He saw a greenjacket lying on his belly. Blood had spewed from the man's mouth to stain a square yard of melting snow. A rifle cracked to Sharpe's left, then one to his right. The greenjackets had taken what cover they could and were trying to kill the Frenchmen above. It occurred to him that the French should have put more men on the heights, that the volume of their fire was too small to overwhelm the road. The thought was so surprising that he stood quite still and gaped at the high skyline.

He was right. The French had just enough men on the heights to pin the ambush down, yet the killing

79

would not be done by those men, but by others. That knowledge gave Sharpe hope, and told him what he must do. He began by striding down the road's centre and shouting for his men. 'Rifles! To me! To me!'

The Riflemen did not move. A bullet slapped into the snow beside Sharpe. The French cavalrymen, more used to the sword than the carbine, were aiming high, but that common fault was small consolation amidst their bullets. Sharpe again shouted for the Riflemen to come to him but, naturally enough, they preferred the small shelter offered at the base of the cliffs. He dragged one man out of a rock cleft. 'That way! Run! Wait for me at the end of the gorge.' He rousted others. 'On your feet! Move!' He kicked more men to their feet. 'Sergeant Williams?'

'Sir?' The reply came from further down the chasm, somewhere beyond the skeins of rifle smoke that were trapped by the rock walls.

'If we stay here we're dead 'uns. Rifles! Follow me!'

They followed. Sharpe had no time to reflect on the irony that men who had so recently tried to kill him now obeyed his orders. They obeyed because Sharpe knew what needed to be done, and the certainty of his knowledge was strong in him, and it was that certainty which fetched the greenjackets out of their scanty shelter. They also followed because the only other man they might have trusted, Harper, was not with them, but still tied to the wounded mule's tail.

'Follow! Follow!' Sharpe jumped a wounded Spaniard, twisted as a bullet slashed past his face, then turned to his right. He had led his men almost to the mouth of the canyon, just behind the place where Vivar still formed his own dismounted cavalrymen into line. Once, years before, a fall of rock had slid down to make a shoulder of scree and turf and, though the slope was perilously steep, and made even more perilous by the melting snow, it offered a short cut to the hillside which, in turn, led to the heights above. Sharpe scrambled up the rockfall, using his rifle as a staff, and behind him, in ones and twos, the Riflemen followed.

'Skirmish order!' Sharpe paused at the top of the first steep slope to shrug off his encumbering pack. 'Spread out!'

Some of the Riflemen suddenly realized what was expected of them. They were supposed to assault a steep and slippery slope at the top of which the French would be protected by the natural bastions of jumbled rock. Some of them hesitated and looked for cover. 'Move!' Sharpe's voice was louder than the gunfire. 'Move! Skirmish order! Move!'

They moved, not because of any confidence in Sharpe, but because the habit of obedience under fire ran deep.

Sharpe knew that to stay in the gorge was to die. The French wanted them in there, pinned by the carbines above to be slaughtered by the Dragoons who would charge from the roadblock. The only way to prise this ambush apart was to attack one of its jaws. Men would die in the attempt, but not so many as would die in the blood-reeking sludge and horror on the roadway.

Sharpe heard Vivar shout a word of command in Spanish, but he ignored it. The Major must do what he thought fit, and Sharpe would do as he thought best, and the strange exaltation of battle suddenly gripped him. Here, in the filthy stench of powder smoke, he felt at home. This had been his life for six-teen years. Other men learned to plough fields or to shape wood, but Sharpe had learned how to use a mus-ket or rifle, sword or bayonet, and how to turn an enemy's flank or assault a fortress. He knew fear, which was every soldier's familiar companion, but Sharpe also knew how to turn the enemy's own fear to his advantage.

High above Sharpe, silhouetted against the grey clouds, a French officer redeployed his men to face the new threat. The dismounted Dragoons who had lined the canyon's edge must now scramble to their right to face this unexpected attack on their flank. They moved urgently, and the first French bullets hissed whip-quick in the freezing air.

'I want fire! I want fire!' Sharpe shouted as he climbed, and was rewarded by the cracks of the Baker rifles. The Riflemen were doing what they were trained to do. One man fired as his partner moved. The Dragoons, still searching for new positions in the high rocks, would hear the bullets spin past their ears. The French did not use rifles, preferring the faster musket, but a musket was a clumsy weapon compared to the slow-loading Baker.

A bullet hissed by Sharpe. He thought it must have been a rifle bullet fired from behind him and he wondered if one of his men, hating him, had aimed at his back. There was no time for that fear now though it was a real fear, for in India he had known more than one unpopular officer shot in the back. 'Faster! Faster! Left! Left!'

Sharpe was gambling on his instinct that the men who had been positioned on the heights were only enough to hold the ambush down, and he hoped he was stretching those men too thin. He went further left, forcing the French to move again. He saw a face in the rocks ahead, a moustached face framed by the odd pigtails of the French Dragoons. *Dragons* was the French and Spanish name for them, and that thought wisped by Sharpe as the face disappeared behind a puff of smoke and again he heard the distinctive smack of a rifle bullet. A rifle! A Baker! He suddenly knew these must be the same men who had split apart Dunnett's four companies of Riflemen at the bridge; they were using captured British rifles, and the memory of that defeat gave him a new anger which drove him onwards.

Sharpe turned abruptly towards the centre of the enemy's weakened line. Somewhere on the hillside behind he had abandoned his unfired rifle and drawn his new sword. The weapon would make him a mark to the Dragoons, an officer to be shot, but it also made him visible to his men.

His legs were hurting with the effort of climbing. The slope was steep and ice-slick, and every footfall slid back before it took purchase. Anger had driven him up the hill, but now fear made him frail. Sharpe was panting, too out of breath to shout any more, conscious only of the need to close the gap on the French. He had a sudden certainty that he would die. He would die here, because even a *Dragon* could not fail to kill him at this short range. But still he climbed. What mattered was to prise open this jaw of the trap so that Vivar's men could escape up the hill. Sharpe's heart pounded in his chest, his muscles burned, his bruises ached, and he wondered whether he would feel the bullet that killed him. Would it strike clean, throwing him back to slide in blood and thawing snow down the slope? At least his men would know he was no coward. He would show the bastards how a real soldier died.

A Spanish volley sounded beneath him, but that was another battle. Further off a trumpet sounded, but it had nothing to do with Sharpe. His world was a few yards of slush with rocks beyond. He saw a shard of white struck by a bullet from a rock and knew some of his men were firing to give cover. He could hear other

Riflemen following him, cursing as they slipped on the icy slope. He saw flashes of pale green in the rocks – Dragoons – and he jerked aside from a puff of smoke and the crash of the carbine rang in his ears. He wondered if he was dreaming, if he was already dead, then his left boot found a firm foothold on an outcrop of stone and he pushed desperately upwards.

Two guns hammered at him. Sharpe was screaming incoherently now; a scream of pure fear turning into a killing rage. He hated the whole world. He saw a Dragoon scrambling backwards with a ramrod in his hand and the big sword, Murray's gift, cleaved down to smash into the man's ribs. There was a moment when the blade was gripped by the flesh, but he twisted the steel free and swung it left so that blood drops spewed into the face of a French officer who lunged with his own sword at Sharpe's belly. Sharpe let the enemy blade come, twisted aside, then rammed the guard of his heavy sword into the Frenchman's face. A bone cracked, there was more blood, then the officer was on the ground and Sharpe was smashing at the man's face with the disc hilt of his sword. A greenjacket ran past, sword-bayonet already bloodied, then another Rifleman was among the rocks.

Sharpe stood, reversed the sword, and stabbed down. On the long slope beneath him he could see two men who, in their green coats, lay like discarded rag dolls. A carbine fired to Sharpe's left and up there, unprotected from the wind, the smoke was snatched clean away to show a frightened Dragoon turning to run.

Sergeant Williams shot the man, then stabbed him with his bayonet. He was shouting like a fiend. Other Riflemen reached the summit. A knot of Frenchmen tried to form a rally square at the canyon's edge and Sharpe shouted for his men to attack. The greenjackets scrambled over patchy snow that was flecked red. Their faces were stained with powder and their lips were drawn back in a snarl as they moved like a wolfpack towards the Dragoons, who did not wait for the charge but broke and fled.

Bullets hissed from the Dragoons positioned on the far side of the gorge. A Rifleman spun, fell, then spat blood as he struggled to his hands and knees.

'Sergeant Williams! Kill those bastards!' Sharpe pointed across the canyon. 'Get their bloody heads down!'

'Sir!'

The trumpet sounded again and Sharpe veered back towards the slope he had climbed. At its foot Vivar had formed his men, but the French had expected it. Their main force had been barricaded on the road and now, from the Spaniard's left flank, a company of Dragoons was lined for the charge. 'You!' Sharpe grabbed a greenjacket. 'You!' Another. 'Kill those buggers.'

The rifles snapped at the horsemen. 'Aim low!' His voice was snatched by the wind. 'Low!' A horse went down. A man fell back from his saddle. Sharpe found a rifle among the rocks, loaded it, and fired downwards. Sergeant Williams had a dozen men sniping over the canyon, but the rest of the greenjackets were now pouring fire at the cavalry. They could not stop the charge, but they could unsettle it. A riderless horse stampeded in the snow, while another dragged a bleeding man across the charge's face.

Vivar retreated. His thin line of men would have been turned into carrion by the Dragoon's swords, and so the Major took shelter in the gorge. The French commander must have realized that his own charge was doomed, for the horsemen were pulled back. If the cavalry had funnelled themselves into the rocks, and done so without the help of cover from above, they would have been massacred by rifle fire.

Stalemate. Somewhere a wounded man sobbed in a terrible wailing voice. A limping horse tried to rejoin the cavalry's ranks, but fell. Cartridge wadding smoked in the snow. Sharpe did not know whether two minutes or two hours had passed. He felt the cold seep back into his bones; a cold that had been vanquished by the sudden emergency. He grinned to himself, proud of his greenjackets' achievement. It had been done with a ruthless speed which had unbalanced the enemy and taken away their advantage, and now there was stalemate.

The French still barred the road, but Sharpe's Riflemen could harass those sheltering behind the low barricade, and they did so with the grim enjoyment of men revenging themselves. Two French prisoners had been taken on the heights; two miserable Dragoons who were shoved into a hollow of the rocks and guarded by a savage-looking Rifleman. Sharpe guessed there had never been more than three dozen Dragoons on each side of the chasm, and he could see no more than sixty or seventy either behind the barricade or in the ranks of the aborted charge. This could only be a detachment of Dragoons, a handful sent into the mountains.

'Lieutenant!' Vivar shouted from beneath Sharpe. The Spaniard was hidden by the loom of the rocks.

'Major?'

'If I reach the barricade, can you give me fire?'

'You'll never make it!' If Vivar attacked the barricade, then his flank would again be open to the horsemen. Sharpe had seen what Dragoons could do to scattered infantry, and he feared for Vivar's dismounted Cazadores. The carbine was not the Dragoons' real weapon; they relished the power of their long straight swords

86

and they prayed for rash fools on whom to wield the killing blades.

'Englishman!' Vivar shouted again.

'Major?'

'I spit on your opinion! Give me fire!'

'Fool,' Sharpe muttered, then shouted at his men, 'Keep their heads down!'

Vivar's men broke cover in a column of threes. The first time he had attacked, Vivar had made a line, but now he aimed his men like a human battering ram at the road's obstruction. The Galicians did not march forward, but ran. Smoke puffed from the barricade and Sharpe's men opened fire.

The mounted Dragoons, just forty strong, saw the scarlet-coated enemy come into the open. The horses wheeled and were spurred into a trot. Vivar ignored them. A Spaniard fell, and his comrades swerved round his body and reformed beyond. A trumpet sounded high and shrill, then at last the Major stopped his men and turned them towards the threatened flank.

Sharpe now saw what Vicar planned, and saw that it was brave to the point of idiocy. Ignoring the Dragoons behind the barricade he would pour all his fire into the horsemen. He was trusting the Riflemen to keep the dismounted Dragoons occupied, and Sharpe paced along his line of marksmen and shouted their targets to them. 'That bugger by the tree. Kill him!' He saw a man fire in a hurry and he kicked his leg. 'Aim properly, you bastard!' Sharpe looked for the telltale scatter of discarded powder which would betray a man who only half-charged his rifle to spare his shoulder the mule-hard kick of the butt, but none of the Riflemen were using that cheap expediency.

Two men at Vivar's right file were down. They were the price Vivar had to pay. The cavalry was galloping at speed now, their hooves flinging up great gobs of dirty snow and soil.

'Take aim!' Vivar stood on the exposed right flank, the one closest to the barricade and where the greatest danger lay. He raised his sword. 'Wait for it, wait for it!'

The snow was thin on the flat ground beside the road. The horses' hooves thrummed the turf, and the long swords reflected the pale light. The trumpet hurled them on, faster, and the horsemen shouted the first challenge. The Spaniards had not formed a square, but were risking all on one crushing volley from men in line. Only disciplined troops could stand in line against a cavalry charge.

'Fire!' Vivar's sword flashed down.

The Spanish carbines flamed. Horses tumbled. Blood, men and snow made a whirling chaos. Something screamed, but whether man or horse, Sharpe could not tell. Then, over the scream, came Vivar's war shout. '*Santiago! Santiago!*'

The Galicians cheered, then charged. Not at the barricade, but towards the broken horsemen.

'Jesus Christ!' a Rifleman close to Sharpe muttered, then lowered his weapon. 'They're bleeding mad!'

But it was a magnificent madness. Sharpe's men watched and he barked at them to keep firing at the enemy behind the barricade. He permitted himself to watch as the tough Galician soldiers discarded their firearms and drew their own long swords. They climbed over the dead horses and stabbed down at dazed Dragoons. Others seized bridles or dragged at riders.

The Frenchmen behind the barricade stood to make their own charge and Sharpe shouted a warning at Vivar, but one which he knew the Spaniard would never hear. He turned. 'Sergeant Williams! Keep your men here! The rest of you! Follow!'

The Riflemen ran in a frenzied scramble down the hill. They made a ragged charge that would take the last Dragoons in the flank, and the French saw them coming, hesitated, then fled. Vivar's men were taking prisoners or rounding up riderless horses, while the surviving Frenchmen scrambled away to safety. The battle was over. The ambushed, outnumbered, had snatched an impossible victory, and the snow stank of blood and smoke.

Then gunfire sounded from the canyon behind Sharpe.

Vivar turned, his face ashen.

A rifle fired, its sound amplified by the echo of rock walls.

'Lieutenant!' Vivar gestured desperately towards the canyon. 'Lieutenant!' There was a genuine despair in his voice.

Sharpe turned and ran towards the chasm. The gunfire was sudden and brusque. He could see Sergeant Williams firing downwards, and he knew there must have been more Frenchmen hidden at the canyon's far end; men who would have blocked the panicked retreat they had expected to provoke. Instead those men must be advancing up the canyon to take Vivar and Sharpe in the rear.

Except they had been stopped by one man. Rifleman Harper had found the rifle of a fallen man and, using the corpse of the mule as a bastion, was holding off the handful of Dragoons. He had cut the bonds from his wrists, using a bayonet that had slashed deep wounds into his hands, but, despite the bleeding cuts, he still loaded and fired his rifle with a fearful precision. A dead French horse and a wounded Dragoon witnessed to the Irishman's skill. He screamed his Gaelic challenge at the others, daring them to come closer. He

turned, wild-eyed, as Sharpe appeared, then turned
scornfully back to face the French.

Sharpe lined his Rifles across the road. 'Take aim!'
The chasseur in his red pelisse and black fur hat was
in the gorge. Next to him rode the tall man in a black
riding coat and white boots.

'Fire!' Sharpe shouted.

A dozen rifles flamed. Bullets whined in ricochet,
and two more horsemen fell. The man in red and the
man in black were safe. They seemed to stare directly
into Sharpe's eyes for an instant, then a fusillade from
above made them turn their horses and spur away to
safety. The Riflemen jeered, and Sharpe snapped them
into silence. 'And reload!'

The French had gone. Water dripped from thawing
icicles that hung from rocks. A wounded horse whinnied. The filthy smoke of gunfire drifted in the gorge.
A Rifleman vomited blood, then sighed. Another man
wept. The wounded horse was silenced by a rifle shot,
and the sound slammed in brutal echoes from the rock
walls.

Footsteps sounded behind Sharpe. It was Blas Vivar
who walked past him, past the greenjackets, and knelt
by the mule. He carefully unstrapped the strongbox
from the dead beast's harness. Then, standing, he
looked up at Harper. 'You saved it, my friend.'

'I did, sir?' It was clear the Irishman had no idea
what value Vivar placed on the chest.

The Spaniard reached up to the huge man and kissed
both his cheeks. One of Sharpe's Riflemen sniggered,
then was shamed to silence by the moment's solemnity.

'You saved it,' Vivar said again, and there were tears
in his eyes. Then he lifted the strongbox and carried
it back up the canyon.

Sharpe followed. His men, silent and cold, came

down to the roadway. There was no exultation in victory for, unnoticed until this moment, and far beyond the abandoned French barricade, a smear of grey smoke rose into the winter air. It rose from the village, and the smoke was grey as a pauper's shroud and carried the stench of death and fire.

And from it, like dark snow, ashes fell on a bloodied land.

CHAPTER 5

The villagers could have sent no warning of the French presence for there was no village any more, nor villagers.

The fires must have been set just as the ambush was sprung, for the houses still burned fiercely. The corpses, though, had frozen hard. The French had killed the people, then sheltered in their houses as they waited for Vivar's small column to reach the high canyon.

It had never been much of a village; a poor place of goats and sheep, and of people who made a living from high pastures. The houses lay in a hollow sheltered by dwarf oaks and chestnut trees. Potatoes had grown in a few small fields that were edged with wild mulberries and furze. The houses had been mere thatched huts with dungheaps at their doors. They had been shared by men and animals alike, just as the houses Sharpe's own Riflemen had known in England had been, and that nostalgic resemblance added to the poignancy of the day.

If anything could add to the poignancy of children and babies killed, of women raped, or of men crucified. Sergeant Williams, who had known his share of horror in a bad world, vomited. One of the Spanish infantrymen turned in silence on a French captive and, before Vivar could utter a word, disembowelled the man. Only then did the Cazador utter a howl of hatred.

Vivar ignored the killing and the howl. Instead, with an odd formality, he marched to Sharpe. 'Would you . . .' he began, but found it hard to continue. The stench of those bodies which burned inside the houses was thick. He swallowed. 'Would you place picquets, Lieutenant?'

'Yes, sir.'

That, at least, took the Riflemen away from the bodies of slaughtered infants and the burning hovels. All that was left of the village's buildings were the church walls; walls of stone which could not be burned, though the church's timber roof still flamed high to spew smoke above the valley's rim where, among the trees, Sharpe placed his sentries. The French, if they still lingered, were invisible.

'Why did they do it, sir?' Dodd, a quiet man, appealed to Sharpe.

Sharpe could offer no answer.

Gataker, as fly a rogue as any in the army, stared empty-eyed at the landscape. Isaiah Tongue, whose education had been wasted by gin, winced as a terrible scream sounded from the village; then, realizing that the scream must have come from a captured Frenchman, spat to show that it had not troubled him.

Sharpe moved on, placing more sentries, finally reaching a spot from which, between two great granite boulders, he could see far to the south. He sat there alone, staring into the immense sky that promised yet more bad weather. His drawn sword was still in his hand and, almost in a daze, he tried to push it home into its metal scabbard. The blade, still sticky with blood, stopped halfway, and he saw to his astonishment that a bullet had pierced the scabbard and driven the lips of metal inwards.

'Sir?'

Sharpe looked round to see a nervous Sergeant Williams. 'Sergeant?'

'We lost four men, sir.'

Sharpe had forgotten to ask, and he cursed himself for the omission. 'Who?'

Williams named the dead, though the names meant nothing to Sharpe. 'I thought we'd have lost more,' he said in wonderment.

'Sims is wounded, sir. And Cameron. There are some others, sir, but those are the worst.' The Sergeant was only doing his job, but he was shaking with nerves as he spoke to his officer.

Sharpe tried to gather his thoughts, but the memory of the dead children was withering his senses. He had seen dead children often enough, who had not? In these past weeks he had passed a score of the army's children frozen to death in the ghastly retreat, but none of them had been murdered. He had seen children beaten till their blood ran, but not till they were dead. How could the French have waited in the village and not first hidden their obscene butchery? How could they have committed it in the first place?

Williams, troubled by Sharpe's brooding silence, muttered something about finding a stream from which the men could fill their canteens. Sharpe nodded. 'Make sure the French haven't fouled the water, Sergeant.'

'Of course, sir.'

Sharpe twisted to look at the burly man. 'And the men did well. Very well.'

'Thank you, sir.' Williams sounded relieved. He flinched as another scream sounded from the village.

'They did very well.' He said it too hastily, as if trying to distract both their thoughts from the scream. The French prisoners were being questioned, then would die. Sharpe stared south, wondering whether the clouds

94

would send rain or snow. He remembered the man in the red coat, the chasseur of the Imperial Guard, and the man in the black coat beside him. Why those two men again? Because, he thought, they had known Vivar was coming, yet the one thing the French had not reckoned on was Riflemen. Sharpe thought of the moment at the hilltop when the first greenjacket had gone past him, sword-bayonet fixed, and he recalled another failing of his own. He had never ordered the swords to be fixed, but the men had done it themselves. 'The men did very well,' Sharpe repeated, 'tell them that.'

Williams hesitated. 'Sir? Wouldn't it be better if you told them?'

'Me?' Sharpe turned abruptly towards the Sergeant.

'They did it for you, sir.' Williams was embarrassed, and made more so because Sharpe did not respond to his awkward words. 'They were trying to prove something, sir. We all were. And hoping you'd . . .'

'Hoping what?' The question was asked too harshly, and Sharpe knew it. 'I'm sorry.'

'We were hoping you'd let Harps go, sir. The men like him, you see, and the army's always let men off punishment, sir, if their comrades fight well.'

The bitterness Sharpe felt for the Irishman was too strong to let him grant the request immediately. 'I'll tell the men they did well, Sergeant.' He paused. 'And I'll think about Harper.'

'Yes, sir.' Sergeant Williams was plainly thankful that, for the first time since he had come under Sharpe's orders, the Lieutenant had treated him with some civility.

Sharpe realized that too, and was shocked by it. He had been nervous of leading these men, and frightened of their insubordination, but he had not understood that they were also frightened of him. Sharpe knew himself to be a tough man, but he had always thought of himself as a reasonable one, yet now, in the mirror of William's nervousness, he saw himself as something far worse; a bullying man who would use the small authority of his rank to frighten men. In fact, the very kind of officer Sharpe had most hated when he himself was under their embittered authority. He felt remorse for all the mistakes he had made with these men, and wondered how to make amends. He was too proud to apologize, so instead he made an embarrassed confession to the Sergeant. 'I wasn't sure any of the men would follow me up that hill.'

Williams grunted, half in amusement and half in understanding. 'Those lads would, sir. You've got the cream of the Battalion there.'

'The cream?' Sharpe could not hide his surprise.

'The rogues, anyway.' Williams grinned. 'Not me, sir. I was never much of a one for a scrap. I always hoped I'd never have to earn my pay, like.' He laughed. 'But these boys, sir, most of them are right bastards.' The words were said with a kind of admiration. 'Stands to reason, sir, if you think about it. I watched the lads when those crapauds attacked at the bridge, sir. Some were just ready to give up, but not these lads. They made sure they got away. You've got the tough ones, sir. Except for me. I was just lucky. But if you give these lads a chance to fight, sir, they'll follow you.'

'They followed you, too,' Sharpe said. 'I saw you on that hilltop. You were good.'

Williams touched the chevrons on his right sleeve. 'I'd be ashamed of the stripes if I didn't muck in. But no, sir, it was you. Bloody madness, it was, to charge that hill. But it worked!'

Sharpe shrugged the compliment away, but he recognized it for one and was secretly rather pleased. He might not be a born officer, but by God he was a born soldier. He was the son of a whore, bereft of God, but a God-damned soldier.

There were spades and shovels in the village that, taken back to the mouth of the canyon, were used to dig graves for the French dead.

Vivar walked with Sharpe to where the shallow graves were being scraped from the hard earth. The Spaniard stopped by one of the Dragoons who had died in the cavalry charge and whose body had since been stripped naked. The skin of the dead man's body was as white as the churned snow, while his face had been turned brown by exposure to wind and sun. The bloodied face was framed by pigtails.

'*Cadenettes*,' Vivar said abruptly. 'That's what they call those. What do you call them, braids?'

'Pigtails.'

'It's their mark.' He sounded bitter. 'Their mark of being special, an elite.'

'Like the rosemary in your men's hats?'

'No, not like that at all.' Vivar's abrupt denial checked the words between the two men. They stood in embarrassed silence above the enemy dead.

Sharpe, feeling uncomfortable, broke the silence. 'I wouldn't have believed it possible for dismounted cavalry to break horsemen.'

The praise delighted the Major. 'Nor would I have believed it possible for infantry to take that hill. It was stupid of you, Lieutenant, very stupid, and more brave that I could have dreamed possible. I thank you.'

Sharpe, as ever made awkward by a compliment, tried to shrug it away. 'It was my Riflemen.'

'They did it to please you, I think?' Vivar spoke

97

meaningfully, trying to offer Sharpe some reassurance. When the Englishman offered no response, the Spaniard's voice became more intense. 'Men always behave best when they know what is expected of them. Today you showed them what you wanted, and it was simple victory.'

Sharpe muttered something about luck.

Vivar ignored the evasion. 'You led them, Lieutenant, and they knew what was expected of them. Men should always know what their officers expect of them. I give my Cazadores three rules. They must not steal unless they will die for not stealing, they must look after their horses before themselves, and they must fight like heroes. Three rules only, but they work. Give men firm rules, Lieutenant, and they will follow you.'

Sharpe, standing on the lonely and cold-swept plateau, knew he was being offered a gift by Major Vivar. Perhaps there were no rules for being an officer, and perhaps the best officers were born to their excellence, but the Spaniard was offering Sharpe a key to success and, sensing the value of the gift, he smiled. 'Thank you.'

'Rules!' Vivar went on as though Sharpe had not spoken. 'Rules make real soldiers, not child-killers like these bastards.' He kicked the dead Frenchman, then shuddered. Other French corpses were being dragged across the slurried snow to the shallow grave. 'I'll have one of my men make some crosses from burnt wood.' Again Sharpe was surprised by this man. One moment he kicked the naked corpse of an enemy, the next he was taking care to mark those enemies' graves with crosses. Vivar saw his surprise. 'It isn't respect, Lieutenant.'

'No?'

'I fear their *estadea*, their spirits. The crosses will keep

98

their filthy souls underground.' Vivar spat onto the body. 'You think I'm a fool, but I've seen them, Lieutenant. The *estadea* are the lost spirits of the doomed dead and they look like a myriad of candles in the night mist. Their moaning is more terrible even than that.' He jerked his head towards another dying scream which sounded from the village. 'For what they did to the children, Englishman, they deserve worse.'

Sharpe could not quarrel with the Major's justification. 'Why did they do it?' He could not imagine killing a child, nor how a man could even dream of such an act.

Vivar walked away from the French corpses, towards the edge of the small plateau across which the cavalry had charged. 'When the French came here, Lieutenant, they were our allies. God damn our foolishness, but we invited them. They came to attack our enemies, the Portuguese, but once they were here they decided to stay. They thought Spain was feeble, rotten, defenceless.' Vivar paused, staring into the great void of the valley. 'And maybe we were rotten. Not the people, Lieutenant. Never think that, never! But the government.' He spat. 'So the French despised us. They thought we were a ripe fruit for the picking, and perhaps we were. Our armies?' Vivar shrugged in hopelessness. 'Men cannot fight if they're badly led. But the people are not rotten. The land isn't rotten,' he slammed his heel into the snow-covered turf. 'This is Spain, Lieutenant, beloved of God, and God will not desert us. Why do you think you and I won today?'

It was a question that expected no answer, and Sharpe made none.

Vivar gazed again at the far hills where the first rain showed as dark stains against the horizon. 'The French despised us,' he picked up his earlier thought, 'but learned to hate us. They found victory hard in Spain. They even learned to taste defeat. We forced an army to surrender at Bailen, and when they besieged Saragossa, the people humiliated them. And for that the French will not forgive us. Now they flood us with armies and think, if they kill us all, they can beat us.'

'But why do they kill children?' Sharp was still haunted by the memory of small and grievously tortured bodies.

Vivar grimaced at the question. 'You fight against men in uniforms, Lieutenant. You know who your enemy is because he dresses in a blue coat for you and hangs gold lace on the coat as a target for your rifles. But the French don't know who their enemies are. Any man with a knife could be their enemy, and so they fear us. And to stop us they will make the price of enmity too high. They will spread a greater fear through Spain, a fear of that!' He turned and jabbed a finger towards the smear of smoke that still rose from the village. 'They fear us, but they will try to make us fear them even more. And maybe they will succeed.'

The sudden pessimism was startling from a man as indomitable as Blas Vivar. 'You truly think so?' Sharpe asked.

'I think men should fear the death of their children.' Vivar, who had buried his own children, spoke very bleakly. 'But I do not think the French will succeed. They're victorious now, and the Spanish people mourn their children and wonder if there is any hope left, but if those people can be given just one small scrap of hope, just one glint in the darkness, then they will fight!' He snarled the last words, then, in a quicksilver change of mood, smiled apologetically at Sharpe. 'I have a favour to ask of you.'

'Of course.'

'The Irishman, Patrick Harper. Release him.'

'Release him?' Sharpe was taken aback, not by the request as such, but by the sudden change in Vivar's manner. A moment before he had been vengeful and steel-hard, now he was diffidently polite, like a petitioner.

'I know,' Vivar said hastily, 'that the Irishman's sin is grievous. He deserves to be flogged half to death, if not beyond death, but he did a thing most precious to me.'

Sharpe, embarrassed by Vivar's humble tone, shrugged. 'Of course.'

'I shall talk to him, and tell him his duties of obedience.'

'He can be released.' Sharpe had already half persuaded himself of the necessity of releasing Harper, if only to prove his own reasonableness to Sergeant Williams.

'I've already released him,' Vivar admitted, 'but I thought it best to seek your approval.' He grinned, saw that Sharpe would offer no protest, then stooped to pick up a fallen French helmet. He ripped away the canvas cover which both protected the fine brass and prevented it from reflecting the sunlight to betray the Dragoon's position. 'A pretty bauble,' he said scathingly, 'something to hang on the staircase when the war's over.'

Sharpe was not interested in a dented Dragoon's helmet; instead he was realizing that the 'thing most precious' Harper had done for Vivar was to protect the strongbox. He remembered the horror on the Spaniard's face when he thought the chest might be lost. Like a stab of sunlight searing through rent in dark clouds, Sharpe at last understood. The chasseur had been chasing Vivar, and that chase had unwittingly drawn the Dragoons across the tail of the British army where they had casually broken four companies of Riflemen, but then they had kept going. Not after the retreating British, but after the strongbox. 'What's in the chest, Major?' he asked accusingly.

'I told you, papers,' Vivar answered carelessly as he tore away the last shreds of canvas from the helmet.

'The French came here to capture that strongbox.'

'The prisoners told me they came for food. I'm sure they were speaking the truth, Lieutenant. Men who face death usually do, and they all told me the same story. They were a forage party.' Vivar polished the helmet's brass with his sleeve, then held the helmet out for Sharpe's inspection. 'Shoddy workmanship. See how badly the chinstrap is riveted?'

Sharpe again ignored the helmet. 'They came here for that chest, didn't they? They've been following you, and they must have known you had to cross these mountains.'

Vivar frowned at the helmet. 'I don't think I shall keep it. I shall find a better one before the killing's done.'

'They're the same men who attacked our rearguard. We're lucky they didn't send the whole Regiment up here, Major!'

'The prisoners said that only the men on fit horses could come this far.' It seemed a partial affirmation of Sharpe's suspicions, but Vivar immediately denied the rest. 'I assure you they only came here for forage and food. They told me they've stripped the villages in the valley bare, so now they must climb high for their food.'

'What's in the chest, Major?' Sharpe persisted.

'Curiosity!' Vivar turned away and began to walk towards the village. 'Curiosity!' He drew back his arm and hurled the helmet far into the void where the plateau dropped steeply away. The helmet glittered, turned, then fell with a crash into the undergrowth. 'Curiosity! An English disease, Lieutenant, which leads to death. Avoid it!'

The fires died in the night, all but for one burning house that Vivar's men fed with wood cut from the surrounding trees in which they roasted hunks of horsemeat that had been threaded onto their swords. The Riflemen cooked the horsemeat on their ramrods. All were glad that the villagers' bodies had been buried. The picquets were pulled back to the very edge of the burnt village where they shivered in the cold wind. The afternoon rain had stopped at dusk, and in the night there were even gaps in the high flying clouds which allowed a wan moonlight to illumine the jagged hills from which the snow had part-melted to leave the land-scape looking strangely leprous. Somewhere in those hills a wolf howled.

Sharpe's men provided the sentries for the first half of the night. At midnight he walked around the village and spoke a few awkward words with each man. The conversations were stilted because none of the greenjackets could forget the morning when they had conspired for Sharpe's death, but a Welshman, Jenkins, more loquacious than the others, wondered where Sir John Moore's army was now.

'God knows,' Sharpe said. 'Far away.'

'Defeated, sir?'

'Maybe.'

'But Boney left, sir?' The question was asked eagerly, as if the Emperor's absence gave the fugitive Riflemen renewed hope.

'So we were told.' Napoleon was supposed to have left Spain already, but that was small reason for opti-mism. He had no need to stay. Everywhere his enemies were in retreat, and his Marshals, who had conquered Europe, could be trusted to finish Spain and Portugal.

Sharpe walked on past the burnt-out houses. The sole of his right boot was hanging loose, and his trousers gaped at his thighs. At least he had repaired the broken scabbard, yet otherwise his uniform hung off him like a scarecrow's rags. He went to the place where the road climbed up towards the canyon and where, beside a stone trough that the women who had once lived in this village had used as a washing place, a three-man picquet was posted. 'See anything?'

'Not a thing, sir. Quiet as a dry alehouse.'

It was Harper who had answered and who now rose up, huge and formidable, from the shadow of the trough. The two men stared at each other, then, awkwardly, the Irishman pulled off his shako in the formal salute. 'I'm sorry, sir.'

'It doesn't matter.'

'The Major talked to me, he did. We was frightened, you see, sir, and . . .'

'I said it doesn't matter!'

Harper nodded. His broken nose was still swollen and would never again be straight. The big Irishman grinned. 'If you'll not mind me saying it, sir, but you've got a punch on you like a Ballinderry heifer.'

The comment might have been offered as a peace-token, but Sharpe's memory of the fight in the ruined farmhouse was too fresh and too sore to accept it. 'I've let you off a damned sharp hook, Rifleman Harper, but that does not give you the God-damned right to say whatever comes into your head. So put your bloody hat on, and go back to work.'

Sharpe turned and walked away, ready to whip round instantly if a single insolent sound was uttered, but Harper had the sense to keep silent. The wind made the only noise, a sighing sound as it passed through the trees before lifting the sparks of the big fire high into the night. Sharpe went close to the fire, letting its heat warm his chilled and wet uniform. He supposed he had blundered again, that he should have accepted the friendly words as the peace-offering they were undoubtedly meant to be, but his pride had stung him into savagery.

'You should get some sleep, sir.' It was Sergeant Williams, muffled against the cold, who appeared in the firelight. 'I'll look after the lads.'

'I can't sleep.'

'No.' The word was said as agreement. 'It's thinking of them dead nippers what does it.'

'Yes.'

'Bastards,' Williams said. He held his hands towards the blaze. 'There was one no older than my Mary.'

'How old is she?'

'Five, sir. Pretty wee thing, she is. Not like her father.'

Sharpe smiled. 'Did your wife come out to Spain with you?'

'No, sir. Helps in her da's bakery, she does. He wasn't too pleased when she married a soldier, but they never are.'

'That's true.'

The Sergeant stretched. 'But I'll have some rare tales to tell when I get back to Spitalfields.' He was silent for a moment, perhaps thinking of home. 'Funny, really.'

'What is?'

'Why these bastards came all this way to get supplies. Isn't that what the Major said, sir?'

'Yes.' French forces were supposed to live off the land, stealing what they could to stay alive, but Sharpe, like Williams, could not believe that the enemy horsemen had climbed to this remote village when other, more tempting places lay in the valleys. 'They were the same men,' he said, 'who attacked us on the road.' Which, in a way, had worked to Sharpe's advantage, because the French Dragoons, unable to resist using the captured rifles, had proved inept with the unfamiliar weapons.

Sergeant Williams nodded. 'Bugger in a red coat, right?'

'Yes. And a fellow in black.'

'It's my belief they're after that box the Spanish lads are carrying.' Williams lowered his voice as though one of the sleeping Cazadores might hear him. 'It's the sort of box you carry jewels in, isn't it? Could be a King's bloody ransom in that thing, sir.'

'Major Vivar says it holds papers.'

'Papers!' The Sergeant's voice was scornful.

'Well, I don't suppose we're going to find out,' Sharpe said. 'And I wouldn't recommend being too inquisitive, Sergeant. The Major doesn't take kindly to curiosity.'

'No, sir.' Williams sounded disappointed at his lack of enthusiasm.

But Sharpe merely hid his own inquisitiveness for, after a few more moments of desultory conversation and after bidding the Sergeant a good night, he went softly and slowly towards the church. He used the stealth he had learned as a child in the London rookery where, if a boy did not steal, he starved.

He walked round the church, then stood for a long time in the shadows by the door. He listened. He heard the fire's crackle and the wind's rising noise, but nothing else. Still he waited, straining to hear a single sound from within the old stone building. He heard nothing. He could smell the fallen and burnt timbers within the building, but he could sense no human presence. The nearest Spaniards were thirty paces away, rolled in their cloaks, asleep.

The church door was ajar. Sharpe edged through and, once inside the church, stopped again.

Moonlight illuminated the sanctuary. The walls were scorched black, the altar was gone, yet Vivar's men had begun to clear the desecration by forcing the burnt roof timbers aside to make an aisle which led to the altar steps. At the top of those steps, black like the walls, was the strongbox.

Sharpe waited. He looked round the building's small interior; watching for movement, but there was none. A small black window opened on the church's southern wall, but that was the only aperture. Nothing showed in the opening, except darkness, suggesting that the small window opened into a cupboard or a deep shelf.

Sharpe walked forward between the fallen timbers, some of which still smouldered. Once his loose right sole crunched a black lump of burnt wood, but that was the only sound he made.

He stopped at the foot of the two steps which had led to the altar and squatted there. Curled on the lid of the strongbox was a jet rosary, its small crucifix shining in the moonlight. Within this box, Sharpe thought, lay something that had drawn French soldiers into the frozen highlands. Vivar had said it was papers, but even the most religious of men would not guard papers with a crucifix.

The chest was wrapped in oilcloth that had been sewn tight. During the fight two bullets had embedded themselves in the big box, breaking the cloth, and Sharpe, fingering under the holes and past the lumpen bullets, felt the hard smoothness of the wood. He traced the shapes of the hasps and padlocks beneath the oil-cloth. The padlocks were old-fashioned ball-locks that

Sharpe knew he could open in seconds with a rifle's cleaning pin.

He rocked back on his heels, staring at the chest. Four Riflemen had died because of it and yet more might die, and that, Sharpe decided, gave him the right to know what lay inside. He knew he would not be able to disguise that the box had been opened, but he had no intention of stealing its contents so had no scruples about leaving the oilcloth torn and the locks picked.

He reached into his jacket pocket and brought out the clasp knife he used for food. He opened its blade and reached forward to cut the cloth.

'Touch it, Englishman, and you die.'

Sharpe twisted to his right. The click of a pistol's lock sounded from the small dark window. 'Major?'

'The sick could watch the Mass from this window, Lieutenant.' Vivar's voice sounded from the blackness. 'It's a good place for a sentry.'

'What is the sentry guarding?'

'Just papers.' Vivar's voice was cold. 'Put your knife away, Lieutenant, and stay there.'

Sharpe obeyed. After a moment the Major appeared in the church doorway. 'Don't do that again, Lieutenant. I will kill to protect what is in that box.'

Sharpe felt like a small boy caught by a watchman, but he tried to brazen out the confrontation. 'Papers?'

'Papers,' Vivar said bleakly. He looked up at the sky where silvered clouds flew fast beside the moon. 'It isn't a night for killing, Englishman. The *estadea* are already restless.' He walked up the aisle. 'Now I think you should try to sleep. We have far to go in the morning.'

Sharpe, chastened, went past Vivar to the church door. With one hand on the jamb, he turned to look back at the chest. Vivar, his back to him, was already on his knees in front of the mysterious strongbox.

Sharpe, embarrassed to see a man praying, paused.

'Yes, Lieutenant?' Vivar had not turned round.

'Did your prisoners tell you who the chasseur is? The man in red who led them here?'

'No, Lieutenant.' The Spaniard's voice was very patient, as though by answering he merely humoured a child's caprice. 'I did not think to ask them.'

'Or the man in black? The civilian?'

Vivar paused for a second. 'Does the wolf know the names of the hounds?'

'Who is he, Major?'

The rosary's beads clicked. 'Goodnight, Lieutenant.'

Sharpe knew he would fetch no answers, only more mysteries to rival the insubstantiality of the *estadea*. He half-closed the charred door, then went to his cold bed of bare earth and listened to the wind moan in the spirit-haunted night. Somewhere a wolf howled, and one of the captured horses whinnied softly. In the chapel a man prayed. Sharpe slept.

CHAPTER 6

The Cazadores and Riflemen still went west but, for fear of the French Dragoons, Vivar avoided the easier paths of the pilgrim way, insisting that safety still lay in the uplands. The road, if it could be called a road at all, struggled through the passes of high mountains and across cold streams swollen by meltwater and by the persistent, stinging rain that made the paths as slippery as grease. The wounded men and those who caught a fever of the cold were carried by the captured French horses, but those precious beasts had to be led with an infinite caution if they were to survive on the treacherous tracks. One of the horses carried the strongbox.

There was no news of the French. During the first two days of the march Sharpe expected to see the threatening silhouettes of the Dragoons on the skyline, but the chasseur and his men seemed to have vanished. The few people who lived in the highland villages assured Vivar that they had seen no Frenchmen. Some of them did not even know that a foreign enemy was in Spain and, hearing the strange language of Sharpe's Riflemen, would stare with a suspicious hostility at the strangers. 'Not that their own dialect isn't strange,' Vivar said cheerfully; then, as fluent in the Galician speech as in the more courtly tongue of Spain, he would reassure the peasants that the men in torn green coats were not to be feared.

After the first few days, and satisfied that the French had lost the scent, Vivar descended to the pilgrim way which proved to be a succession of mingling tracks that twisted through the deeper valleys. The largest roads were reinforced with flint so that carts and carriages could use them, and even though the winter had drowned the flints in mud, the men marched fast and easily on the firmer surface. Chestnuts and elm trees grew thick beside the road which led through a country that had so far been free of scavenging armies. The men ate well. There was maize, rye, potatoes, chestnuts, and salted meat in winter store. One night there was even fresh mutton.

Yet, despite the food and the easier footing, it was not a soft country. One midday, beside a bridge which crossed a deep, dark stream, Sharpe saw three human heads stuck high on wooden poles. The heads had been there for months, and their eyes, tongues, and softer flesh had been eaten by ravens, while what shreds of skin were left on the grisly skulls had turned as black as pitch. '*Rateros*,' Vivar told Sharpe, 'highwaymen. They think that pilgrims give easy pickings.'

'Do many pilgrims go to Santiago de Compostela?'

'Not so many as in the old days. A few lepers still go to be cured, but even they will be stopped by the war.' Vivar nodded towards the lank-haired skulls. 'So now those gentlemen will have to use their murderous skills against the French.' The thought cheered him, just as the easier going on the pilgrim way cheered Sharpe's Riflemen. Sometimes they sang as they marched. They rediscovered old comforts. Vivar bought great blocks of tobacco that had to be rasped into shreds before it could be smoked and some of the Riflemen imitated the Spanish soldiers and twisted the tobacco in paper rather than smoking it in clay pipes. The small villages would always yield generous quantities of a rough, strong cider. Vivar was astonished at the Riflemen's capacity for the drink, and even more astonished when Sharpe told him that most of the men had only joined the army to get the daily ration of a third of a pint of rum.

There was no rum to be had but, perhaps because of the plentiful cider, the men were happy; even treating Sharpe with a wary acceptance. The greenjackets had welcomed Harper back into their ranks with unfeigned delight, and Sharpe had again seen how the big man was the real leader of the men. They liked Sergeant Williams, but instinctively expected Harper to make their decisions, and Sharpe noted sourly how it was Harper, rather than himself, who melded these survivors of four separate companies into a single unit.

'Harps is a decent fellow, sir.' Sergeant Williams persevered in his role as peacemaker between the two men. 'He says he was wrong now.'

Sharpe was irritated at this second-hand compliment. 'I don't give a damn what he says.'

'He says he was never hit so hard in his life.'

'I know what he says.' Sharpe wondered if the Sergeant would talk in this way to other officers, and decided he would not. He supposed it was only because Williams knew he was an ex-Sergeant that he felt able to use such intimacy. 'You can tell Rifleman Harper,' Sharpe said with deliberate harshness, 'that if he steps out of line once more, he'll be hit so hard that he'll remember nothing.'

Williams chuckled. 'Harps won't step out of line again, sir. Major Vivar had a word with him, sir. God knows what he said, but he scared the bloody daylights out of him.' He shook his head in admiration of the Spaniard. 'The Major's a tough bugger, sir, and a rich

112

one. He's carrying a bloody fortune in that strongbox!'

'I told you it's nothing but papers,' Sharpe said carelessly.

'It's jewels, sir.' Williams took an evident pleasure in revealing the secret. 'Just like I guessed. Diamonds and things. The Major told Harps as much, sir. Harps says the jewels belong to the Major's family, and that if we get them safe to this Santy-aggy place, then the Major will give us all a piece of gold.'

'Nonsense!' Sharpe said sourly, and he knew that his sourness was provoked by an irrational jealousy. Why should Vivar tell Rifleman Harper what he would not tell him? Was it because the Irishman was a Catholic? For that matter, why would Vivar reverently lodge a family's jewels in a church? And would mere jewels have brought enemy Dragoons across wintry hills to set an ambush?

'They're ancient jewels.' Sergeant Williams was oblivious to Sharpe's doubts. 'One of them's a necklace made from the diamonds of a crown. A blackamoor's crown, sir. He was an old King, sir. An 'eathen.' It was clear that the greenjackets had been fearfully impressed. The Riflemen might march through rain and across bad roads, but their hardships were given dignity because they escorted the pagan jewels of an ancient kingdom.

'I don't believe a bloody word of it,' Sharpe said.

'The Major said you wouldn't, sir,' Williams said respectfully.

'Did Harper see these jewels?'

'That would mean bad luck, sir.' Williams had his answer ready. 'If the chest is opened, like, without all the family's permission, then the bad spirits will get you. Understand, sir?'

'Oh, entirely,' Sharpe said, but the Sergeant's belief in the jewels was beyond any of Sharpe's ironic doubts.

That afternoon, in a flooded field that was pitted with rain, Sharpe saw two gulls fly down from the west. The sight, even if it did not promise journey's end, was full of hope. To reach the sea would be an accomplishment; it denoted the end of the westward march and the beginning of the journey south, and in his eagerness he even fancied he could smell the salt in the rain-stinging air.

That night, an hour before dusk, they came to a small town built about a bridge that spanned a deep, fast river. An old stump of a fortress dominated the town, but the stronghold had long been abandoned. The *alcalde*, the mayor, assured Major Vivar there were no Frenchmen within five leagues, and that assurance persuaded him to rest in the town. 'We'll make an early start,' he told Sharpe. 'If the weather holds, we'll be in Santiago de Compostela this time tomorrow.'

'Where I turn south.'

'Where you turn south.'

The *alcalde* offered his own house to Vivar and his stables to the Cazadores, while the Riflemen were billeted in a Cistercian monastery which, sworn to offer hospitality to pilgrims, proved equally generous to the foreign soldiers. There was freshly killed pork, with beans, bread, and skins of red wine. There were even black bottles of a raw and fierce brandy called *aguardiente*, offered by a brawny monk whose scars and tattoos made him look like an old soldier. The monk also brought a sack of hard-baked bread, and intimated by dumb show that the food was for their march on the morrow. The monks' generosity convinced Sharpe that, after the cold horrors of the last weeks, he and his Riflemen would truly reach safety. The danger of the enemy at last seemed far away and, relieved of the need to set picquets against a night's alarms, Sharpe slept.

Only to be woken in the very depths of the night.

A white-robed monk, holding a lantern, searched among the dark forms of the Riflemen who slept in a cloister's arcade. Sharpe grunted and propped himself up on an elbow. He could hear noises in the street outside; the rumble of wheels and the crack of hooves.

'*Señor! Señor!*' The monk beckoned urgently to Sharpe who, cursing his broken sleep, scooped up his boots and weapons and followed the monk across the frosted cloister to the monastery's candle-lit hallway.

Standing in that hallway, with a handkerchief pressed against her mouth as though she feared a contagion, was a woman of fearsome size. She was as tall as Sharpe, as broad in the shoulders as Harper, and as large about the waist as any wine-tun. She wore a multiplicity of cloaks and capes that made her bulk seem even more massive, while her small-eyed, thin-lipped face was surmounted by a tiny bonnet of ludicrous delicacy. She ignored the importunate monks who clamoured at her in pleading tones. The great doors of the monastery stood open behind her and, in the light of torches bracketed in the street, Sharpe could see a carriage. As he arrived, the woman pushed the handkerchief into her sleeve. 'Are you an English officer?'

Sharpe was so astonished that he said nothing. It was not the demand that surprised him, nor even the stentorian voice in which it was made, but the fact that the huge woman was clearly English. 'Well?' she demanded.

'Yes, ma'am.'

'I cannot say I am glad to find an officer who has sworn allegiance to a Protestant King in such a place as this. Now put your boots on. Hurry, man!' The woman shrugged off the monks who tried to attract her attention, much as a massive milch-cow might have ignored the bleating of sheep. 'Tell me your name,' she ordered Sharpe.

'Sharpe, ma'am. Lieutenant Richard Sharpe of the Rifles.'

'Find me the most senior English officer. And button your jacket.'

'I am the senior officer, ma'am.'

The woman stared with malevolent suspicion at him. 'You?'

'Yes, ma'am.'

'You will have to suffice, then. Take your filthy hands off me!' This was to the Abbot who, with an exquisite politeness, had tried to draw the woman's attention by a tentative hand placed tremulously on the edge of one of her voluminous cloaks. 'Find me some men!' This was to Sharpe.

'Who are you, ma'am?'

'My name is Mrs Parker. You have heard of Admiral Sir Hyde Parker?'

'Indeed, ma'am.'

'He was my husband's kinsman, before God chose to translate him to glory.' Having established that she outranked Sharpe, at least by marriage, Mrs Parker returned to her more vituperative tone. 'Hurry, man!'

Sharpe, pulling on his torn boots, tried to make sense of an Englishwoman appearing at the dead of night in a Spanish monastery. 'You want men, ma'am?'

Mrs Parker looked at him as though she would wring his neck. 'Are you deaf, man? Touched? Or merely witless? Get your Papist hands off me!' This last admonition was again addressed to the Cistercian Abbot who, as if stung, jumped backwards. 'I shall wait in the carriage, Lieutenant. Hurry!' Mrs Parker, to the evident relief of the monks, stalked back to her coach.

Sharpe buckled on his sword, slung his rifle and,

without bothering to fetch any men, went out to the street which was crowded with wagons, coaches, and horsemen. There was a feeling of panic in the crowd, engendered by people who knew they must be moving, but did not know where safety might lie. Sharpe, sensing disaster, went to Mrs Parker's coach. Its plush interior was lit by a shielded lantern which showed a tall and painfully thin man trying to assist the woman to her seat.

'There you are!' Mrs Parker, succeeding at last in twisting her vast bulk onto the leather bench, frowned at Sharpe. 'You have men?'

'Why do you want them, ma'am?'

'Why do I want them? Did you hear that, George? One of his Majesty's officers discovers a defenceless Englishwoman, stranded in a Papist country and endangered by the French, and he asks questions!' Mrs Parker leaned forward to fill the open carriage door. 'Get them!'

'Why?' Sharpe barked the word, astonishing Mrs Parker who was clearly not accustomed to opposition.

'For the testaments.' It was the man who replied. He peered around Mrs Parker to offer Sharpe a very tentative smile. 'My name is Parker, George Parker. I have the honour to be a cousin to the late Admiral Sir Hyde Parker.' He said the last in a weary tone, revealing that whatever glory Mr George Parker might have achieved in this life was due solely to the reflected lustre of his cousin. 'My wife and I have need of your assistance.'

'We have Spanish translations of the New Testament,' Mrs Parker interrupted, 'hidden in this town, Lieutenant. The Spanish confiscate such scriptures unless we hide them. We require your men to rescue them.' Such an explanation clearly constituted a conciliatory

117

speech, and one that her husband rewarded with an eager nod.

'You want my Rifles to rescue testaments from the Spanish?' Sharpe asked in utter confusion.

'From the French, you fool!' Mrs Parker bellowed out of the carriage.

'They're here?'

'They entered Santiago de Compostela yesterday,' Mr Parker said sadly.

'Jesus Christ!'

The blasphemy had the happy effect of silencing Mrs Parker. Her husband, seeing Sharpe's shock, leaned forward. 'You haven't heard of the events at Corunna?'

Sharpe almost did not want to hear. 'I've heard nothing, sir.'

'There was a battle, Lieutenant. It seems the British army succeeded in escaping to sea, but at the expense of many lives. Sir John Moore is said to be dead. The French, it seems, are now masters of this part of Spain.'

'Good God.'

'We were told of your presence when we arrived here,' George Parker explained, 'and now we beg your protection.'

'Of course.' Sharpe glanced up the street, understanding the panic. The French had taken the Atlantic ports at the north-western corner of Spain. The British were gone, the Spanish armies squandered, and soon Napoleon's troops would turn southwards to complete their victory. 'How far is Corunna from here?'

'Eleven leagues? Twelve?' George Parker's face, pale in the candlelight, was drawn and worried. And no wonder, Sharpe thought. The French were scarcely a day's march away.

'Will you hurry?' Mrs Parker, recovered from the

118

shock of Sharpe's blasphemy, leaned vengefully forward.

'Wait, ma'am.' Sharpe ran back into the monastery. 'Sergeant Williams! Sergeant Williams!'

It took ten minutes to rouse and parade the Riflemen who staggered sleepily into the street where, under the torchlight, Sharpe shouted them into their ranks. The men's breath steamed in the flamelight as he felt the first stinging drops of rain. The monks were generously bringing small sacks of bread out to the soldiers who seemed bemused by the shouting chaos in the small street.

'Lieutenant! Will you hurry!' It was Mrs Parker, making the carriage springs creak as she leaned forward. It was then that Rifleman Harper let out a piercing whistle, the other men cheered, and Sharpe whipped round to make a most unwelcome discovery.

There was a third person in the carriage; a person who, till now, had been concealed by Mrs Parker's great bulk. It seemed Mrs Parker must have a maid, or perhaps a companion, or else a daughter, and the girl, if indeed she was Mrs Parker's daughter, did not take after her mother. Not in the least. Sharpe saw a bright-eyed face, dark curls, and a mischievous smile which, among soldiers, could only mean trouble. 'Oh, shit,' he muttered.

Sharpe had roused and paraded his men and, not knowing what to do with them now, and while he waited for Blas Vivar to appear from the *alcalde*'s house where a council of town elders had been hurriedly convened, he let his men rescue the Spanish New Testaments from the stable of a bookseller who had hidden the books for George Parker.

'The Church of Rome doesn't approve, you understand?' George Parker, away from his wife, proved a courtly and somewhat sad character. 'They wish to keep their people in the darkness of ignorance. The Archbishop of Seville confiscated a thousand testaments and burned them. Can you credit such behaviour? That's why we came north. I believed Salamanca might prove a more fertile field for our endeavours, but the Archbishop there threatened a similar confiscation. So we went to Santiago, and on the way we sheltered our precious books with this good man,' Parker gestured towards the bookseller's home. 'I believe he sells a few on his own account, but I can scarce blame him for that. Indeed not. And if he spreads the gospel, Lieutenant, unadulterated by the priests of Rome, it can only be to God's glory, don't you agree?'

Sharpe was too befuddled by the night's strange happenings to offer agreement. He watched as another stack of the black bound books was brought out into the street and packed into the carriage's rear box. 'You're in Spain to distribute bibles?'

'Only since the peace treaty between our two countries was signed,' Parker said as though that explained everything, then, seeing that puzzlement remained on Sharpe's face, he offered further information. 'My dear wife and I, you must understand, are followers of the late John Wesley.'

'The Methodist?'

'Exactly and precisely so,' Parker nodded vigorously, 'and when my late cousin, the Admiral, was gracious enough to remember me in his will, my dear wife deemed that the money might most appropriately be spent upon the illumination of the Popish darkness that so envelops southern Europe. We saw the declaration of a peace between England and Spain as a providence of God that directed our steps hither.'

'To much success?' Sharpe could not resist asking,

though the answer was clearly visible on Parker's lugubrious face.

'Alas, Lieutenant, the people of Spain are obstinate in their Romish heresy. But if just one soul is brought to a knowledge of God's saving and Protestant grace, then I will feel amply justified in this endeavour.' Parker paused. 'And you, Lieutenant? May I enquire if you have a personal knowledge of your Lord and Saviour?'

'I'm a Rifleman, sir,' Sharpe said firmly, anxious to avoid a Protestant attack on his already Catholic-besieged soul. 'Our religion is killing crapauds and other such heathen bastards who don't like good King George.'

The belligerence of Sharpe's answer silenced Parker for a moment. The middle-aged man stared gloomily at the refugees in the street, then sighed. 'You are a soldier, of course. But perhaps you will forgive me, Lieutenant?'

'Forgive you, sir?'

'My cousin, the late Admiral, was much given to strong oaths. I do not wish to offend, Lieutenant, but my dear wife and niece are not accustomed to the strong language of the military man, and . . .' His voice faded away.

'I apologize, sir. I'll try and remember.' Sharpe gestured towards the bookseller's house where Mrs Parker and the girl had taken temporary shelter. 'She's your niece, sir? She seems a little young to be travelling in such a troubled place?'

If Parker suspected that Sharpe was fishing for information about his niece, he showed no resentment. 'Louisa is nineteen, Lieutenant, but sadly orphaned. My dear wife offered her employment as a companion. We had no conception, of course, that the war would take such a disadvantageous course. We believed that, with a British army campaigning in Spain, we would be both welcome and protected.'

'Perhaps God's a Frenchman these days?' Sharpe said lightly.

Parker ignored the levity. Instead he watched the stream of refugees who straggled through the night with their bundles of clothes. Children cried. A woman dragged two goats on lengths of rope. A cripple swung by on crutches. Parker shook his head. 'There is a great fear of the French here.'

'They're bastards, sir. Forgive me,' Sharpe blushed. 'Were you in Santiago de Compostela when they arrived?'

'Their cavalry reached the northern edge of the town yesterday evening, which gave us time to make our escape. The Lord was very providential, I think.'

'Indeed, sir.'

Sergeant Williams, grinning broadly, stood to attention before Sharpe. 'That's all the holy books loaded up, sir. Want me to fetch the ladies?'

Sharpe looked at Parker. 'Are you travelling on tonight, sir?'

Parker was clearly bemused by the question. 'We'll do whatever you think best, Lieutenant.'

'It's up to you, sir.'

'Me?'

It was obvious that George Parker was as indecisive as his cousin, Sir Hyde, whose prevarication had nearly lost the battle of Copenhagen. Sharpe tried to explain what choices the family faced. 'This road, sir, only goes east or west, and the French lie in both directions. I assume that now your books are safe, sir, you'll have to choose one way or the other? They say the French behave well enough to innocent English travellers.

You'll doubtless be questioned, and there'll be some inconvenience, but they'll probably give you permission to travel south. Might I suggest Lisbon, sir? I've heard there's still a small British garrison there, but even if the garrison's sailed away, you should be able to find a British merchant ship.'

Parker stared worriedly at Sharpe. 'And you, Lieutenant? What is your intention?'

'I can hardly depend on French forbearance, sir.' He smiled. 'No, we're going south, sir. We'd hoped to take the road from Santiago de Compostela, but since the bast – since the French are there, sir, we'll cut across the hills.' Sharpe slapped one of the muddy wheels of the big coach. 'No chance of that thing going with us, sir, so I fear you'll have to ask French permission to cross their territory.'

Parker had been shaking his head for a few seconds. 'I do assure you, Lieutenant, that my wife and I have no intention of humbling ourselves before the enemy so long as there is a viable escape for us. We shall travel south with you. And I can further assure you that there is a perfectly good southern road from this town. There!' He pointed to the bridge. 'Just the other side of the river.'

Sharpe's astonishment made him silent for a second. 'There's a road that goes south from here?'

'Precisely and exactly so? Otherwise I would hardly have dared come here for my testaments.'

'But I was told . . .' Sharpe realized abruptly that there was no point in retelling Vivar's assertion that no such southern road existed. 'Are you sure, sir?'

'I travelled it but a month ago.' Parker saw Sharpe's hesitation. 'I have a map, Lieutenant. You wish to see it?'

Sharpe followed Parker into the bookseller's house.

Mrs Parker, sitting massively by the fire, offered the greenjacket a suspicious glance.

'All the testaments are safe, my dear,' Parker said meekly, 'and I wondered if we might peruse the map?'

'Louisa?' Mrs Parker demanded of her niece. 'The map.'

The girl obediently crossed to a leather valise and searched among the papers. Sharpe deliberately kept his eyes away from her. Louisa Parker, from the glimpses he had already caught of her, was disturbingly pretty. She had a tall and slender grace, a brightly inquisitive face, and a clear skin unscarred by hardship or disease. A girl, Sharpe thought, to make a soldier twitch in his dreams, even if she was a God-damned Methodist.

Louisa brought the map to the table. George Parker attempted an introduction. 'Louisa, my dear, you have not been named to Lieutenant . . .'

'Louisa!' Mrs Parker, evidently well aware of the dangers that soldiers presented to young girls, interrupted. 'You will come here and sit!'

Sharpe unfolded the map in the ensuing silence.

'It isn't a very accurate map,' Parker said humbly, as if he was personally responsible for its vagaries, 'but I assure you the road exists.' He traced a thin black line which meant little to Sharpe who was still trying to find just where he was on the ill-printed sheet. 'The road meets the coastal route here, well south of Villagarcia,' Parker continued, 'and I was hoping we might find a vessel here, at Pontevedra. I believe the Royal Navy patrols this coast and, God willing, perhaps a friendly fisherman can be persuaded to take us to one of their ships?'

Sharpe was not really listening. He was staring at the map, trying to discover the tortuous route he had followed with Vivar. He could not find the exact course of the journey, but one thing was very clear: in the last days, he and his Riflemen had passed at least two southern roads. Vivar had told Sharpe again and again that there was no southern road, that the Riflemen must go to Santiago de Compostela before they turned towards Lisbon. The Spaniard had lied.

George Parker mistook Sharpe's grim expression for pessimism. 'I do assure you the road exists.'

Sharpe was suddenly very aware of the girl's gaze on him, and all his soldier's protective instincts were warmed by that examination. 'You say you travelled the road a month ago, sir?'

'Indeed.'

'And a coach can manage it in winter?'

'Indeed it can.'

'Do you intend to fritter away this whole night?' Mrs Parker stood threateningly. 'Or do British soldiers no longer care for the fate of British womanhood?'

Sharpe folded the map and, without permission, thrust it into his pouch. 'We can leave very soon, ma'am, but first I have business in the town.'

'Business!' Mrs Parker was clearly stoking the fires of her awesome wrath. 'What possible business can a Lieutenant have, Mr Sharpe, that will take precedence over our safety?'

Sharpe pulled open the door. 'I shall be a quarter of an hour at the most. You will do me the kindness, ma'am, of being ready in ten minutes. I have two wounded men who will need to travel inside your carriage.' He saw another protest boiling up inside her. 'And my men's packs will travel on the roof. Otherwise, ma'am, you can find your way south without me.' He offered a trace of a bow. 'Your servant, ma'am.'

Sharpe turned away before Mrs Parker could argue

125

with him, and he could have sworn he heard an amused chuckle from the girl. God damn it! God damn it! God damn it! He had enough to worry about without that perennial soldier's problem. He went to find Vivar.

'Good news!' Vivar greeted Sharpe the moment the Rifleman appeared in the *alcalde*'s house. 'My reinforcements are a mere half-day away! Lieutenant Davila has found fresh horses and fresh men! Did I tell you about Davila?'

'You didn't tell me about the road, did you?'

'Road?'

'You told me we had to go west before we could go south!' Sharpe had not meant to speak with such anger, but he could not hide his bitterness. He and his men had crossed a cold country, clambering wet hills and struggling through icy streams, and all for nothing. They could have headed south days ago. By now they could be across the Portuguese border. Instead they were within a few hours' march of the enemy. 'The road!' He slammed George Parker's map onto the table. 'There's a road, Vivar! A God-damned road! And you marched us past two other God-damned roads! And the God-damned French are just a day's bloody march away. You bloody lied to me!'

'Lied to you?' Blas Vivar's anger flared as fiercely as Sharpe's. 'I saved your miserable lives! You think your men would have lasted a week in Spain without me? If you're not fighting amongst yourselves, you're all getting drunk! I've brought a pack of useless drunkards across Spain and I get no thanks, none. I spit on your map!' Vivar seized the precious map and, instead of spitting on it, tore it into shreds which he tossed onto the fire.

The *alcalde*, together with a priest and half a dozen

other elderly and serious men, watched the confrontation in perturbed silence.

'Damn you!' Sharpe had grabbed at the map a second too late.

'Damn me?' Vivar shouted. 'I'm fighting for Spain, Lieutenant. I'm not running away like a frightened little boy. But that's the British way, isn't it? One setback and they run home to their mothers. Very well! Run away! But you won't find a garrison at Lisbon, Lieutenant. They'll have run away too!'

Sharpe ignored the insults to ask the question that boiled indignantly inside him. 'Why did you bring us here at all, you bastard?'

Vivar leaned over the table. 'Because for once in your benighted life, Lieutenant, I thought an Englishman could do something for Spain. Something for God. Something useful! You're a nation of pirates, of barbarians, of heathens! God alone knows why He put the English on this earth, but I thought, just once, you might do something of use to His creation!'

'To protect your precious strongbox?' Sharpe gestured at the mysterious chest which stood against one wall. 'You'd have lost the bloody thing without us, wouldn't you? And why, Major? Because your precious Spanish armies are bloody useless, that's why!'

'And your army's broken, beaten, and gone. It's less than useless. Now get out! Run away!'

'I hope the French get your bloody box.' Sharpe twisted away, then heard the rasp of a sword being drawn. He whipped back, scraping his own sword quickly from its mended scabbard as Vivar, blade already flickering in the candlelight, came towards him.

'*Basta!*' It was the priest who threw himself between the two furious men. He pleaded with Vivar, who stared contemptuously at Sharpe. Understanding none of the conversation, the Rifleman held his ground with his sword still raised.

Vivar, reluctantly persuaded by the priest, dropped his blade. 'You won't last a day without me, Lieutenant, but get out!'

Sharpe spat on the floor to show his own contempt, then, his sword still drawn, went back into the night. The French had gained the north, and he must flee.

CHAPTER 7

Progress during the first day of the southward journey proved better than Sharpe had dared to hope. The Parkers' carriage was cumbersome, but it had broad-rimmed wheels designed to cope with rutted and muddy roads and a patient Spanish coachman who skilfully handled its team of six big draught horses. Only twice in that first day was it necessary for the Riflemen to help pull the carriage out of difficulty; once on a steep incline and the second time when a wheel dropped into a roadside morass. Of Louisa Parker Sharpe saw nothing, for the girl's aunt made certain that she stayed safely mewed up behind the coach's drawn leather curtains.

The size and cost of the carriage impressed Sharpe. The Parkers' self-imposed mission to enlighten the Papist heathens of Spain clearly lacked for little and George Parker, who seemed to prefer walking with Sharpe to the company of his wife, explained that it was the bequest of the Admiral's prize money that had made such comforts possible.

'Was the Admiral a religious man, sir?' Sharpe asked.

'Alas, no. Far from it. But a wealthy one, Lieutenant. Nor do I see,' Parker was clearly piqued by Sharpe's questions about the carriage's cost, 'why the Lord's work should be constrained by a paucity of funds, do you?'

'Indeed not,' Sharpe cheerfully agreed. 'But why Spain, sir? I'd have thought there were enough heathens in England without bothering the Spanish.'

'Because the Spanish labour under the darkness of Rome, Lieutenant. Do you have any idea what that means? The horror of it? I can tell you tales of priestly behaviour that would make you shudder! Do you know what superstitions these people harbour?'

'I've an idea, sir.' Sharpe turned to check on the carriage's progress. His two wounded men were travelling on the roof, banished there on Mrs Parker's insistence. 'But the Dons don't seem quite ready for Methodism, sir, if you'll forgive me saying as much.'

'It is stony ground,' Parker agreed glumly.

'Mind you, I knew an officer in India who converted the heathen to Christianity,' Sharpe said helpfully, 'and he was most successful.'

'Truly?' Mr Parker was pleased to hear of this evidence of God's grace. 'A godly man?'

'Mad as a hatter, sir. One of the Royal Irish, and they've all got wormscrew wits.'

'But you say he was successful?'

'He threatened to blow their heads off with a musket unless they were baptized, sir. That queue went twice round the armoury and clear back to the guardhouse.'

Mr Parker fell silent, plunged into a gloom that was matched only by the rebellious mood of the trudging Riflemen. Sharpe's own cheerfulness was forced, for he was unwilling to admit that the small progress he had so far made in gaining the Riflemen's confidence had been shattered by his decision to strike off south alone. He told himself that the men's sullenness was due to lack of sleep, while in truth he knew it was because they had been forced to leave Major Vivar. They trusted Vivar, while his own authority over them was still on

130

trial, and that knowledge fretted at Sharpe's fragile dignity.

Confirmation of the Riflemen's unhappiness came from Sergeant Williams, who fell into step with Sharpe as the small column marched between wide apple orchards. 'The lads really wanted to stay with the Major, sir.'

'For Christ's sake why?'

'Because of his jewels, sir! He was going to give us gold when we got to Santy-aggy.'

'You're a bloody fool, Sergeant. There was never going to be any gold. There may have been jewels in that damned box, but the only reason he wanted our company was to give him protection.' Sharpe was certain he was right. Vivar's encounter with the Riflemen had almost doubled the Major's small force, and Sharpe's duty was not to some damned strongbox but to the British army. 'We'd never have reached Santiago anyway. It's full of the damned Frogs.'

'Yes, sir,' Williams said dutifully, but with regret.

They stopped that night in a small town where George Parker's command of Spanish secured space in an inn. The Parkers hired themselves one of the rooms off the tavern's large chamber, while the Riflemen were given the use of a stable.

The remains of the monastery's gift of bread was the only food the men carried, and Sharpe knew they needed more. The innkeeper had meat and wine, but would not part with either unless Sharpe paid. He had no money, so approached George Parker who confessed, sadly, that his wife controlled the family purse.

Mrs Parker, divesting herself of cloaks and scarves, seemed to swell with indignation at his request. 'Money, Mr Sharpe?'

'The men need meat, ma'am.'

'We are to make a subvention to the army?'

'It will be repaid, ma'am.' Sharpe felt Louisa's gaze on him but, in the interests of his men's appetites, he resisted looking at the niece for fear of offending the aunt.

Mrs Parker jangled her leather purse. 'This is Christ's money, Lieutenant.'

'We're only borrowing it, ma'am. And my men can offer you no protection if they're starving.'

That argument, put so humbly, seemed to convince Mrs Parker. She demanded the presence of the inn-keeper with whom she negotiated the purchase of a pot of goat-bones which, she told Sharpe, could be seethed into a nourishing broth.

When the haggling was done, Sharpe hesitated before writing out the receipt that Mrs Parker demanded. 'And some money for wine, ma'am?'

George Parker raised eyes to the ceiling, Louisa busied herself with candle-wicks, and Mrs Parker turned to stare with horror at Sharpe. 'Wine?'

'Yes, ma'am.'

'Your men are bibbers of strong drink?'

'They're entitled to wine, ma'am.'

'Entitled?' The rising inflection presaged trouble.

'British army regulations, ma'am. One third of a pint of spirits a day, ma'am, or a pint of wine.'

'Each?'

'Of course, ma'am.'

'Not, Lieutenant Sharpe, while they are escorting Christian folk to safety.' Mrs Parker thrust the purse into a pocket of her skirt. 'Our Lord and Saviour's money, Lieutenant, will not be frittered away on liquor. Your men may drink water. My husband and I drink nothing but water.'

'Or small beer,' George hastened to correct her.

Mrs Parker ignored him. 'The receipt, Lieutenant, if you please.'

Sharpe dutifully signed the piece of paper, then followed the innkeeper into the large room where, for lack of any other currency, he sliced off four of the silver buttons sewn on the outside seams of his uniform trousers. The buttons purchased enough wineskins to give each man a cupful. The issue, like the pot of gristly bones, was received in sullen silence that was only broken by a mutinous muttering when Sharpe announced a reveille for four o'clock in the morning. Stung by this new evidence of the Riflemen's most unco-operative behaviour, he snapped that if any man preferred to be a French prisoner, then that man could leave now. He gestured to the stable door, beyond which the frost was already forming on the stableyard.

No one spoke or moved. Sharpe could see Harper's eyes glittering from the back of the stable, and he saw again how the Riflemen had instinctively grouped themselves about the big Irishman. But there was no point in looking to Harper for help. He, more than any man, seemed to resent leaving Major Vivar, though what purpose any of them imagined would be served by staying at the Major's side was beyond Sharpe's imagination. 'Four o'clock!' he said. 'And we'll be marching at five!'

Mrs Parker was no happier at the news than the Riflemen. 'Rising at four? You think a body can survive without sleep, Lieutenant?'

'I think, ma'am, that it's best to be travelling before the French.' Sharpe hesitated, not willing to make another request of this disobliging woman, but knowing he could not trust himself to judge the hours in the night's blackness. 'I was wondering, ma'am, if you had a clock, or a watch?'

'A timepiece, Lieutenant?' Mrs Parker asked the question to gain time in which to marshal her forces of rejection.

'Please, ma'am.'

Louisa smiled at Sharpe from her seat on the shelf in the alcove which formed the bed. Her aunt, seeing the smile, snatched the alcove's curtain closed. 'You, of course, will sleep outside this door. Lieutenant?'

Sharpe, thinking of timepieces, was taken aback by the peremptory demand. 'I beg your pardon, ma'am?'

'There are defenceless females in this room, Lieutenant! British females!'

'I'm certain you will be safe, ma'am.' Sharpe pointed at the heavy bolt inside the door.

'Have you no conception of your responsibilities, Lieutenant?' Mrs Parker advanced in wrath. 'Is it any wonder that you have never secured promotion beyond your lowly rank?'

'Ma'am, I . . .'

'Do not interrupt me! I will have none of your barrack manners here, Lieutenant. Have you seen the Papist creatures who are drinking like animals in this tavern? Do you know what horrors strong drink provokes? And let me remind you that Mr Parker paid his taxes in England, which entitles us to your protection.'

George Parker, trying to read his scriptures by the light of a tallow dip, looked beseechingly at Sharpe. 'Please, Lieutenant?'

'I shall sleep outside, ma'am, but I need a timepiece.'

Mrs Parker, pleased with her small victory, smiled. 'If you are to guard us, Lieutenant, then you will want to be wakeful. Turning an hourglass will keep you from slumbering. George?'

George Parker rooted about in his valise to produce an hourglass that he handed, with an apologetic grimace, to Sharpe. Mrs Parker nodded satisfaction. 'It lacks twenty-five minutes of ten o'clock, Lieutenant, and the glass takes one hour to evacuate itself.' She waved an imperious hand in dismissal.

Sharpe leaned on the wall outside the Parker's room. He put the hourglass on a window sill and watched the first grains trickle through. Damn the bloody woman. No wonder the army discouraged the spread of Methodism in its ranks. Yet in one way Sharpe was glad to be a bodyguard, even to someone as disobliging as Mrs Parker, for it gave him an excuse not to go back to the stable where his Riflemen would make their displeasure and disdain clear once more. There had been a time when the company of such men had been his life and pleasure, but now, because he was an officer, he was bereft of such companionship. He felt an immense and hopeless weariness, and wished this damned journey was over.

He cut one more button from his trousers which already gaped to show a length of scarred thigh, and bought himself a skin of wine. He drank it quickly and miserably, then dragged a bench close to the family's door. The tavern customers, suspicious of the ragged, harsh-faced, foreign soldier, kept clear of him. The bench was close to a small unshuttered window that gave Sharpe a view of the stables. He half suspected that the Riflemen might attempt another mutiny, perhaps sneaking off in the darkness to rejoin their beloved Major Vivar, but except for a few men who appeared in the stableyard to urinate, all seemed calm. Calm, but not quiet. Sharpe could hear the Riflemen's laughter and it galled his loneliness. Gradually the laughter turned to silence.

He could not sleep. The tavern emptied, except for two drovers who snored cheerfully by the dying fire and the potman who made his bed under the serving hatch. Sharpe felt the beginnings of a headache. He suddenly missed Vivar. The Spaniard's cheerfulness and certainty had made the long march bearable, and now he felt adrift in chaos. What if the British garrison had left Lisbon? Or what if there were no naval ships off the coast? Was he doomed to wander through Spain till, at last, the French solved his problems by making him a prisoner? And what if they did? The war must soon end with French victory, and the French would send their prisoners home. Sharpe would go back to England as just another failed officer who must eke out a bare existence on half-pay. He turned the hourglass and scratched another mark on the limewashed wall.

There was a half-collapsed skin of wine beside the sleeping drovers and Sharpe stole it. He squirted the foul liquid into his mouth, hoping that the raw taste would cut through his burgeoning headache. He knew it would not. He knew that in the morning he would feel foul-tempered and sore. So, doubtless, would his men, and the memory of their sullenness only depressed him more. Damn them. Damn Williams. Damn Harper. Damn Vivar. Damn Sir John Moore for ruining the best damned army that had ever left England. And damn Spain and damn the bloody Parkers and damn the bloody cold that slowly seeped into the tavern as the fire died.

He heard the bolt shifting in the door behind him. It was being drawn surreptitiously and with excruciating care. Then, after what seemed a long time, the heavy door creaked ajar. A pair of nervous eyes stared at Sharpe. 'Lieutenant?'

'Miss?'

'I brought you this.' Louisa closed the door very, very carefully and crossed to the bench. She held out a thick silver watch. 'It's a striking watch,' she said quietly, 'and I have set it to ring at four o'clock.'

Sharpe took the heavy watch. 'Thank you.'

'I have to apologize,' Louisa said hastily.

'No . . .'

'Indeed I do. I spend many hours apologizing for my aunt's behaviour. Perhaps tomorrow you would be kind enough to return the watch without her noticing?'

'Of course.'

'I also thought you might like this, Lieutenant.' She smiled mischievously as she brought a black bottle from beneath her cloak. To Sharpe's astonishment it held Spanish brandy. 'It's my uncle's,' she explained, 'though he's not supposed to drink it. He'll think my aunt found it and threw it away.'

'Thank you.' Sharpe swallowed some of the fierce liquid. Then, with awkward courtesy, he wiped the bottle's mouth on his dirty sleeve and offered it to Louisa.

'No, thank you.' She smiled at the clumsy gesture but, recognizing it as a friendly invitation, sat in decorous acceptance at the far end of Sharpe's bench. She was still dressed in skirts, cloak and bonnet.

'Your uncle drinks?' Sharpe asked in amazement.

'Wouldn't you? Married to her?' Louisa smiled at his expression. 'Believe me, Lieutenant, I only came with my aunt for the opportunity to see Spain. It was hardly because I desired months of her company.'

'I see,' Sharpe said, though he really did not understand any of it, and certainly not why this girl had sought his company in the middle of the night. He did not think she had risked her aunt's wrath just to lend him a watch, but she seemed eager to talk and, even though her presence made him shy and tongue-tied, he wanted her to stay. The dying fire cast just enough light to give a red sheen to her face. He thought her very beautiful.

'My aunt is uncommonly rude,' Louisa said in further apology. 'She had no cause to comment on your rank in the manner that she did.'

Sharpe shrugged. 'She's right. I am old to be a Lieutenant, but five years ago I was a Sergeant.'

Louisa looked at him with new interest. 'Truly?'

'Truly.'

She smiled, thus striking darts of desire into Sharpe's soul. 'I think you must be an extremely remarkable man, Lieutenant, though I should tell you that my aunt thinks you are extremely uncouth. She continually expresses amazement that you hold His Majesty's commission, and avers that Sir Hyde would never have allowed a ruffian like you as an officer on one of his ships.'

For an instant Sharpe's battered self-esteem made him bristle at the criticism, then he saw that Louisa's face was mischievous rather than serious. He saw, too, a friendliness in the girl. It was a friendliness that Sharpe had not received from anyone in months and, though he warmed to it, his awkwardness made his response clumsy. A born officer, he thought sourly, would know how to reply to the girl's dry humour, but he could only ask a dull question. 'Was Sir Hyde your father?'

'He was a cousin of my father's, a very distant cousin indeed. I'm told he was not a good Admiral. He believed Nelson was a mere adventurer.' She froze, alerted by a sudden noise, but it was only the fall of a log in the smouldering fire. 'But he became a very rich Admiral,' Louisa went on, 'and the family benefited from all that prize money.'

'So you're rich?' Sharpe could not help asking.

'Not I. But my aunt received a sufficiency to create

trouble in the world.' Louisa spoke very gravely. 'Have you any idea, Mr Sharpe, just how embarrassing it is to be spreading Protestantism in Spain?'

Sharpe shrugged. 'You volunteered, miss.'

'True. And the embarrassment is the price I pay for seeing Granada and Seville.' Her eyes lit up, or perhaps it was just the reflected flare of glowing embers. 'I would like to see more!'

'But you're returning to England?'

'My aunt thinks that is wise.' Louisa's voice was carefully mocking. 'The Spanish, you see, are not welcoming her attempts to free them from Rome's shackles.'

'But you'd like to stay?'

'It's scarcely possible, is it? Young women, Mr Sharpe, do not have the freedom of this world. I must return to Godalming where a Mr Bufford awaits me.'

Sharpe had to smile at her tone. 'Mr Bufford?'

'He's entirely respectable,' Louisa said, as though Sharpe had intimidated otherwise, 'and, of course, a Methodist. His money comes from the manufacture of ink, a trade of such profitability that the future Mrs Bufford may look forward to a large house and a life of great, if tedious, comfort. Certainly it will never be discoloured by the ink, which is manufactured in far-away Deptford.'

Sharpe had never before talked with a girl of Louisa's evident education, nor heard the monied class spoken of with such deprecation. He had always believed that anyone born to great, if tedious, comfort would be eternally grateful for the gift. 'You're the future Mrs Bufford?'

'That is the intention, yes.'

'But you don't want to be married?'

'I do desire that, I think.' Louisa frowned. 'Are you married?'

'I'm not rich enough to marry.'

'That's rarely stopped others, I think. No, Mr Sharpe, I simply do not desire to marry Mr Bufford, though my reluctance is doubtless very selfish of me.' Louisa shrugged away her indiscretions. 'But I did not hope to find you awake just to impose my small unhappiness on you. I wished to ask of you, Lieutenant, whether our presence makes it more likely that you and your men will be captured by the French?'

The answer was clearly yes, but equally clearly Sharpe could not say so. 'No, miss. So long as we keep going at a fair clip, we should keep ahead of the bast— of them.'

'I was going to enjoin you, should you have answered me truthfully, to abandon us to the bast— to them.' Louisa smiled her gravely mischievous smile.

'I wouldn't abandon you, miss,' Sharpe said clumsily, glad that the gloom hid his blush.

'My aunt does provoke great loyalty.'

'Exactly.' Sharpe smiled, and the smile turned into a laugh which Louisa hushed by holding a finger to her lips.

'Thank you, Lieutenant.' She stood. 'I hope you do not feel badly about our encumbering you?'

'Not now, miss.'

Louisa crept to her door. 'Sleep well, Lieutenant.'

'And you, miss.' Sharpe watched as she slipped through the door, and held his breath until he heard the bolt slide safely shut on its far side. His sleep would be turbulent now, for all his thoughts and desires and dreams had been turned inside out and upside down by a gentle, mocking smile. Richard Sharpe was far from home, endangered by a conquering enemy and, just to make things worse, he had fallen in love.

*   *   *

At four in the morning Sharpe was woken by the tinkling alarm of Louisa's silver watch. He hammered on the Parkers' door until a groan assured him the family was awake. Then he went to the stable and found that his men had not absconded in the night. They were all present, and they were nearly all drunk.

They were not as drunk as the men who had been abandoned to the French during the retreat, but they had come close. All but a handful of them were insensible, soused, unconscious. The wineskins which Sharpe had purchased lay empty on the floor, but among the bedding straw were also numerous empty bottles of *aguardiente* and he knew that the Cistercian monks, when they had brought out the sacks of bread, had secreted the brandy as part of their gift. Sharpe swore.

Sergeant Williams was groggy, but managed to stagger to his feet. 'It was the lads, sir,' he said helplessly. 'They was upset, sir.'

'Why didn't you tell me about the brandy?'

'Tell you, sir?' Williams was astonished that he should expect such a thing.

'God damn them.' Sharpe's head was thick, his own belly sore, but his hangover was as nothing compared to the state of the greenjackets. 'Get the bastards up!'

Williams hiccupped. The lantern revealed just how hopeless was the task of rousing the Riflemen but, scared by Sharpe's demeanour, he made some feeble attempts to stir the nearest man.

Sharpe brushed Williams aside. He shouted at the men. He kicked them awake, dragged them up from stupor, and he punched tender bellies so that suffering men vomited on the stable floor. 'Up! Up! Up!'

The men reeled in dazed confusion. This was ever the danger in this army. The men joined for drink. They could only be kept in the ranks by the daily issue of rum. They took every opportunity to drown themselves in liquor. Sharpe had done it himself as a redcoat, but now he was an officer and his authority once again had been flouted. He primed his loaded rifle with dry powder, and cocked the flint. Sergeant Williams flinched from the expected noise, Sharpe pulled the trigger, and the explosion hammered about the stable. 'Up, you bastards! Up, up!' Sharpe kicked out again, his anger made worse by his own incompetence in not knowing about the brandy. He was also keenly and miserably aware of how badly this behaviour would appear to Miss Louisa Parker.

By a quarter past five, in a drizzle that promised to persist all day, Sharpe finally paraded the men on the road. The Parkers' carriage was being manoeuvred out of the tavern yard as Sharpe, in the light of a lantern carried by Sergeant Williams, inspected weapons and equipment. He smelt each canteen and poured what was left of the brandy onto the road.

'Sergeant Williams?'

'Sir?'

'We'll go at the quick!' The quick march of the Rifles was immensely fast and, anticipating the pain to come, the men groaned. 'Silence!' Sharpe bellowed. 'Rifles will turn to the right! Right turn!' The men's unshaven faces were bleary, their eyes reddened, their drill sloppy. 'Quick march!'

They marched into a grey and dispiriting dawn. Sharpe forced the pace so hard that some men had to drop out to vomit into the flooded ditches. He kicked them back into line. At this moment he thought he probably hated these men, and almost wanted them to defy him so that he could swear and lash out at the ill-disciplined bastards. He forced them so fast that the Parkers' carriage fell behind.

Sharpe ignored its slow progress. Instead he made the Riflemen's pace still quicker until Sergeant Williams, fearing the men's mutinous mood, fell back to his side. At this point the road twisted down a long slope towards a wide stream that was crossed by a stone bridge. 'They can't do it, sir.'

'They can get drunk, though, can't they? So let them bloody suffer now.'

Sergeant Williams was clearly suffering. He was pale and breathless, dragging his feet, seemingly on the point of being sick. Other men were in a far worse state. 'I'm sorry, sir,' he said feebly.

'I should have abandoned you to the French. All of you.' Sharpe's anger was made worse by remorse. He knew it was his own fault. He should have had the courage to inspect the stables in the night, but instead he had tried to hide from the men's dislike by staying in the inn. He remembered the drunks who had been abandoned during Sir John Moore's retreat; hopeless men left to the untender mercies of the pursuing French and, though he had just threatened them with the same fate, Sharpe knew he would not abandon these men. It was a matter of pride now. He would bring this group of Riflemen out of disaster. They might not thank him for it, they might not like him for it, but he would take them through hell if it led to safety. Vivar had said it could not be done, but Sharpe would do it.

'I'm sorry, sir.' Williams still tried to assuage him.

Sharpe said nothing. He was thinking how much easier this ordeal would be if he had a Sergeant who could keep the men to order. Williams cared too much about being liked, but there was no one else he could see taking the stripes. Gataker was too fly and too eager for the good opinion of his fellow Riflemen. Tongue was educated, but the worst drunkard in the company. Parry Jenkins, the Welshman, could have made a Sergeant, but Sharpe suspected he lacked the necessary ruthlessness. Hagman was too lazy. Dodd, the quiet man, was too slow and diffident. There was only Harper, and he, Sharpe knew, would do nothing to help the despised Quartermaster. Sharpe was stuck with Williams, just as Williams and the company were stuck with Lieutenant Sharpe who, when he reached the stone bridge, ordered the men to halt.

They halted. There was relief on their faces. The coach was out of sight, still negotiating the boulders beyond the hill's crest.

'Company!' Sharpe's loud voice made some of the men wince. 'Ground arms!'

There was more relief as they grounded their heavy weapons, then as they unbuckled their bayonets and pouches. Sharpe separated the handful of men who had been sober that morning and ordered the rest to take off their packs, greatcoats, and boots.

The men thought he was mad, but all soldiers were used to humouring eccentric officers and so they removed their boots under the Lieutenant's sour gaze. The coach appeared at the top of the slope and Sharpe snapped at the men to look to their front and not gape at it. The squeal of the carriage's brake-blocks was like a nail scratching on slate. 'You did not have my permission to get drunk.' Sharpe's voice was flat now, no longer angry. 'I hope, as a result, that you feel Goddamned awful.'

It was apparent to the men that Sharpe's rage had passed and some of them grinned to show that they did indeed feel dreadful.

He smiled. 'Good. So now jump in the stream. All of you.'

They stared at him. The thunder and squeal of the carriage wheels grew louder.

Sharpe loaded his rifle with the swift movements of a man long trained to the army. The men stared in disbelief as he brought the brass butt into his shoulder and aimed the weapon at their front file. 'I said jump in the stream! Go!'

He cocked the rifle.

The men jumped.

The drop from the bridge parapet was perhaps eight feet and the stream, swollen by melting snow and winter rains, was four feet deep. The water was icy cold, but Sharpe stood on the parapet and ordered each man to soak himself in the bitter flood. He used the rifle as an encouragement. 'You! Get your bloody head under! Harper! Duck, man, duck!' Only the sober, the wounded and, in deference to his flimsy authority, Sergeant Williams, were spared the ordeal. 'Sergeant! Form threes on the bank. Hurry now!'

The shivering men waded from the stream and formed three miserable ranks on the grass. The coach lumbered to a halt and George Parker, his face nervous, was ejected from the door. 'Lieutenant? My dear wife is concerned that you might abandon us by your swift pace.' Parker then saw the soaked parade and his jaw fell.

'They're drunk.' Sharpe said it loudly enough for the men to hear. 'Pickled. Stewed. God-damn useless! I've been sweating the bloody liquor out of the bastards.'

Parker flapped a hand in protest at the blasphemy but Sharpe ignored him. Instead he shouted at his men. 'Strip!'

There was a pause of disbelief. 'Strip!'

They stripped themselves naked. Forty freezing men, pale and miserable, stood in the drizzle.

Sharpe stared down at them. 'I don't care if you all bloody die.' That got their attention. 'At any moment now, you bastards, the bloody French could be coming down that road,' he jerked his thumb back up the hill, 'and I've a good mind to leave you here for them. You're good for nothing! I thought you were Rifles! I thought you were the best! I've seen bloody militia Battalions that were better than you! I've seen bloody cavalrymen who looked more like soldiers!' That was a difficult insult to beat, but Sharpe tried. 'I've seen bloody Methodists who were tougher than you bastards!'

Mrs Parker ripped back the leather curtain to demand an end to the cursing, saw the naked men, and screamed. The curtain closed.

Sharpe stared his men down. He did not blame them for being frightened, for any soldier could be forgiven terror when defeat and chaos destroyed an army. These men were stranded, far from home, and bereft of the commissary that clothed and fed them, but they were still soldiers, under discipline, and that word reminded Sharpe of Major Vivar's simple commandments. With one simple change, those three rules would suit him well.

Sharpe made his voice less harsh. 'From now on we have three rules. Just three rules. Break one of them and I'll break you. None of you will steal anything unless you have my permission to do so. None of you will get drunk without my permission. And you will fight like bastards when the enemy appears. Is that understood?'

Silence.

'I said, is that understood? Louder! Louder! Louder!'

The naked men were shouting their assent; shouting frantically, shouting to get this madman off their freezing backs. They looked a good deal more sober now.

'Sergeant Williams!'

'Sir?'

'Greatcoats on! You have two hours. Light fires, dry the clothes, then form up in threes again. I'll stand guard.'

'Yes, sir.'

The carriage stood immobile, its Spanish coachman expressionless on his high box. Only when the Riflemen were in their dry greatcoats did the door fly open and a furious Mrs Parker appear. 'Lieutenant!'

Sharpe knew what that voice portended. He whipped round. 'Madam! You will keep silent!'

'I will . . .'

'Silence, God damn you!' Sharpe strode towards the coach and Mrs Parker, fearing violence, slammed the door.

But Sharpe went instead to the luggage box from which he took a handful of the Spanish testaments. 'Sergeant Williams? Kindling for the fires!' He threw the books down to the meadow while George Parker, who thought the world had gone mad, kept a politic silence.

Two hours later, in a very chastened silence, the Riflemen marched south.

At midday it stopped raining. The road joined a larger road, wider and muddier, which slowed the coach's lumbering progress. Yet, as if in promise of better things to come, Sharpe could see a stretch of water far to his right. It was too wide to be a river, and thus was either a lake or an arm of the ocean which, like a Scottish sea-loch, stretched deep inland. George Parker opined that it was indeed a *ria*, a valley flooded by the sea, which could therefore lead to the patrolling ships of the Royal Navy.

That thought brought optimism, as did the country

they now traversed. The road led through pastureland interspersed with stands of trees, stone walls, and small streams. The slopes were gentle and the few farms looked prosperous. Sharpe, trying to remember the map that Vivar had destroyed, knew they must be well south of Santiago de Compostela. His despair of the night before was being eroded by the hopes of this southern road, and by the subdued look on his men's faces. The glimpse of the sea had helped. Perhaps, in the very next town, there might be fishermen who could take these refugees out to where the Navy's ships patrolled. George Parker, walking with Sharpe, agreed. 'And if not, Lieutenant, then we certainly won't need to go as far as Lisbon.'

'No, sir?'

'There'll be English ships loading with wine at Oporto. And we can't be more than a week from Oporto.'

One week to safety! Sharpe rejoiced in the thought. One week of hard marching on his broken boots. One week to prove that he could survive without Blas Vivar. One week of whipping these Riflemen into a disciplined unit. One week with Louisa Parker, and then at least two more weeks at sea as their ship beat north against the Biscay winds.

Two hours after midday, Sharpe called a halt. The sea was still invisible, yet its salt odour was thin among the straggly pine trees beneath which the carriage horses were given a feed of dried maize and hay. The Riflemen, after breaking apart the last of the monastery's loaves, lay exhausted. They had just crossed a stretch of flooded meadows where the road had proved a morass from which the men had had to push the great carriage free. Now the road led gently upwards between mossy walls towards a stone farmhouse which lay, perhaps a mile to the south, on the next crest.

The Parkers sat on rugs beside their carriage. Mrs Parker would not look at Sharpe since his outburst beside the stream, but Louisa gave him a happy and conspiratorial smile that caused Sharpe instant embarrassment for he feared his men would see it and jump to the correct and unavoidable conclusion that the Lieutenant was smitten. To avoid betraying his feelings, Sharpe walked from beneath the stand of pines to where a single picquet squatted beside the road.

'Anything?' he asked.

'Nothing, sir.' It was Hagman, the oldest Rifleman, and one of the very few not to have drunk himself insensible during the night. He was chewing tobacco and his eyes never left the northern skyline. 'It's going to rain again.'

'You think so?'

'Know so.'

Sharpe squatted. The clouds seemed endless, black and grey, rolling from the invisible sea. 'Why did you join the army?' he asked.

Hagman, whose toothless mouth gave his already ugly face a nutcracker profile, grinned. 'Caught poaching, sir. Magistrate gave me a choice, sir. Clink or the ranks.'

'Married?'

'That's why I chose the ranks, sir.' Hagman laughed, then spat a stream of yellow spittle into a puddle. 'God-damned sawny-mouthed bitch of a sodding witch she was, sir.'

Sharpe laughed, then went utterly still.

'Sir!' Hagman said softly.

'I see them.' Then Sharpe was standing, turning, shouting, for on the southern skyline, silhouetted against the dark clouds, were cavalry.

The French had caught up.

CHAPTER 8

It was a bad place to be caught; a stretch of open
country where cavalry could manoeuvre almost at will.
It was true that there were patches of bog at the edges
of the fields which, like the road, were lined with low
stone walls, but Sharpe knew he would be hard put to
extricate his men from the enemy.

'You're certain it's the French?' Parker asked.

Sharpe did not even bother to answer. A soldier who
could not recognize enemy silhouettes did not deserve
to live, but neither did a soldier who hesitated. 'Go!
Go!' This was to the coachman who, jarred by Sharpe's
sudden anger, cracked his long whip at his lead pair.
Traces jangled, splinter bars jerked with the strain, and
the carriage lunged forward.

The Riflemen tore rags from their weapon locks.
Sharpe said a silent prayer of thanks to whichever deity
looked after soldiers that, on the day when they had
been cut off from the army, these men had been issued
with so much ammunition. They would need it, for they
were horribly outnumbered and their only hope lay in
the ability of the rifle to delay the enemy's pursuit.

Sharpe estimated it would take the French horsemen
ten minutes to reach the stand of pines which presently
shrouded the Riflemen. There was no escape to east or
west, where only empty fields lay; instead he needed to
reach the southern crest where the farm stood and

hope that, beyond the crest and by some miracle, he would find an obstacle impassable to horsemen. If there was no escape, then the farmhouse must be barricaded into a fortress. But ten minutes was not enough time to reach the farm, so Sharpe held back a dozen men at the pines. The rest, under Williams's command, went with the coach.

Sharpe kept Hagman, for the old poacher had an uncanny skill with his rifle, and he retained Harper with his closest cronies, for Sharpe suspected that they were his best fighters. 'We can't hold them up for long,' he told the few men, 'but we can buy some time. But when we do move, we'll have to run like the devil.'

Harper crossed himself. 'God save Ireland.' There were at least two hundred Dragoons now filing along the boggy road that had mired the coach an hour earlier.

The Riflemen lay at the edge of the trees. To the French, still half a mile off, they would be invisible. 'Lie still,' Sharpe warned his men. 'Aim at the horses. It's going to be a very long shot.' He would have liked to have waited till the enemy was just two hundred yards away before opening fire, but that would let the horsemen come far too close. Instead he would be forced to fire at the very limit of the rifle's killing range in the hope that the bullets created enough surprise and panic to check the French advance for a few precious moments.

Sharpe, concealed by the darkness beneath the pines, stood a few paces behind his men. He drew out his telescope and steadied its long barrel against a pine trunk.

He saw pale green coats, pink facings, and pigtails. The telescope foreshortened the advancing French column so that the lens seemed filled with men rising and falling in their saddles. Scabbards, carbines, pouches, and sabretaches jiggled. At this distance the French faces, dark beneath their forage caps, were expressionless and menacing. There were curious bundles strapped behind the saddles which Sharpe realized were netfuls of fodder for the horses. The French halted.

Sharpe swore softly.

He panned the telescope left and right. The Dragoons had left the worst of the marshland behind and had spread into a line that was now quite motionless. Horses lowered their heads to crop at the damp grass.

'Sir?' Hagman called. 'On the road, sir? See the buggers?'

Sharpe jerked the telescope back to the centre of the enemy line. A group of officers had appeared there, their aiguillettes and epaulettes a dark gold in the wintry light, and in their midst were the chasseur in his red pelisse, and the civilian in his black coat and white boots. Sharpe wondered by what weird skill those two men followed his scent across the winter land.

The chasseur opened his own telescope and it seemed to Sharpe that the Frenchman stared directly into the betraying circle of his own lens. He kept his glass motionless until the other telescope was snapped shut. Then he watched as the chasseur gave an order to a Dragoon officer, apparently an aide, who galloped his horse westward.

The result of the order was that a small detachment of Dragoons lifted the heavy helmets which hung from their saddles' pommels. The six men pulled the helmets onto their heads; a sure sign they had been ordered to advance. Sensible to the fact that the pines could hide an ambush, the chasseur was sending a picquet ahead. Sharpe had lost surprise, for even though the enemy did not know that he waited for them, they were prepared for trouble. He slammed his glass shut, and cursed the French commander's caution that now imposed a delicate choice on him.

Sharpe could kill the six men, but would that stop the other Dragoons? Or would they, judging his strength from the paucity of shots fired, spur into an instant gallop that would bring the mass of horsemen into the trees long before the Riflemen could reach the southern crest? Instead of ten minutes, he might have five.

He hesitated. But if he had learned one thing as a soldier it was that any decision, even a bad one, was better than none. 'We're pulling back. Fast! Keep hidden!'

The Riflemen slithered backwards, stood when the trees shielded them from the French, then followed Sharpe onto the road. They ran.

'Jesus!' The imprecation came from Harper and was caused by the sight of the Parkers' carriage which, just two hundred yards ahead, was stuck fast. The coachman, in his haste, had rammed a wheel against a stone wall at a bend in the road. Williams and his men were vainly trying to free the vehicle.

'Leave it!' Sharpe bellowed. 'Leave it!'

Mrs Parker's head appeared at the window of the coach to countermand his orders. 'Push! Push!'

'Get out!' Sharpe floundered in the road's mud. 'Get out!' If the coach was to be rescued then the horses would have to be coaxed backwards, slewed, then whipped forward, and that would take time which he did not have, so it must be abandoned.

But Mrs Parker was in no mood to sacrifice the carriage's comfort. She ignored Sharpe, instead leaning perilously from the opened window to threaten her coachman with a furled umbrella. 'Whip them harder, you fool! Harder!'

Sharpe seized the door handle and tugged it down. 'Get out! Out!'

Mrs Parker flailed the umbrella at him, knocking his mildewed shako over his eyes, but Sharpe seized her wrist, tugged, and heard her scream as she fell in the mud. 'Sergeant Williams?'

'Sir?'

'Two men to get those packs off the roof!' They contained all Sharpe's spare ammunition. Gataker and Dodd scrambled up, slashed at the ropes with their sword-bayonets, and tossed the heavy packs down to the waiting riflemen. George Parker tried to speak with Sharpe, but the officer had no time for his nervousness. 'You'll have to run, sir. To the farm!' Sharpe physically turned the tall man and pointed him towards the stone house and barn which were the only refuges left in this bare country.

There was nervous excitement in Louisa's eyes, then the girl was pushed aside by Mrs Parker who, muddied by her fall and made incoherent by the loss of her carriage and luggage, tried to reach Sharpe, but he shouted at the family to start running. 'You want to die, woman? Move! Sergeant Williams! Escort the ladies! Get into the farmhouse!' Mrs Parker screamed for her valise that Mr Parker, shaking like a leaf, rescued from inside the carriage. Then, surrounded by Riflemen, the family and their coachman fled uphill.

'Sir?' Harper checked Sharpe. 'Block the road?' He gestured at the coach.

Sharpe did not have the time to be astonished at the Irishman's sudden willingness. He did, however, recognize the value of the suggestion. If the road was blocked then the French would be forced to negotiate the stone walls which barred the fields on either side. It would not buy much time, but even a minute would help in this desperate plight. He nodded. 'If we can.'

'No trouble at all, sir.' Harper unhooked the chain-traces, splinter bars, and lead bars while other men slashed at the harness and reins. The Irishman slapped the horses' rumps to drive the loosened team uphill. 'Right, lads! We're going to tip the bastard!'

The Riflemen gathered on the coach's right side. Sharpe was staring at the trees, waiting for the enemy picquet, but he could not resist turning to watch as the Irishman commanded the men to lift.

For a moment the coach refused to budge, then Harper seemed to take all the carriage's weight into his own huge body and thrust it skywards. The wheels shifted in the mud and the axle boss scraped against the stone where it was stuck. 'Heave!' Harper drew the word out into a long bellow as the coach rose ever higher into the air. For a second it threatened to collapse back, crushing the greenjackets, and Sharpe ran and put his own weight into the huge vehicle. It teetered for a second, then, with a splintering thump, collapsed onto its side in the road. Luggage and seat cushions tumbled inside, and Spanish testaments were strewn thick into the road's mud.

'Cavalry, sir!' Hagman shouted.

Sharpe turned north to see the six enemy horsemen curbing in at the edge of the trees. He aimed swiftly, too swiftly, and his shot missed. Hagman, firing a second later, made one of the horses rear in pain. The other Dragoons wrenched their reins about. Two more shots were fired before the enemy picquet was safe among the pines.

'Run!' Sharpe shouted.

The Riflemen ran. Their scabbards flapped and their

packs thumped on their backs as they scrambled up the road. A carbine bullet, fired at long range, fluttered above Sharpe's head. He could see Mrs Parker being bodily dragged by two greenjackets and the sight made him want to laugh. It was ludicrous. He was trapped by cavalry and he wanted to double over in laughter.

Sharpe caught up with Sergeant Williams's group. Mrs Parker, furious, was too breathless to shout at him, but she was equally too fat to move fast. Sharpe looked for Harper. 'Drag her!'

'You can't mean it, sir!'

'Carry her if you must!'

The Irishman pushed Mrs Parker in the rump. Louisa laughed, but Sharpe yelled at the girl to run. He himself, with the remainder of his squad, filed into the field beside the road where, sheltered by a stone wall, they watched for the pursuit.

Sharpe could hear the cavalry trumpets talking with each other. The picquets had sent the call that the enemy was in sight and running, so now the other Dragoons would be spurring forward, exchanging forage caps for canvas-covered helmets. Swords would be rasping out of scabbards, carbines would be unslung. 'They'll have to come through the trees, so we'll give the bastards a volley, then run! Aim where the road comes through the trees, lads!' Sharpe hoped to delay the Dragoons by at least a minute, maybe more. When the head of the enemy column appeared beneath the trees he would hammer it with one well-aimed volley, and it would take time for the cavalrymen who followed to negotiate the wounded horses.

Hagman was carefully reloading his rifle with the best powder and shot. He eschewed the ready-made cartridges which were made with coarser powder, charging his rifle instead with the best fine powder which each Rifleman carried in a horn. He wrapped the ball in the greased leather patch which, when the weapon was fired, would grip the seven spiralling grooves and lands which imparted spin to the bullet. He rammed the leather-patched ball down past the resistance of the lands' quarter turn, then primed the lock with a pinch of good powder. It took a long time to load a rifle thus, but the resultant shot could be wickedly accurate. When Hagman was done he levelled the gun across the top of the stone wall and spat a stream of tobacco-stained spittle. 'Aim a pace left for the wind.'

A spot of rain landed on the wall beside Sharpe. He prayed it would hold off long enough to let his rifles fire. He paced behind the men. 'Make this shot hurt! One volley, then we run like hell.'

'Sir?' A man at the end of the line pointed to the trees east of the road and, staring there, Sharpe wondered if he saw movement among the pines. He unbuttoned the pocket in which his telescope was stored, but before he could even draw the glass from its protective case, the enemy burst in a great line from the trees.

Sharpe had expected them to file in column through the gap where the road pierced the pines, but instead the Dragoons had spread left and right in the woodland and now, helmeted and carrying drawn swords, the enemy's whole strength erupted into the light.

'Fire!'

It was a puny volley. If the rifles had been able to concentrate their bullets into the head of a packed column of cavalry, they might have turned the road into a charnel of screaming horses and bleeding men. But against a whole spread of horsemen, coming in single line abreast, the bullets were scarcely more of a nuisance than horseflies. Only one horse, struck by Hagman's careful bullet, staggered and fell.

'Run!' Sharpe shouted.

The Rifles ran as if the devil was on their heels. The French had foreseen that volley, guarded against it, and now were in the open and hullooing forward like hunters smelling blood. Ahead of Sharpe the other Riflemen were angling towards the farm. Louisa, he saw, was carrying the wounded Cameron's pack and pulling the man along by his hand.

'Bastards on the right!' Hagman called the warning and Sharpe twisted to see that the horsemen to the east were on the firmest ground and thus the likeliest to catch his small group. The Dragoons were riding like steeple chasers, victory in their nostrils, and a gap in a stone wall lent them speed, just as it made them bunch together like men racing for a turn. Sharpe saw the water spray up from their hooves as the cavalry charged through a damp patch, then, extraordinarily, he saw red blood appear on two of the horses, a sword circle through the air, then he saw a man twisting in the saddle, falling, and being dragged by a screaming, frightened horse. Only then did Sharpe hear the crack of the rifles ahead.

Harper had abandoned Mrs Parker and formed a line of Riflemen at the edge of the farm's outer wall. Their volley had scattered the easternmost cavalry to give Sharpe's group a ghost of a chance. 'Run! Run!'

The men slung their rifles and ran. Sharpe could hear the enemy hooves behind. He could hear the creak of the saddles and the shout of the officers and Sergeants. More rifle bullets flicked past, firing from the farm to give him cover. Louisa stared, eyes wide.

'Left, sir!' A man shouted. 'Left!' Cavalrymen were coming from the west; men who had ridden around the roadblock and who now put their beasts to jump the stone wall that edged the road. One man, his horse in midflight, was hit by a bullet and slewed sideways. The others came on unscathed and Sharpe knew his squad would be trapped. He dragged the big sword free, planted his feet, and let the first Frenchman ride at him. 'Run on!' he shouted at his men. 'Run on!'

The first Frenchman was a Dragoon officer who leaned low in his saddle and speared his sword forward so that, like a lance, it would rip into Sharpe's belly. The Rifleman backswung his own sword, left to right, in a two-handed blow that was aimed at the horse's mouth. It struck home on bone and teeth, the animal wrenched aside, and Sharpe threw himself against its body so that the Frenchman's sword went past and outside him. He tried to reach up to drag the rider from the saddle, missed, and his shako went flying as the forage net thumped him down on to the road. The horse's rear leg struck his hip, then the Dragoon was gone and Sharpe scrambled to his feet.

'Down!' It was Harper's voice and he instinctively dropped flat as another volley crashed overhead. A horse screamed, then slid and fell in the road's muck. One of the beast's flailing hooves missed Sharpe's skull by an inch.

'Run!' Harper bellowed.

Sharpe caught a glimpse of the carnage on the road. Harper's volley, aimed at the congestion formed by the constriction of the stone walls, had stopped the horsemen dead. Sharpe ran through the farm gate. There was an open pasture to cross before he was safe. Riflemen were already filing into the farmhouse and he saw the first shutter pushed aside by a rifle barrel.

'Behind you!' Hooves again, this time from the left, and Sharpe snarled as he turned. His sword swung towards the horse which swerved away and forced its rider to try the dificult cross-cut down and across his own body. Lunging, the Rifleman felt his own sword pierce the Dragoon's left thigh. The impetus of man and horse dragged the rider free of the blade. More rifles fired, one bullet going so close to Sharpe that he felt its passage like a thump of wind.

'Run!' Harper called again.

Sharpe ran. He reached the farmhouse just as the last Rifleman scrambled over its threshold. Harper was ready to shut the door and jam it tight with a chest. 'Thank you!' Sharpe gasped as he cannoned through the door. Harper ignored him.

Sharpe found himself in a passage which ran clean through the farmhouse from north to south. Doors barred the passage's outer entrances, while two other doors led into the house itself. He chose the door on the left which opened into a spacious kitchen where, quivering with fright, a man and a woman crouched beside the hearth in which, suspended from a pothook, a seething cauldron stank of lye. The Parkers' coach-man offered the couple urgent explanation, then began loading a huge horse-pistol. Louisa was trying to prise a small ivory-hilted pistol from its snug-fitting case.

'Where's your aunt?' Sharpe asked.

'There.' She pointed to a door at the back of the kitchen.

'Get in there.'

'But . . .'

'I said get in there!' Sharpe closed the pistol case and, despite Louisa's indignation, pushed her towards the scullery where her aunt and uncle crouched among tall stone jars. He limped to the closest window and saw the Dragoons milling about just beyond the small barn. His men were firing at them. A horse reared, a French-man clapped a hand to a wounded arm, and a trumpet screamed.

The Dragoons scattered. They did not go far; only to find shelter behind the stone barn or the field walls, and Sharpe knew it would only be seconds before, dismounted, they began to rattle the farmhouse with their carbine fire. 'How many windows are there, Sergeant?'

'Dunno, sir.' Williams was panting from the effort of running uphill.

A bullet lashed through the kitchen from outside. It struck a high beam above Sharpe. 'Keep your bloody heads down! And fire back!'

There were three rooms downstairs; the large kitchen which had a window facing north and another south. The small scullery where the Parkers crouched had no windows. Beyond the passage was a much larger, windowless room, this one a byre for the animals. Two pigs and a dozen scared chickens were its only occupants.

A ladder from the kitchen led upstairs where there was a single room for sleeping. The farm's relative prosperity was witnessed by a massive bed and a chest of drawers. The room had two windows, also facing north and south. Sharpe put Riflemen in both windows, then ordered Sergeant Williams to take charge of the upstairs room and to make loopholes in the eastern and western walls. 'And break through the roof.'

'The roof?' Williams gaped up at the thick beams and the timbers which hid the tiles.

'To keep watch east and west,' Sharpe ordered. Until he could see to his flanks then he was vulnerable to French surprise.

Downstairs again, Sharpe ordered a loophole to be hacked next to the chimney breast. The Spanish farmer, understanding what needed to be done, produced a pickaxe and began to pound at his wall. A crucifix, hanging on the limewashed stone, juddered with the force of the man's blows.

'Bastards right!' Harper shouted from the window. Rifles cracked. The greenjackets who fired ducked back, letting others take their places. Some dismounted Dragoons had tried to rush the farm, but three of them now lay in a puddle; two scrambled up and limped to safety, the third was still. Sharpe saw the splash of rain in the blood-rippled water.

Then, for a few moments, there was relative peace.

None of Sharpe's men was wounded. They were breathless and damp, but safe. They stayed crouched low under the threat of carbine fire that flayed at the windows, but the bullets did no harm except to the house. Sharpe, peering out, saw that the enemy was hidden in ditches or behind the dunghill. The farmer's wife was nervously offering sliced sausage to the greenjackets.

George Parker crept on hands and knees from the scullery. He nervously waited for Sharpe's attention which, once gained, he used to enquire what course of action Lieutenant Sharpe planned to follow.

Lieutenant Sharpe informed Mr Parker that he intended to wait for darkness to fall.

Parker swallowed. 'That could be hours!'

'Five at the most, sir.' Sharpe was reloading his rifle, 'unless God makes the sun stand still.'

Parker ignored Sharpe's levity. 'And then?'

'Break out, sir. Not till it's dead of night. Hit the bastards when they're not expecting it. Kill a few of them, and hope the others get confused.' Sharpe righted the rifle and primed its pan. 'They can't do much damage to us so long as we stay low.'

'But . . .' Parker flinched as a bullet smacked into the wall above his head. 'My dear wife, Lieutenant, wishes your assurance that our carriage will be retrieved?'

'Afraid not, sir.' Sharpe knelt up, saw a flicker of a

shadow beyond the dunghill, and fired his rifle. Smoke billowed from the weapon, and a wad of burning paper smoked on the floor. 'There won't be time, sir.' He crouched, took a cartridge from his pouch, and bit the bullet away.

'But my testaments!'

Sharpe did not like to reveal that the testaments, when last seen, had been strewn in the Spanish mud. He spat the bullet into his rifle's muzzle. 'Your testaments, sir, are now in the hands of Napoleon's army.' He rammed ball, wadding and powder down his rifle barrel. The saltpetre from the powder was rank and dry in his mouth.

'But . . .' Again Parker was silenced by a carbine bullet. This one clanged against a saucepan that hung from a beam. The bullet punched a hole in the metal, hit the next beam, and dropped at Sharpe's feet. He picked it up, juggling it because of its heat, then smelt it. Parker frowned in perplexity.

'There's a rumour that the Frogs poison their bullets, sir.' Sharpe said it loud enough so that his men, some of whom half-believed the story, could hear. 'It ain't true.'

'It isn't?'

'No, sir.' Sharpe put the bullet into his mouth, grinned, then swallowed it. His men laughed at the expression on George Parker's face. Sharpe turned to see how the farmer was progressing with the loophole. The walls of the farm were hugely thick and, though the man's pick had pierced a foot into the centre rubble, he still had not reached daylight.

A volley of carbine shots crashed through the rear window. The Riflemen, unharmed, jeered their defiance, but it was a defiance that the grey-haired Parker could not share. 'You're doomed, Lieutenant!'

'Sir, if you've nothing better . . .'

'Lieutenant! We are civilians! I see no reason why we should stay here and share your death!' George Parker had found courage under fire; the courage to assert his timorous soul and demand surrender.

Sharpe primed his rifle. 'You want to walk out there, sir?'

'A flag of truce, man!' Parker flinched as another carbine bullet ricocheted over his head.

'If that's what you want, sir . . .' But before Sharpe could finish his sentence, there was a panicked shout from Sergeant Williams upstairs, then a rattling crash as a massive enemy volley flogged the front of the house. A Rifleman was jerked back from the window with blood spurting from his head. Two rifles fired, more shot from upstairs, then the northern window was darkened as French Dragoons, who had charged about the blind western angle of the house, filled the frame. Sharpe and several other men fired; but the Dragoons were dragging at the chairs which blocked the window. They were repulsed only when the farmer's wife, screaming with despair and using a strength that seemed remarkable in so scrawny a woman, snatched the cauldron from the pothook and threw it at the enemy. The scalding lye snatched the French back as though a cannon had fired at them.

'Sir!' Harper was by the kitchen door. A crash sounded in the passage as the French broke down the southern door which the Irishman had not blocked as securely as the northern. A group of Dragoons had taken advantage of the larger attack to make a charge at the other side of the house and were now within the central passage. Harper fired his rifle through the kitchen door, which instantly splintered in two places as the French replied. Both bullets struck the table.

The kitchen filled with powder smoke. Men were taking turns to fire through the windows, then reloading with frantic haste. The coachman emptied his huge pistol through the door and was rewarded with a shout of pain.

'Open it!' Sharpe said.

Harper obeyed. An astonished Frenchman, levelling his carbine, found himself facing Sharpe's sword which skewered forward so savagely that the blade's tip jarred against the far wall of the passage after it had gone clean through the Dragoon's body. Harper, screaming his weird battle-shouts, followed Sharpe with an axe he had plucked from the kitchen wall. He hacked down at another man, making the passage slithery with blood.

Sharpe gouged and twisted his sword free. A Frenchman's blade scraped up his forearm, springing warm blood, and he threw himself onto the man, forcing him against the passage wall and hammering the sword hilt at his face. A rifle exploded beside his head to throw another Dragoon back from the door. The pigs squealed in terror, while Sharpe tripped over a crawling Frenchman who was bleeding from the belly. Another rifle hammered in the passage, then Harper shouted that the enemy was gone.

A carbine bullet slammed into the passage, ricocheted from the walls, and buried itself in the far door. Sharpe pushed into the room where the animals were kept and saw a wooden trough that would serve as some kind of barricade in the passage. He dragged it out, and the pigs took the opportunity to escape before he could slam the damaged outer door closed and ram the trough under its cross-members. 'Lucky bloody French,' Harper said. 'Pork for supper.'

The action lulled again. Dreadful squeals announced the death of the pigs; squeals which momentarily stilled the fusillade of carbine shots which raked the farm-house. No more Frenchmen appeared as targets. One Rifleman was dead in the kitchen, another wounded. Sharpe went to the ladder. 'Sergeant Williams?'

There was no answer.

'Sergeant Williams! How are those loopholes?'

It was Dodd who answered. 'He's dead, sir. Got one in the eye, sir.'

'Jesus Christ.'

'He was looking out the roof, sir.'

'Make sure someone keeps looking out!'

Williams was dead. Sharpe sat at the foot of the ladder and stared at Patrick Harper. He was the obvious replacement, the only choice, but Sharpe suspected the big Irishman would scathingly reject the offer. So, he thought, the rank should not be offered but simply imposed. 'Harper?'

'Sir?'

'You're a Sergeant.'

'I'm bloody not.'

'You're a Sergeant!'

'No, sir! Not in this damned army. No.'

'Jesus Christ!' Sharpe spat the blasphemy at the huge man, but Harper merely turned to stare out of the window to where puffs of smoke betrayed the position of some Dragoons in a ditch.

'Mister Sharpe?' A tentative hand touched Sharpe's wounded arm. It was George Parker again. 'My dear wife and I have discussed it, Lieutenant, and we would appreciate it if you would communicate with the French commander.' Parker suddenly saw Sharpe's blood on his own fingers. He blanched and stuttered on: 'Please don't think we wish to desert you at this time, but . . .'

'I know,' Sharpe cut him short, 'you think we're doomed.' He spoke savagely, not because he disapproved of Parker's wish to be safe, but because, if the Parkers went, he would lose Louisa. He could have left the Parkers on the road, safe in their carriage, but he had panicked them into flight because he did not want to lose the girl's company. Yet now Sharpe knew he had no choice, for the two women could not be expected to endure the French assault, nor the danger of a ricocheting bullet. Louisa must go.

On the table, where the dead Rifleman lay among shattered crockery with the blood still dripping from his sopping hair, there was a piece of cheesecloth which, though grey and dirty, might pass for a flag of truce. Sharpe speared the flimsy material onto the tip of his sword, then shuffled over to the window. The Riflemen made way for him.

He reached up and pushed the sword clear of the window frame. He waved it left and right, and was rewarded with a shout from outside. There was a pause in which, tentatively, Sharpe stood upright.

'What do you want, Englishman?' a voice shouted.

'To talk.'

'Come out then. Just one of you!'

Sharpe plucked the cheesecloth from his sword, sheathed the blade, and went into the passage. He stepped over a dead Dragoon, pulled the chest clear of the northern door, then, feeling oddly naked and exposed, walked into the rain.

To talk to the man in the red pelisse.

CHAPTER 9

A dozen French wounded lay in the barn, filling its cavernous space with the stench of blood, pus, and camphorated vinegar. The casualties lay on rough beds of hay at one end while at the other, in front of a stack of woven sheep hurdles, the officers had made a crude command post out of an upturned water barrel. A half-dozen officers stood about the barrel and among them was the chasseur in his red pelisse, who greeted Sharpe warmly and in fluent English. 'My name is Colonel Pierre de l'Eclin, and I have the honour to be a chasseur of His Majesty's Imperial Guard.'

Sharpe returned the hint of a bow. 'Lieutenant Richard Sharpe of the Rifles.'

'The Rifles, eh? You make it sound like a very proud boast.' De l'Eclin was a handsome man; as tall as Sharpe, strongly built, and with a square-jawed face and golden hair. He gestured at a flask of wine which stood on the makeshift table. 'Will a Rifle take some wine?'

Sharpe was not certain whether he was being mocked or complimented. 'Thank you, sir.'

The chasseur waved away a Lieutenant, insisting on filling the two small silver cups himself. He handed one towards Sharpe but, before the Rifleman could take the cup, de l'Eclin withdrew it slightly as though giving himself a chance to study his scarred face. 'Have we met, Lieutenant?'

'By a bridge, sir. You broke my sabre.'

De l'Eclin seemed delighted. He gave the cup to Sharpe and clicked his fingers as the memory came back. 'You parried! A quite remarkable parry! Or was it luck?'

'Probably luck, sir.'

'Soldiers should be lucky, and consider how lucky you are that I didn't catch up with you in open ground today. All the same, Lieutenant, I salute your Rifles' excellent defence. It's a pity it must end like this.'

Sharpe drank the wine to scour the sour taste of powder from his mouth. 'It isn't ended, sir.'

'No?' De l'Eclin raised a polite eyebrow.

'I'm here, sir, solely on behalf of some English civilians, trapped inside the farm, who desire to leave. They are willing to trust to your kindness, sir.'

'My kindness?' De l'Eclin gave a gleeful bellow of laughter. 'I told you that I am a chasseur of the Emperor's Imperial Guard, Lieutenant. A man does not achieve that signal honour, let alone a colonelcy, by kindness. Still, I'm grateful for what was indubitably meant as a compliment. Who are these civilians?'

'English travellers, sir.'

'And these are their books?' De l'Eclin gestured at two muddy Spanish testaments which lay on the upturned barrel. The French had clearly been curious about the spilt books, a curiosity which Sharpe tried to satisfy. 'They're Methodist missionaries, sir, trying to turn Spain from the Papacy.'

De l'Eclin inspected Sharpe for evidence of levity, found none, and burst into laughter. 'They've as much hope, Lieutenant, of turning tigers into cows! What strange people it is a soldier's privilege to meet. Do I have your word that these Methodists have not carried weapons?'

Sharpe conveniently forgot Louisa's small pistol. 'You have, sir.'

'You can send them out. God knows what we'll make of them, but we won't shoot them.'

'Thank you, sir.' Sharpe turned to go.

'But don't leave me yet, Lieutenant. I'd like to talk to you.' De l'Eclin saw the flicker of worry on Sharpe's face, and shook his head. 'I won't keep you against your will, Lieutenant. I do respect flags of truce.'

Sharpe went to the barn door and shouted to the farmhouse that the Parker family could leave. He also suggested that the three Spaniards in the farm might take this chance to escape, but it seemed none of them wanted to risk French hospitality, for only the Parker family emerged from the besieged house. Mrs Parker was the first to appear, stumping through the mud and rain with her umbrella carried like a weapon. 'Dear God,' de l'Eclin murmured behind Sharpe. 'Why don't you recruit her?'

George Parker stepped hesitantly into the rain, then Louisa emerged and de l'Eclin breathed a sigh of appreciation. 'It seems we have to thank you.'

'You might not, sir, when you meet the aunt.'

'I don't intend to bed the aunt.' De l'Eclin ordered a Captain to take care of the civilians, then drew Sharpe back into the barn. 'So, my Rifle Lieutenant, what do you plan to do now?'

Sharpe ignored the patronizing tone and pretended incomprehension. 'Sir?'

'Let me tell you your plans.' The tall Frenchman, whose pelisse hung so elegantly from his right shoulder, paced up and down the barn. 'You've succeeded in loopholing the end walls of the farm's upstairs room, which means I cannot surprise you until it is dark. A night attack might succeed, but it will be risky, especially as you will doubtless have a stock of combustibles inside the house with which you plan to illuminate the exterior.' He cocked an amused eye to catch a reaction from the Rifleman, but Sharpe betrayed nothing. De l'Eclin paused to refill Sharpe's cup. 'I suspect you feel you can survive at least one more attack and you also gauge that, once that attack fails, I will wait for first light. So, at about two or three in the morning, when my men are at their weariest, you will make a sally. I imagine you'll head west, because there's a gully of brushwood just a hundred paces away. Once there you will be relatively safe, and there are woodland paths up to the hills.' De l'Eclin had begun his pacing again, but now swivelled back to stare at Sharpe. 'Am I right?'

The chasseur had been entirely, utterly accurate. Sharpe had not known about the gully, though he would have seen it from the hole in the roof and would undoubtedly have chosen to make his attack in that direction.

'Well?' de l'Eclin insisted.

'I was planning something different,' Sharpe said.

'Oh?' The chasseur was exquisitely polite.

'I was planning to capture your men and do to them what they did to those Spanish villagers in the highlands.'

'Rape them?' de l'Eclin suggested, then laughed. 'Some of them might even enjoy that, but I assure you that most will resist your bestial, though doubtless very English, lusts.'

Sharpe, made to feel extremely foolish by the Frenchman's poise, said nothing. He also felt unbearably ragged. His jacket was torn and blood-stained, he was hatless, his trousers were gaping because of the missing silver buttons and his cheap boots were in shreds. De l'Eclin, in contrast, was exquisitely uniformed. The chasseur wore a tight red dolman jacket with loops and buttons of gold. Over it hung his scarlet pelisse; a garment of utter uselessness but high fashion for cavalrymen. A pelisse was merely a jacket that was worn on one shoulder like a cloak. Decorated with golden braid, de l'Eclin's was fastened about his neck with a golden chain, and edged with soft black lamb's fleece. Its empty sleeves hung down to the gold-coloured chains of his sabre slings. The inner legs and lower cuffs of his dark green overalls had been reinforced with black leather to resist the chafing of a saddle, while their outer seams were red stripes brightened with golden buttons. His tall boots were of soft black leather. Sharpe wondered how much such a uniform cost, and knew it was probably more than his salary for a year.

De l'Eclin opened his sabretache and took out two cigars. He offered one to the Rifleman, who saw no reason to refuse it. The two men companionably shared the flame of a tinder-box, then the Frenchman, blowing a stream of smoke over Sharpe's head, sighed. 'I think, Lieutenant, that you and your Rifles should surrender.'

Sharpe kept a stubborn silence.

De l'Eclin shrugged. 'I will be honest with you, Lieutenant,' he paused, 'Sharpe, did you say?'

'Yes, sir.'

'I will be honest with you, Lieutenant Sharpe. I do not wish my men to be in this place at night. We have the honour to be the vanguard of our army and we are, therefore, exposed. The Spanish peasantry is sometimes tempted to make itself a nuisance. If I am here tonight, then I might lose a handful of men to knives in the dark. Those men will die horribly, and I do not think that the best cavalry in the world should suffer such an ignoble and painful death. So I expect you to surrender long before nightfall. Indeed, if you do not do so now, I shall not accept a surrender later. Do I make myself plain?'

Sharpe hid his astonishment at the threat. 'I understand you, sir.'

De l'Eclin, despite Sharpe's assent, could not resist embroidering his menace. 'You will all die, Lieutenant. Not slowly, as we kill the Spanish peasants, but die all the same. Tomorrow the army will catch up with me, and I shall deploy artillery to grind your Rifles into mincemeat. It will be a lesson to other enemies of France not to waste the Emperor's time.'

'Yes, sir.'

De l'Eclin smiled pleasantly. 'Does that affirmative signify your surrender?'

'No, sir. You see, sir, I don't believe in your guns. You're carrying forage nets,' Sharpe gestured through the barn's gaping rear door at the officers' horses which, tethered safely out of sight of the Rifles, all had heavy nets of hay slung from their saddle spoons. 'If your army was going to catch up with you, sir, you'd let the waggons carry your feed. You're on a patrol, nothing more, and if I resist long enough, you'll leave.'

The French Colonel gazed thoughtfully at him for a few seconds. It was plain that, just as de l'Eclin had correctly guessed Sharpe's tactics a moment before, so Sharpe had now guessed the Frenchman's. De l'Eclin shrugged. 'I admire your courage, Lieutenant. But it won't avail you. There really is no choice. Your army is defeated and fled home, the Spanish armies are broken and scattered. No one will help you. You can surrender now or you can be stubborn, which means that you will be cut to shreds by my blades.' His voice had lost its light and bantering tone, and was now deadly serious.

'One way or another, Lieutenant, I will see you all killed.'

Sharpe knew he had no chance to win this siege, but was too pig-headed to give way. 'I want time to think about it, sir.'

'Time to delay, you mean?' The chasseur shrugged scornfully. 'It won't help, Lieutenant. Do you really think we've come this far just to let Major Vivar escape?' Sharpe stared blankly at him. De l'Eclin entirely misunderstood Sharpe's expression; mistaking the Rifleman's incomprehension for guilty astonishment. 'We know he's with you, Lieutenant. He and his precious strongbox!'

'He's . . .' Sharpe did not know what to say.

'So you see, Lieutenant, I really will not abandon the hunt now. I was charged by the Emperor himself to take that strongbox to Paris, and I do not intend to fail him.' De l'Eclin smiled condescendingly. 'Of course, if you send the Major out to me, with his box, I might let you continue south. I doubt if a few ragged Rifles will endanger the future of the Empire.'

'He's not with me!' Sharpe protested.,

'Lieutenant!' de l'Eclin chided.

'Ask the Methodists! I haven't seen Major Vivar in two days!'

'He's lying!' The voice came from behind the stack of sheep hurdles, from where the tall civilian in the black coat and white riding boots appeared. 'You're lying, Englishman.'

'Piss on you, you bastard.' Sharpe snarled at the insult to his honour.

Colonel de l'Eclin moved swiftly to interpose himself between the two angry men. He addressed himself in English to the man in the black coat, though he still stared at the Rifleman. 'It seems, my dear Count, that your brother might have successfully spread a false rumour? He is not, after all, travelling south to find remounts?'

'Vivar is his brother?' Sharpe's confusion was absolute. Vivar, whose hatred of the French was so overwhelming, had a brother who rode with the enemy? Who must have watched as the Dragoons raped and killed Spanish women and children? His disbelief must have shown on his face for de l'Eclin, clearly astonished that Sharpe had not known of the relationship, made a formal introduction. 'Allow me to name the Count of Mouromorto, Lieutenant. He is indeed Major Vivar's brother. You have to understand that, contrary to the lies told in the English newspapers, there are many Spaniards who welcome the French presence. They believe it is time to sweep away the old superstitions and practices that have crippled Spain for so long. The Count is such a man.' De l'Eclin bowed to the Spaniard at the end of that description, but the Count merely glared at the Englishman.

Sharpe returned the hostile stare. 'You let these bastards kill your own people?'

For a second it seemed as if the Count would lash out at him. He was taller than Blas Vivar, but now that he was close, Sharpe could see the familiarity. He had the same pugnacious jaw and fervent eyes, which now regarded Sharpe with hostility. 'What would you know of Spain, Lieutenant?' the Count asked, 'or of Spain's desperate needs? Or of the sacrifices its people must make if they are to know liberty?'

'What do you know of liberty? You're nothing but a bloody murdering bastard.'

'Enough!' De l'Eclin raised his left hand to check Sharpe's anger. 'You say Major Vivar is not with you?'

'He is not with me, nor is his damned strongbox. If

it's any business of yours, which it is not, I parted from Major Vivar in anger and I don't much care if I never see him again! But he's sent you on a wild goose chase, hasn't he?'

De l'Eclin seemed amused at Sharpe's anger. 'Maybe, but you're the goose, Lieutenant, and you're the one who'll be plucked. You and your Rifles.' The Colonel was entranced by the word. He knew Hussars, chasseurs, lancers, Dragoons, and gunners, he was familiar with sappers and cuirassiers, grenadiers and fusiliers, but he had never before heard a man described as a 'Rifle'. 'On the other hand,' de l'Eclin continued, 'if Major Vivar is with you, then you are bound to deny his presence, are you not? Just as you are bound to defend him, which might explain your persistence in this hopeless fight.'

'He isn't here,' Sharpe said wearily. 'Ask the Methodists.'

'I shall certainly ask the girl,' de l'Eclin said happily.

'Do that.' Sharpe spat the words. Blas Vivar, he thought, had been superbly clever, using a rumour to persuade the French that he had fled south with the Riflemen, thereby sacrificing them. But Sharpe could feel no anger against the Spaniard, only a reluctant admiration. He threw his cigar onto the floor. 'I'm going back.'

De l'Eclin nodded. 'I shall give you ten minutes to make up your mind about surrender. *Au revoir, Lieutenant.*'

'And go to hell yourself.'

Sharpe went back to the farmhouse. The wild goose was trapped, and would now be killed and plucked. That, in a way, was Vivar's revenge for Sharpe's abandonment and Sharpe laughed at it, for there was nothing else to do. Except fight.

* * *

'What did the bugger want, sir?' Harper asked.

'He wants us to surrender.'

'Bugger would.' Harper spat towards the fire.

'If we don't surrender now, they won't let us do it later.'

'So he's got the wind up his backside, has he? He's scared of the night?'

'He is, yes.'

'So what are you going to do, sir?'

'Tell him to go to hell. And make you a Sergeant.'

Harper grimaced. 'No, sir.'

'Why the hell not?'

The big man shook his head. 'I don't mind telling the lads what to do in a fight, sir. Captain Murray always let me do that, so he did, and I'll do it whether you wanted me to or not. But I'll go no further. I won't run your punishments for you or take a badge from you.'

'For Christ's sake, why not?'

'Why the hell should I?'

'Why the hell did you save my life out there?' Sharpe gestured beyond the farmhouse to where, in the panicked scramble to escape the Dragoons, he had been rescued by Harper's volleys.

The big Irishman looked embarrassed. 'That would be Major Vivar's fault, sir.'

'What the hell does that mean?'

'Well, sir, he told me that, with one exception, you were the best man in a fight he'd ever seen. And that so long as the heathen English were fighting for a free Catholic Spain, sir, that I was to keep you alive.'

'The best?'

'With the one exception.'

'Who is?'

'Me, sir.'

'The Major's a lying bastard,' Sharpe said. He

supposed he must accept what was offered, which was Harper's support on the battlefield. Even that would be better than no support at all. 'So if you are such a God-damned good fighter, tell me how we get out of this God-damned hole?'

'We probably don't, sir, and that's the truth. But we'll give the buggers a hell of a damned fight, and they won't be so cocksure the next time they meet the Rifles.'

A carbine bullet whiplashed through the kitchen window. De l'Eclin's ten minutes were over, and the fight had started again.

From one of the holes in the roof, Sharpe saw the wooded gully of which de l'Eclin had spoken. Just to its north, in a walled paddock, most of the Dragoon's horses were pastured. 'Hagman!'

The old poacher climbed the ladder. 'Sir?'

'Make yourself a firing position and start killing horses. That'll keep the buggers busy.'

Downstairs the farmwife was busy with food. She produced a cask of salted mackerel and whiting, evidence of how close the sea lay, which she distributed among the soldiers. Her husband, his loophole completed, had charged a fowling piece with powder and shot that he discharged deafeningly towards the east.

The French moved their horses further north. From the barn came the tantalizing smell of pork being cooked. The rain seethed harder, then stopped. The carbine fire never stopped, but neither did it do much damage. One Rifleman suffered a flesh wound in the arm and, when he yelped, was scornfully jeered by his colleagues.

In the late afternoon a few Dragoons made a half-hearted charge through the orchard which lay to the north, but they were easily discouraged. Sharpe, going from window to window, wondered what devilry de l'Eclin plotted. He also wondered what Blas Vivar was doing with the time he had gained by sending de l'Eclin on this wild goose chase. The strongbox was clearly of even more importance than Sharpe had suspected; so important that the Emperor himself had sent the chasseur to capture it. Sharpe supposed he would never know what it contained. Either he would be captured or killed here, or else, when the French tired of this vigil, they would leave and Sharpe would continue south. He would find a ship home, rejoin the mainstream of the army and he supposed, with a sudden lurch of his heart, once again become a Quartermaster. He had not realized until this second just how much he loathed that God-damn job.

'Sir!' The voice was scared. 'Sir!'

Sharpe ran to the front kitchen window. 'Fire!'

The French had made screens from the sheep hurdles. They had lashed them together to make heavy mats of birch-wattle that were large enough to hide half a dozen men and resilient enough to stop rifle bullets. The cumbersome shields were being inched across the yard, coming ever closer, and Sharpe knew that, once they reached the house, the French would use axes and bars to break down the doors. He fired his own rifle, knowing that the bullet was wasted against the supple wood. The carbine fire rose to a new pitch.

Sharpe twisted about the table to the northern window. Powder smoke spurted from the orchard, showing that Dragoons barred that escape, yet it was his only hope. He shouted up the ladder. 'Come down!'

He turned to Harper. 'We'll take the Spaniards with us. We're breaking southwards.'

'They'll catch us.'

'Better that than dying like rats in a pit. Fix swords!'

179

He looked up the ladder to the bedroom. 'Hurry!'

'Sir!' It was Dodd who called back; quiet Dodd who stared out of the loophole in the roof and who sounded most unnaturally excited. 'Sir!'

Because a new trumpet challenged the sky.

Major Blas Vivar scraped his sword free of its scabbard. He raised it high, then, as the trumpet reached its screaming high note, he lashed the blade down.

The horses spurred forward. There were a hundred of them; all that Lieutenant Davila had brought from Orense. They scrambled up from the gully, found firm footing on the pasture, and charged.

The crimson-uniformed Galician who held the guidon on its lance-like stave lowered the point. The flag snapped in the wind. Dismounted French Dragoons turned in shock.

'Santiago! Santiago!' Vivar drew out the last syllable of his war cry as his Cazadores pounded behind him. The remnants of his scarlet-clad elite company were here, reinforced by their blue-coated comrades who had come north with Lieutenant Davila. Clods of earth were flung high into the air from the horses' hooves. 'Santiago!' There was a ditch ahead, lined with Dragoons who had been firing at the farmhouse and who now rose, twisted, and aimed at the Spanish cavalry. A bullet hissed past Vivar's face. 'Santiago!' He came to the ditch, jumped it, and his blade hissed down to slice blood from a Frenchman's face.

The lance slammed into a Dragoon, burying the guidon flag in his chest. The standard-bearer rode the staff free, screaming his own challenge, then was hit in the neck by a carbine bullet. A horseman coming behind seized the toppling staff and raised the blood-soaked flag high again.

'Santiago!'

Dismounted Dragoons were fleeing in the farmyard. The Spanish cavalry crashed into them. Blades chopped down. Frightened horses twisted, snapped with yellow teeth and lashed with their hooves. Swords clashed, ringing like blacksmith's hammers. A Spaniard fell from the saddle, a Frenchman screamed as a sword pinned him against the barn. The hurdle screens were abandoned in the mud.

The charge had scoured the French clean out of the farmyard, and had made carnage of the eastern ditch. The trumpeter was sounding the call to reform as Vivar reined in, turned his horse, and started back. A French Dragoon, reeling from the first attack, made a feeble thrust at the Major and was rewarded with a cut throat. 'Rifles! Rifles!' Vivar shouted.

Some French officers ran from the barn and Vivar slewed his horse towards them, his men close behind him. The Frenchmen turned and fled. The Cazadores rode right into the barn, ducking under the lintel, and screams sounded inside. Mounted Dragoons appeared and Vivar shouted at his men to form a line, to charge home, to fight for Santiago.

It was then that the Riflemen appeared from the house, splintering down the bullet-riddled door and running into the yard with sword-bayonets fixed. They cheered the Spaniard. 'East!' Vivar shouted above their cheers, pointing with his sword. 'East!'

The Riflemen ran eastwards, away from the sea, into the wooded gully where there would be temporary safety from the French Dragoons. Those Dragoons, recovering from the shock of Vivar's attack, and realizing how they outnumbered the Spanish horsemen, were reforming their ranks on the road beneath the farmhouse. The French trumpet sounded the advance.

Vivar let the counterattack come. He was yielding ground, content that the French should regain the farm buildings while he withdrew to the gulley. His men fired from the saddle. When they reloaded they rammed the bullets down their carbine barrels with ramrods that were attached by a hinged sleeve at the weapons' muzzles and so could not be dropped. The farmer, his wife, and the Parkers' coachman fled with the green-jackets.

The last of the Spanish Cazadores crashed down the gully's slope. Sharpe's Riflemen lined the brink, firing at the Frenchmen whose pursuit, though enthusiastic, was doomed. The gully's brush and thorn would force the Dragoons to funnel into the narrow paths that were covered by the Rifles and, realizing the danger, de l'Eclin called his men back. A few Frenchmen, stung to anger, spurred onwards and Sharpe watched as the rifle bullets destroyed their scattered charge. 'Cease fire!'

'Follow us!' Vivar called from the gully's far crest.

'Sir!' Harper shouted the warning, making Sharpe turn back.

Sprinting over the pasture, her skirt held up in her right hand and her bonnet grasped in her left, came Louisa Parker. A bellow of rage sounded from the farm, evidently her aunt's despairing protest, but the girl ignored it. She skirted a fallen, bleeding horse. A Frenchman began running in pursuit, but Hagman dropped the man with a single shot.

'Lieutenant! Lieutenant!' Louisa shouted.

'God Almighty!' Harper laughed as the girl, gasping for breath and eyes wide with the excitement of the moment, crashed into the gully and threw herself at Sharpe as though he could protect her against all the world.

Sharpe, exhilarated by her arrival, opened his arms to check her headlong flight. For a second she clung to him, laughing and breathless, then she drew away. Sharpe's men cheered the girl's defiance.

'Lieutenant!' Vivar had spurred back to hasten the Riflemen's retreat, and now stared with amazement at the girl at Sharpe's side. 'Lieutenant?'

But there was no time for explanations, no time for anything but the panicked flight eastwards, away from the sea's safety, and back to the mysteries enshrined in Blas Vivar's strongbox. The wild goose was safe.

CHAPTER 10

They journeyed throughout that night, climbing ever higher and always into the teeth of a wind that brought the chill from the snow which lay in the gullies of the upper slopes. Past midnight, from a wooded spur, Sharpe saw the far off gleam of the western sea. Much closer, and beneath him in the dark tangle of the lowlands, a smear of camp fires betrayed where men bivouacked. 'The French,' Vivar said softly.

'Who believed I was escorting you southwards,' Sharpe said accusingly.

'Later! Later!' Vivar responded, just as he had to every other attempt Sharpe had made to invite an explanation for the Spaniard's behaviour. Beyond Vivar the Riflemen, bowed under their heavy packs, trudged up the hill path. The Cazadores led their horses to conserve the strength of the animals for the long journey which lay ahead. Only the wounded were allowed to ride. Even Louisa Parker had been told she must walk. Vivar, seeing the girl go past, scowled at Sharpe. 'I leave you alone for two days and you find an English girl?'

Sharpe heard the hostility in the Spaniard's voice and chose to answer it mildly. 'She ran away from her aunt and uncle.'

Vivar spat towards the distant lights. 'I heard all about them! The Parkers, yes? They call themselves missionaries, but I think they are English busybodies. I was told that the Bishop was going to eject them from Santiago de Compostela, but I see the French have done that favour for us. Why did she run away?'

'I think she craves excitement.'

'We can provide that,' Vivar said sourly, 'but I have never considered soldiers to be fit company for a girl; even a Protestant girl.'

'You want me to shoot her?' Sharpe suggested acidly.

Vivar turned back towards the path. 'I'll shoot her myself, Lieutenant, if she makes any difficulties. We have our own mission, and that must not be put at risk.'

'What mission?'

'Later! Later!'

They climbed higher, leaving the shelter of the trees to emerge onto a wind-scoured slope of thin grass and treacherous rocks. The night was dark, but the cavalrymen knew their path. They crossed a high valley, splashing through a stream, then climbed again. 'I'm going,' Vivar said, 'to a remote place. Somewhere the French won't disturb us.' He walked in silence for a few paces. 'So you met Tomas?'

Sharpe sensed that it was a great effort for Vivar to make the question sound casual. He tried to respond in the same careless manner. 'That's your brother's name?'

'If he is my brother. I can count no traitor as a brother.' Vivar's shame and bitterness was now undisguised. He had been unwilling to discuss the Count of Mouromorto earlier, yet the subject was unavoidable. Sharpe had met the Count, and explanations must be offered. Vivar had obviously decided that now, in the clean cold darkness, was the right time. 'How did he seem to you?'

'Angry,' Sharpe said inadequately.

'Angry? He should be filled with shame. He thinks

Spain's only hope is to ally itself with France.' They were walking along a high ridge and Vivar had to shout above the wind's noise. 'We call such men *anfrancesados*. They believe in French ideas, but in truth they are Godless traitors. Tomas was ever seduced by northern notions, but such things bring no happiness, Lieutenant, only a great discontent. He would cut out Spain's heart and put a French encyclopaedia in its place. He would forget God, and enthrone reason, virtue, equality, liberty, and all the other nonsenses which make men forget that bread has doubled in price and only tears are more plentiful.'

'You don't believe in reason?' Sharpe let the conversation veer away from the painful subject of the Count of Mouromorto's loyalty.

'Reason is the mathematics of thinking, nothing more. You don't live your life by such dry disciplines. Mathematics cannot explain God, no more can reason, and I believe in God! Without Him we are no more than corruption. But I forget. You are not a believer.'

'No,' Sharpe said lamely.

'But that disbelief is better than Tomas's pride. He thinks he is greater than God, but before this year is out, Lieutenant, I will deliver him to the justice of God.'

'The French may think otherwise?'

'I do not give a damn what the French think. I only care about victory. That is why I rescued you. That is why, this night, we travel in the dark.' Vivar would explain no more, for all his energies were needed to cajole the flagging men further and higher. Louisa Parker, exhausted beyond speech, was lifted onto a horse. Still the path climbed.

At dawn, beneath a sky scoured clean of cloud in which the morning star was a fading speck above the frosted land, Sharpe saw that they travelled towards a fortress built on a mountaintop.

It was not a modern fort, built low behind sloping earthen walls that would bounce the cannon shot high over ditches and ravelins, but a high fortress of ancient and sullen menace. Nor was it a gracious place. This was not the home of some flamboyant lord, but a stronghold built to defend a land till time itself was finished.

The fort had lain empty for a hundred years. It was too distant and too high to be easily supplied, and Spain had not needed such places. But now, in a cold dawn, Blas Vivar led his tired Cazadores under the old, moss-thick arch and into a cobbled courtyard that was rank with weed and grass. Some of his men, commanded by a Sergeant, had garrisoned the old fortress while the Major was gone, and the smell of their cooking fires was welcome after the chill of the night. Not much else was welcoming; the ramparts were overgrown, the keep was a home for ravens and bats, and the cellar was flooded, but Vivar's delight, as he led Sharpe about the walls, was infectious.

'The first of the Vivars built this place almost a thousand years ago! It was our home, Lieutenant. Our flag flew from that tower and the Moors never took it.'

He led Sharpe to the northern bastion which, like the eyrie of some massive bird of prey, jutted above immeasurable space. The valley far below was a blur of streams and frosted tracks. From here, for centuries, steel-helmed men had watched for the glint of reflected sunlight from far-off heathen shields. Vivar pointed to a deep shadowed cleft in the northern mountains where the frost lay like snow. 'You see that pass? A Count of Mouromorto once held that road for three days against a Muslim horde. He filled hell with their miserable souls, Lieutenant. They say you can still find rusted arrowheads and scraps of their chain mail in the crevices of that place.'

Sharpe turned to look at the high tower. 'The castle now belongs to your brother?'

Vivar took the question to be a goad to his pride. 'He has disgraced the family's name. Which is why it is my duty to restore it. With God's help, I shall.'

The words were a glimpse into a proud soul, a clue to the ambition which drove the Spaniard, but Sharpe had intended to elicit a different response; one that he now sought directly. 'Won't your brother know you're here?'

'Oh, indeed. But the French would need ten thousand men to surround this hill, and another five thousand to assault the fortress. They won't come. They are just beginning to discover what problems victory will give them.'

'Problems?' Sharpe asked.

Vivar smiled. 'The French, Lieutenant, are learning that in Spain great armies starve, and small armies are defeated. You can only win here if the people feed you, and the people are learning to hate the French.' He led the way down the rampart. 'Think of the French position! Marshal Soult pursued your army north-west, to where? To nowhere! He is stranded in the mountains, and around him is nothing but snow, bad roads, and a vengeful peasantry. Everything he eats he must find, and in winter, in Galicia, there is not much to be found if the people wish to hide it. No, he is desperate. Already his messengers are being killed, his patrols ambushed, and so far only a handful of the people are resisting him! When all the countryside rises against him, then his life will be a torment of blood.'

It was a chilling prophecy and spoken with so much verve that Sharpe was convinced by it. He remembered how de l'Eclin had frankly expressed his fear of the night; his fears of peasant knives in the dark.

Vivar turned again to stare at the notch in the mountains where his ancestor had made carnage of a Muslim army. 'Some of the people fight already, Lieutenant, but the rest are frightened. They see the French victorious, and they feel abandoned of God. They need a sign. They need, if you like, a miracle. These are peasants. They don't know reason, but they do know their Church and their land.'

Sharpe felt his skin creep, not with the morning's cold, nor with fear, but with the apprehension of something beyond his imaginings. 'A miracle?'

'Later, my friend, later!' Vivar laughed at the mystery he deliberately provoked, then ran down the steps towards the courtyard. His voice was suddenly mischievous, full of joy and nonsense. 'You still haven't thanked me for rescuing you!'

'Rescuing me! Good God! I was about to destroy those bastards, only you interfered!' Sharpe followed him down the steps. 'You haven't apologized for lying to me.'

'Nor do I intend to. On the other hand, I do forgive you for losing your temper with me when last we met. I told you that you wouldn't last a day without me!'

'If you hadn't sent the damned French after me, I'd be halfway to Oporto by now!'

'But there was a reason for sending them after you!' Vivar had reached the foot of the rampart steps where he waited for Sharpe. 'I wanted to clear the French out of Santiago de Compostela. I thought that if they pursued you, then I could enter the town when they were gone. So I spread the rumour, it was believed, but the town was garrisoned anyway. So!' He shrugged.

'In other words, you can't win a war without me.'

'Think how bored you would be if you'd gone to Lisbon! No Frenchmen to kill, no Blas Vivar to admire!' Vivar linked his arm through Sharpe's in the intimate Spanish manner. 'In all seriousness, Lieutenant, I beg your pardon for my behaviour. I can justify my lies, but not my insults. For those, I apologize.'

Sharpe was instantly excruciated with embarrassment. 'I behaved badly, too. I'm sorry.' Then he remembered another duty. 'And thank you for rescuing us. We were dead men without you.'

Vivar's ebullience returned. 'Now I have another miracle to arrange. We must work, Lieutenant! Work! Work! Work!'

'A miracle?'

Vivar loosed his arm so he could face Sharpe. 'My friend, I will tell you all, if I can. I will even tell you tonight after supper, if I can. But some men are coming here, and I need their permission to reveal what is in the strongbox. Will you trust me till I've spoken with those men?'

Sharpe had no choice. 'Of course.'

'Then we must work.' Vivar clapped his hands to attract his men's attention. 'Work! Work! Work!'

Everything that Vivar's men needed had to be carried up the mountain. The cavalry horses became pack-horses for firewood, fuel, and fodder. The food came from mountain villages, some of it fetched for miles on the backs of mules or men. The Major had sent word throughout the land which had been his father's domain that supplies were needed, and Sharpe watched the response in astonishment. 'My brother,' Vivar said with grim satisfaction, 'ordered his people to do nothing which might hinder the French. Ha!'

All that day the supplies arrived in the castle. There

were jars of grain and beans, boxes of cheese, nets of bread, and skins of wine. There was hay for the horses. Cords of wood were dragged up the steep path, and bundles of brushwood brought for tinder. Some of the brushwood was made into brooms that were used to clean out the keep. Saddle blankets made curtains and rugs, while fires seeped warmth into cold stone.

The men whom Vivar expected arrived at noon. A trumpet call announced the visitors' approach, and there was a flourish of celebration in its sound. Some of the Cazadores went down the steep path to escort the two men into the fortress. The newcomers were priests.

Sharpe watched their arrival from the window of Louisa Parker's room. He had gone to see her to discover why she had fled from her family. She had slept all morning and now seemed entirely recovered from the night's exertions. She looked past him at the dismounting priests and gave an exaggerated shudder of pretended horror. 'I can never properly rid myself of feeling there's something very sinister about Romish clergy. My aunt is convinced they have tails and horns.' She watched as the priests advanced through a guard of honour to where Blas Vivar waited to greet them. 'I expect they do have tails and horns, and cloven hooves. Don't you agree?'

Sharpe turned away from the window. He felt embarrassed and awkward. 'You shouldn't be here.'

Louisa widened her eyes. 'You do sound grim.'

'I'm sorry.' Sharpe was speaking more abruptly than he would have liked. 'It's just that . . .' His voice tailed away.

'You think your soldiers will be unsettled by my presence?'

Sharpe did not like to say that Blas Vivar had already been unsettled by Louisa's impulsive act. 'It isn't a fit place for you,' he said instead. 'You're not used to this kind of thing.' He waved his hand around the room, as though to demonstrate its shortcomings, though in truth Vivar's Cazadores had done everything they could to make the foreign girl comfortable. Her room, though small, had a fireplace in which logs smouldered. There was a bed of cut bracken and crimson saddle blankets. She had no other belongings, not even a change of linen.

She seemed crestfallen by Sharpe's strict tone. 'I'm sorry, Lieutenant.'

'No.' Sharpe tried to dismiss her apology, even though he had elicited it.

'My presence embarrasses you?'

Sharpe turned back to the window and watched the Cazadores gather about the two priests. Some of his Riflemen looked on in curiosity.

'Would you like me to go back to the French?' Louisa asked tartly.

'Of course not.'

'I think you would.'

'Don't be so damned stupid!' Sharpe turned on her viciously, and was instantly ashamed. He did not want her to know just how glad he was that she had run from her aunt and uncle and, in his effort to disguise that gladness, he had let his voice snap uncontrollably. 'I'm sorry, miss.'

Louisa was just as contrite. 'No, I'm sorry.'

'I shouldn't have sworn.'

'I can't imagine you giving up swearing, even for me.' There was a trace of her old mischievousness, a hint of a smile, and Sharpe was glad of it.

'It's just that your aunt and uncle will worry about you,' he said lamely. 'And we're probably going to have to fight again, and a fight's no place for a woman.'

Louisa said nothing for a moment, then shrugged.

'The Frenchman, de l'Eclin? He offended me. I think he perceived me as a spoil of war.'

'He was offensive?'

'I imagine he thought he was being very gallant.' Louisa, dressed in the blue skirts and coat in which she had fled the travelling coach, paced about her small room. 'Would I offend you by saying that I preferred your protection to his?'

'I'm flattered, miss.' Sharpe felt himself being drawn into her conspiracy. He had come here to warn Louisa that Blas Vivar disapproved of her presence, and to tell her to avoid the Spaniard as much as was possible; instead he felt the attraction of her vivacity.

'I was tempted to stay with the French,' Louisa confessed, 'not because of the Colonel's intrinsic charms, but because Godalming would surely have been agog to hear of my adventures with the army of the Corsican ogre, would it not? Perhaps we would have been sent to Paris and paraded before the mob like Ancient Britons displayed before the Romans.'

'I doubt that,' Sharpe said.

'I rather doubted it, too. Instead I foresaw a most tedious time in which I would be forced to listen to my aunt's interminable complaints about the war, the lost testaments, her discomforts, French cooking, your shortcomings, her husband's timidity, my forwardness, the weather, her bunions – do you wish me to continue?'

Sharpe smiled. 'No.'

Louisa teased out her dark curls with her fingers, then shrugged. 'I came, Lieutenant, because of a whim. Because if I am to be stranded in a war then I would rather be stranded with my own side than with the enemy.'

'I think Major Vivar fears you'll be a hindrance to us, miss.'

'Oh,' Louisa said with mock foreboding, then walked to the window and frowned down at the Spaniard who still stood with the two priests. 'Does Major Vivar not like women?'

'I think he does.'

'He just thinks they get in the way?'

'In battle, they do. If you'll pardon me, miss.'

Louisa mocked Sharpe with a deprecating smile. 'I promise not to stand in the way of your sword, Lieutenant. And I'm sorry if I have caused you inconvenience. Now you can tell me just why we're here, and what you plan to do. I can't stay out of the way unless I know exactly where the way leads, can I?'

'I don't know what's happening, miss.'

Louisa grimaced. 'Does that mean you don't trust me?'

'It means I don't know.' Sharpe told her about the strongbox and Vivar's secretiveness, and about their long journey which had been dogged by the French Dragoons. 'All I know is that the Major wants to take the box to Santiago, but why, I don't know, and what's in it, I don't know.'

Louisa was delighted with the mystery. 'But you will find out?'

'I hope so.'

'I shall ask Major Vivar directly!'

'I don't think you should, miss.'

'Of course not. The ogre-ish Papist Spaniard doesn't want me interfering in his adventure.'

'It's not an adventure, miss, but war.'

'War is the moment, Mr Sharpe, when we loose the bonds of convention, do you not think so? I do. And they are very constricting bonds, especially in Godalming. I insist upon knowing what is in Major Vivar's box! Do you think it is jewels?'

'No, miss.'

'The crown of Spain! The sceptre and orb! Of course it is, Mr Sharpe. Napoleon wishes to put the crown on his head, and your friend is denying it him! Don't you see? We are carrying a dynasty's regalia to safety!' She clapped her hands with delight. 'I shall insist upon seeing these treasures. Major Vivar is going to reveal everything to you, is he not?'

'He said he might tell me after supper. I think it rather depends on those priests.'

'In that case we might never know.' Louisa grimaced. 'But I can have supper with you?'

The request embarrassed Sharpe, for he doubted whether Vivar would want Louisa present, but nor did he know a tactful way of telling the girl that she was being too persistent. 'I don't know,' he said weakly.

'Of course I can dine with you! You don't expect me to starve, do you? Tonight, Mr Sharpe, we shall look upon the jewels of an empire!' Louisa was enchanted with the whole idea. 'If only Mr Bufford could see me now!'

Sharpe recalled that Mr Bufford was the ink-manufacturing Methodist who hoped to marry Louisa. 'He would doubtless pray for you?'

'Most devoutly.' She laughed. 'But it is cruel to mock him, Mr Sharpe, especially as I merely delay the time when I must accept his hand.' Her enthusiasm visibly evaporated in the face of reality. 'I presume that once you have solved this mystery, you will go to Lisbon?'

'If there's still a garrison there, yes.'

'And I shall have to go with you.' She sighed, as a child might sigh for the ending of a treat that had yet to begin. Then her face cleared, reverting to an expression of mischievous delight. 'But you will ask Major Vivar's permission for me to dine with the gentlemen? I promise to behave myself.'

* * *

To Sharpe's surprise, Blas Vivar was not at all disconcerted by Louisa's request. 'Of course she may have supper with us.'

'She's very curious about the strongbox,' Sharpe warned.

'Naturally, aren't you?'

Thus Louisa was present that night when Sharpe at last discovered why Blas Vivar had lied to him, why the Cazadores had ridden to rescue him, and why the Spanish Major had journeyed so obsessively westward through the chaos of winter and defeat.

That night, too, Sharpe felt himself drawn ever more deeply into a world of mystery and weirdness; a world where the *estadea* drifted like flames in the night and sprites inhabited streams; Blas Vivar's world.

Sharpe, Louisa, Vivar and Lieutenant Davila dined in a room punctuated by thick pillars which supported a barrel-vaulted ceiling. They were joined by the two priests. A fire was lit, blankets were spread on the floor, and dishes of millet, beans, fish, and mutton were served. One of the priests, Father Borellas, was a short, plump man who spoke passable English and seemed to enjoy practising it on Sharpe and Louisa. Borellas told them that he had a parish in Santiago de Compostela; a small, very poor parish. Pouring Sharpe wine and ever eager that the Rifleman's plate did not empty, he seemed at pains to exaggerate his humble status. The other priest, he explained, was a rising man, a true *hidalgo*, and a future prince of the church.

That other priest was the sacrist of Santiago's cathedral, a canon and a man who, from the very first, made it plain that he disliked and distrusted Lieutenant Richard Sharpe. If Father Alzaga spoke English then he did not betray that skill to Sharpe. Indeed, Alzaga barely acknowledged his presence, confining his conversation to Blas Vivar whom he perhaps perceived as his social equal. His hostility was so blatant, and so jarring, that Borellas felt constrained to explain it. 'He does not love the English.'

'Many Spaniards don't,' Louisa, who seemed unnaturally subdued by the evident hostility in the room, commented drily.

'You're heretics, you see. And your army has run away.' The priest spoke in soft apology. 'Politics, politics. I do not understand the politics. I am just a humble priest, Lieutenant.'

But Borellas was a humble priest whose knowledge of Santiago de Compostela's alleyways and courtyards had saved the sacrist from the French. He told Sharpe how they had hidden in a plasterer's yard while the French cavalrymen searched the houses. 'They shot many people.' He crossed himself. 'If a man had a fowling gun, they said he was an enemy. Bang. If someone protested at the killing, bang.' Borellas crumbled a piece of hard bread. 'I did not think I would live to see an enemy army on Spanish soil. This is the nineteenth century, not the twelfth!'

Sharpe looked at the haughty-faced Alzaga who clearly had not expected, nor liked, to see Protestant English soldiers on Spanish soil. 'What is a sacrist?'

'He is the cathedral's treasurer. Not a clerk, you understand,' Borellas was eager that Sharpe should not underestimate the tall priest, 'but the man responsible for the cathedral's treasures. That is not why he is here, but because he is a most important churchman. Don Blas would have liked the Bishop to come, but the Bishop would not talk to me, and the most important man I could find was Father Alzaga. He hates the French, you see.' He flinched as the sacrist's voice was raised in anger and, as if to cover his embarrassment, offered Sharpe more dried fish and began a long explanation of the kinds of fish caught on the Galician coast.

Yet no discussion of fish could hide the fact that Vivar and Alzaga were involved in a bitter altercation; each man deeply entrenched in opposing views which, equally plainly, involved Sharpe himself. Vivar, making some point, would gesture at the Rifleman. Alzaga, refuting it, seemed to sneer in his direction. Lieutenant Davila concentrated on his food, evidently wanting no part in the fierce argument while Father Borellas, abandoning his attempts to distract Sharpe's attention, reluctantly agreed to explain what was being said. 'Father Alzaga wants Don Blas to use Spanish troops.' He spoke too softly for the other to overhear.

'Spanish troops for what?'

'That is for Don Blas to explain.' Borellas listened for another moment. 'Don Blas is saying that to find Spanish infantry would mean persuading a Captain-General, and all the Captain-Generals are in hiding; and anyway a Captain-General would hesitate, or he would say he must have the permission of the Galician Junta, and the Junta has fled Corunna, so he might apply to the Central Junta in Seville instead, and in one or two months' time the Captain-General might say that perhaps there were men, but then he would insist that one of his own favourite officers be placed in charge of the expedition, and anyway by that time Don Blas says it would be too late.' Father Borellas shrugged. 'I think Don Blas is right.'

'Too late for what?'

'That is for Don Blas to explain.'

Vivar was speaking adamantly now, chopping his hand down in abrupt, fierce gestures that appeared to mute the priest's opposition. When he finished, Alzaga seemed to yield reluctantly on some part of the argument, and the concession made Blas Vivar turn towards Sharpe. 'Would you mind very much describing your career, Lieutenant?'

'My career?'

'Slowly? One of us will translate.'

Sharpe, embarrassed by the request, shrugged. 'I was born . . .'

'Not that bit, I think,' Vivar said hastily. 'Your fighting career, Lieutenant. Where was your first battle?'

'In Flanders.'

'Start there.'

For ten uncomfortable minutes Sharpe described his career in terms of the battles he had fought. He spoke first of Flanders, where he had been one of the Duke of York's unfortunate ten thousand, then, with more confidence, of India. The pillared room, lit by its pinewood fire and cheap rushlights, seemed an odd place to be talking of Seringapatam, Assaye, Argaum, and Gawilghur. Yet the others listened avidly, and even Alzaga seemed intrigued by the translated tales of far-off battles on arid plains. Louisa, her eyes shining, followed the story closely.

When Sharpe had finished his description of the savage assault on the mud walls of Gawilghur, no one spoke for a few seconds. Resin flared in the fire. Alzaga, in his harsh voice, broke the silence and Vivar translated. 'Father Alzaga says he heard that the Tippoo Sultan had a clockwork model of a tiger mauling an Englishman to death.'

Sharpe looked into the priest's eyes. 'A lifesize model, yes.'

Vivar translated again. 'He would dearly like to have seen that model.'

'I believe it's in London now,' Sharpe said.

The priest must have recognized the challenge in

those words for he said something which Vivar did not interpret.

'What was that?' Sharpe asked.

'It was nothing,' Vivar said a little too carelessly. 'Where did you fight after India, Lieutenant?'

'Father Alzaga said,' Louisa astonished the room by raising her voice, and by her evident knowledge of Spanish which she had concealed till this moment, 'that this night he will pray for the soul of the Tippoo Sultan, because the Tippoo Sultan slew many Englishmen.'

Till now Sharpe had been embarrassed in describing his career, but the priest's scorn touched his soldier's pride. 'And I killed the Tippoo Sultan.'

'You did?' Father Borellas's voice was sharp with disbelief.

'In the water gate's tunnel at Seringapatam.'

'He had no bodyguard?' Vivar asked.

'Six men,' Sharpe said. 'His picked warriors.' He looked from face to face, knowing he need say no more. Alzaga demanded a translation, and grunted when he heard it.

Vivar, who had been pleased with Sharpe's performance, smiled at the Rifleman. 'And where did you fight after India, Lieutenant? Were you in Portugal last year?'

Sharpe described the Portuguese battlefields of Rolica and Vimeiro where, before he was recalled to England, Sir Arthur Wellesley had trounced the French. 'I was only a Quartermaster,' he said, 'but I saw some fighting.'

Again there was silence and Sharpe, watching the hostile priest, sensed he had passed some kind of a test. Alzaga spoke grudgingly, and the words made Vivar smile again. 'You have to understand, Lieutenant, that I need the blessing of the church for what I have to do, and, if you are to help me, then the Church must approve of you. The Church would prefer that I use Spanish troops, but that, alas, is not possible. With some reluctance, therefore, Father Alzaga accepts that your experience of battle will be of some small use.'

'But what . . .'

'Later.' Vivar held up a hand. 'First, tell me what you know of Santiago de Compostela.'

'Only what you've told me.'

So Vivar described how, a thousand years before, shepherds had seen a myriad of stars shining in a mist above the hill on which the city was now built. The shepherds reported their vision to Theudemirus, Bishop of Iria Flavia, who recognized it as a sign from heaven. He ordered the hill to be excavated and, in its bowels, was found the long lost tomb of Santiago, St James. Ever since the city had been known as Santiago de Compostela; St James of the field of stars.

There was something in Vivar's voice that made Sharpe shiver. The taper flames shimmered uncertain shadows beyond the pillars. Somewhere on the ramparts a sentry stamped his boots. Even Louisa seemed unnaturally subdued by the chill in the Spaniard's voice.

A shrine had been built above the long lost tomb and, though the Muslim armies had captured the city and destroyed the first cathedral, the tomb itself had been spared. A new cathedral had been built when the heathen were repulsed, and the city of the field of stars had become a destination second only to Rome for pilgrims. Vivar looked at Sharpe. 'You know who Santiago is, Lieutenant?'

'You told me he was an apostle.'

'He is far more.' Vivar spoke softly, reverently, in a voice that made Sharpe's skin creep. 'He is St James, brother of St John the Evangelist. St James, the patron saint of Spain. St James, Child of the Thunder. St James the Great. Santiago.' His voice had been growing louder, and now it rang out to fill the high-arched ceiling with the last, the greatest, and the most resonant of all the saint's titles: 'Santiago Matamoros!'

Sharpe was utterly still. 'Matamoros?'

'The Slayer of Moors. Slayer of Spain's enemies.' From Vivar, it sounded like a challenge.

Sharpe waited. There was no sound except for the fire's crackle and the grate of boots on the ramparts. Davila and Borellas stared down at their empty plates, as if to move or speak would be to jeopardize the moment.

It was Alzaga who broke the silence. The sacrist made some protest which Vivar interrupted harshly and swiftly. The two men argued for a moment, but it was plain that Vivar had won the night. As if signalling his victory, he stood and crossed to a dark archway. 'Come, Lieutenant.'

Beyond the archway was the fortress's ancient chapel. On its stone altar a cross of plain wood stood between two candles.

Louisa hurried to see the mystery revealed, but Vivar barred her entrance to the chapel until she had covered her head. She hastily pulled a shawl over her dark curls.

Sharpe stepped past her and stared at the object which lay in front of the altar, the object he had known must be here: the very heart of the mystery, the lure which had drawn French Dragoons across a frozen land, and the treasure for which Sharpe himself had been fetched to this high fortress.

The strongbox.

CHAPTER 11

Vivar stood to one side so that Sharpe could approach the altar steps. The Spaniard nodded towards the strongbox. 'Open it.' His voice was curt and matter-of-fact, almost as if the long haverings about revealing the secret had never taken place.

Sharpe hesitated. It was not fear, but rather a sense that some ceremony should attend this moment. He heard the priests come into the chapel behind him as Louisa went to stand beside Vivar. The girl's face was solemn.

'Go on,' Vivar urged Sharpe.

The oilcloth had already been cut away from the chest, and the padlocks removed from the two hasps. Sharpe stooped to lift the hasps, felt the resistance in their ancient hinges, then glanced at Vivar as if to receive his blessing.

'Proceed, Lieutenant,' Vivar said. Father Alzaga made a last protest, but Vivar waved it down before reassuring Sharpe: 'It is right that you should know what it is I want of you. I don't doubt you will consider it a nonsense, but there are things in England you might consider sacred which I would regard as similar nonsenses.'

Sharpe's metal scabbard scraped on the chapel's stone floor as he knelt. He did not make the obeisance out of reverence, but because kneeling would make it easier to explore the chest's interior. He pushed at the heavy lid and winced as the big hinges grated and screeched.

Inside was another box. It was made from a leather that seemed as old as the wood which encased it. The leather had been red, but was now so faded and worn as to appear the colour of dried blood. The box was much smaller than the chest; just eighteen inches long, a foot deep, and a foot wide. Incised into its lid was a design that had once been picked out with gold leaf, of which only shreds remained. The design was an intricately patterned border surrounding a thick-bladed and curved sword. 'Santiago was killed by the sword,' Vivar said softly, 'and it is still his symbol.'

Sharpe lifted the leather box out of the chest, stood, and placed it on the altar. 'Was Santiago killed here?'

'He brought Christianity to Spain,' there was a faint note of reluctance in Vivar's explanation, 'but then returned to the Holy Land where he was martyred. Afterwards his body was placed in a ship that had neither oars nor sails, nor even a crew, but which brought him safely back to the coast of Galicia where he wished to be buried.' Vivar paused. 'I said you would find it a nonsense, Lieutenant.'

'No.' Sharpe, overwhelmed by the moment, fingered the golden catch which fastened the leather box.

'Open it gently,' Vivar said, 'but do not touch what you find inside.'

Sharpe lifted the golden catch. The lid was stiff, so much so that he thought he would break the leather spine which served as a hinge, but he forced it back until the box lay open before him.

The two priests and the two Spanish officers crossed themselves, and Sharpe heard Father Alzaga's deep voice quietly intoning a prayer. The candlelight was dim. Dust floated above the newly opened box. Louisa held her breath and stood on tiptoe to see what lay within it.

The leather box was lined with sarsenet that Sharpe supposed had once been of royal purple, but was now so faded and worn as to be of the palest and most threadbare lilac. Encased in the sarsenet was an embroidered tapestry bag about the size of a Rifleman's canteen. The bag was plump, and drawn tight by a golden cord. The design of the tapestry was a pattern of swords and crosses.

Vivar offered Sharpe the smallest glimmer of a smile. 'As you can see, there are no papers.'

'No.' Nor were there family jewels, nor even the crown of Spain; just a tapestry bag.

Vivar climbed the altar steps. 'Nearly three hundred years ago, the treasures of Santiago's shrine were put into hiding. Do you know why they were hidden?'

'No.'

'Because of the English. Your Francis Drake raided close to Santiago de Compostela, and it was feared he would reach the cathedral.'

Sharpe said nothing. Vivar's mention of Drake had been in a voice so bitter that it was clearly best to keep quiet.

Vivar stared down at the strange treasure. 'In England, Lieutenant, you still have Drake's Drum. Have you seen it?'

'No.'

The candlelight made the Spaniard's face appear to be carved from some fiery stone. 'But you do know the legend of Drake's Drum?'

Sharpe, very conscious that everyone in the room watched him, shook his head.

'The legend,' Louisa interrupted in a soft voice, 'proclaims that if England is in peril, then the drum must be beaten and Drake will come from his watery grave to scour the Dons from the ocean.'

'Only it isn't the Dons any more, is it?' There was still bitterness in Vivar's voice. 'Whatever the enemy, the drum can be beaten?'

Louisa nodded. 'So I've heard.'

'And there is yet another story in your country; that if Britain faces defeat, King Arthur will rise from Avalon to lead his knights into battle once more?'

'Yes,' Louisa said. 'Just as the Hessians believe that Charlemagne and his knights lie sleeping in Oldenburg, ready to wake when the Antichrist threatens Christendom.'

Louisa's words pleased Vivar. 'You are looking at the same thing, Lieutenant. You are looking at the gonfalon of Santiago, the banner of St James.' He stepped quickly forward and stooped to the bag. Alzaga tried to protest, but Vivar ignored him. He put his strong, blunt fingers onto the golden cord and, rather than untie the knot, simply snapped it. He opened the tapestry bag and Sharpe saw, folded inside, a length of dusty white cloth. He thought it was silk, but he could not be sure, for the folded material was so old that a single touch of a finger might have crumpled it into dust. 'For years now,' Vivar said quietly, 'the gonfalon has been a royal treasure, but always my family has been its guardians. That is why I rescued it before the French could take it. It is my responsibility, Lieutenant.'

Sharpe felt a flicker of disappointment that the treasure was not some ancient crown, nor jewels heaped to catch the candlelight, yet he could not deny the awe which filled the chapel because of the folded length of silk. He stared, trying to sense what magic lay within its dusty creases.

Vivar stepped away from the box. 'A thousand years

ago, Lieutenant, it seemed that the Muslims would capture all of Spain. From Spain their armies would have gone north, across the Pyrenees, to assault the whole of Christendom. Their heresy would even now rule Europe. There would be no cross, only a crescent.'

A cold wind, coming through the unglazed lancet window, shivered the candles. Sharpe stood transfixed by the gonfalon as Vivar's voice continued the old story.

'You must understand, Lieutenant, that though the Moors conquered nearly all of Spain, they were checked in these northern mountains. They were determined to break our resistance here, so they came in their thousands, while we were numbered only in our hundreds. We could not win, but nor could we surrender, and so our knights rode into unequal battle after unequal battle.' Vivar was speaking very softly now, but his voice held every person in the room motionless. 'And we lost battle after battle. Our children were taken into slavery, our women for Islam's pleasure, and our men to their fields and galleys. We were losing, Lieutenant! The light of Christianity was nothing but a candle's dying flicker that must defy the light of a great, but evil sun. Then there was one last battle.'

Blas Vivar paused. Then, in a voice as proud as Spain itself, he told how a small band of Christian knights rode their tired horses against a Muslim army. He told the story so well that Sharpe felt he could actually see the Spanish knights lowering their lances and lumbering into a gallop beneath banners bright as the sun. Swords clashed on scimitars. Men hacked and gouged and lunged. Arrows hissed from strings and banners fell into the bloodied dust. Men, their entrails cut from their bellies, were trampled by war-horses, and the screams of the dying were drowned by the thunder of new attacks and the shouts of pagan victory.

'The heathen were winning, Lieutenant,' Vivar spoke as if he had himself tasted the dust of that far-off battlefield, 'but in the last extremities, in the candle's final flicker, a knight called on Santiago. It was Santiago who had brought the news of Christ to Spain; would the saint now let Christ be driven out? So the knight prayed, and the miracle happened!'

Sharpe's flesh crawled. He had stared so long at the tapestry bag that the shadows in the chapel seemed to curl and shift like strange beasts all around him.

'Santiago appeared!' Vivar's voice was triumphant and loud now. 'He came on a white horse, Lieutenant, and in his hand was a sword of sharpest steel, and he cut his way through the enemy like an angel of vengeance. They died in their thousands! We filled hell that day with their miserable souls, and we stopped them, Lieutenant! We stopped them dead! It would take centuries to clear Spain of their filth; centuries of battle and siege, yet it all began on that day when Santiago earned his name Matamoros. And this,' Vivar stepped to the box and lightly touched the folded silk within the open bag, 'is the banner he carried, Lieutenant. This is Santiago's banner, his gonfalon, which has been in my family's trust ever since the day when the first Count of Mouromorto prayed that Santiago would come to snatch a victory from the death of Christ.'

Sharpe looked to his left and saw that Louisa seemed to be in a trance. The priests watched him, judging the effect of the story on the foreign soldier.

Vivar closed the leather box and placed it carefully back in the strongbox. 'There are two legends concerning the gonfalon, Lieutenant. The first says that if it is captured by the enemies of Spain, then Spain itself will be destroyed. That is why Father Alzaga does not want your help. He believes the English will ever be our enemies, and that the present alliance is merely an expedience that will not last. He fears you will steal the banner of St James.'

Sharpe turned uneasily towards the tall priest. He did not know if Alzaga spoke English, but he tried in a stumbling way to assure him that he had no intention of doing such a thing. He felt a fool saying it, and Alzaga's contemptuous silence only deepened Sharpe's uneasiness.

Vivar, like the priest, ignored his protestation. 'The second legend is more important, Lieutenant. It says that if Spain lies endangered, if once again the barbarians are trampling our country, then the banner must be unfurled before the high altar of Santiago's shrine. Then Matamoros will arise and fight. He will bring victory. It is that miracle I wish to rouse, so that the people of Spain, however many lives they must lose, will know that Santiago rides.'

The hinges creaked as Vivar closed the strongbox lid. The wind seemed suddenly colder and more threatening as it sliced through the narrow window and fluttered the candle flames. 'Your brother,' Sharpe stumbled over the words, 'wants to take the gonfalon to France?'

Vivar nodded. 'Tomas does not believe the legend, but he does understand its power. As does the Emperor Napoleon. If the people of Spain were to learn that the banner of Santiago was just another trophy in Paris, they might despair. Tomas understands that, just as he understands that if the banner can be unfurled in Santiago, then the people of Spain, the good people of Spain, will believe in victory. It will not matter, Lieutenant, if a thousand-thousand Frenchmen ride our roads because, if Santiago is with us, no French Emperor can defeat us.'

Sharpe stepped away from the altar. 'So the banner must reach Santiago de Compostela?'

'Yes.'

'Which is held by the French?'

'Indeed.'

Sharpe hesitated, then plunged. 'So you want my help to make a raid on the city?' Even as he spoke it sounded like madness, but the atmosphere in the chapel entirely freed his voice of any scepticism. He stared at the strongbox as he continued. 'We have to go through their defences, penetrate the cathedral, and hold it long enough for your ceremony? Is that it?'

'No. We need a victory, Lieutenant. Santiago must be seen to have a victory! This will not be some dark deed, done in secret and haste. This will be no raid. No, we will take the city from the French. We'll capture it, Lieutenant, and we'll hold it long enough for the people to know that this new enemy can be humiliated. We'll win a great victory, Lieutenant, for Spain!'

Sharpe stared in disbelief. 'Good God.'

'With his help, of course.' Vivar smiled. 'And, perhaps, because I cannot find any Spanish infantry, with the help of your Rifles?'

Somehow Sharpe had not thought he was being given a choice. Instead, by the very act of seeing Vivar's secret, he had assumed he was entering into the conspiracy. Now, standing in the cold chapel, he knew he could refuse. What Vivar wanted was madness. A handful of beaten men, British and Spanish, was supposed to take a city from a conquering enemy, and not just take it but hold it against the bulk of the French army that would be only a day's march away.

'Well?' Vivar was impatient.

'Of course he'll help!' Louisa said with a fervour that showed in the brightness of her eyes.

The men ignored her, and still Sharpe said nothing.

'I cannot make you help me,' the Major said softly, 'and if you refuse, Lieutenant, I shall give you supplies and a guide to see you safely to the south. Perhaps the British are still in Lisbon? If not, you will find a ship somewhere along the coast. Good military practice demands that you forget this superstitious nonsense and march south, does it not?'

'Yes,' Sharpe replied bleakly.

'But victory is not always won by sense, Lieutenant. Logic and reason can be tumbled by faith and pride. I have the faith that an ancient miracle will work, and I am driven by pride. I must avenge my brother's treachery, or else the name Vivar will stink through the annals of Spain.' Vivar spoke these words in a commonplace manner, as if avenging fraternal treachery was an everyday part of any humdrum existence. Now he looked into Sharpe's eyes and spoke in a very different tone. 'So I beg your help. You are a soldier, and I believe God has provided you as an instrument for this work.'

Sharpe knew how difficult it was for Vivar to make the appeal, for he was a proud man, not used to being a supplicant. Father Alzaga protested with an incoherent and throaty growl as Sharpe still hesitated. Nearly half a minute passed before the Englishman at last spoke. 'There is a price for my help, Major.'

Vivar bridled immediately. 'A price?'

Sharpe told him and, by telling Vivar, he accepted the madness. For the sake of his Riflemen, he would rouse a saint from an eternity's sleep. He would go to the city of the field of stars and take it from the enemy. But only for a price.

The next day, after the morning parade, Sharpe left the fortress and walked to a place from where he could see for miles across the winter landscape. The far hills were stark and pale, sharp as steel against the sky's whiteness. The wind was cold; a wind to sap the strength of men and horses. If Vivar did not move soon, he thought, then the Spaniard's horses would be unable to march.

Sharpe sat alone at the track's edge where the hillside fell steeply away. He gathered a handful of pebbles, each about the size of a musket ball, and shied them at a white boulder some twenty paces down the hill. He told himself that if he hit it five times running then it would be safe to march on the cathedral city. The first four pebbles struck clean, bouncing off into the weeds and scree of the slope. He was almost tempted to throw the fifth askew, but instead the pebble bounced plumb from the boulder's centre. God damn it, but he was mad! Last night, overcome with the solemnity of the occasion, he had allowed himself to be swept away by Vivar's skilled telling of an ancient myth. The banner of a saint dead two thousand years! He threw another pebble and watched it skim over the boulder to fall into a patch of ragweed which, in Spain, was called St James's grass.

He stared into the far distance where a frost still lay in those folds of the hills which the sun had not yet touched. A wind fretted at the high tower and thick bulwarks of the fort behind him. The wind felt immeasurably clean and cold, like a dose of common-sense after the wit-fuddling darkness and candle-stench of the night before. It was madness, God-damned madness! Sharpe had let himself be talked into it, and he knew he had also been influenced by Louisa's enthusiasm for the whole idiotic business. He threw a whole handful of the pebbles which, like canister splitting apart from a cannon's muzzle, spattered about the white boulder.

Footsteps sounded behind Sharpe, stopping a few paces away. There was a pause, then a surly voice. 'You wanted me, sir?'

Sharpe stood. He pulled his sword straight, then turned to stare into Harper's resentful eyes.

Harper hesitated, then took off his hat in the formal salute. 'Sir.'

'Harper.'

Another pause. Harper glanced away from the officer, then looked back. 'It isn't fair, sir. Not at all, sir.'

'Don't be so bloody pathetic. Who ever expected fairness in a soldier's life?'

Harper stiffened at Sharpe's tone, but would not flinch from it. 'Sergeant Williams was a fair man. So was Captain Murray.'

'And they're dead men. We don't stay alive by being agreeable, Harper. We stay alive by being quicker and nastier than the enemy. You've got the stripes?'

Harper hesitated again, then nodded reluctantly. He fished in his ammunition pouch and brought out a set of Sergeant's chevrons that had been newly stitched in white silk. He showed them to Sharpe, then shook his head. 'I still say it ain't fair, sir.' This had been Sharpe's price: that Vivar would persuade the Irishman of his duty. If Harper would accept a Sergeantcy, then Sharpe would march on Santiago de Compostela. The Major had been amused by the price, but had agreed to exact it.

'I'm not accepting the stripes to please you, sir.' Harper was deliberately provocative, as though he hoped to change Sharpe's mind by a display of insolence. 'I'm just doing it for the Major. He told me about his flag, sir, and I'll take it into the cathedral for him, then throw these stripes back at you.'

'You're a Sergeant at my pleasure, Harper. For as

long as I need you and want you. That's my price, and that's what you accept.'

There was silence. The wind fretted at the hill's crest and fluttered the silk stripes in Harper's hand. Sharpe wondered where such a rich and lustrous material had been found in this remote fortress, then forgot the speculation as he realized that once again he had taken the wrong course. He had let his hostility show when instead he should have demonstrated his need of this big man's co-operation. Just as Blas Vivar had humbled himself to ask for Sharpe's help, so Sharpe now had to show some humility to bring this man to his side.

'I didn't want the stripes when I was first offered them,' Sharpe said awkwardly.

Harper shrugged as if to show that Sharpe's odd admission was of no interest to him.

'I didn't want to become an officer's guard dog,' Sharpe went on. 'My friends were in the ranks, my enemies were Sergeants and officers.'

That must have touched a sympathetic chord for the Irishman gave a half-grudging and half-amused grimace.

Sharpe stooped and picked up some pebbles. He flicked one at the white rock and watched it ricochet down the hill. 'When we rejoin Battalion they'll probably put me back in the stores and you can go back to the ranks.' Sharpe said it as a sop to the Irishman's pride, as a half-promise that Harper would not be forced to keep the white stripes, but he could not keep the resentment from his voice. 'Does that satisfy you?'

'Yes, sir.' Harper's agreement sounded neither heartfelt nor bitter, merely the acknowledgement of a wary truce.

'You don't have to like me,' Sharpe said, 'but just remember I was fighting battles when this Battalion was still being formed. When you were growing up, I was carrying a musket. And I'm still alive. And I haven't stayed alive by being fair, but by being good. And if we're going to survive this shambles, Harper, we've all got to be good.'

'We are good. Major Vivar said so.' Harper spoke defensively.

'We're half-good,' Sharpe spoke with a sudden intensity, 'but we're going to be the bloody best. We're going to be the cocks of the dirtiest dunghill in Europe. We're going to make the French shiver to think of us. We're going to be good!'

Harper's eyes were unreadable; as cold and hard as the stones of the hillside, but there was a stirring of interest in his voice now. 'And you need me to do it?'

'Yes, I do. Not to be a bloody lapdog. Your job is to fight for the men. Not like Williams, who wanted you all to like him, but by making them good. That way we all stand a chance of going home when this war's over. You want to see Ireland again, don't you?'

'Aye, I do.'

'Well, you won't see it again if you fight against your own side as well as the bloody French.'

Harper blew out a great breath, almost in exasperation. It was plain he had accepted the stripes, however reluctantly, because Vivar had pressed them on him. Now, with equal reluctance, he was being half-persuaded by Sharpe. 'A good few of us will never see home,' he said guardedly, 'not if we go to this cathedral for the Major.'

'You think we shouldn't go?' Sharpe asked with genuine curiosity.

Harper considered. He was not weighing what answer he should give, for his mind was already made up, but rather what tone he should use. He could be surly, thus ensuring that Sharpe knew of his continuing hostility, or he could match Sharpe's conciliatory manner. He chose neither, but rather spoke in a flat and dutiful voice. 'I think we should go, sir.'

'To see a saint on a white horse?'

Again the Irishman teetered between his choices. He stared at the stark horizon, then shrugged as he chose his new course. 'It never does to question a miracle, sir. You just take the guts and belly out of it and you're left with nothing at all.'

Sharpe heard the acquiescence, and knew his price was being paid. Harper would co-operate, but Sharpe wanted that co-operation to be willing. He wanted their fragile truce to become more than an agreement of convenience. 'You're a good Catholic?' he asked, wondering just what sort of a man his new Sergeant was.

'I'm not so devout as the Major, sir. Not many are, are they?' Harper paused. He was making his peace with Sharpe, but there would be no formal declaration of hostility's end, nor any regrets about the past, but rather a new beginning that must find its halting start on this cold hillside. Both men were too proud for apology, so apologies must be forgotten. 'Religion's for the women, so it is,' Harper went on, 'but I make my nod to the Church when I must, and I hope God's not looking when I don't want Him to see what I'm doing. But I believe, aye.'

'And you think there's some usefulness in taking an old flag to a cathedral?'

'Aye, I do,' Harper said flatly, then frowned as he tried to think of an explanation for his bald faith. 'Did you see that wee church in Salamanca where the Virgin's statue had eyes that moved? Your priest there said it was a miracle, but you could see the string the fellow jerked to make the wooden eyeballs twitch!' More relaxed now, he laughed at the memory. 'But why go to the trouble of having a string? I asked myself. Because the people want a miracle, that's why. And just because some people invent a miracle doesn't mean there aren't real ones, does it now? It means the opposite, so it does, for why would you imitate something that doesn't exist? Perhaps it is the real banner. Perhaps we will see St James himself, in all his glory, riding in the sky.' Harper frowned for a second. 'But we'll never know if we don't try, will we?'

'No.' Sharpe's agreement was half-hearted, for he could put no credence in Vivar's superstition. Yet he had wanted Harper's opinion, for he keenly felt the worry of the night's decision on him. By what right could a mere Lieutenant order men into battle? His duty, surely, was to take these men to safety, not march them against a French-held city. Yet there was an impulse to adventure which led him there, and Sharpe had wanted to know if Harper would follow the same impulse. It seemed he would, which meant that the other greenjackets would also. 'You think the men will fight?' Sharpe asked openly.

'One or two of them will make a fuss.' Harper was scornful of the prospect. 'Gataker will squeal, I dare say, but I'll knock his bloody brains about. Mind you, they'll want to know what it is they're fighting for, sir.' He paused. 'Why the hell do they call it a gonfalon? It's a bloody flag, so it is.'

Sharpe, who had had to ask Vivar the same question, smiled. 'A gonfalon's different. It's a long stringy banner you hang off a cross-staff on a pole. Old-fashioned sort of thing.'

An awkward silence followed. Like strange dogs meeting they had growled at each other, made a rough peace, and now kept a cautious distance. Sharpe ended the silence by nodding down into the valley where, far beneath the high track, men were arriving. They were villagers; tough Galicians from across the Mouromorto domain; herdsmen, miners, blacksmiths, fishermen, and shepherds. 'In one week,' he asked Harper, 'can we knock that lot into infantry?'

'We have to do that, sir?'

'The Major will provide interpreters, and we teach them to be infantry.'

'In a week?' Harper sounded astonished.

'You believe in miracles, don't you?' Sharpe said lightly.

Harper replied in kind. He fluttered the stripes in his hand, and grinned. 'I believe in miracles, sir.'

'Then let's get to work, Sergeant.'

'Bloody hell.' It was the first time Harper had heard himself addressed as Sergeant. It seemed to surprise him, then he gave a sly grin and Sharpe, who had trodden the same path years before, knew that the Irishman was secretly pleased. Harper might have fought against the stripes, but they were a recognition of his worth, and he doubtless believed that no other man in the company deserved them. So now Harper had the chevrons, and Sharpe had a Sergeant.

And both men had a miracle to perform.

CHAPTER 12

At night the men would sing around the fire in the courtyard. They did not sing the rumbustious marching songs which could make the miles melt beneath hard boots, but the soft, melancholic tunes of home. They sang of the girls left behind, of mothers, of children, of home.

Each night there was the flicker of campfires in the deep valley beneath the ramparts where Vivar's volunteers made their encampment. The volunteers came from throughout the Mouromorto domains. They bivouacked where chestnuts grew beside the stream in a sheltered crook of the hill, and they made wood and turf huts. They were peasants who obeyed the ancient call to arms, just as their ancestors had shouldered a scythe blade and marched to face the Moors. Such men would not leave their womenfolk behind, and at night the skirted shapes flickered between the fires and the children cried from the turf huts. Sharpe heard Harper warn the Riflemen against the temptation of the women. 'One touch,' he said, 'and I'll crack your skull open like a bloody egg.' There was no trouble, and Sharpe marvelled at the ease with which Harper had assumed his unwanted authority.

By day there was work. Hard work, urgent work, to fashion a victory from defeat. The priests drew a map of the city on which, in careful detail, Vivar plotted the

French defences. News of the enemy preparations came daily, fetched to the hills by refugees who fled from the invader and told tales of arrests and killings.

The city was still bounded by the decayed walls of its medieval defences. Those walls were gone in places, and in others the houses had spilt outside to make suburbs, yet the French were basing their defence on the ancient line of ramparts. Where the stones had fallen they had made barricades. The defences were not fearsome; Santiago de Compostela was no frontier city, enwrapped in star-trace and ravelins, but the ramparts could still be a terrible obstacle to an infantry attack. 'We attack just before dawn,' Vivar announced early in the week.

Sharpe grunted agreement. 'What if they have picquets beyond the walls?'

'They will. We ignore them.'

Sharpe heard the first risk being taken, the first corner cut in this desperate lunge for an impossible victory. Vivar was relying on darkness and weariness to fuddle the wits of the French. Yet it would only take one soldier to stumble in the night, for his musket to spark and fire, and the whole attack would be betrayed. Vivar proposed attacking without loaded muskets. There would be time, he said, after the initial surprise for the men to load their guns. Sharpe, an infantryman who relied on his gun far more than a cavalryman like Vivar, hated the idea. Vivar pressed, but the most Sharpe would yield was that he would consider it.

The plans grew more detailed and, as they did, so Sharpe's fears gathered like dark clouds looming on the skyline. It was easy to win a victory on paper. There were no dogs to bark, no stones to trip a man, no rain to soak powder, and the enemy performed as dozily as Vivar could wish; on paper. 'They'll know we're coming?' Sharpe asked him.

'They'll suspect we're coming,' Vivar allowed. The French could hardly have failed to hear of the gathering in the hills, though they might well dismiss such a threat as negligible. They had, after all, broken the armies of Spain and Britain, so what did they have to fear from a few peasants? Yet the Count of Mouromorto and Colonel de l'Eclin would know exactly what ambition spurred Blas Vivar, and they were both in Santiago. The refugees confirmed it. Marshal Ney's cavalry had taken the city and then ridden back to Corunna to join Marshal Soult, leaving two thousand French cavalrymen inside the circuit of broken walls.

They had not been left there to stop an ancient banner reaching a shrine, but rather to collect forage from the coastal valleys of Galicia. Having thrown the British out of Spain, Marshal Soult was now planning to march south. His officers, bragging in the taverns of Corunna, spoke openly of their plans, and those words were faithfully retailed to Vivar. The French, once their wounded and frostbitten ranks were mended, would turn south on Portugal. They would conquer that country and expel the British from Lisbon. The coast of Europe would thus be sealed against British trade, and the Emperor's stranglehold would be complete.

Soult's route south would lead through Santiago de Compostela and thus he had ordered that the city become his forward supply base. His army would collect those supplies to fuel its southern attack. French cavalry was aggressively patrolling the countryside in search of the food and fodder which, the refugees told Vivar, was being stockpiled in houses about the cathedral's plaza. 'So you see,' Vivar said to Sharpe on a night later in the week when they met as usual to stare at the city's map and hone their plan of assault, 'you have a proper reason for attacking, Lieutenant.'

'Proper?'

'You can claim that you are not just humouring a mad Spaniard. You are protecting your Lisbon garrison by destroying French supplies. Is that not true?'

But Sharpe was in no mood for such reassurance. He stared at the city's plan, imagining the French sentries staring into the night. 'They'll know we're coming.' Sharpe could not rid himself of the fear of the enemy's preparedness.

'But not where we'll attack, nor when.'

'I wish de l'Eclin wasn't there.'

Vivar scorned his fears. 'You think Imperial Guards don't sleep?'

Sharpe ignored the question. 'He isn't there to collect forage. His job is to take the gonfalon, and he knows we'll bring it to him. Whatever we plan, Major, he's already thought of. He's waiting for us! He's ready for us!'

'You're frightened of him.' Vivar leaned against the wall of the tower room where the map was kept. Firelight flickered in the courtyard below where a Spaniard sang a slow, sad song.

'I'm frightened of him,' Sharpe confirmed, 'because he's good. Too good.'

'He's only good in attack. He can't defend! When you attacked his ambush, and I attacked him in the farmyard, he wasn't so clever, was he?'

'No,' Sharpe allowed.

'And now he's trying to defend a city! He's a chasseur, a hunter like a Cazador, and he's no good at defence.' Vivar would brook no defeatism. 'Of course we'll win! Thanks to your ideas, we'll win.'

The praise was calculated to elicit enthusiasm from Sharpe who had suggested an inside-out stratagem for the assault. The attack would not try to take the city house by house, or street by street, but instead it would strike fast and hard for the city's centre. Then, split into ten parties, one party for each of the roads that broke the circuit of the ancient defences, the attackers would drive the French outwards towards the open country. 'Let them get away!' Sharpe had argued. 'So long as you take the city.'

If they took the city, which Sharpe doubted, they could hope to hold it for no more than thirty-six hours. Soult's infantry, marching from Corunna and reinforced with the superb French artillery, would soon make mincemeat of the Major's men. 'I only need a day,' Vivar hesitated. 'We capture it at dawn, we find the traitors by noon, we destroy the supplies, and that night we unfurl the gonfalon. The next day we leave in glory.'

Sharpe went to the narrow window. Bats, woken from their winter's sleep by the arrival of soldiers in the fortress, flickered in the red light. The hills were dark. Somewhere on those black slopes Sergeant Harper led a patrol of Riflemen on a long, looping march. The patrol was not just to search for a bivouacking French cavalry patrol, but also to keep the men hard and accustom them to the vagaries of marching at night. All of Vivar's small force, including the half-trained volunteers, would have to make such a journey and, having seen what chaos a night march could inflict on troops, Sharpe flinched inwardly. He thought, too, of the dreadful odds. There were two thousand French cavalrymen in Santiago de Compostela. Not all would be there when Vivar attacked; some would be bivouacking in the farmlands which they pillaged, but there would still be a mighty preponderance of enemy.

Against whom would march fifty Riflemen, one hundred and fifty Cazadores of whom only a hundred had horses, and close to three hundred half-trained volunteers.

Madness. Sharpe turned on the Spaniard. 'Why don't you wait till the French have marched south?'

'Because to wait wouldn't make a story which will be told in every Spanish tavern. Because I have a brother who must die. Because, if I wait, I will be thought as spineless as the other officers who've fled south. Because I've sworn to do it. Because I cannot believe in defeat. No. We go soon, we go very soon.' Vivar was almost speaking to himself, staring down at the charcoal marks which showed the French defences. 'Just as soon as our volunteers are ready, we go.'

Sharpe said nothing. The truth was that he now believed that the attack was madness, but it was a madness he had helped to plan and sworn to support.

Just as the innocent scrabbling of an unfledged owlet in an attic could be turned by a child's dread into the night-steps of a fearful monster, so Sharpe let his fears feed and grow as the days passed.

He could tell no one of his certainty that the assault would end in disaster. He did not want to earn Vivar's scorn by such an admission, and there was no one else in whom he could confide. Harper, like the Spanish Major, seemed imbued by a blithe confidence that the attack would work. 'Mind you, sir, the Major will have to wait another week.'

The thought of postponement spurted hope into Sharpe. 'He'll have to wait?'

'Those volunteers, sir. They're not ready, not ready at all.' Harper, who had taken on himself the job of training the volunteers in the art of platoon fire, sounded genuinely concerned.

'Have you told the Major?'

'He's coming to inspect them in the morning, sir.'

'I'll be there.'

And in the morning, in a rain which darkened the rocks and dripped from the trees, Sharpe went down to the valley where Lieutenant Davila and Sergeant Harper demonstrated to Blas Vivar the results of a week's training.

It was a disaster. Vivar had asked merely that the three hundred men be taught the rudiments of musket drill; that, like a half Battalion, they could stand in three ranks and fire the rippling platoon volleys which could gut an attacking force.

But the volunteers could not hold the rigid, tight ranks which concentrated the musket fire into deadly channels. The trouble began as the men in the rear rank instinctively stepped backwards to give themselves adequate space in which to wield their long ramrods, while the centre rank also took a step back to distance itself from the men in front, and thus the whole formation was shaken ragged. Under fire, the instinct would be for that backward movement to continue and, in just a few volleys, the French would have these men running. Nor were they even training with ammunition, for there was not enough powder and shot for that. They merely went through the musket motions. How the front rank would react to the percussion of the rear ranks' musket shots in their ears, Sharpe dared not think.

The 'muskets' were any gun that a man could contrive to bring. There were ancient fowling pieces, musketoons, horse-pistols, and even a matchlock. Some of the miners did not even have guns, carrying their pick instead. Doubtless such men would make fearsome fighters if they could first close on their enemy, but the French would never let them. They would make mincemeat of these men.

It was not that the volunteers lacked bravery; their very presence in this remote valley attested to their willingness to fight, but they could not be turned into soldiers. It took months to make an infantryman. It took a steel-hard discipline to enable a man to stand in the battle-line and face the massed drums and shining bayonets of a French attack. Natural bravery or a cock-sure stubbornness were no substitutes for training; a fact the Emperor had proved again and again as his veterans had destroyed Europe's ill-trained armies.

A French infantry attack was a thing of awe. French troops did not attack in line, but in vast columns. Rank after rank of men, massed tight, with bayonets glinting above their heads, marched to the beat of the boy drum-mers who were hidden in their midst. Men fell at the front and flanks as skirmishers bit at the column; some-times a cannon ball flayed through the packed ranks, yet always the French closed up and marched forward. The sight was fearsome, the sense of power was terrify-ing, and even the bravest men could break at the mere sight unless months of training had taught them to stand hard.

'But we won't be facing infantry.' Vivar tried to find a scrap of hope in the face of disaster. 'Only cavalry.'

'No infantry?' Sharpe sounded doubtful.

'There's a few to protect the French headquarters,' Vivar said dismissively.

'But if they shake out like that,' Sharpe gestured at the dispirited volunteers, 'they'll never stand against cavalry, let alone infantry.'

'The French cavalry are tired.' Vivar was clearly piqued by Sharpe's insistent pessimism. 'They've worn their horses to the bone.'

'We should wait,' Sharpe said. 'Wait till they've marched south.'

'You think they won't garrison Galicia?' Vivar was stubborn in his refusal to wait. He gestured for Davila and Harper to join him. How long before the volunteers would be hammered into shape?

Davila, no infantryman, looked at Harper. The Irishman shrugged. 'It's desperate, sir. Bloody desperate.'

Harper's response was so unlike his usual cheerfulness that it depressed even Vivar. The Spaniard only needed these volunteers brought to a minimum of efficiency before launching his attack, but the Irishman's gloom seemed to presage indefinite postponements, if not outright abandonment.

Harper cleared his throat. 'But what I don't understand, sir, is why you're trying to turn them into soldiers at all.'

'To win a battle?' Sharpe suggested acidly.

'If it comes to a straight scrap between these lads and French Dragoons, we're not going to win,' Harper paused, 'begging your pardon, sir.' None of the officers spoke. His voice took on a note of authority, like a practical man demonstrating a simplicity to fools. 'What's the point in training them to fight an open battle when that's not what you're expecting? Why do they need to learn platoon fire? These lads have to fight in the streets, sir. That's just gutter fighting, so it is, and I'll wager they're as good at that as any Frenchman. Get them into the city, then set them loose. I wouldn't want to face the bastards.'

'Ten trained men can see off a rabble.' Sharpe, hearing his hopes of a postponement being dashed by Harper's words, spoke harshly.

'Aye, but we've got two hundred trained men,' Harper said, 'and we just push them to wherever there's real trouble.'

'My God!' Vivar was suddenly elated. 'Sergeant, you are right!'

'Nothing, sir.' Harper was obviously delighted at the praise.

'You are right!' Vivar slapped the Irishman's shoulder. 'I should have seen it. The people, not the army, will free Spain, so why turn the people into an army? And we forget, gentlemen, just what forces will be on our side in the city. The citizens themselves! They'll rise and fight for us, and we would never think of refusing their help because they're not trained!' Vivar's optimism, released by Harper's words, was in full flood. 'So, we can go soon. Gentlemen, we are ready!'

So now, Sharpe thought, even the training would be abandoned. An outnumbered rabble would march on a city. Vivar made it all sound so easy, like filling a pit with rats then letting in the terriers. Yet the pit was a city, and the rats were waiting.

Vivar's volunteers might not be trained soldiers, but the Major insisted on swearing them into the service of the Spanish Crown. The priests conducted the ceremony, and each man's name was solemnly recorded on paper as a duly sworn soldier of His Most Christian Majesty, Ferdinand VII. Now the French could have no excuse for treating Vivar's volunteers as civilian criminals.

Yet soldiers needed uniforms, and there was no dyed cloth to make bright coats, nor any of the other accoutrements of a soldier like shakos, belts, pouches, or gaiters. But there was plenty of coarse brown homespun to be had, and from that humble material Vivar ordered simple tunics to be made. There was also some white linen, fetched from a nunnery twenty miles away, which was made into sashes. It was a very crude uniform, fastened with loops about bone buttons, but, if any rules of war could be applied to Vivar's expedition, the brown tunics passed as soldiers' coats.

The wives of the volunteers cut and sewed the brown tunics while Louisa Parker, high in the fortress, helped the Riflemen mend their green jackets. The coats were ragged, torn, threadbare and scorched, yet the girl proved to have an extraordinary skill with the needle. She took Sharpe's green jacket and, in less than a day, made it seem almost new. 'I even ironed out the bugs,' she said happily, and folded back a seam at the collar to prove that the lice had truly been exterminated by the stub of a broken sabre which he had used as a flatiron.

'Thank you.' Sharpe took the coat and saw how she had turned the collar, darned the sleeves, and patched the black facings. His trousers could not be restored to their original grey, so she had sewn patches of brown homespun over the worst rents. 'You look like a harlequin, Lieutenant.'

'A fool?'

It was the evening of the day on which Harper had convinced Vivar of the uselessness of training the volunteers. Sharpe, as on previous evenings, walked the ramparts with Louisa. He prized these moments. As the fears of defeat grew on him, these snatched conversations were passages of hope. He liked to stare at the firelight reflected from her face, he liked the gentleness which sometimes softened her vivacity. She was gentle now as she leaned against the parapet. 'Do you suppose my uncle and aunt are in Santiago?'

'Perhaps.'

Louisa was swathed in a Cazador's scarlet cloak and wore a close fitting bonnet. 'Perhaps my aunt won't take me back. Perhaps she will be so scandalized by my terrible behaviour that I will be cast from chapel and home.'

'Is that likely?'

'I don't know.' Louisa was wistful. 'I sometimes suspect that's what I want to happen.'

'Want?' Sharpe was surprised.

'To be cast adrift in the middle of the biggest adventure in the world? Why ever not?' Louisa laughed. 'When I was a child, Lieutenant, I was told it was perilous to cross the village green in case the gypsies took me. And if soldiers ever appeared in the village –' she shook her head to demonstrate the enormity of such an occasion's danger. 'Now I'm in the middle of a war and accompanied only by soldiers!' She smiled at the predicament, then gave Sharpe a look which mingled curiosity and warmth. 'Don Blas says you're the best soldier he's ever known.'

Sharpe thought it odd that she used Vivar's Christian name, then supposed it was the polite usage of an *hidalgo*. 'He exaggerates.'

'What he actually said,' Louisa spoke more slowly, and Sharpe sensed she was delivering a message to him, 'was that if you had more confidence in yourself, you'd be the best. I suppose I shouldn't have told you that?' He wondered if the criticism were true and Louisa, mistaking his silence for hurt, apologized.

'I'm sure it is true,' Sharpe said hastily.

'Do you like being a soldier?'

'I always dreamed of having a farm. God knows why, because I know nothing of the business. I'd probably plant the turnips upside down.' He stared at the camp-fires in the deep valley; tiny sparks of warmth and light in an immensity of cold darkness. 'I imagined I'd have a couple of horses in a stable, a stream to fish,' he paused, shrugged, 'children.'

Louisa smiled. 'I used to dream of living in a great castle. There would be secret passages, dungeons, and mysterious horsemen bringing messages in the night. I think I should have preferred to have lived in the days of Queen Elizabeth. Catholic priests in the shrubbery and Spaniards in the channel? Except those old enemies are now our friends, aren't they?'

'Even the priests?'

'They aren't the ogres I thought they were.' She was silent for a second. 'But if you're brought up too firmly in one persuasion then you're bound to be curious about the enemy, are you not? And we English were always taught to hate Catholics.'

'I wasn't.'

'But you know what I mean. Aren't you curious about the French?'

'Not really.'

Louisa frowned. 'I find myself curious about the Catholics. I even find myself with a most unprotestant affection for them now. I'm sure Mr Bufford would be scandalized.'

'Will he ever know?' Sharpe asked.

Louisa shrugged. 'I shall have to describe my adventures to him, shall I not? And I shall have to confess that the Inquisition didn't torture me or try to burn me at the stake.' She stared into the night. 'One day this will all seem like a dream?'

'Will it?'

'Not for you,' she said ruefully. 'But one day I will find it hard to believe that any of this even happened. I will be Mrs Bufford of Godalming, a most respectably dull lady.'

'You could stay here,' Sharpe said, and felt immensely brave for saying it.

'Could I?' Louisa turned to him. There was a glow

231

to their left where a Rifleman drew on his pipe, but they both ignored it. She turned away and traced some indeterminate pattern on the parapet. 'Are you saying that the British army will stay in Portugal?'

The question surprised Sharpe, who thought he had broken through to a more intimate layer of conversation. 'I don't know.'

'I think the Lisbon garrison must have gone already,' Louisa said flatly. 'And if not, what possible use would such a small garrison be when the French march south? No, Lieutenant, the Emperor has taught us a smart lesson, and I fear we'll not dare risk our army again.'

Sharpe wondered where she had gained such firm opinions on strategy. 'What I meant when I said you could stay here . . .' he began clumsily.

'Forgive me, I know,' Louisa interrupted him quickly, and there was a very awkward silence between them until she spoke again. 'I do know what you're saying, and I am very sensible of the honour you do me, but I do not want you to ask anything of me.' The formal words were said in a very small voice.

Sharpe had wanted to say that he would offer her everything that was in his power. It might not be much; in terms of money it was nothing, yet in slavish adoration it was everything. He had not said that, yet Louisa, out of his incoherence, had understood everything and now he felt embarrassed and rejected.

Louisa must have sensed that embarrassment, and regretted causing it. 'I don't want you to ask anything of me yet, Lieutenant. Will you give me until the city's captured?'

'Of course.' Hope flared again in Sharpe, to mingle with the shame left by his clumsy proposal. He supposed he had spoken too soon, and too impetuously, yet Louisa's evident desire to stay in Spain and avoid the fate of matrimony to Mr Bufford had provoked his words.

The sentry paced further away from them, the smell of his tobacco drifting back along the ramparts. The fire in the courtyard blazed bright as a man threw a log onto it. Louisa turned to watch the sparks whirl up to the height of the tower's crenellations. From somewhere deep in the fortress came the wailing noise of one of the Galician bagpipes that inevitably provoked cries of feigned horror from Sharpe's men. She smiled at the sound of the dutiful protests, then frowned accusingly at Sharpe. 'You don't think Don Blas will succeed in taking the city, do you?'

'Of course I . . .'

'No,' she interrupted him. 'I listen to you. You think there are too many Frenchmen in Santiago. And in private you say that this is Don Blas's madness.'

Sharpe was somewhat disconcerted by the accusation. He had not admitted his real fears to Louisa, yet she had truly perceived them. 'It is madness,' he said defensively. 'Even Major Vivar says it is.'

'He says it is God's madness, which is different,' Louisa said in gentle reproof. 'But it would work better, wouldn't it, if there were fewer Frenchmen in the city?'

'It would work better,' Sharpe said drily, 'if I had four Battalions of good redcoats, two batteries of nine pounders, and two hundred more Rifles.'

'Suppose,' Louisa began, then checked her words. 'Go on.'

'Suppose the French thought that you had marched to a hiding place near the city. A place where you planned to wait during the day so you could attack just after dark? And suppose,' she hurried on to prevent him interrupting, 'that the French knew where you were hiding?'

233

Sharpe shrugged. 'They'd send men out to slaughter us, of course.'

'And if you were in another place entirely,' Louisa spoke now with the same enthusiasm with which she had greeted the mystery of the strongbox, 'you could attack while they were out of the city!'

'It's all very complicated,' Sharpe said in muted criticism.

'But supposing I was to tell them that?'

Sharpe, astonished, said nothing. Then he shook his head abruptly. 'Don't be ridiculous!'

'No, truly! If I went to Santiago,' Louisa rode over his protest by raising her voice, 'if I went there and said that's what you were doing, they'd believe me! I'd say that you wouldn't let me come with you, and that you insisted I had to go on my own to Portugal, but I preferred to find my aunt and uncle. They'd believe me!'

'Never!' Sharpe wanted to stop this outburst of nonsense. 'Major Vivar's already played that trick on them. He spread rumours that he'd travelled with me, which sent the French haring off south. They won't fall for it again.' He regretted extinguishing such enthusiasm, but her idea was quite hopeless. 'Even if you tell the French that we're hiding somewhere, they won't send cavalry out to find us until after dawn. And by then it will be too late to attack. If there was a way of stripping the garrison at night . . .' He shrugged, intimating that there was no way.

'It was just a notion.' Louisa, chastened, stared at the bats which flickered past the ramparts in the night.

'It was kind of you to want to help.'

'I do want to help.'

'Just by being here, you help.' Sharpe tried to sound gallant. The sentry turned at the rampart's end and paced slowly back towards them. Sharpe sensed that the girl would retire to her room at any moment and, though he risked further embarrassment, he could not bear to let the moment pass without reinforcing his thin hopes. 'Did I offend you earlier?' he asked clumsily.

'Don't think such a thing. I am flattered.' Louisa stared at the lights in the deep valley.

'I can't believe that we're going to run away from Spain.' If that was Louisa's objection to accepting him, then Sharpe would scotch it, not because he knew that the Lisbon garrison would stay in place, but because he could not accept that the British intervention had been defeated. 'We're going to stay. The Lisbon garrison will be reinforced, and we'll attack again!' He paused, then plunged closer to the heart of the matter. 'And there are officers' wives with the army. Some live in Lisbon, some stay a day or so behind the army, but it isn't unusual.'

'Mr Sharpe.' Louisa laid a gloved hand on his sleeve. 'Give me time. I know you'd tell me that I should seize the moment, but I don't know if that moment is now.'

'I'm sorry.'

'There is nothing to regret.' She gathered her cloak about her. 'Will you let me retire? I am quite wearied by sewing.'

'Goodnight, miss.'

No man, Sharpe thought, felt as foolish as a man rejected, yet he persuaded himself that he had not been rejected, rather that she had promised an answer after Santiago de Compostela was taken. It was his impatience which demanded an answer sooner. It was an impatience that would obsess him, and drive him onto a city from which he would return, triumphant or defeated, to receive the answer he craved.

*   *   *

The next day was a Sunday. Mass was celebrated in the fort's courtyard, and afterwards a group of horsemen arrived from the north. They were fierce-looking men, festooned with weapons, who treated Vivar with a wary courtesy. Later he told Sharpe that the men were *rateros*, highwaymen, who for the moment had turned their violence against the common enemy.

The *rateros* brought news of a French messenger, captured with his escort four days before, who had carried a coded despatch. The despatch was lost, but the gist of the message had been extracted from the French officer before he died. The Emperor was impatient. Soult had waited too long. Portugal must fall and the British, if they still lingered in Lisbon, must be expelled before February was done. Marshal Ney was to stay in the north and clear away all hostile forces from the mountains. So, even if Vivar waited till Soult was gone, there would still be French troops in Santiago de Compostela.

But if Vivar attacked now, while Soult was still twelve leagues to the north, and while the precious fodder was still stored in the city, then a double blow could be struck: the supplies could be destroyed, and the gonfalon unfurled.

Vivar thanked the horsemen, then went to the fortress chapel where, for an hour, he prayed alone.

When he emerged, he found Sharpe. 'We march tomorrow.'

'Not today?' If haste was so desperately needed, why wait the extra twenty-four hours?

But Vivar was adamant. 'Tomorrow. We march tomorrow morning.'

The next dawn, before he had shaved, and before he had even swallowed a mug of the hot bitter tea which the Riflemen loved so much, Sharpe discovered why

Vivar had waited that extra day. The Spaniard was trying to deceive the French with another false trail, to which end, the previous night, he had sent Louisa from the fortress. Her room was empty, her bed lay cold, and she was gone.

CHAPTER 13

'Why?' Sharpe's question was both a challenge and a protest.

'She wanted to help,' Vivar said blithely. 'She was eager to help, and I saw no reason why she should not. Besides, Miss Parker has eaten my food and drunk my wine for days, so why should she not repay that hospitality?'

'I told her it was a nonsense! The French will see through her story in minutes!'

'You believe so?' Vivar was sitting close to a water-butt just inside the fort's inner gateway, where he was smearing footcloths with the pork fat that was issued to every soldier as a specific against blisters. He broke off the distasteful task to stare indignantly at Sharpe. 'Why should the French think it strange that a young girl wishes to rejoin her family? I don't find such a thing strange. Nor, Lieutenant, would I have thought it necessary for me to have either your approval or your opinion.'

Sharpe ignored the reproof. 'You just sent her off into the night?'

'Don't be ridiculous. Two of my men are escorting Miss Parker as far as is possible, after which she may walk the remaining distance to the city.' Vivar wrapped one of the greasy cloths about his right foot, then turned with feigned astonishment as though he had just understood the true cause of Sharpe's displeasure. 'You are in love with her!'

'No!' Sharpe protested.

'Then I cannot think why you should be perturbed. Indeed, you should be delighted. Miss Parker will reluctantly inform the French that our attack had been abandoned.' Vivar pulled on his right boot.

Sharpe gaped. 'You told her the attack was cancelled?'

Vivar began wrapping his left foot. 'I also told her that we will capture the town of Padron at dawn tomorrow. The town lies some fifteen miles or so south of Santiago de Compostela.

'They'll never believe that!'

'On the contrary, Lieutenant, they will find it a most likely tale, far more likely than a hare-brained attack on Santiago de Compostela! Indeed, they will be amused that I ever contemplated such an attack, but my brother will entirely understand why I have chosen the lesser town of Padron. It is where Santiago's funeral boat landed on the coast of Spain, and is thus accounted as a holy place. Not, I agree, as sanctified as Santiago's burial site, but Louisa's other indiscretions will explain why Padron will suffice.'

'What other indiscretions?'

'She will tell them that the gonfalon is so far destroyed by time and corruption that it cannot be unfurled. So, instead my plan is to crumble its tattered shreds into a dust that I shall scatter on the sea. That way, though I cannot perform the miracle I wish, I can at least ensure that the gonfalon will never pass into the hands of Spain's enemies. In brief, Lieutenant, Miss Parker will tell Colonel de l'Eclin that I am abandoning the attack because I fear the strength of their defences. You should appreciate the force of that argument, should you not? You keep telling me how fearsome our enemy is.' Vivar pulled on his left boot and stood. 'My hope is that Colonel de l'Eclin will leave the city tonight to ambush our approach march on Padron.'

At least Vivar's false trail had a plausibility that Louisa's enthusiastic ideas had lacked, but even so Sharpe was astonished that the Spaniard would risk the girl's life. He broke the skim of ice on the water-butt and took out his razor which he laid on the butt's rim. 'The French have more sense than to leave the city at night.'

'If they think they have a chance of ambushing our march, and of capturing the gonfalon? I think they might. Louisa will also inform them that you and I have quarrelled, and that you have taken your Riflemen south towards Lisbon. She will say it was your ungentlemanly attentions which drove her to seek her family's protection. Thus de l'Eclin will not fear your Riflemen, and I think he might be enticed out of his lair. And if they do not march? What have we lost?'

'We may have lost Louisa!' Sharpe said a little too forcefully. 'She could be killed!'

'True, but many women are dying for Spain, so why should Miss Parker not die for Britain?' Vivar took off his shirt and brought out his razor and mirror-fragment. 'I think you are fond of her,' he said accusingly.

'Not especially,' Sharpe tried to sound offhand, 'but I feel responsible.'

'That is a most dangerous thing to feel for a young woman; responsibility can lead to affection, and affection thus born, I think, is not so lasting as . . .' Vivar's voice faded away. Sharpe had pulled his ragged and torn shirt over his head, and the Spaniard stared with horror at his naked back. 'Lieutenant?'

'I was flogged.' Sharpe, so used to the terrible scars, was always surprised when other people found them remarkable. 'It was in India.'

'What had you done?'

'Nothing. A Sergeant didn't like me, that's all. The bastard lied.' Sharpe plunged his head under the frigid water, then came up gasping and dripping. He unfolded his razor and began scraping at his chin's dark stubble. 'It was a very long time ago.'

Vivar shuddered, then, sensing that Sharpe would not talk further about it, dipped his own razor in the water. 'Myself, I do not think the French will kill Louisa.'

Sharpe grunted, as if to intimate that he did not really care one way or the other.

'The French, I think,' Vivar went on, 'do not hate the English as much as they hate the Spanish. Besides, Louisa is a girl of great beauty, and such girls provoke men's feelings of responsibility.' Vivar waved his razor towards Sharpe as proof of the assertion. 'She also has an air of innocence which, I think, will both protect her and make de l'Eclin believe her.' He paused to scrape at the angle of his jaw. 'I told her she should weep. Men always believe weeping women.'

'That could make him take her damned head off,' Sharpe said harshly.

'I would be most sorry if they did,' Vivar said slowly. 'Most sorry.'

'Would you?' Sharpe, for the first time, heard the betrayal of genuine emotion in the Spaniard's voice. He stared at Vivar, and repeated the question accusingly, 'Would you?'

'Why ever should I not? Of course, I hardly know her, but she seems a most admirable young lady.' Vivar paused, evidently contemplating Louisa's virtues, then shrugged. 'It's a pity she's a heretic, but better to be a

Methodist than an unbeliever like yourself. At least she's halfway to heaven.'

Sharpe felt a pang of jealousy. It was evident that Blas Vivar had taken more of an interest in Louisa than he had either detected or believed possible.

'Not that it matters,' Vivar said casually. 'I hope she lives. But if she dies? Then I shall pray for her soul.'

Sharpe shuddered in the cold, wondering how many souls would need prayers spoken before the next two days were done.

Vivar's expedition trudged through a thin cold rain which pecked at the day's dying.

They followed mountain paths that twisted over barren spurs and led through wild valleys. Once they passed a village sacked by the French. Not a building remained intact, not a person was in sight, not an animal still lived. Nor did one of Vivar's men speak as they passed the charred beams from which the rain dripped slow.

They had started well before noon, for there were many miles to travel before dawn. Vivar's Cazadores led. One squadron of the cavalry was mounted to patrol the land ahead of the march. Behind those picquets came the dismounted Cazadores, leading their horses. Behind them were the volunteers. The two priests rode just in front of Sharpe's Riflemen, who formed the rearguard. The strongbox travelled with the two priests. The precious cargo had been strapped to a *macho*, a mule whose vocal cords had been slit so it could not bray to warn the enemy.

Sergeant Patrick Harper was pleased to be marching to battle. The white silk stripes were bright on his ragged sleeve. 'The lads are just fine, sir. My boys are delighted, so they are.'

'They're all your boys,' Sharpe said, by which he

meant that Harper's especial responsibility extended beyond the group of Irish soldiers.

Harper nodded. 'So they are, sir, and so they are.' He gave a quick glance at the marching greenjackets and was evidently satisfied that they needed no injunction to move faster. 'They'll be glad to be having a crack at the bastards, so they will.'

'Some of them must be worried?' Sharpe asked, hoping to draw Harper out about a rumoured incident earlier in the week, but the Sergeant blithely disregarded the hint.

'You don't fight the bloody crapauds without being worried, sir, but think how worried the French would be if they knew the Rifles were coming. And Irish Rifles, too!'

Sharpe decided to question him directly. 'What happened between you and Gataker?'

Harper shot him a look of perfect innocence. 'Nothing at all, sir.'

Sharpe did not press the matter. He had heard that Gataker, a fly and shifty man, had opposed their involvement in Vivar's scheme. The greenjackets had no business fighting private battles, he had claimed, especially ones likely to leave most of them dead or maimed. The pessimism could have spread swiftly, but Harper had put a ruthless stop to it and Gataker's black eye had been explained as a tumble down the gatehouse stairs. 'Terrible dark steps there,' was all Harper would say on the matter.

It was for just such swift resolutions of problems that Sharpe had wanted the Irishman's promotion, and it had proved an instant success. Harper had assumed the authority easily, and if that authority stemmed more from his strength and personality than from the silk stripes on his right sleeve, then so much the better.

Captain Murray's dying words had been proved right; with Harper on his side, Sharpe's problems were halved.

The Riflemen marched into the night. It became dark as Hades and, though an occasional granite outcrop loomed blacker than the surrounding darkness, it seemed to Sharpe that they moved blind through a featureless landscape.

Yet this was the country of Blas Vivar's volunteers. There were herdsmen among them who knew these hills as well as Sharpe had known his childhood alleys about St Giles in London. These men were now scattered throughout the column as guides, their services abetted by the cigars which Vivar had distributed amongst his small force. He was certain no Frenchmen would be this deep in the hills to smell the tobacco, and the small glowing lights acted as tiny beacons to keep the marching men closed up.

Yet, despite the guides and the cigars, their pace slowed in the night and became even slower as the rain made the paths slippery. The frequent streams were swollen, and Vivar insisted that each one was sprinkled with holy water before the vanguard splashed through. The men were tired and hungry, and in the darkness their fears became treacherous; the fears of men who go to an unequal battle and in whom apprehension festers until it becomes close to terror.

The rain stopped two hours before the dawn. There was no wind. Frost made the grass brittle. The cigars were finished, but their usefulness was ended anyway for a mist silted the last valleys before the city.

When the rain stopped, Vivar called a halt.

He stopped because there was a danger that the French might have put heavy picquets into the villages which lay in the hills about the city. Refugees from Santiago de Compostela knew of no such precautions, but Vivar guarded against it by ordering that any piece of equipment which might rattle or clang must be tied down. Musket and rifle-slings, canteens and mess tins, all were muffled. It still seemed to Sharpe, as they moved off, that the troops made sufficient noise to wake the dead; horseshoes clicked on stone, iron boot-heels thumped frosted earth, but no French picquet startled the darkness with a volley of musketry to warn the distant city.

The Riflemen now led the march. Vivar followed with his cavalry, but the greenjackets led because they were the experienced infantry who would spearhead the attack. Cavalry could not assault a barricaded town; only infantry could achieve such a thing, and this time it had to be done without loaded firearms. Sharpe had reluctantly agreed that his Riflemen would make the assault with the bayonet alone.

A flintlock was a precarious thing. Even uncocked the weapon could fire if the flint's doghead snagged on a twig, was dragged back, then released. Such a shot, however accidental, would alert French sentries.

It was one thing to order men not to fire; to tell them that their lives depended on a silent approach, but in the misted darkness just before dawn, when a man's blood was at its coldest and his fears warmest, a cat's squawl could be enough to scare a Rifleman and make him fire blind into the night. Just one such shot would bring Frenchmen tumbling from their guardhouses.

And so, though yielding the point had added to Sharpe's dread, he had seen the force of Vivar's pleading and so had agreed to advance with empty weapons. Now no shot could startle the night.

Yet still the French could be forewarned. Such fears were Sharpe's tumultuous companions on the long and ever more halting march. Perhaps the French had their

245

own spies in the mountains who, just as the refugees had betrayed information to Vivar, had betrayed Vivar to the city? Or perhaps de l'Eclin, a man whose ruthlessness was absolute, had whipped the truth from Louisa? Perhaps artillery had been fetched from Corunna and waited, charged with canister, to greet the fumbling attackers? Attackers, moreover, who would be tired, cold, and without loaded guns. The first moments of such a fight would be slaughter.

Sharpe's fears burgeoned and, away from Vivar's indomitable cheerfulness, he let the doubts gnaw at him. He could not express those doubts, for to do so would destroy whatever confidence his men might have in his leadership. He could only hope that he conveyed the same certainty as Patrick Harper who seemed to march eagerly over the last steep miles. Once, as they splashed through a soggy reach of grassland beneath the dark line of a pinewood, Harper spoke enthusiastically of just how grand it would be to see Miss Louisa again. 'She's a brave lass, sir.'

'And a foolish one,' Sharpe replied sourly, still angry that her life had been risked.

Yet Louisa was the reverse of Sharpe's fear; the consolation which, like a tiny beacon in an immense darkness, kept him going. She was his hope, but arrayed against that hope were the demons of fear. Those demons became more sinister with every forced halt. Sharpe's guide, a blacksmith from the city, was leading a circuitous route that would avoid the villages and the man stopped frequently to sniff the air as though he could find his way by scent alone.

At last satisfied, he increased his pace. The Riflemen slithered down a steep hill, reaching a stream that had flooded the meadows and turned the valley's bottom into a morass of frost and shallow water. Sharpe's guide stopped at the margin of the marsh. '*Agua, señor.*'

'What does he want?' Sharpe hissed.

'Saying something about water,' Harper replied.

'I know it's God-damned water.' Sharpe started forward, but the guide dared to pluck at the Rifleman's sleeve.

'*Agua bendita! Señor!*'

'Ah!' It was Harper who understood. 'He wants the holy water, sir, so he does.'

Sharpe swore at the idiocy of the request. The Riflemen were late and this fool demanded that he sprinkle a morass with holy water? 'Come on!'

'Are you sure . . .' Harper began.

'Come on!' Sharpe's voice was made harsher by the fears which seethed inside him. This whole expedition was misbegotten and mad! Yet pride would not let him turn back, nor would it let him make an obeisance towards Vivar's water-sprites. 'I haven't got any bloody holy water!' he growled. 'Anyway, it's superstitious bloody nonsense, Sergeant, and you know it.'

'I don't know that at all, sir.'

'Come on!' Sharpe led the way through the stream and cursed because his tattered boots let in cold water. The Riflemen, oblivious to the cause of the small delay at the water's edge, followed. This mist seemed thicker in the valley's bottom and the guide, who had splashed through the stream with Sharpe, hesitated on the far bank.

'Hurry!' Sharpe growled, though it was a pointless admonition for the blacksmith spoke no English. 'Hurry! Hurry!'

The guide, clearly flustered, indicated a narrow sheep track that angled up the further slope. As he climbed, Sharpe realized they must have come very close to the city, which was betrayed by the mephitic stink of its streets that seemed to him to be a foretaste of the horror that awaited his men.

Sharpe suddenly realized that the thump and chink of moving cavalry had been left behind, and he knew Vivar must have sent the Cazadores on their northward detour which was designed to take them far from the ears of French sentries. The ill-trained volunteer infantry should be some two or three hundred yards behind Sharpe by now. The Riflemen were isolated, ahead of the attack, and now very close to the holy city of St James.

And they were late, for the mist was being silvered by the first hint of the false dawn. Sharpe could see Harper beside him, he could even see the beads of moisture on the peak of Harper's shako. He had lost his own shako in the battle at the farm, and now wore a Cazador's forage cap instead. The cap was a pale grey and Sharpe was seized with the sudden irrational knowledge that the light-coloured cloth would make his head a target for some French marksman on the hill above. He snatched it off and threw it into some brambles. He could feel the thump of his heart. His belly was tender and his mouth dry.

The blacksmith, going very cautiously now, led the Riflemen across a rough pasture and into a grove of elm trees that grew at the hill's summit. The bare branches dripped and the mist wavered in the darkness. Sharpe could smell a fire, though he could not see it. He wondered if it belonged to one of the French guardposts and the thought of the waiting sentries made him feel horribly alone and vulnerable. The dawn was coming. This was the moment when he should be attacking, but the mist masked the landmarks which Vivar had coached him to expect. To his right there should be a church, to his left the loom of the city, and he should not be on a hilltop, but in a deep ravine which would hide the Riflemen's approach.

Sharpe, lacking those landmarks, supposed there was still further to go, that they yet had to drop down into the ravine, but the blacksmith checked under the trees and, in dumbshow, indicated that the city lay to their left. Sharpe did not respond, and the guide plucked again at the Rifleman's green sleeve and pointed to the left. 'Santiago! Santiago!'

'Jesus bloody wept.' Sharpe dropped to one knee.

'Sir?' Harper knelt beside him.

'We're in the wrong bloody place!'

'God save Ireland.' The Sergeant's voice was scarce above a whisper. The guide, unable to gain an understandable response from the greenjackets, disappeared into the darkness.

Sharpe swore again. He was in the wrong place. That mistake worried and irritated him, but what angered him more was the knowledge that Vivar would say it was because the spirits of the stream, the *xanes*, had been slighted. God damn it, but that was nonsense! All the same Sharpe had gone astray, he was late, and he did not know where Vivar's other troops were. The fears took hold of him. This was not how an attack should start! There should be bugles and banners in the mist! Instead he was alone, lost, far ahead of the Cazadores and volunteers. He told himself he had known this would happen! He had seen it happen before, in India, where good troops, forced to a night attack, had become lost, frightened, and beaten.

'What do we do, sir?' Harper asked.

Sharpe did not answer, because he did not know. He was tempted to say they would pull back in an abandonment of the whole attack, but then a shape moved to his left, boots rustled the frosted grass, and the blacksmith

249

re-appeared in the mist with Blas Vivar at his side. 'You've come too far,' Vivar whispered.

'God damn it, I know!'

The blacksmith was evidently trying to explain how the Riflemen had risked the mischief of the *xanes*, but Vivar could spare no time for such regrets. He waved the man away and knelt beside Sharpe. 'It's two hundred paces to the church. That way.' Vivar pointed to his left. The church should have been to their right.

Vivar's force had curled around the city in the night and now approached from the north. The city's northern wall had long been destroyed, its stone taken to build the newer houses which spread beyond the line of mediaeval fortifications along the road which led to Corunna. He had chosen that road for his approach, not only because it lacked the barrier of a mediaeval wall, but also because the guards might think that any approaching troops were Frenchmen coming from Soult's army.

The church, which served the newer suburb, had been turned into a French guardpost. It lay three hundred yards outside the main defence line that was composed of barricades. Every road into the city had such a guardhouse, intended to give an early alarm should Santiago be assaulted. The sentries of such posts might be killed in an attack, but the noise of their sacrifice would serve as a warning to the city's main defences. 'I think,' Vivar whispered to Sharpe, 'that God is with us. He's sent the mist.'

'He's sent us to the wrong God-damned place.'

The Riflemen should have been a quarter-mile to the south, in the marshy ravine, and they should have been there an hour before. The ravine snaked behind the church and led up to the houses just outside the main defences. They had lost the chance to make that secretive approach. Nor, so close to the enemy and so near to the treacherous wolf-light of dawn, could they spare the time to creep back through the mist.

'Leave the guardhouse to me,' Vivar said.

'You want me to charge straight past it?'

'Yes.'

Which was easy for Vivar to ask, but it meant a change of plan which put the whole assault in jeopardy. Because they had come late and to the wrong place, the Riflemen would lose surprise. Vivar proposed that Sharpe's assault ignore the guardhouse. That was possible, but the French sentries would not ignore them. Their reaction would take time. Astonished men lose precious seconds, and further seconds could be lost if the enemy muskets, dampened by the mist, misfired. The darkness might even have swallowed the Riflemen before the French fired, but fire they would, startling the dawn long before the greenjackets had covered the three hundred yards from the church to the city's defences. The guards at the barricades would be warned. They would be waiting and, at best, Vivar's force could find itself clinging to a few houses on the northern side of the city and, as the day lightened and the mist shredded, the cavalry would cut off their retreat. By midday, Sharpe knew, they could all be prisoners of the French.

'Well?' Vivar sensed from Sharpe's silence and immobility that the Rifleman already believed the battle lost.

'Where's your cavalry?' Sharpe asked, not out of interest, but to delay the horrid decision.

'Davila's leading them. They'll be in place. The volunteers are in the pasture behind.' Receiving no response, Vivar touched Sharpe's arm. 'With or without you, I'll do it. I have to do it, Lieutenant. I would not care if the Emperor himself and all the forces of hell guarded the city, I would have to do it. There is no other way of expunging my family's shame. I have a brother who is a traitor, so the treason must be washed away with enemy blood. And God will look mercifully upon such a wish, Lieutenant. You say you do not believe, but I think on the verge of battle every man feels the breath of God.'

It was a fine speech, but Sharpe did not relent. 'Will God keep the guardhouse quiet?'

'If he wills it, yes.' The mist was lightening. Sharpe could see the bare pale branches of the elm above him. Every second's delay was puting the assault in more jeopardy, and Vivar knew it. 'Well?' he asked again. Still Sharpe said nothing and the Spaniard, with a gesture of disgust, stood. 'We Spanish will do it alone, Lieutenant.'

'Bugger you, no! Rifles!' Sharpe stood. He thought of Louisa; she had said something about seizing the moment and, despite his demons, Sharpe thought he might lose her if he did not act now. 'Coats and packs off!' The Riflemen, so they could fight unencumbered, obeyed. 'And load!'

Vivar hissed a caution against loading the rifles, but Sharpe would not go into the attack with neither surprise nor loaded weapons. The risk of a misfire must be endured. He waited till the last ramrod had been thrust home and the last lock primed. 'Fix swords!'

Blades scraped, then clicked as the bayonets' spring-loaded catches slotted onto the rifle muzzles. Sharpe slung his own rifle and drew his big clumsy sword. 'In file, Sergeant. Tell the men not to make a bloody sound!' He looked at Vivar. 'I'll not have you thinking we didn't have the courage.'

Vivar smiled. 'I would never have thought that. Here.' He reached up and took the tiny sprig of dead rosemary from his hat and tucked it into a loose loop on Sharpe's jacket.

'Does that make me one of your elite?' Sharpe asked.

Vivar shook his head. 'It's a herb that averts evil, Lieutenant.'

For a second Sharpe was tempted to reject the superstition, then, remembering his defiance of the *xanes*, he let the shred of rosemary stay where it was. The morning's task had become so desperate that he was even prepared to believe that a dead herb could give him protection. 'Forward!'

In for a penny, Sharpe thought and, God damn it, but he had put his approval on Vivar's madness back in the fort's chapel when he had let the mystery of the gonfalon overwhelm him like the heady fumes of some dark and heated wine. Now was not the time to let the fears stop the insanity.

So forward. Forward through the trees, past a stone wall, and suddenly Sharpe's boots grated on flint and he saw they had come to the road. A building loomed dark to his right, while ahead of him he could at last see the guardhouse fire. Its flames were dim, smeared vague by the mist, but it had been lit outside the church and thus illumined the roadway. Any second now the challenge might sound. 'Close up!' Sharpe whispered to Harper. 'And fingers off triggers!'

'Close up!' Harper hissed. 'And don't bloody fire!'

Sharpe proposed to go past the guardhouse at a run. The noise would begin then, but that could not be helped. It would begin with the smatter of musket and rifle fire, and end in the full cacophony of death. For now, though, there was only the scrape of boots on flint, the thump of muffled equipment, and the hoarse breathing of men already tired by hours and hours of marching.

Harper crossed himself. The other Irishmen in the company did the same. They grinned, not with pleasure,

253

but fear. The Riflemen were shaking, and their bellies wanted to empty. Mary, Mother of God, Harper repeated to himself time and time again. He supposed he should say a prayer to St James, but he knew none, and so he nervously repeated the more familiar invocation. *Be with us now and at the hour of our death. Amen.*

Sharpe led the advance. He walked slowly; ever staring at the smeared light of the watch-fire. The flamelight glinted up his sword blade which he held low. Far beyond the first blaze, he could now see the blur of other fires which must be burning at the margin of the main French defence. The mist was silvering, lightening, and he even thought he could see the faint tangle of pinnacles and domes that was the city's roofline. It was a small city, Vivar had said; a mere handful of houses about the abbey, hostels, cathedral, and plaza, but a city held by the French that must be taken by a motley little army.

A motley, brown-dressed, ill-trained little force that was inspired by one man's faith. Vivar, Sharpe thought, must be drunk on God if he believed the moth-eaten shred of silk could work its miracle. It was madness. If the British army knew that an ex-Sergeant was leading Riflemen on such a mission, they would court-martial him. Sharpe supposed he was as mad as Vivar; the only difference was that Vivar was goaded by God, and Sharpe by the stubborn, stupid pride of a soldier who would not admit defeat.

Yet, Sharpe reminded himself, other men had achieved glory on dreams just as impractical. Those few knights, forced a thousand years before to their fastnesses in the mountains by the overwhelming armies of Mahomet, must have felt just this same despair. When those knights had tightened their girths and lifted their lances from the stirrup-couches and stared at the great crescent of the enemy beneath the rippling banners that had brought blood from the desert, they must have known that this was the hour of their death. Yet still they had slammed down the visors of their helmets, raked back their spurs, and charged.

A stone grated beneath Sharpe's foot and brought his thoughts back to the present. They were in a street now, the countryside left behind. The windows of the silent houses had iron grilles. The road was climbing, not steeply, but enough of a slope to make the charge more difficult. A shape moved by the fire, then Sharpe saw there was a crude barrier placed across the road that would stop his mad dash to the city's main defences. The barrier was nothing but two handcarts and some chairs, but it was still a barrier.

The moving shape by the watch-fire resolved itself into a human silhouette; a Frenchman who stooped to light a pipe with a burning spill taken from the flames. The man suspected nothing, nor did he look northwards to where he might have seen the reflection of firelight on fixed bayonets.

Then a dog barked in a house to Sharpe's right. He was so tense that he jumped sideways. The dog became frantic. Another dog took up the alarm, and a cockerel challenged the morning. The Riflemen instinctively quickened their pace.

The Frenchman by the fire straightened and turned. Sharpe could see the distinctive shape of the man's shako; an infantryman. Not a dismounted cavalryman, but a Goddamned French infantryman who unslung his musket and pointed it towards the Riflemen. '*Qui vive?*'

The challenge began the day's fight. Sharpe took a breath, and ran.

CHAPTER 14

It was extraordinary how, once the waiting was over, the fears sloughed away.

Sharpe ran. It was uphill. His bootsole, so carefully sewn into place the day before, flapped free. Though he ran on the road's flint-hardened surface, it seemed as if he pounded through a thick and cloying mud, yet the fears went because the die was cast and the game must be seen to its end.

'*Qui vive?*'

'*Ami! Ami! Ami!*' Vivar had given him a whole French phrase that might confuse an alert enemy sentry, but Sharpe had been unable to commit the strange words to memory, and so had settled on the simpler word for 'friend'. He shouted it louder, at the same time pointing behind him as though he fled from some enemy hidden in the mist.

The sentry hesitated. Four other Frenchmen had come from the church porch. One had a Sergeant's stripe on his blue sleeve, but he evidently did not want the responsibility of firing on his own side for he shouted into the church for an officer to come. '*Capitaine! Capitaine!*' Then, shako-less and still buttoning his blue jacket, the Sergeant turned back towards the approaching Riflemen. '*Halte là!*'

Sharpe held up his left hand as though he was ordering his men to slow down. He slowed himself,

256

gasping again: '*Ami! Ami!*' He appeared to stumble forward, exhausted, and the clumsy subterfuge took him to within two paces of the enemy Sergeant. Then he looked into the Frenchman's eyes and saw the sudden terror of realization.

It was too late. All Sharpe's fears, and all the relief from those fears, went into his first sword stroke. One pace forward, the snarling lunge, and the Sergeant was folding over the twisting blade and the first sentry was opening his mouth to shout as Harper's bayonet came up into his belly. The Frenchman's finger closed in spasm on his musket's trigger. Sharpe was so close to the man that he did not see the muzzle flame, only the explosion in the pan. A spark of burning powder fizzed over his head, smoke billowed around him, then he was twisting and wrenching his sword free of the Frenchman's flesh. The Sergeant fell backwards into the watch-fire and his hair, which had served as his towel for greasy hands, flared bright and high for an instant.

The remaining three Frenchmen were retreating towards the porch, but the Riflemen were faster. Another musket shot stunned the dawn, then the sword-bayonets did their work. A Frenchman screamed terribly.

'Silence the bastard!' Harper snapped. A blade ripped, there was a choking sound, then nothing.

A pistol banged from the church door. A greenjacket gasped, turned, and fell into the fire. Two rifles fired, throwing a dark shape back into the church's shadowed interior. The burning Rifleman screamed foully as he was dragged from the flames. The dogs were barking like the hounds of hell.

Surprise was gone, and there were yet three hundred yards of road to cover. Sharpe was pulling the handcart aside, opening the road to the cavalry that must follow.

'Leave the buggers!' There were still Frenchmen inside the church but they must be ignored if the assault was to have any chance of success. Even Sharpe's own wounded must be abandoned if the city was to fall. 'Leave them! Come on!'

The Riflemen obeyed. One or two hung back, seeking safety in the shadows, but Harper demanded to know whether they would prefer to fight him or the French and the laggards found their courage. They followed Sharpe into the dark mist that was not so dark any longer. There were bugles sounding in the city, not in alarm yet, merely ordering the stand-to, but the calls served to instil urgency into the greenjackets. The haste made them lose all semblance of military order; they advanced neither in file nor line, but as a pounding mass of men who ran up the slope towards the looming city.

Where the defences would have been alerted. Now the fear had time to surge back, and it was made worse because Sharpe saw how the French had pulled down the houses nearest the old wall so that the guards behind the barricades would have a clear field of fire.

Shots came from the Frenchmen in the church behind. A bullet fluttered overhead, another skipped between the Riflemen to smash into a broken wall ahead. Sharpe imagined the muskets and carbines sliding over the city's barricades. He imagined a French officer ordering the troops to wait until the enemy was close. Now was the moment of death. Now, if there were cannon in the defences, the great barrels would gout their spreading canisters. Riflemen would be flensed alive, their bellies ripped out, their guts spread ten yards along a cold road.

No such shots came, and Sharpe realized that the city's defenders must be confused by the shots from the church. To a man on the main defence line it must seem as if the approaching Riflemen were the remnants of the guardhouse's garrison being pursued by the musketry of a distant enemy. He shouted the magic word as loud as he could, hoping it would reinforce the mistaken identity. '*Ami! Ami!*'

Sharpe could see the main defences now. A high-sided farm-waggon had been pushed across the nearest street entrance to make a temporary barricade which, by day, could be hauled aside to let the cavalry patrols enter or leave the city. It was illuminated by a fire which also showed the shapes of men climbing onto the waggon bed. Sharpe could see them fixing their bayonets. He could also see a narrow gap to the left of the waggon where the harness pole formed the only obstacle.

A question was shouted from the waggons, and Sharpe had no answer beyond the single word, '*Ami!*' He was panting with the uphill run, but managed to snarl an order to his men. 'Don't bunch! Spread!'

Then, from the church behind him, a bugle sounded.

It must have been an agreed signal, but one which had been delayed by the death of the picquet's officer and Sergeant. It was the alarm; shrill and desperate, and it provoked an instant volley from the waggon.

The muskets banged, but the defenders had fired too soon and, like so many troops firing downhill, too high. The realization gave Sharpe a sudden burst of hope. He was shouting a war cry now, nothing coherent, just a scream of murderous rage that would carry him to the very edge of the enemy's position. Harper was beside him, feet pounding, and the Riflemen were spreading across the road so that they did not make a bunched target for the French soldiers who scrambled onto the waggon to take the places of the men who had fired.

'*Tirez!*' An enemy officer's sword slashed down.

The musket flames leaped three feet clear of the French muzzles, smoke pumped to hide the cart, and a Rifleman was jerked back as though a rope had yanked him off his feet.

Sharpe had gone to the left of the road where he stumbled on the rubble from the dismantled houses. He saw a Rifleman stop to take aim and he shouted at him to keep running. There could be no pause now, none, for if this attack lost its momentum, the enemy would merely swat it away. Sharpe clenched himself for the awful moment when the gap must be faced.

He leaped for the gap, screaming his challenge that was meant to strike fear into whoever waited for him. Three Frenchmen were there, lunging with bayonets, and Sharpe's sword clanged from the blades to bite into a musket stock. He stumbled on the waggon pole, then was thumped aside as Sergeant Harper crashed through the narrow gap. Other Riflemen were clawing at the cart's side, trying to climb it. A Frenchman stabbed down with a bayonet, but was hurled back by a rifle bullet. More rifles fired. A Frenchman aimed at Sharpe but, in his nervousness, he had forgotten to prime his musket. The flint sparked on an empty pan, the man screamed, then Sharpe had found his footing and drove forward with the sword. Harper was twisting his sword bayonet from an enemy's ribs. More Riflemen were crowding through the gap, chopping and slashing, while others came over the waggon to drive the Frenchmen back. The defenders had been too few, and had waited too long before the bugle had turned their uncertainty into action. Now they died or fled.

'The waggon! The waggon!' Sharpe jerked his sword free of the man who had forgotten to prime his gun. Harper slammed down with his rifle butt to stun the last Frenchman, then bellowed at the Riflemen to drag the cart out of the way. 'Pull, you bastards! Pull!' The greenjackets threw themselves at the wheels and slowly the waggon creaked into the space which the French had cleared for their killing ground.

Most of the French picquet had fled down the street ahead. It was a narrow, cobbled street with a central gutter. Other streets led left and right, following the line where the walls had once stood. In all the streets, Frenchmen were spilling from the houses and some paused to fire at the Riflemen. A pistol bullet ricocheted from the window grille beside Sharpe's head.

'Load! Load!' Sharpe was kicking the watch-fire aside, trying to make a passage for Vivar's horsemen. He booted flaming debris into an alley, scorching his boots and trousers. The Riflemen took shelter in doorways, spitting bullets into muzzles and thrusting down with their iron ramrods. There were shouts from the street and the first Riflemen to be reloaded sniped at the enemy. Sharpe turned and saw the cathedral's three bell-towers just two hundred yards away. The narrow street went uphill, turning slightly to the right after fifty paces. The misted light was growing, though the dawn proper had not yet come. A few Frenchmen in breeches, boots, and shirts still ran from houses with weapons and helmets clutched in their hands. One enemy cuirassier, panicking, ran towards the greenjackets and was thumped on the head by a rifle butt. Others took cover in doorways to fire at the invaders.

'Fire!' Sharpe called. More rifles snapped to drive the disorganized enemy further into the city. Sharpe's rifle kicked his shoulder like a mule and the flaming powder from the pan stung his cheek. Harper was dragging French corpses aside, pulling the bodies through the frosted nightsoil in the central gutter.

There was a curious silence. The Rifles had achieved surprise, and the silence marked the precious, and precarious moments as the French tried to make sense of the sudden alarm. Sharpe knew a counterattack would come, but now there was just the eerie, unexpected, and menacing silence. He broke it by shouting his men into their places. He put one squad to cover the western street, a second to watch eastwards, while he held the largest number of Riflemen to guard the narrow way which led to the city's centre. His voice echoed back from the stone walls. He suddenly felt the impertinence of what he had done, of what Blas Vivar had dared to order done, of this chilling moment in the dawn. A French bugle sounded the reveille, then, in betrayal of the spreading warnings, slurred into the alarm. A bell began an urgent clamour and a thousand pigeons clattered up from the cathedral's pinnacled roof to fill the air with panicked wings. Sharpe turned to stare north and wondered when Vivar's main force would arrive.

'Sir!' Harper had kicked in the door of the closest house where half a dozen Frenchmen, scared half-witless, cowered in the guardroom. A fire flickered in the hearth, and their bedding lay in confusion on the bare wood floor. They had been sleeping, and their muskets were still racked beside the door. 'Get the guns out!' Sharpe ordered. 'Sims! Tongue! Cameron!'

The three Riflemen ran to him.

'Cut their belts, braces, bootlaces, belts and buttons. Then leave the bastards where they are. Take their bayonets. Take anything you damn well want, but hurry!'

'Yes, sir.'

Harper crouched beside Sharpe in the street outside the guardroom. 'That was all easier than I thought.'

Sharpe had imagined the big Irishman to have felt no fear, and the words hinted at a relief which he shared. They were also true words. As he had run uphill from the church, Sharpe had expected an overwhelming defence to blaze and crash from the line of buildings; instead a half-dazed picquet had fired two volleys, then crumpled. 'They weren't expecting us,' he offered in explanation.

Another enemy bugle snatched its urgent summons to rival the barking of dogs and the clangour of the bells. The closest streets were empty now but for the shredding mist and the humped shapes of two Frenchmen killed as they came from their billets. Sharpe knew that this was the moment for the enemy to counterattack. If one French officer had his wits and could find two companies of men, then the Riflemen were beaten. He looked to his right, but there was still no sign of the Cazadores. 'Load! Then hold your fire!'

Sharpe loaded his own rifle. When he bit the bullet from the cartridge the saltpetre tasted bitter and foul. After a couple more shots he knew that the thirst would be raging in him because of the powder's salty taste. He spat the bullet into the rifle's muzzle and rammed it down on the wadding. He pushed the ramrod home and primed the pan.

'Sir! Sir!' It was Dodd, one of the men covering the street which led west. He fired. 'Sir!'

'Steady! Steady!' Sharpe ran to the corner and saw a single French officer on horseback. Dodd's bullet had missed the man who was seventy paces away. 'Steady now!' Sharpe called. 'Hold your fire!'

The French officer, a cuirassier, pushed back the edges of his cloak in a gesture that was as disdainful as it was brave. His steel breastplate shone pale in the misty light. The man drew his long sword. Sharpe cocked his rifle. 'Harvey! Jenkins!'

'Sir?' Both Riflemen answered at once.

'Take that bastard when he comes.'

Sharpe twisted, wondering where the hell Vivar's Cazadores were. The sound of hooves turned him back,
and he saw that the officer had begun to trot down the
street. Other cuirassiers joined him from the side alleys.
Sharpe counted ten horsemen, then ten more. It was
all the enemy could muster. The other cavalrymen in
the city must still be saddling their horses or waiting
for orders.

The Frenchman, who was as brave a man as any
Sharpe had seen, barked a command. '*Casques en tête!*'
The plumed helmets were pulled on. The street was
only wide enough for three horsemen to ride abreast.
The cuirassiers' swords were drawn. 'Stupid bastard,'
Harper said in savage condemnation of the French
officer who, in his bid for fame, led men to destruction.

'Take aim!' Sharpe almost hated the moment. There
were half a dozen rifles for each of the leading Frenchmen who, when they died, would block the street for
those behind. 'Steady, lads! We're going to take all
these bastards! Aim low!'

The rifles were levelled. Swan-necked cocks were
pulled back. Hagman knelt on his right knee, then
rocked back to squat on his ankle so that his left hand,
supported by his left knee, could better take the weight
of the rifle and bayonet. Some of the Riflemen were
similarly posed, while others propped their guns against
door lintels. Remnants of the scattered watch-fire
smoked in the street, hazing their view of the horsemen
who now spurred into a canter.

The French officer raised his sword. '*Vive l'Empereur!*'
He lowered the sword to the lunge.

'Fire!'

The rifles spat. Sharpe heard the strike of bullets on
the breastplates. It sounded like pebbles thrown hard

against a sheet of tin. A horse screamed, reared, and its rider fell in the path of a tumbling horse. Sword clanged on cobbles. The officer was on the ground, jerking in spasms, and retching blood. A riderless horse clattered into an alleyway. A cuirassier turned and fled. Another, unseated, limped towards an open door. The cavalrymen at the rear did not try to force their way through, but slewed round and fled.

'Reload!'

Smoke spurted from windows down the street. A bullet smacked with horrid force into the stone beside Sharpe, while another snicked up from the cobbles to thump into a Rifleman's leg. The man hissed with the pain, fell, and clutched at the blood which spread thick on his black trousers. It was hard to spot the Frenchmen behind the windows with their black grilles, and harder still to pick such men off. More of them appeared as shadows at the street's far end, and from those shadows musket flames stabbed towards the Riflemen. It was light enough now for Sharpe to see a French tricolour flying from the cathedral's high dome, and he saw that it was going to be a clear and cold day, a day for killing, and unless Vivar threw in his main force soon, it would be the Riflemen who did the dying.

Then the trumpet sounded behind.

The Cazadores did not just fight for pride, nor just for their country, though either cause would have driven them through the gates of hell itself, they fought for the patron saint of Spain. This was Santiago de Compostela, where the angels had sent a cloud of stars to light a forgotten tomb, and the Spanish cavalry charged for God and Santiago, for Spain and Santiago, for Blas Vivar and Santiago.

They came like a terrible flood. Hooves struck sparks

from the road as their horses plunged past Sharpe. Their swords struck shards of light in the grey dawn. They lunged into the city's heart, led by Blas Vivar who shouted an incomprehensible thanks as he galloped past the Riflemen.

And behind the Cazadores, scrambling up from the ravine where Sharpe should have been at first light, the volunteer infantry followed. They too shouted the saint's name as their warcry. Despite their makeshift uniforms of brown tunics and white sashes, they looked more like an avenging mob armed with muskets, picks, swords, knives, lances, and scythe-blades.

As they ran past, Sharpe thrust the captured French muskets towards the men who had no firearms, but the volunteers were too intent on reaching the city's centre. For the first time Sharpe saw they might win, not through skilled tactics, but by harnessing a nation's hate.

'What do we do, sir?' Harper came from the guard-house with a bundle of captured bayonets.

'Follow them! Forward! Watch your flanks! Keep an eye on the upper windows!'

Not that any advice would be heeded now. The Riflemen were infected by the madness of the morning, and all that mattered was to take the city. The fears of the long cold night were gone, replaced with a surging and extraordinary confidence.

They advanced into chaos. Frenchmen, waking to slaughter, ran into alleys where vengeful Spaniards hunted and killed them. Inhabitants of the city joined the chase, abetting Vivar's men who were spreading into the arcaded medieval streets which made a labyrinth about the central buildings. Screams and shots sounded everywhere. Cazadores, split into squads, clattered from street to street. A few Frenchmen still fought from the upper windows of their billets, but one by one they were killed. Sharpe saw his erstwhile guide, the blacksmith, smashing a lancer's skull with a hammer. The gutters were slick with blood. A priest knelt by a dying volunteer.

'Stay together!' Sharpe was fearful that in the horror of the moment, a dark-uniformed Rifleman might be mistaken for a Frenchman. He came to a small square, chose a turning at random, and led his men along a street where three Frenchmen lay dead in pools of trickling blood. A woman was stripping one man of his uniform on the steps of a church. A fourth Frenchman lay dying as two children, neither over ten years old, stabbed at him with kitchen knives. A legless cripple, eager for plunder, swung on calloused knuckles to a corpse's side.

Sharpe turned left into another street and shrank aside as Spanish cavalrymen clattered past. A Frenchman fled from a house into the horseman's path, he screamed, then a sword cut into his face and he went down under the iron-shod hooves. Somewhere in the city a volley of musketry crashed like thunder. A French infantryman came from an alleyway, saw Sharpe, and fell to his knees; literally begging to be taken prisoner. Sharpe pushed him behind, into the keeping of the Riflemen, as more Frenchmen came from the alley. They threw away their muskets, only wanting to be under protection.

There was light and space ahead now, a contrast to the dank shadow of the tiny streets, and Sharpe led his men towards the wide plaza which surrounded the cathedral. There was the incongruous smell of bread in a bakery, then that homely smell was instantly overlaid by the stench of powder smoke. The Riflemen advanced cautiously towards the plaza from which another huge volley jarred the morning. Sharpe could see bodies lying among the weeds which grew between the plaza's flagstones. There were dead horses and a score of dead men, most of them Spanish. Musket smoke was thicker than the mist. 'Bastards are making a stand,' Sharpe shouted to Harper.

He edged forward to the street corner. To his left was the cathedral. Three men in brown tunics lay on the cathedral steps with blood trickling from their bodies. To Sharpe's right, and directly opposite the cathedral, was a richly decorated building. A tricolour hung above its central door, while every window was wreathed in powder smoke. The French had turned the huge building into a fortress that dominated the plaza.

This was not the time to fight a battle against a cornered band of desperate Frenchmen, but rather to determine that the rest of city was taken. The Riflemen used back alleys to circumvent the plaza. The prisoners stayed with them, terrified of the vengeance which the townspeople were exacting on other captured Frenchmen. The city had spawned a vengeful mob, and Sharpe's soldiers had to use their rifle butts to keep the prisoners safe.

Sharpe led his men south. They passed a dying horse which Harper shot. Two women immediately attacked the corpse with knives, sawing off great joints of warm meat. A hunchback with a bleeding scalp grinned as he cut off a dead Dragoon's pigtails, and it occurred to Sharpe that the dead man was the first Dragoon he had seen in Santiago de Compostela. He wondered whether Louisa's deception had truly worked, and the bulk of the green-coated French cavalry had ridden south.

'In there!' Sharpe saw a courtyard to his left and he

pushed his prisoners through the archway. He left half a dozen greenjackets to guard them, then went back to the medieval maze that was a confusion of fighting. Some alleys were peaceful, while in others there were brief, furious fire-fights as desperate Frenchmen were cornered. One cuirassier, trapped in an alley, laid about with his sword and put six volunteers to flight before a crash of musket bullets smashed his defiance. Most of the French barricaded themselves in their billets. Spanish muskets blasted doors open, men died as they charged up narrow stairs, but the French were out-numbered. Two houses caught fire, and men screamed horribly as they were burned alive.

Most of the surviving enemy, except those who held the great building in the plaza, were to the south of the city where, in a slew of houses, their officers enjoined them to a sturdy defence. Sharpe's men took over two housetops and their rifle fire drove the French from windows and courtyards. Vivar led a dis-mounted charge of Cazadores and Sharpe watched the red and blue-coated cavalry flood into the enemy-held buildings.

Vivar's careful plan, which would have sent men to each of the city's exits, had crumbled in the heat of victory so that men who should have been driving the enemy eastwards were killing and plundering wherever they could. Yet it was this very savagery which drove the attackers through the city, and made the French flee, either to the countryside, or to the French headquarters in the plaza.

The rising sun revealed that the tricolour was gone from the cathedral's high dome. In its place, bright as a jewel, a Spanish standard caught the small breeze. It bore the coat of arms of Spanish royalty; a banner for the morning, but not the banner of Santiago that would be unfurled in the cathedral. Sharpe thought how beautiful the city's skyline was in this dawn. It was an intricate tangle of spires, domes, pinnacles, cupolas and towers, all misted by smoke and sunlight. Above the whole scene was the great cathedral itself. A group of blue-coated Frenchmen appeared on the balustraded balcony of one of the bell towers. They fired downwards, then a volley from below drove them back. One of the Spanish bullets clanged against a bell. The other church bells of the city rang their peals of victory, even though the stammer of musket fire still testified to the last vestiges of French resistance.

A Rifleman beside Sharpe tracked two Frenchmen scrambling across a roof fifty yards away. The Baker rifle slammed back into his shoulder and one of the enemy slid bloodily down the tiles and fell into the street. The other, in desperation, hurled himself across the roof ridge to disappear. Vivar's men had hunted forward with sabre and carbine, and Sharpe could see French soldiers running into the southern fields. He told his men to hold their fire, then led them down to the street where the beauty of the city's skyline was replaced by the curdling stench of blood. One of the Riflemen laughed because a child was carrying a human head. A dog lapped at blood in a gutter and snarled when the Riflemen came too close.

Sharpe went back to the edge of the plaza where musket fire still whip-cracked above the flagstones. The wide space was empty but for the dead and dying. The French were still barricaded inside the vast and elegant building from which, whenever a Spaniard dared show himself in the plaza, a thunder of musketry crashed out.

Sharpe kept his Riflemen out of sight. He sidled to the very corner of the street from where he could see what lavish wealth a dead saint had brought to the city's centre. The wide plaza was surrounded by buildings of spectacular beauty. A scream turned him, and he saw a Frenchman being thrown from one of the cathedral's bell towers. The body twisted as it fell, then was mercifully hidden by a lower terrace. The cathedral was a miracle of delicately carved stone and intricate design, but on this day, in the labyrinth of its carved roofs, men died. Another Spanish standard was hung from the bell tower as the last Frenchman was killed there. The great bells began their joyful sound, even as a volley of musketry from the French-held side of the plaza tried to take revenge on the Spaniards who had hung the banner into the dawn.

A Spaniard burst from the cathedral's western doors to brandish a captured French flag. Immediately a fusillade splintered from the west of the plaza, and its bullets buzzed and cracked about the man. By a miracle he lived and, clearly knowing that this day he was both invincible and immortal, he pranced mockingly down the cathedral steps and through the scattered corpses of the plaza. Each step of the way the enemy's captured flag was riddled by the hissing bullets, but somehow the man lived and the Riflemen cheered as, at last, he stalked into the cover of the street with his tattered trophy safe.

Standing in the shadows, Sharpe had watched the French-held building and had tried to gauge how many muskets or carbines had fired from its façade. He estimated at least a hundred shots, and knew that, if the French had as many men on every other side of the great building, then this would prove a stubborn place to take.

He turned as hooves sounded behind him. It was Blas Vivar, who must have known what threat waited in the plaza for he slid out of the saddle well short of the street's ending. 'Have you seen Miss Louisa?'

'No!'

'Nor me.' Vivar listened to the musketry from the plaza. 'They're still in the palace?'

'In force,' Sharpe said.

Vivar peered round the corner to stare at the building. It was under fire from men on the cathedral roof. Window panes shattered. French muskets answered the fire, spurting smoke into the rising sun. He swore. 'I can't leave them in the palace.'

'It'll be damned hard to get them out.' Sharpe was wiping blood from his sword blade. 'Have we found any artillery?'

'None that I've seen.' Vivar jerked back as a musket ball slapped the wall close to his head. He grinned as though apologizing for a weakness. 'Perhaps they'll surrender?'

'Not if they think they'll get slaughtered.' Sharpe gestured to the street behind, where a disembowelled French corpse witnessed to the fate awaiting any enemy who was caught by the townspeople.

Vivar stepped away from the corner. 'They might surrender to you.'

'Me!'

'You're English. They trust the English.'

'I have to promise them life.'

A Spaniard must have shown himself somewhere on the plaza's edge, for there was a sudden, echoing crash of musket fire which bore witness to just what strength the French had crammed inside the palace. Vivar waited until the splintering volleys were done. 'Tell them I'll set the palace on fire if they don't surrender.'

Sharpe doubted whether the stone building could be fired, but that was not the threat the French feared most. They feared torture and horrid death. 'Can the officers keep their swords?' he asked.

Vivar hesitated, then nodded. 'Yes.'

'And you guarantee that every Frenchman will be safe?'

'Of course.'

Sharpe did not want to negotiate the surrender; he felt such diplomacy would be done better by Blas Vivar, but the Spaniard seemed convinced that an English officer would be more reassuring to the French. A Cazador trumpeter sounded the cease-fire.

A bedsheet was found, tied to a broom handle, and waved around the street corner. The trumpeter repeated the call to cease fighting, but it took a full quarter-hour just to convince the vengeful Spaniards about the plaza's rim that the call was genuine. It was a further ten minutes before a French voice called suspiciously from the palace.

Vivar translated. 'They'll see one man only. I hope it isn't a trick, Lieutenant.'

'So do I.' Sharpe sheathed his sword.

'And ask them about Louisa!'

'I was going to,' Sharpe said, and stepped into the sunlight.

CHAPTER 15

No fusillade greeted Sharpe; only silence. The rising sun threw the intricate shadow of the cathedral's pinnacles onto the palace's bullet-pocked stone, through the haze of dawn mist that had been thickened by musket smoke. The sound of his footsteps echoed from the buildings. A wounded man moaned and turned over in his own blood.

Sharpe could tell some of the morning's events from the manner in which the wounded and dead lay in the plaza. Frenchmen, fleeing to the safety of the palace, had been cut down by pursuing Spaniards who, in turn, had been repulsed by volleys from the Frenchmen already safe inside. Those Frenchmen now watched him thread his way through the extraordinary litter of battle.

There were bodies lying with curled fists. A dead horse bared yellow teeth to the dawn. A cuirassier's half-polished breastplate lay beside a single drumstick. Scraps of cartridge paper lay black and curled on the flagstones. A block of pipeclay had crumbled to white dust. A Spanish spur that had come unscrewed from its boot socket glinted beside a bent ramrod. There was an empty sabre scabbard, a helmet cover, cartouches, and French shakos abandoned among the weeds which thrust through the cracks in the paving. A cat bared its teeth at Sharpe, then slunk quickly away.

Sharpe paced through the litter, conscious of the watching eyes in the palace. He also felt ill-accoutred for the diplomatic task he faced. His boot sole flapped and scraped on the flagstones. He had no hat, the seams of his trousers had opened again, while his face and lips were stained black by powder. His rifle was slung on his right shoulder, and he supposed he should have discarded the weapon as inappropriate to this mission.

Sharpe noted the *rejas* of black iron that barred the windows of the palace's lowest storey; bars that would force an assault to attack the double doors. As he approached, one of those doors was opened a few cautious inches. Loopholes had been smashed in its timbers. Shards of glass, broken when the French punched out the windows with their musket butts, lay on the paving amidst misshapen musket balls. Skeins of powder smoke, stinking like rotten eggs, clung to the palace façade.

Sharpe stepped carefully through the broken glass. A voice from the doorway demanded something of him in harsh Spanish. 'English,' he called in reply, 'English.' There was a pause, then the door was pulled back.

Sharpe stepped through, finding himself in a high, pillared hall where a group of French infantrymen faced him with bayonets. The men were stationed behind a makeshift battlement of plump sacks; evidence that they had foreseen that the doors might be assaulted. Surely, Sharpe reasoned, the French would not allow him to see such careful preparations if they had not already decided to surrender. That thought gave him confidence.

'You're English?' An officer spoke from the shadows to Sharpe's left.

'I'm English. My name is Sharpe, and I command a detachment of His Majesty's 95th Rifles present in this city.' It seemed best, at this moment, not to betray his lowly rank which would hardly impress men in such desperate danger as these French.

Not that the small deception mattered, for another voice spoke from the gloom of the big stairway ahead of him. 'Lieutenant Sharpe!' It was Vivar's brother, the Count of Mouromorto. 'Are you the best emissary they could find, Lieutenant?'

Sharpe said nothing. He wiped his face on his sleeve, thereby smudging his cheeks with the sootlike powder. Somewhere on the city's edges a volley of musketry sounded, then, closer to the plaza, a cheer. The French officer pulled his sword belt straight. 'This way, Lieutenant.' He led him up the stairs, past the Count who, as always dressed in his black riding coat and odd white topboots, fell into step behind. Sharpe wondered if Louisa was in the palace. He was tempted to ask the officer, but supposed the question was better posed to Colonel de l'Eclin or whoever waited to negotiate the surrender upstairs.

'I must congratulate you, Lieutenant.' The French officer, like Sharpe, had a voice made hoarse from the effort of shouting orders in battle. 'I understand it was your Riflemen who made the first assault?'

'Indeed.' Sharpe always found the politeness of such truces incongruous. Men who had been trying to disembowel each other at sunrise talking, an hour later, in flowery compliments.

'The Lieutenant was fool enough to sacrifice his men for my brother's madness.' The Count of Mouromorto was evidently not disposed to compliments, flowery or otherwise. 'I thought the British had more sense.'

Sharpe and the French officer both ignored the comment. Sharpe deduced from the Count's presence that Colonel de l'Eclin would indeed be waiting at the top of these stairs, and he found himself dreading the meeting. He did not think he could deceive de l'Eclin into surrender; the chasseur officer was too good, and Sharpe knew his own fragile confidence would wane before the Colonel's knowing and sceptical gaze.

'This way, Lieutenant.' The French officer ushered him past another barricade on the half landing, then up to doors which opened into a tall and once gracious room which served as a passage to other, similar rooms. To their right were the palace windows, where infantrymen crouched with loaded weapons amidst the shards of broken glass. Upturned shakos full of cartridges lay beside the men at the firing positions. The upper part of the room's rear wall was pitted by musket strikes, as was the fine moulding of the plaster ceiling. A huge mirror above the mantel had been shattered into savage glass spikes which leaned dangerously from the gilt frame. A portrait of a stern man, dressed in an ancient ruff, was punctured with bullet holes. The soldiers turned to watch Sharpe with silent and hostile curiosity.

The next room had a score of soldiers embrasured in its windows, too. Like the men in the first room they were mostly infantry, with just a smattering of dismounted cuirassiers or lancers. No Dragoons, Sharpe noted. The men were protected by cushions and upturned furniture, or by sacks which, struck by musket fire, had leaked flour or grain onto the parquet floor. Sharpe's confidence that the French would surrender was beginning to erode. He could see that this French headquarters had plenty of both men and ammunition for a siege. His feet scrunched the shards of a shattered chandelier as he was led into the third room where a group of officers awaited his arrival.

To Sharpe's relief de l'Eclin was not among the Frenchmen who stiffened as he appeared in the doorway.

Instead it was a blue-coated Colonel of infantry who stepped forward and gave the smallest bow.

'Sir,' Sharpe acknowledged the courtesy, though his voice was little more than a croak because of his hoarseness.

The Colonel's left arm was in a sling, while his cheek had been scratched by a splinter that had drawn enough blood to soak the white silk stock at his neck. The left tip of his moustache was similarly discoloured by blood. 'Coursot,' he said curtly. 'Colonel Coursot. I have the honour to command the Headquarter's Guard of this city.'

'Sharpe. Lieutenant Sharpe. 95th Rifles, sir.'

The Count of Mouromorto, having followed Sharpe in silence from the stairway, went to one of the windows from which he could stare at the cathedral's shadowed façade. He seemed to disdain the proceedings, as though the fate of Spain was above such petty negotiations.

Yet Colonel Coursot's opening struck Sharpe as anything but petty. The Frenchman took a watch from his waistcoat pocket and touched the button which sprang open its lid. 'You have one hour to leave the city, Lieutenant.'

Sharpe was non-plussed. He had come expecting to deliver the ultimatum, but instead it was this tall, grey-haired Frenchman who so confidently dictated terms. Coursot snapped the watch shut. 'You should know, Lieutenant, that an army corps is approaching this city from the north. It will arrive here in a matter of hours.'

Sharpe hesitated, not knowing what to say. His mouth was dry and, to give himself time, he uncorked his canteen, swilled the taste of salty gunpowder from his tongue, then spat into the ashes of the grate. 'I don't believe you.' It was, and Sharpe knew it, a feeble response, but probably a truthful one. If either Marshal

Soult or Marshal Ney had left Corunna, then news would have reached Vivar by now.

'Disbelief is your privilege, Lieutenant,' Coursot said, 'but I assure you the army corps is coming.'

'And I assure you,' Sharpe said, 'that we shall defeat you before they arrive.'

'That assumption is also your privilege,' the Colonel said equably, 'but it will not make me surrender to you. I assume you have come here to seek my surrender?'

'Yes, sir.'

There was a tense silence. Sharpe wondered if some of the officers in this room had urged a surrender on Coursot; these Frenchmen were vastly outnumbered, surrounded, and every moment of continued fighting would make more casualties to join the wounded who lay in the corners of the room. 'If you don't surrender now,' Sharpe pressed his case awkwardly, 'we shall give you no further opportunity. You wish the palace to burn down around you?'

Coursot chuckled. 'I assure you, Lieutenant, that a stone building does not catch fire easily. You, I think, lack artillery? So what are you hoping for? That St James will send down heavenly fire?'

Sharpe blushed. The Count of Mouromorto translated the jibe and the tension in the room relaxed as the French officers laughed.

'Oh, I know all about your miracle,' Coursot said mockingly. 'What astonishes me is to find an English officer involved in such nonsense. Ah, the coffee!' He turned as an orderly entered the room with a tray of cups. 'Do you have time for coffee?' he asked Sharpe. 'Or must you hurry away to pray for a divine thunderbolt?'

'I'll tell you what I'll do.' Sharpe, stung out of his efforts at diplomacy, spoke with a biting savagery. 'I'll put my best Riflemen on those bell towers.' He pointed through the window at the cathedral. 'Your muskets aren't accurate at that range, but my men can pick the eyes out of your French skulls at twice that distance. They've got all day to do it, Colonel, and they'll turn these rooms into a charnel house. Frankly, I don't give a bugger. I'd rather shoot Frenchmen than talk to them.'

'I do believe you.' If the Colonel was rattled by Sharpe's threat he did not betray it, but nor did he press his own threat of an approaching army corps which Sharpe sensed had been made purely as a formality. Instead he placed a cup of coffee on the table in front of the Rifleman. 'You can kill a lot of my men, Lieutenant, and I can make myself a considerable nuisance to your miracle.' Coursot took a cup from the orderly, then looked with amusement at Sharpe. 'The gonfalon of Santiago? Isn't that right? Don't you think you're clutching at straws if you need such a nonsensical bauble for victory?'

Sharpe neither confirmed nor denied it.

The Colonel sipped coffee. 'Of course I'm no expert, Lieutenant, but I would imagine miracles are best performed in an atmosphere of reverent peace, wouldn't you agree?' He waited for a reply, but Sharpe kept silent. Coursot smiled. 'I am suggesting a truce, Lieutenant.'

'A truce?' Sharpe could not keep the astonishment from his voice.

'A truce!' Coursot repeated the word as though he was explaining it to a child. 'I assume you do not think your occupation of Santiago de Compostela will be forever? I thought not. You have come here to make your little miracle, then you wish to leave. Very well. I promise not to fire on your men, nor on any other person in the city, not even upon St James himself, so long as you promise not to fire on my men, nor make an attack on this building.'

The Count of Mouromorto made a sudden and impassioned protest against the suggestion, then, when Coursot ignored it, turned away in disgust. As he drank his coffee, Sharpe thought he could understand the Count's displeasure. He had tried again and again to capture the gonfalon, now he was supposed to stand idly by while it was unfurled in the cathedral. Yet would these Frenchmen stand idle?

Coursot saw Sharpe's hesitation. 'Lieutenant. I have two hundred and thirty men in this building; some of them wounded. What damage can I do to you? You wish to inspect the palace? You may, indeed you should!'

'I can search it?' Sharpe asked suspiciously.

'From top to bottom! And you will see that I tell the truth. Two hundred and thirty men. There are also some twenty Spaniards who, like the Count of Mouromorto, are friends of France. Do you really think, Lieutenant, that I will surrender those men to the vengeance of their countrymen? Come!' Almost angrily, Coursot threw open a door. 'Search the palace, Lieutenant! See just what a paucity of men frighten you!'

Sharpe did not move. 'I'm in no position to accept your suggestion, sir.'

'But Major Vivar is?' The Colonel seemed annoyed that Sharpe had not greeted his offer of a truce with immediate enthusiasm. 'I assume Major Vivar is in command?' he persisted.

'Yes, sir.'

'So tell him!' Coursot waved his hand, as though the errand was negligible. 'Finish your coffee, and tell him! In the meantime, I want an assurance from you. I presume you have taken some French prisoners today? Or have you slaughtered them all?'

Sharpe ignored the bitterness in the Frenchman's tone. 'I have prisoners, sir.'

'I want your word, as a British officer, that they will be treated properly.'

'They will be, sir.' Sharpe paused. 'And you, sir, have a British family under your protection?'

'We have one English girl in the palace.' Coursot still seemed nettled by Sharpe's suspicions of his truce. 'A Miss Parker, I believe. Her family was sent to Corunna last week, but I assure you Miss Parker is entirely safe. I assume she was sent here to mislead us?'

The calmness of the question did not indicate whether the deception had worked or failed, though Sharpe, at that instant, was only concerned with Louisa's fate. She was alive and in the city, and thus his hopes were alive too. 'I don't know that she was sent to mislead you, sir,' he said dutifully.

'Well, she did!' Coursot said testily. The Count of Mouromorto scowled at Sharpe as though the Rifleman was personally responsible.

'Miss Parker deceived you?' Sharpe tried to seek more information without betraying any anxiety.

Coursot hesitated, then shrugged. 'Colonel de l'Eclin left at three o'clock this morning, Lieutenant, with a thousand men. He believes you have gone south, and that Major Vivar is at Padron. I congratulate you on a successful *ruse de guerre.*'

Sharpe's heart missed a beat. It had worked! He tried to keep his face expressionless, but he was certain it must betray his delight.

Coursot grimaced. 'But be assured, Lieutenant, that Colonel de l'Eclin will return by this afternoon, and I advise you to finish your miracle before he does so. Now! Will you seek Major Vivar's consideration of my proposal?'

'Yes, sir.' Sharpe did not move. 'And can I assume you will release Miss Parker to our protection?'

'If she so wishes, then I will release her to you when you return with Major Vivar's answer. Remember, Lieutenant! We will not fire on you, so long as you do not fire on us!' With ill-disguised impatience, the French Colonel conducted Sharpe towards the doorway. 'I give you half an hour to return with your answer, otherwise we shall assume you have turned down our generous offer. *Au revoir*, Lieutenant.'

Once Sharpe had left the room, Coursot went to stand in one of the deep window bays. He opened his watch again and stared with apparent incomprehension at its filigreed hands. He only looked up when he heard the sound of Sharpe's footsteps on the plaza's flagstones. Coursot watched the Rifleman walk away. 'Bite, little fish, bite,' he spoke very softly.

'He's stupid enough to bite,' the Count of Mouromorto had overheard the murmured words, 'as is my brother.'

'You mean they have a sense of honour?' Coursot asked with a surprising malevolence, then, sensing he had spoken too sharply, smiled. 'I think we need more coffee, gentlemen. More coffee for our nerves.'

Blas Vivar was less astonished at Coursot's suggestion than Sharpe expected. 'It isn't unusual,' he said. 'I can't say that I'm delighted, but it isn't such a bad idea.' The Spaniard took advantage of the cease-fire to walk into the plaza and stare at the palace façade. 'Do you think we can capture it?'

'Yes,' Sharpe said, 'but we'll lose fifty men killed and double that with bad wounds. And they'll be our best men. You can't send half-trained volunteers against those bastards.'

Vivar nodded agreement. 'Colonel de l'Eclin's gone south?'

283

'That's what Coursot said.'

Vivar turned and shouted towards the civilians who crowded the streets leading from the plaza. A chorus of voices answered, all confirming that yes, French cavalry had left the town in the middle of the night, going south. How many cavalry? he asked, and was told that hundreds and hundreds of mounted men had filed through the city.

Vivar looked back at the palace, not seeing its severe beauty, but judging the thickness of its stone walls. He shook his head. 'That flag will have to come down,' he gestured at the bullet-riddled tricolour that hung over the doorway, 'and they'll have to agree to close all the window shutters. They can keep observers at a single window on each side of the building, but nothing more.'

'Can you barricade the doors from the outside?' Sharpe asked.

'Why not?' Vivar looked at his watch. 'And why don't I tell them our terms? If I'm not back in fifteen minutes, attack!'

Sharpe wanted to be the one to greet Louisa and draw her safe from the French Headquarters. 'Shouldn't I go back?'

'I think I shall be safe,' Vivar said, 'and I want to search the palace for myself. It isn't that I don't trust you, Lieutenant, but that I think this responsibility is mine.'

Sharpe nodded his understanding. It was the French willingness to allow the palace to be searched that had convinced him of their good faith but, if he was Vivar, he would insist on conducting that search himself. His reunion with Louisa would have to wait, and it would be no less piquant because it was delayed.

Vivar did not set out at once; instead he clapped his

hands with delight and danced two steps of clumsy joy. 'We've done it, my friend! We have truly done it!'

They had gained victory.

Victory brought work. Captured muskets and carbines were piled in the plaza south of the cathedral, and the French prisoners were locked into the town jail where they were guarded by greenjackets. The Riflemen's packs and greatcoats were retrieved from the elm trees north of the city. Corpses were dragged to the city ditch, and defences properly set up. Sharpe went from guardpost to guardpost, ensuring that Vivar's volunteers were in place. A few French fugitives were still in sight to the south of the city, but a scatter of rifle shots drove them off. The road south, Sharpe saw, was heavily dunged and thickly patterned with hoofmarks; testimony to Colonel de l'Eclin's absence. Lookouts in the cathedral bell towers and Cazador picquets on the outlying roads would give warning of the Dragoons' return, against which eventuality he ordered his men to clean their rifles and sharpen their bayonets.

A victory had been won, and now the spoils could be taken. There were uniforms from the French billets, and horses from their stables. Every house that the French had commandeered for quarters yielded a small hoard of food. There were sacks of twice-baked bread, bags of flour, baked sausages, cured hams, salted pork, dried mackerel, skins of wine, and thick-rinded cheeses. Much of the food was snatched by the townspeople, but Vivar's Cazadores retrieved enough to fill a score of mule panniers.

Sharpe searched for the larger plunder; the forage that had been collected in the last weeks and stored against Soult's southward advance. In two of the city churches he found hay, flour and wine, but the amounts were scarcely sufficient to keep Soult's men and horses fed. In a third, which had been plundered of its treasures like every other church in Santiago de Compostela, Sharpe found the remnants of more supplies. The church's flagstone floor was thick with spilled oats and smeared with the traces left by sacks which had been dragged away. The parish priest, in halting English, explained that the French had emptied the church of its supplies on the previous afternoon and taken the sacks to the Raxoy Palace.

'Raxoy Palace? In the plaza?'

'*Si, señor.*'

Sharpe swore softly. The French had begun to collect the supplies into one central distribution point, and Vivar's capture of the city had interrupted that process too late. Most of the precious fodder was in the sacks Sharpe had seen inside the palace; sacks that now made breastworks for the Frenchmen trapped inside. The realization angered him. There had only ever been three justifications for taking this city. The first, to unfurl the gonfalon, was a piece of superstitious madness. The second, to rescue Louisa, was a personal whim of Sharpe's and irrelevant to the war. The third, to destroy Soult's supplies, was the only justification of true value, and it had largely failed.

Yet, if most of the supplies were safe inside the palace, Sharpe could still deny Marshal Soult what was left. The nets of hay were taken for Vivar's horses, while the flour was given away to the townspeople. He ordered the wine to be thrown away.

'Throw it away?' Harper sounded appalled.

'You want the men drunk if de l'Eclin counter-attacks?'

'It's a sinful waste, sir, so it is.'

'Throw it away!' Sharpe suited action to his words by

286

skewering a pile of wineskins with his sword. The red liquid gushed onto the church flagstones and trickled through the gaps into the crypt beneath. 'And if any man does get drunk,' he raised his voice, 'he'll answer to me, personally!'

'Very good, sir!' Harper waited till Sharpe was gone, then summoned Gataker. 'Find a tavern keeper, bring him here, and see what cash he offers. Quick now!'

Sharpe took a squad of Riflemen to search for any other French caches of grain or hay. They found none. They did discover a store of French infantry packs, made from oxhide and much better than the standard British ones. The packs were commandeered, as were three dozen pairs of riding boots though, to Sharpe's disgust, none of the boots was large enough for him. The Riflemen found French cartridges to refill their cartouches; the French musket-ball, fractionally smaller than its British equivalent, could be used in Baker rifles, though enemy ammunition was only used as a last resort because the coarse French powder fouled the rifle barrels. They found greatcoats and stockings, shirts and gloves, but no more grain or hay.

The townspeople were also seeking booty. The citizens of Santiago de Compostela did not care that the bulk of the French forage was safe inside the palace, they cared only that, at least for a day, they were free. They turned the winter's day into a carnival, costumed by plunder, so that it seemed as if the city was inhabited by a gleeful crowd of half-dressed enemy soldiers. Even the women were dressed in French coats and shakos.

At midday a convoy of mules carried much of the fodder, together with the Riflemen's packs, to a safe place in the eastern hills. Vivar did not want his men encumbered by personal belongings if the city had to be defended, and so the cache of packs and trophies would wait to be collected after the withdrawal. Once the mules had gone, Sharpe ordered most of his Riflemen to rest while he, fighting off a vast weariness, went in search of Blas Vivar. He walked first to the big plaza which he found almost deserted; all but for a picquet of Cazadores who warily watched the shuttered windows of the palace. There were also a few civilians making a crude barrier of furniture, empty wine vats, and carts which would eventually surround the whole building that was conveniently bounded on its other three sides by streets.

A single window was unshuttered in the palace façade, though no observer was visible there. The flag was gone from above the double door which had been barricaded by planks supported by timber buttresses. The French were thus penned inside their huge building.

They were also being taunted by crowds who, prevented by Cazadores from filling the big plaza, jeered from the smaller open spaces to north and south of the cathedral. They cheered when they saw Sharpe, then went back to insulting the hidden Frenchmen. Bagpipes added their squalling to the noise. Children danced derision of the enemy, while the city bells still rang their mad cacophony of victory. Sharpe, smiling his tired happiness at the citizens' celebrations, climbed the flight of steps which twisted towards the cathedral's ornate western entrance. He stopped halfway up, not from tiredness, but because he was suddenly overwhelmed by the beauty of the façade. Pillars and arches, statues and balustrades, escutcheons and scrolls: all were superbly carved to the glory of Santiago who was buried inside. After the weeks of hardship and cold, of battle and anger, the cathedral seemed to dwarf the ambitions of the men who fought across Spain. Then he thought that this cathedral was like Vivar's ambition. The Spaniard fought for something he believed in, while Sharpe only fought like a pirate; out of a stubborn and bloody pride.

'Do I perceive admiration in a soldier's eyes?' The question, asked in a voice of gentle teasing, came from a figure who moved forward on the stone platform at the top of the flight of steps.

Sharpe instantly forgot the cathedral's glories. 'Miss Parker?' He knew he was smiling like a fool, but he could not help it. It was not just a pirate's pride that had made him fight, but his memory of this girl who, in her blue skirt and rust-coloured cape, smiled back at him. He turned and gestured at the silent French-held palace. 'Isn't it dangerous to be here?'

'My dear Lieutenant, I was inside the ogre's den for a whole day! You think I am in more peril now that you have gained such a victory?'

Sharpe smiled at the compliment, then, as he climbed to the top of the steps, returned it. 'A victory, Miss Parker, to which you signally contributed.' He bowed to her. 'My humblest congratulations. I was wrong, and you were right.'

Louisa, delighted with the praise, laughed. 'Colonel de l'Eclin believes he will ambush you in the Ulla valley east of Padron. I watched him at three o'clock this morning.' She walked to the very centre of the cathedral's platform which made a kind of stage dominating the wide plaza. 'He stood in this very place, Lieutenant, and made a speech to his men. They filled the plaza! Rank after rank of helmets gleaming in the torchlight, and all of the men cheering their Colonel. I never thought to see such a thing! They cheered, then they rode off to their great victory.'

Sharpe thought how slender had been this day's

margin of victory. An extra thousand men, under de l'Eclin's ruthlessly efficient command, would have destroyed Vivar's attack. Yet the chasseur Colonel, utterly deceived by Louisa, had been lured southwards. 'How did you convince him?'

'With copious tears and an evident reluctance to tell him anything. Eventually, though, he wheedled the fatal truth from me.' Louisa seemed to mock her own cleverness. 'In the end he gave me a choice. I could stay in the city or rejoin my aunt in Corunna. I think he believed that if I chose to stay here then I must have hopes of rescue, and that to express such a hope would reveal that I lied to him. So I pleaded to rejoin my grieving family, and the Colonel rode away.' She did a pirouette of joy. 'I was supposed to leave for Corunna at midday today. Do you see what a fate you have spared me?'

'Weren't you frightened of staying?'

'Of course, weren't you frightened of coming?'

He smiled. 'I'm paid to be frightened.'

'And to be frightening. You look very grim, Lieutenant.' Louisa walked to some crates that lay open beside the cathedral door, sat on one of them, and pushed an errant curl from her eyes. 'These crates,' she said, 'were filled with plunder from the cathedral. The French took most of it away last week, but Don Blas has saved some.'

'That will please him.'

'Not very much,' Louisa said tartly. 'The French desecrated the cathedral. They plundered the treasury and tore down most of the screens. Don Blas is not happy. But the gonfalon arrived safely and is under guard, so the miracle can proceed.'

'Good.' Sharpe sat, drew sword and, with the blade across his knees, scrubbed at the blood which would pit the steel with rust if it were not removed.

'Don Blas is inside. He's preparing the high altar for his nonsense.' Louisa defused the word with a smile. 'Doubtless you wish he would get it over with swiftly, so you can withdraw?'

'Indeed, yes.'

'But he won't,' Louisa said firmly. 'The priests are insisting that the nonsense must be done properly and with due ceremony. This is a miracle, Lieutenant, that must be observed by witnesses who can carry news of it throughout Spain. We wait for the coming of some monks and friars.' She laughed delightedly. 'It's like something out of the Middle Ages, isn't it?'

'Indeed.'

'But Don Blas is serious, so we must both treat it with the utmost gravity. Shall we go inside to see him?' Louisa spoke with sudden enthusiasm. 'You should also see the Gate of Glory, Lieutenant, it really is a very remarkable piece of masonry. Much more impressive than the doors to a Methodist meeting house, though it's monstrously disloyal of me to say as much.'

Sharpe was silent for a few seconds. He did not want to see the Gate of Glory, whatever that might be, nor share this girl with the Spaniards who prepared the cathedral for the evening's rigmarole. He wanted to sit here with her, sharing the moment of victory.

'I do believe,' Louisa said, 'that these have been the happiest days of my life. I do envy you.'

'Envy me?'

'It's the lack of restraint, Lieutenant. Suddenly there are no rules any more, are there? You wish to tell a lie? You lie! You desire to tear a town into tatters? You do it! You wish to light a fire? Then strike the flint! Perhaps I should become one of your Riflemen?'

Sharpe laughed. 'I accept.'

'But instead,' Louisa folded her arms demurely, 'I

must travel south to Lisbon, and there take a ship to England.'

'Must you?' Sharpe blurted out.

Louisa was silent for a second. The smell of smoke from one of the burning houses drifted across the plaza, then was dispelled by a gust of wind. 'Isn't that what you're going to do?' she asked.

The hope soared in him. 'It depends on whether we keep a garrison is Lisbon. I'm sure we will,' he added lamely.

'It seems unlikely, after our defeats.' Louisa turned to watch a group of Spanish youths who had succeeded in slipping past the Cazadores who guarded the plaza. The boys held a captured tricolour which they first set alight, then brandished towards the trapped enemy. If they hoped to stir the Frenchmen in the palace by their defiance, they failed.

'So I am doomed to return home,' Louisa gazed at the capering boys as she spoke, 'and for what, Lieutenant? In England I shall resume my needlework and spend hours with my watercolours. Doubtless I shall be a curiosity for a while; the squire will want to hear of my quaint adventures. Mister Bufford will resume his courtship and reassure me that never again, so long as there is breath in his body, shall I be exposed to such foul danger! I shall play the pianoforte, and spend weeks deciding whether to buy pink ribbons or blue for next year's gowns. I shall take alms to the poor, and tea with the ladies of the town. It will all be so very unarduous, Lieutenant Sharpe.'

Sharpe felt adrift in an irony he was not clever enough to understand. 'So you have decided to marry Mr Bufford?' he asked in trepidation, fearing that the answer would dash all his fragile hopes.

'I'm not heiress enough to attract anyone more

exalted,' Louisa said with a feigned self-pity. She brushed a scrap of fallen ash from her skirts. 'But it's surely the sensible thing for me to do, is it not, Lieutenant? To marry Mr Bufford and live in his very pleasant house? I shall have roses planted against the south wall and once in a while, a very long while, I shall see a paragraph in the newspapers and it will tell of a battle faraway, and I'll remember how very horrid powder smoke smells and how sad a soldier can look when he's scraping blood off his sword.'

Her last words, which seemed so very intimate, restored Sharpe's optimism. He looked up at her.

'You see, Lieutenant,' Louisa forestalled anything he might say, 'there comes a moment in anyone's life when a choice presents itself. Isn't that true?'

The hope, so ill-based, so impractical, so irresistible, soared inside Sharpe. 'Yes,' he said. He did not know exactly how she could stay with the army, or how the finances, which were the bane of most impractical romances, would be worked through, but other officers' wives had houses in Lisbon, so why not Louisa?

'I'm not convinced I want the roses and the embroidery.' Louisa seemed nervous and febrile suddenly, like an untrained horse edging skittishly towards the skirmish line. 'I know that I should want those things, and I know I am most foolish in despising them, but I like Spain! I like the excitement here. There isn't much excitement in England.'

'No.' Sharpe hardly dared move for fear he would scare away her acceptance.

'You think I am wrong to crave excitement?' Louisa did not wait for an answer, but instead asked another question. 'Do you really think a British army will stay to fight in Portugal?'

'Of course!'

'I don't think it will.' Louisa turned to stare at the youths who were stamping on the ashes of the burnt French flag. 'Sir John Moore is dead,' she continued, 'his army is gone, and we don't even know if the Lisbon garrison still remains. And if it does, Lieutenant, how can such a small garrison hope to resist the armies of France?'

Sharpe stubbornly clung to his belief that the British army had not surrendered its hopes. 'The last news we heard from Lisbon was that the garrison was in place. It can be reinforced! We won two battles in Portugal last year, why not more this year?'

Louisa shook her head. 'I think we British have been trounced, Lieutenant, and I suspect we shall abandon Spain to its fate. It's been a hundred years since a British army was successful in Europe, what makes us think we can be successful now?'

Sharpe at last sensed that Louisa's ambitions and his own hopes were not, after all, in step. Her nervousness was not that of a girl shyly accepting a proposal, but of a girl anxious not to cause hurt by her rejection. He looked up at her. 'Do you believe that, Miss Parker? Or is that Major Vivar's opinion?'

Louisa paused, then spoke so softly that her voice scarcely carried to Sharpe over the din of the church bells. 'Don Blas has asked me to stay in Spain, Lieutenant.'

'Oh.' Sharpe closed his eyes as though the sunlight in the plaza was hurting him. He did not know what to say. There was nothing so foolish, he thought, as a man rejected.

'I can take instruction in the faith,' Louisa said, 'and I can become a part of this country. I don't want to run away from Spain. I don't want to go back to England and think of all the excitement that beckons here. And I cannot . . .' She stopped in embarrassment.

She did not need to finish. She could not throw herself away on a common soldier, an ageing Lieutenant, a pauper in a tattered uniform whose only prospect was to decay in some country barracks. 'Yes,' Sharpe said helplessly.

'I cannot ignore the moment,' she said dramatically.

'Your family . . .' Sharpe began.

'Will hate it!' Louisa forced a laugh. 'I am trying to persuade myself that is not the sole reason why I intend to accept Don Blas's offer.'

Sharpe made himself look up at her. 'You will marry?'

She looked very gravely at him. 'Yes, Mr Sharpe, I shall marry Don Blas.' There was relief in her voice now that the truth was out. 'It is a sudden decision, I know, but I must have the bravery to seize the moment.'

'Yes.' He could think of nothing else to say.

Louisa watched him in silence. There were tears in her eyes, but Sharpe did not see them. 'I'm sorry,' she began.

'No.' Sharpe stood. 'I had no expectations, none.'

'I am pleased to hear that,' Louisa said very formally. She stepped back as Sharpe walked to the platform's edge, then frowned as he went down the cathedral steps. 'Didn't you have to see Don Blas?'

'No.' Sharpe did not care any longer. He sheathed his sword and walked away. He felt he had fought for nothing, there was nothing left worth fighting for, and his hopes were like the ashes of the burnt flag in the empty plaza. It was all for nothing.

CHAPTER 16

For Lieutenant Richard Sharpe to aspire to Miss Louisa Parker was, in its way, as daring as Vivar's plan to capture an enemy-held city. She came from a respectable family which, though it sometimes trembled on the edges of genteel poverty, was far above Sharpe's ignoble station. He was a peasant by birth, an officer by accident, and a pauper by profession.

And what, Sharpe asked himself, had he expected of the girl? Did he imagine that Louisa would willingly tramp behind the campaigning army, or find some squalid home near the barracks and eke out his inadequate pay on scraps of meat and day-old bread? Was she to have abandoned silk dresses for woollen shifts? Or would he have expected her to follow him to the West Indian garrison where the yellow fever wiped out whole Regiments? He told himself that his hopes of the girl had ever been as stupid as they were unrealistic, yet that did not heal the sudden hurt. He told himself that he acted childishly for even feeling the hurt, but that did not make it any easier to bear.

He plunged from the plaza's wintry sunshine into the foetid reek of an alley where, beneath an arcade, he found a wineshop. Sharpe had no money to pay for the wine, but his demeanour and the hammer of his hand on the counter persuaded the tavern keeper to fill a big flask from the barrel. Sharpe took the flask and a tin cup to an alcove at the back of the room. The few customers, huddled round the fire and seeing his bitter face, ignored him; all but for a whore who, at the tavern keeper's bidding, edged onto the bench beside the foreign soldier. For a second Sharpe was tempted to push her away, but instead he beckoned for a second mug.

The tavern keeper wiped the mug on his apron and set it on the table. A sacking curtain was looped back over the alcove's arch and he took hold of it and raised an interrogatory eyebrow.

'Yes,' Sharpe said harshly. '*Sí.*'

The curtain dropped, plunging Sharpe and the girl into dark shadow. She giggled, put her arms about his neck, and whispered some Spanish endearment until he silenced her with a kiss.

The curtain was snatched back, making the girl squeal in alarm.

Blas Vivar stood in the archway. 'It's very simple to follow a foreigner through Spanish streets. Did you hope to hide from me, Lieutenant?'

Sharpe put his left arm around the whore and pulled her towards him so that her head leaned on his shoulder. He moved his hand to cup her breast. 'I'm busy, sir.'

Vivar ignored the provocation, sitting instead on the bench opposite Sharpe. He rolled a cigar across the table. 'By now,' he said, 'Colonel de l'Eclin must have realized that Miss Parker lied to him?'

'I'm sure,' Sharpe said carelessly.

'He will be returning. Soon he will meet a fugitive from the city and he will learn the extent of his mistake.'

'Yes.' Sharpe tugged at the laces of the whore's bodice. The girl made a desultory effort to stop him, but he insisted, and succeeded in pulling her dress apart.

Vivar's voice was very patient. 'So I would expect de l'Eclin to attack us, wouldn't you?'

'I suppose he will.' Sharpe put his hand beneath the girl's unlaced dress and dared Blas Vivar to make a protest.

'The defence is ready?' Vivar asked in a tone of gentle reasonableness. The tavern whore might not have existed for all the notice he took of her.

Sharpe did not answer at once. He poured himself wine with his free hand, drank the cupful, and poured more. 'Why in Christ's name don't you just get your damned nonsense over with, Vivar? We're lingering in this bloody deathtrap of a city just so you can work a conjuring trick in the cathedral. So do what you have to do quickly, then get the hell out!'

Vivar nodded as though Sharpe's words made sense. 'Let me see now. I've sent Cazadores on patrol north and south. It will take me two hours to recall them, maybe longer. We have yet to find every man in the city who has cooperated with the French, but the searches go on and may take another hour. Are all the supplies destroyed?'

'There are no bloody supplies. The bloody crapauds took them all into the palace yesterday.'

Vivar flinched at the news. 'I feared as much. I saw great piles of grain and hay when I looked into the cellars of the palace. That is a pity.'

'So do your miracle, and run.'

Vivar shrugged. 'I'm waiting for some churchmen to arrive, and I've sent men to destroy the nearest bridges over the Ulla, which cannot be completed till late this afternoon. I don't really see that haste is so very feasible. We should be ready in the cathedral by sundown, and we can certainly leave tonight rather than tomorrow, but I do think we must be ready to defend the city against de l'Eclin, don't you?'

Sharpe tipped the whore's face to his own and kissed her. He knew he was behaving boorishly, yet the hurt was strong and the jealousy like a fever.

Vivar sighed. 'If Colonel de l'Eclin has failed to take the city back by nightfall, then he will be blinded by the darkness and we shall simply walk away. That's why I think it best to wait till nightfall before we leave, don't you?'

'Or is it so you can unfurl your magic banner in the dark? Miracles are best done in darkness, aren't they? So that no one can see the bloody trickery.'

Vivar smiled. 'I know my magic banner is not as important to you, Lieutenant, as it is to me, but that is why I am here. And when it is unfurled I want as many witnesses as can be assembled. The news must travel out from this city; it must go to every town and village in all of Spain. Even in the far south they must know that Santiago has stirred in his tomb and that the sword is drawn again.'

Sharpe, despite all his scepticism, shuddered.

Vivar, if he saw Sharpe's betrayal of emotion, pretended not to notice. 'I estimate that Colonel de l'Eclin will be here within the next two hours. He will approach from the south of the city, but I suspect he will attack from the west in hope that the setting sun dazzles us. Will you undertake to conduct the defence?'

'Suddenly you need the bloody English, do you?' Sharpe's jealousy flared vivid. 'You think the British are running away, don't you? That we'll abandon Lisbon. That your precious Spain will have to beat the French without us. Then bloody well do it without me!'

For a second Vivar's immobility suggested a proud fury that might snap like Sharpe's temper. The whore shrank back, expecting violence, but when Vivar did move it was only to reach across the table to pick up

Sharpe's flask of wine. His voice was very controlled and very placid. 'You once told me, Lieutenant, that no one expected officers who had risen from the ranks of Britain's army to be successful. What was it you said? That the drink destroyed them?' He paused, but Sharpe made no answer. 'I think you could become a soldier of great repute, Lieutenant. You understand battle. You become calm when other men become frightened. Your men, even when they disliked you, followed you because they understood you would give them victory. You're good. But perhaps you're not good enough. Perhaps you're so full of self-pity that you'll destroy yourself with drink or,' Vivar at last designed to notice the straggly-haired girl who leaned against the Rifleman, 'with the pox.'

Throughout this lecture, Sharpe had stared at the Spaniard as if wishing to draw the big sword and slash across the table.

Vivar stood and tipped the wine flask to pour what was left of its contents onto the floor rushes. Then he dropped it contemptuously.

'Bastard,' Sharpe said.

'Does that make me as good as you?' Vivar again paused to let Sharpe reply, and again Sharpe kept silent. The Spaniard shrugged. 'You feel sorry for yourself, Lieutenant, because you were not born to the officer class. But have you ever thought that those of us who were so fortunate sometimes regret it? Do you think we're not frightened by the tough, bitter men from the rookeries and hovels? Do you think we don't look at men like you and feel envy?'

'You patronizing bastard.'

Vivar ignored the insult. 'When my wife and children died, Lieutenant, I decided there was nothing to live for. I took to drink. I now thank God that a man cared enough for me to give me patronizing advice.' He picked up his tasselled hat. 'If I have given you cause to hate me, Lieutenant, I regret it. It was not done purposefully; indeed you gave me to believe that I would not cause any bitterness between us.' It was as near as Vivar had come to a reference to Louisa. 'Now all I ask is that you help me finish this job. There's a hill to the west of the city which should be occupied. I shall put Davila under your command with a hundred Cazadores. I've reinforced the picquets to the south and west. And thank you for everything you have done so far. If you had not taken that first barricade, we would now be fleeing in the hills with lancers stabbing at our backsides.' Vivar stepped free of the bench. 'Let me know when your defences are in place and I shall make an inspection.' He disdained any acknowledgement, but merely strode from the wineshop.

Sharpe picked up his winecup which was still full. He stared at it. He had threatened his own men with punishment if any became worse for drink, yet now he wished to God that he could drown his disappointment in an alcoholic haze. Instead he threw the cup away and stood. The girl, seeing her earnings lost, whimpered.

'Damn them all,' Sharpe said. He tore at two of the remaining silver buttons on his breeches, ripping a great swatch of the cloth away with the buttons which he dropped into the girl's lap. 'Damn them all.' He snatched up his weapons and left.

The tavern keeper looked at the girl who was relacing her bodice. He shrugged sympathetically. 'The English, yes? Mad. All mad. Heretics. Mad.' He made the sign of the cross to defend himself from the heathen evil. 'Like all soldiers,' the tavern keeper said. 'Just mad.'

*   *   *

Sharpe walked with Sergeant Harper to the west of the city and forced himself to forget both Louisa and the shame of his behaviour in the tavern. Instead he tried to judge what approach the French might choose if they attacked Santiago de Compostela.

The Dragoons had gone to Padron, and the road from that small town approached Santiago from the south-west. That made an attack from the south or west the likeliest possibility. De l'Eclin could emulate Vivar and make an assault from the north, but Sharpe doubted if the chasseur would choose that approach because it needed surprise. The ground to the city's east was broken, and the most easily defended. The land to the south was hedged and ditched, while the ground to the west, from where Vivar believed the attack would come, was open and inviting like an English common field.

The western open ground was flanked to the south by the low hill which Vivar wanted garrisoned and on which Sharpe's Riflemen now waited for orders. The French, knowing the value of the hill, had chopped down most of the trees which had covered the high ground and made a crude fortification of brushwood jammed between the fallen trunks. Further west was dead ground where de l'Eclin's Dragoons could assemble unseen. Sharpe stopped at the edge of that lower ground and stared back at the city. 'We might have to hold the bloody place till after nightfall.'

Harper instinctively glanced to find the sun's position. 'It won't be full dark for six hours,' he said pessimistically, 'and it'll be a slow dusk, sir. No damned clouds to hide us.'

'If God was on our side,' Sharpe essayed one of the stock jokes of the Regiment, 'he'd have given the Baker rifle tits.'

Harper, recognizing from the feeble jest that Sharpe's grim mood was passing, grinned dutifully. 'Is it true about Miss Louisa, sir?' The question was asked very carelessly and without evident embarrassment, making Sharpe think that none of his men had suspected his attachment to the girl.

'It's true.' Sharpe tried to sound as though he took little interest in the matter. 'She'll have to become a Catholic, of course.'

'There's always room for another. Mind you,' Harper stared down into the dead ground as he spoke, 'I never thought it was a good thing for a soldier to be married.'

'Why ever not?'

'You can't dance if you've got one foot nailed to the bloody floor, can you now? But the Major isn't a soldier like us, sir. Coming from that big castle!' Harper had clearly been mightily impressed by the wealth of Vivar's family. 'The Major's a grand big fellow, so he is.'

'So what are we? The damned?'

'We're that, sure enough, but we're also Riflemen, sir. You and me, sir, we're the best God-damned soldiers in the world.'

Sharpe laughed. Just weeks ago he had been bitterly at odds with his Riflemen, now they were on his side. He did not know how to acknowledge Harper's compliment, so he resorted to a vague and meaningless cliché. 'It's a bloody odd world.'

'Difficult to do a good job in six days, sir,' Harper said wryly. 'I'm sure God did his best, but where was the sense in putting Ireland plum next to England?'

'He probably knew you bastards needed smacking around.' Sharpe turned to look south. 'But how the hell do we smack this French bastard back into his tracks?'

'If he attacks.'

'He'll attack. He thinks he's better than us, and he's damned annoyed at being tricked again. He'll attack.' Sharpe walked to the southern edge of the common ground, then swivelled back to stare at the city. He was putting himself in de l'Eclin's glossy boots, seeing what the Frenchman would see, trying to anticipate his plans.

Vivar was certain that de l'Eclin would come from the west, that the chasseur would wait till the setting sun was a blinding dazzle behind his charge, then launch his Dragoons across the open ground.

Yet, Sharpe reasoned, a cavalry charge was of dubious value to the French. It might sweep the Dragoons in glorious style to the city's margin, but there the horses would baulk at walls and barricades, and the glory would be riven into blood and horror by the waiting muskets and rifles. De l'Eclin's attack, just like Vivar's, would best be done by infantry that could open the city to the cavalry's fierce charge; and the best infantry approach was from the south.

Sharpe pointed to the south-western corner of the city. 'That's where he'll make his attack.'

'After dark?'

'At dusk.' Sharpe frowned. 'Maybe earlier.'

Harper followed him over a ditch and an embankment. The two Riflemen were walking towards a slew of buildings that straggled like a limb from the city's south-western corner and which could shelter de l'Eclin's men as they approached. 'We'll have to put men in the houses,' Harper said.

Sharpe seemed not to hear. 'I don't like it.'

'A thousand Dragoons? Who would?'

'De l'Eclin's a clever bastard.' Sharpe was half-talking to himself. 'A clever, clever bloody bastard. And he's especially clever when he's attacking.' He turned and stared at the city's barricaded streets. The obstacles were manned by Cazadores and by the brown-coated volunteers who were piling brushwood into fires that could illuminate a night attack. They were doing, in fact, exactly what the French had done the night before, yet surely Colonel de l'Eclin would foresee all these preparations? So what would the Frenchman do? 'He's going to be bloody clever, Sergeant, and I don't know how clever.'

'He can't fly,' Harper said stoically, 'and he doesn't have time to dig a bloody tunnel, so he has to come in through one of the streets, doesn't he?'

The stolid good sense made Sharpe suppose he was seeing danger where there was none. Better, he thought, to rely on his first instincts. 'He'll send his cavalry on a feint there,' he pointed to the smooth western ground, 'and when he thinks we're all staring that way, he'll send dismounted men in from the south. They'll be ordered to break that barricade,' he pointed to the street which led from the city to the church, 'and his cavalry will swerve in behind them.'

Harper turned to judge for himself, and seemed to find Sharpe's words convincing. 'And so long as we're on the hill or in those houses,' he nodded towards the straggling buildings that lay outside the defences, 'we'll murder the bastard.' The big Irishman picked up a sprig of laurel and twisted the pliant wood in his fingers. 'But what really worries me, sir, is not holding the bastard off, but what happens when we withdraw? They'll be flooding into those streets like devils on a spree, so they will.'

Sharpe was also worried about that moment of retreat. Once Vivar's business in the cathedral was done, the signal would be given and a great mass of people would flee eastwards. There would be volunteers, Riflemen, Cazadores, priests, and whatever townspeople no longer cared to stay under French occupation; all jostling and running into the darkness. Vivar had planned to have his cavalry protect the retreat, but Sharpe knew what savage chaos could overtake his men in the streets when the French Dragoons realized that barricades had been abandoned. He shrugged. 'We'll just have to run like hell.'

'And that's the truth,' Harper said gloomily. He tossed away the crumpled twig.

Sharpe stared at the twisted scrap of laurel. 'Good God!'

'What have I done now?'

'Jesus wept!' Sharpe clicked his fingers. 'I want half the men in those houses,' he pointed at the line of buildings which led from the south-western barricade, and enfiladed the southern approach to the city, 'and the rest on the hill.' He began running towards the city. 'I'll be back, Sergeant!'

'What's up with him?' Hagman asked when the Sergeant returned to the hilltop.

'The doxie turned him down,' Harper said with evident satisfaction, 'so you owes me a shilling, Dan. She's marrying the Major, so she is.'

'I thought she was soft as lights on Mr Sharpe!' Hagman said ruefully.

'She's got more sense than to marry him. He ain't ready for a chain and shackle, is he? She needs someone a bit steady, she does.'

'But he was sotted on her.'

'He would be, wouldn't he? He'll fall in love with anything in a petticoat. I've seen his type before. Got the sense of a half-witted sheep when it comes to women.' Harper spat. 'It's a good job he's got me to look after him now.'

'You!'

'I can handle him, Dan. Just as I can handle you lot.

Right, you Protestant scum! The French are coming for supper, so let's be getting ready for the bastards!'

Newly cleaned rifles pointed south and west. The greenjackets were waiting for the dusk and for the coming of a chasseur.

The idea buzzed in Sharpe's head as he ran uphill towards the city centre. Colonel de l'Eclin could be clever, but so could the defenders. He stopped in the main plaza and asked a Cazador where Major Vivar might be. The cavalryman pointed to the smaller northern plaza beyond the bridge which joined the bishop's palace to the cathedral. That plaza was still crammed with people, though instead of yelling defiance at the trapped Frenchmen, the crowd was now eerily quiet. Even the bells had fallen silent.

Sharpe elbowed his way through the crush and saw Vivar standing on a flight of steps which led to the cathedral's northern transept. Louisa was with him. Sharpe wished she was not there. The memory of his boorish behaviour with the Spaniard embarrassed him, and he knew he should apologize, but the girl's presence inhibited any such public repentance. Instead he shouted his idea as he forced his way up the crowded steps. 'Caltrops!'

'Caltrops?' Vivar asked. Louisa, unable to translate the unfamiliar word, shrugged.

Sharpe had picked up two wisps of straw as he ran through the city and now, just as Harper had unwittingly twisted the laurel twig, Sharpe twisted the straw. 'Caltrops! But we haven't got much time! Can we get the blacksmiths working?'

Vivar stared at the straw, then swore for not thinking of the idea himself. 'They'll work!' He ran down the steps.

307

Louisa, left with Sharpe, looked at the twisted straw which still meant nothing to her. 'Caltrops?'

Sharpe scooped some damp mud from the instep of his left boot and rolled it into a ball. He snapped the straw into four lengths, each about three inches long, and he stuck three of them into the mud ball to form a three-pointed star. He laid the star on the flat of his hand and pushed the fourth spike into the mud ball so that it stood vertically. 'A caltrop,' he said.

Louisa shook her head. 'I still don't understand.'

'A medieval weapon made of iron. The cleverness of it is that, whatever way it falls, there's always a spike sticking upwards.' He demonstrated by turning the caltrop, and Louisa saw how one of the spikes, which had first formed part of the three-pointed star, now jutted upwards.

She understood then. 'Oh, no!'

'Oh, yes!'

'Poor horses!'

'Poor us, if the horses catch us.' Sharpe crumpled the straw and mud into a ball that he tossed away. Proper caltrops, made from iron nails which would be fused and hammered in the fire, should be scattered thick on the roadways behind the retreating Riflemen. The spikes would easily pierce the soft frog tissue inside a horse's hoof walls, and the beasts would rear, twist, plunge, and panic. 'But the horses recover,' he assured Louisa, who seemed upset by the simple nastiness of the weapon.

'How did you know about them?' she asked.

'They were used against us in India . . .' Sharpe's voice faded away because, for the first time since he had climbed the cathedral steps, he saw why the crowd was packed so silently in the plaza.

A rough platform had been constructed at its centre;

a platform of wooden planks laid across wine vats. On it was a high-backed chair which Sharpe at first took to be a throne.

The impression of royal ceremony was heightened by the strange procession which, flanked by red-uniformed Cazadores, approached the platform. The men in the procession were robed in sulphurous yellow and capped with red conical hats. Each carried a scrap of paper in his clasped hands. 'The paper,' Louisa said quietly, 'is a confession of faith. They've been forgiven, you see, but they must still die.'

Sharpe understood then. The tall chair, far from being a throne, was a garotte. On its high back was a metal implement, a collar and screw, that was Spain's preferred method of execution. It was the first such machine he had seen in Spain.

Priests accompanied the doomed men. 'They're all *anfrancesados*,' Louisa said. 'Some served as guides to French cavalry, others betrayed partisans.'

'You intend to watch?' Sharpe sounded shocked. If Louisa blanched at the thought of pricking a horse's hoof, how was she to bear watching a man's neck being broken?

'I've never seen an execution.'

Sharpe glanced down at her. 'And you want to?'

'I suspect I shall be forced to see many unfamiliar things in the next years, don't you?'

The first man was pushed up to the platform where he was forced into the chair. The iron collar was prised around his neck. The sacrist, Father Alzaga, stood beside the executioner. '*Pax et misericordia et tranquillitas!*' He shouted the words into the victim's ear as the executioner went behind the chair, and shouted them again as the lever which turned the screw was snatched tight. The screw constricted the collar with impressive speed so that, almost before the second Latin injunction was over, the body in the chair jerked up and slumped back. The crowd seemed to sigh.

Louisa turned away. 'I wish . . .' she began, but could not finish.

'It was very quick,' Sharpe said in wonderment.

There was a thump as the dead body was pushed off the chair, then a scraping sound as it was dragged off the platform. Louisa, no longer watching, did not speak till after the next shout from Father Alzaga signified that another traitor had met his end. 'Do you think badly of me, Lieutenant?'

'For watching an execution?' Sharpe waited till the second body was released from the collar. 'Why on earth should I? There are usually more women at a public hanging than men.'

'I don't mean that.'

He looked down at her and was instantly embarrassed. 'I would not think badly of you.'

'It was that night in the fortress.' There was a plea in Louisa's voice, as if she desperately needed Sharpe to understand what had happened. 'You remember? When Don Blas showed us the gonfalon and told us the tale of the last battle? I think I was trapped then.'

'Trapped?'

'I like his nonsense. I was brought up to hate Catholics; to despise them for their ignorance and fear them for their malevolence, but no one ever told me of their glory!'

'Glory?'

'I'm bored with plain chapels.' Louisa watched the executions as she spoke, though Sharpe doubted whether she was even aware that men died on the crude scaffold. 'I'm bored with being told I'm a sinner and that my salvation depends only on my own dogged repentance. I want, just once, to see the hand of God come in all its glory to touch us. I want a miracle, Lieutenant. I want to feel so very small in front of that miracle, and that doesn't make any sense to you at all, does it?'

Sharpe watched a man die. 'You want the gonfalon.'

'No!' Louisa was almost scornful. 'I do not believe for one small second, Lieutenant, that Santiago fetched that flag from heaven. I believe the gonfalon is merely an old banner that one of Don Blas's ancestors carried into battle. The miracle lies in what the gonfalon does, not in what it is! If we survive today, Lieutenant, then we will have achieved a miracle. But we would not have done it, nor even tried to do it, without the gonfalon!' She paused, wanting some confirmation from Sharpe, but he said nothing. She shrugged ruefully. 'You still think it's all a nonsense, don't you?'

Still Sharpe said nothing. For him the gonfalon, whether nonsensical or not, was an irrelevance. He had not come to Santiago de Compostela for the gonfalon. He had thought it was for this girl, but that dream was dead. Yet there was something else that had fetched him to this city. He had come to prove that a whoreson Sergeant, patted on the head by a patronizing army and made into a Quartermaster, could be as good, as God-damned bloody good, as any born officer. And that could not be proved without the help of the men in green jackets who waited for the enemy, and Sharpe was suddenly swept with an affection for those Riflemen. It was an affection he had not felt since he had been a Sergeant and had held the power of life and death over a company of redcoats.

A scream jerked his attention back to the plaza where a recalcitrant prisoner fought against the hands which pushed him up to the platform. The man's fight was useless. He was forced to the garotte and strapped into the chair. The iron was bent around his neck and the collar's tongue inserted into the slot where the screw would draw it tight. Alzaga made the sign of the cross. '*Pax et misericordia et tranquillitas!*'

The prisoner's yellow-frocked body jerked in a spasm as the collar gripped his neck to break his spine and choke the breath from him. His thin hands scrabbled at the arms of the chair, then the body slumped down. Sharpe supposed that swift death would have been the Count of Mouromorto's fate if he had not stayed safe inside the French-held palace. 'Why,' he asked Louisa suddenly, 'did the Count stay in the city?'

'I don't know. Does it matter?'

Sharpe shrugged. 'I've never seen him apart from de l'Eclin before. And that Colonel is a very clever man.'

'You're clever, too,' Louisa said warmly. 'How many soldiers know about caltrops?'

Vivar pushed through the crowd and climbed the steps. 'The forges are being heated. By six o'clock you'll have a few hundred of the things. Where do you want them?'

'Just send them to me,' Sharpe said.

'When you hear the bells next ring, you'll know the gonfalon is unfurled. That's when you can withdraw.'

'Make it soon!'

'Shortly after six,' Vivar said. 'It can't be sooner. Have you seen what the French did to the cathedral?'

'No.' But nor did Sharpe care. He only cared about a clever French Colonel, a chasseur of the Imperial Guard, then a single rifle shot sounded from the south-west, and he ran.

CHAPTER 17

The shot warned, not of de l'Eclin's arrival, but of the approach of a Cazador patrol. Their horses were whipped to blood and lather. Vivar, who had returned with Sharpe to discover what had prompted the shot, translated the picquet's message. 'They saw French Dragoons.'

'Where?'

'About two leagues to the south-west.'

'How many?'

'Hundreds.' Vivar interpreted his patrol's anxious report. 'The Frenchmen chased them and they were lucky to escape.' He listened to more excited words. 'And they saw the chasseur.' Vivar smiled. 'So! We know where they are now. All we must do is hold them out of the city.'

'Yes.' Somehow the news that the enemy was at last approaching served to calm Sharpe's apprehension. Most of that nervousness had been concentrated on Colonel de l'Eclin's cleverness, but the prosaic knowledge of which road the enemy was on, and how far away his forces were, made him seem a less fearsome opponent.

Vivar followed the tired horsemen through the gap in the barricade. 'You hear the hammers?' he called back.

'Hammers?' Sharpe frowned, then did indeed hear

the echoing ring of hammers on anvils. 'Caltrops?'

'I'll send them to you, Lieutenant.' Vivar started up the hill. 'Enjoy yourselves!'

Sharpe watched the Major walk away, then, on an impulse, he threaded the barricade and followed him up the cobbled street. 'Sir?'

'Lieutenant.'

Sharpe made certain he was out of his men's earshot. 'I want to apologize for what happened in the tavern, sir, I . . .'

'What tavern? I haven't been in a tavern all day. Tomorrow, maybe, when we're safely away from these bastards, we'll find a tavern. But today?' Vivar's face was entirely serious. 'I don't know what you're talking about, Lieutenant.'

'Yes, sir. Thank you, sir.'

'I don't like it when you call me "sir",' Vivar smiled. 'It means you're not being belligerent. I need you belligerent, Lieutenant. I need to know Frenchmen are going to die.'

'They'll die, sir.'

'You've put men in the houses?' Vivar meant the houses which lay along the road outside the city's perimeter.

'Yes, sir.'

'They can't defend against an attack from the west there, can they?'

'It won't be from the west, sir. We'll see them to the west first, but they'll attack from the south.'

It was plain as a pikestaff that Vivar was unhappy with Sharpe's deployment, but he also had faith in the Rifleman's skills and that faith made him swallow his protest. 'You're a typical British soldier,' he said instead, 'talking of taverns when there's work to do.' He laughed and turned away.

Feeling shriven, Sharpe went back to the fortified hilltop where, behind a brushwood breastwork strung between tree stumps, two dozen Riflemen waited. They had a fine view from the hill-crest, but Sharpe had no doubt that, once the enemy committed himself to the attack, this strong picquet would go down to the houses where the rest of his men waited. The attack would be from the south, not the west. 'You heard the Major!' he warned his Riflemen. 'The bastards are coming! They'll be here in another hour.'

In fact it took nearer three hours. Three hours of increasing worry that the Dragoons were hatching wickedness, and three hours during which the first clinking sacks of caltrops were delivered to the hilltop. Only then did the two-man picquet of Cazadores which had been posted at the brink of the dead ground rowel their horses back to the city. '*Dragons! Dragons!*' They made gestures over their heads to imitate the shape of the French helmets, and pointed west to the dead ground.

'*Si!*' Sharpe shouted, '*Gracias!*'

The Riflemen, some of whom had been laughing over the wicked small spikes of the caltrops, went back to their barricades. The landscape stayed empty. Sharpe looked south, expecting to see the other close picquet withdrawing, but there was no sign of the Cazadores who had been posted to guard the southern approach to the city.

'Bloody hell!' Hagman spat in horror at the sudden smell which came across the grassland. It was the rancid stench of saddle and crupper sores that came on the chill west wind from the dead ground. The Riflemen wrinkled their noses against the foul odour.

Sharpe watched the innocent and empty scene which hid the attackers. Doubtless the French officers, concealed by the ragged bushes at the valley's edge, were watching the city. Behind those officers the Dragoons would be preparing for battle. He imagined helmets being crammed onto pig-tailed heads, and long swords scraping out of metal scabbards. The horses, knowing what was to come, would be pawing the ground. Men would be nervously shortening stirrup leathers or wiping sweat from their reins. Sharpe wondered if he had been wrong; if, instead of feinting from the west and attacking from the south, the French would simply charge to the barricades and then just claw at the defences.

'Jesus Christ!' The blasphemy was torn from Hagman as the hidden valley suddenly sprouted a line of cavalry; a great line of Dragoons who trotted forward with billowing cloaks and drawn swords. They had taken the cloth covers from their helmets so that the gold-coloured metal shone in the afternoon light. 'There's thousands of the buggers!' Hagman pushed his rifle forward.

'Don't fire!' Sharpe called. He did not want the Riflemen to fire for fear that they would trigger the fingers of the Cazadores behind the barricades. The Spanish muskets and carbines, being smooth-bored, were far less accurate than the rifles, and a volley fired at this distance was a volley wasted.

Sharpe could have saved his breath for, within seconds of the cavalry's appearance, the first muskets fired. He swore, turned, and saw that the city's roofs were crammed with civilians who wanted to kill the French. Immediately the first shots sounded, so all the men behind the barricades began to fire. A huge volley crackled and spat flames, smoke belched to hide the city's flank, and scarce a single Frenchman fell. The range, over three hundred yards, was hopelessly long.

Even if a bullet struck it was likely to be spent, and would bounce harmlessly off a thick uniform coat or a horse's winter pelt.

The horsemen checked their slow advance. Sharpe looked for de l'Eclin's red pelisse and could not see it. He mentally divided the line into quarters and made a swift count of one quarter, then multiplied the result by four to reach a total of three hundred. This was not the attack. This was a display of strength, spread into an impressive line, but only meant to draw eyes westward. 'Watch the south!' Sharpe called to his men. 'Watch the south!'

The firing from the city had drawn Sergeant Harper up from the buildings that guarded the southern approach. He stared at the line of Dragoons and whistled. 'That's a rare lot of mischief, sir.'

'Only three hundred men,' Sharpe said calmly.

'Is that all, now?'

A French officer drew his sword and cantered forward. After a few strides he spurred his horse into a gallop and curved its path so that he would swoop within a hundred yards of the city's defence. Muskets crackled from the barricades, but he galloped safe through the wild shots. Another officer started forward, and Sharpe guessed the Frenchmen would keep tantalizing the defenders until the real attack erupted.

Hagman pulled back his rifle cock as the second French officer spurred to full speed. 'Can I teach the bugger a lesson, sir?'

'No. Let them be. This is just a fake. They think it's working, so let them play.'

Minutes passed. A whole squadron of Dragoons trotted down the front of the line, then reversed their path to gallop derisively back. Their defiance prompted another huge volley to ripple down the city's western

317

buildings, and Sharpe saw the ground flecked by the strike of the balls and knew that the Spaniards' shots were falling short. A second squadron, holding a guidon high, trotted northwards. Some of the stationary Frenchmen sheathed their swords and fired carbines from the saddle, and every French shot provoked an answering and wasteful volley from the city.

Another officer displayed his bravery by galloping as close as he dared to the city's defences. This one had less luck. His horse went down in a flurry of blood and mud. A great cheer went up from the barricades, but the Frenchman slashed his saddle free and ran safely back towards his comrades. Sharpe admired the man, but schooled himself to keep watching the south.

South! That was where the attack would come, not here! De l'Eclin's absence from the west meant that the chasseur must be with the men who crept about the city's southern flank. Sharpe was sure of it now. The French were waiting for the sun to sink even lower so that the shadows would be long in the broken southern ground. In the meantime this western diversion was calculated to stretch the defenders' nerves and waste the city's powder, but the attack would come from the south; Sharpe knew it, and he stared obsessively south where nothing moved among the falling ground. Somewhere beyond that ground was the southern picquet of mounted Cazadores, and he became obsessed that the Spaniards had been overwhelmed by a French attack. There could be seven hundred Dragoons hidden to the south. He wondered whether to send a patrol of Riflemen to explore the shadows.

'Sir?' Harper had stayed on the hilltop and now called urgently. 'Sir?'

Sharpe turned back to the west, and swore.

Another squadron of Dragoons had come from the

dead ground, and this one was led by a horseman wearing a red pelisse and a black fur colback. A horseman on a big black horse. De l'Eclin. Not to the south, where the bulk of Sharpe's Riflemen were deployed, but to the west where the Frenchman could wait until the sinking sun was a dazzling and blinding ball of fire in the defenders' eyes.

'Do I pull the lads out of the buildings?' Harper asked nervously.

'Wait.' Sharpe was tempted by the thought that de l'Eclin was clever enough to make himself a part of the deception.

The French waited. Why, Sharpe wondered, if this was their main attack, would they signal it so obviously? He looked south again, seeing how the shadows darkened and lengthened. He stared at the rutted road and scanned the hedgerows. Something moved in a shadow; moved again, and Sharpe clapped his hands in triumph. 'There!'

The Riflemen twisted to look.

'Cazadores, sir.' Harper, knowing that he disappointed Sharpe's expectations, sounded subdued.

Sharpe pulled open his telescope. The approaching men were in Spanish uniform, suggesting that they were either the southern picquet bringing news or else one of the parties that had gone south-east to break down the bridges over the river. Or perhaps they were disguised Frenchmen? Sharpe looked back at the chasseur, but de l'Eclin was not moving. There was something very threatening in his utter stillness; something that spoke of a rampant and chilling confidence.

Sharpe obstinately clung to his certainty. He knew that his men no longer believed him, that they prepared themselves to fight the enemy who paraded so confidently in the west, but he could not surrender his obsession with the south. Nor could he rid himself of the conviction that de l'Eclin was too subtle a soldier to put all his hopes in a straightforward and unsubtle attack.

Sharpe opened his telescope to inspect the horsemen who came slowly from the south. He swore softly. They were Spaniards. He recognized one of Vivar's Sergeants who had white side-whiskers. The mud on the horses' legs and the picks strapped to the Cazadores' saddles showed that they were a returning bridge-breaking party.

'Damn. Bloody hell and bloody damnation!' He had been wrong, utterly wrong! The Spaniards who approached from the south had just ridden clean through an area which should have been rife with de l'Eclin's seven hundred missing men. Sharpe had been too clever by half! 'Fetch the men out of the houses, Sergeant.'

Harper, relieved at the order, ran down the slope and Sharpe turned his glass back to the west. Just as he settled the long tube and adjusted the barrels to focus the image, Colonel de l'Eclin drew his sabre and Sharpe was momentarily dazzled by the reflection of sunlight from the curved steel.

He blinked the brightness away, remembering the moment when de l'Eclin had so nearly cut him down by the bridge. It seemed so long ago now; before he had met Vivar and Louisa. Sharpe remembered the black horse charging and his astonishment as the superbly trained beast had swerved right to allow the Colonel to hack down with a left-handed stroke. A man did not expect to face a cack-handed swords-man, and perhaps that explained why so many soldiers were superstitious of fighting against a left-handed opponent.

Sharpe peered through the telescope again. Colonel

de l'Eclin was resting his curved blade on his saddle pommel, waiting. The horses behind him moved restlessly. The sun was sinking and reddening. Soon a flag would be unfurled in Santiago's cathedral, and the faithful would plead with a dead saint to come to their country's aid. Meanwhile, a soldier of the Emperor's favourite elite waited for the charge that would break the city's defences. The feint and the attack, Sharpe realized, would both come from the west. These three hundred horsemen would draw the defenders' fire while the rest of the Dragoons, hidden in the dead ground, prepared a sudden lunge that would burst from the fog of powder smoke like a thunderbolt.

Harper was urging the Riflemen uphill. 'Where do you want them, sir?'

But Sharpe did not answer. He was watching Colonel de l'Eclin who cut the sabre in flashing practice strokes, as though he was bored. The sun's reflection from the gleaming blade provoked a ragged and inaccurate volley from the city's defenders. De l'Eclin ignored it. He was waiting for the sun to become a weapon of awesome power, dazzling the defenders, and that moment was very close.

'Sir?' Harper insisted.

But still Sharpe did not answer for, at that very instant, he had a new certainty. He knew at last what the French planned. He had been wrong about the southern attack, but if he was wrong now then the city, the gonfalon, and all his own men would be lost. All would be lost. He felt the temptation to ignore the new knowledge, but to hesitate was fatal and the decision must be taken. He slammed the telescope shut and pushed it into his pocket. He kicked the sacks of caltrops. 'Bring them, and follow me. All of you!'

'On your feet!' Harper bawled at the Riflemen.

Sharpe began to run. 'Follow me! Hurry! Come on!' He cursed himself for not seeing the truth earlier. It was so God-damned simple! Why had the French moved the supplies into the palace? And why had Colonel Coursot stacked grain and hay in the cellars? A cellar was no place to store forage a day or so before it was to be distributed! And there was the business of a thousand horsemen. Even a soldier as experienced as Harper had stared at the Dragoons and been impressed by their numbers. Men often saw a horde where there was only a small force, and how much easier it was for a civilian to make that mistake in the middle of the night. Sharpe ran even harder. 'Come on! Hurry!'

For the city was almost lost.

The cathedral's nave was plainer than the exterior of the building might suggest, but the plainness did not detract from the magnificence of its pillared height. Beyond the long nave, the domed transepts, and the screen was a sanctuary as sumptuous as any in Christendom, and still sumptuous even though the French had torn away the silverwork, wrenched down the statues, and ripped the triptychs from their frames. Behind the altar was an empty void, the space of God, that this dusk was lit by the scarlet rays of the setting sun which slashed through the cathedral's dusty and smoky interior.

Beneath the altar and above the crypt where the saint lay buried, the opened strongbox stood before the altar.

From the top of the dome which covered the meeting of transepts and aisle, a great silver bowl hung from ropes. It smoked with incense that filled the huge church with a sweet and musty smell. A thousand candles added their smoke to make the shrine a place of mystery, scent, shadows and hope; a place for a miracle.

Two hundred people knelt in the transepts. There were priests and soldiers, monks and merchants, scholars and friars; the men who could carry a message throughout Spain that Santiago Matamoros lived. They would tell an invaded people that the due obeisance had been made, the proper words said, and that the great gonfalon, which had once flared above the massacre of pagans, had been unfurled again.

It was as if Drake's Drum was at last beaten, or the soil of Avalon erupted in a violent darkness to release a band of woken knights, or as if Charlemagne, roused from his sleep of centuries, drew his battle-sword again to drive away the enemies of Christ. All nations had their legend, and this night, in the great ringing vault of the cathedral, Spain's legend would be stirred from a thousand years of silence. The candles shivered in a cold wind as the robed priests bowed before the altar.

As they bowed, one of the cathedral's western doors banged open as though a violent wind had snatched the wood and crashed it against stone. Feet pounded on paving. The soldiers who knelt before the altar twisted towards the sound and reached for their swords. Louisa, kneeling veiled beside Blas Vivar, gasped. The priests checked their words to see who had dared to interrupt the invocations.

Vivar stood. Sharpe had burst into the cathedral and now appeared beneath the Gate of Glory. The Spaniard ran down the long nave. 'Why are you here?' There was outrage in his voice.

Sharpe, wild-eyed, did not reply. He stared about the cathedral as though expecting to find enemies. He saw none, and turned back to the western doors.

Vivar reached out a hand to stop the Rifleman. 'Why aren't you at the barricades?'

'He was holding his sabre in his right hand!' Sharpe said. 'Don't you understand? His right hand! Colonel de l'Eclin's left-handed!'

Vivar stared uncomprehendingly. 'What are you talking about?'

'There are three hundred of the bastards out there,' Sharpe's voice rose to echo from the tall stone of the nave, 'only three hundred! And none to the south. So where are the rest? Did you look behind the sacks in the cellars?'

Vivar said nothing. He did not need to.

'Did you search the cellars?' Sharpe insisted.

'No.'

'That's why your brother's there! That's why they wanted a truce! That's why they saved the supplies! That's why they had the place prepared! Don't you see? De l'Eclin is in the palace! He's been there all day, laughing at us! And he's coming here!'

'No!' Vivar's tone did not imply disagreement, only horror.

'Yes!' Sharpe pulled himself from Vivar's grasp. He ran back through the Gate of Glory, oblivious of its majesty, and tore open the cathedral's outer doors.

A shout of triumph and a trumpet's peal of victory turned him back. Sharpe saw, dim through the smoke and incense, a flag unfurl. Not an old, threadbare, motheaten flag which crumbled to the air, but a new and glorious white banner of shining silk, crossed with red; the gonfalon of Santiago, and as it spread, so the bells began to ring.

And, at the same instant, the sledgehammers drove down the planking which had locked the French into the palace. The bells rang for a miracle, and the French, as they had always intended, broke their truce.

* * *

French Dragoons attacked from either side of the palace. They must have come from the rear gates of the building, where the stables lay, and as the infantry debouched from the central door, the horsemen burst into the western plaza. The only obstacle to their charge was the low barricade where a handful of dismounted Cazadores fired a ragged volley, then fled.

'Sergeant! Caltrops!' Sharpe shoved Harper towards the cathedral's southern flank and, seizing two of the sacks himself, shouted at his men to follow him to the northern plaza.

Cavalry could not climb the intricate flights of steps at the cathedral's western front. Instead the Dragoons planned to surround the shrine, so that no one inside could escape. 'Rifles! Hold your fire! Hold your fire!' Sharpe knew there was no point in wasting a volley. Instead the caltrops must hold up this first French onslaught.

It was a threateningly high jump from the platform on the cathedral's façade to the plaza, but Sharpe had no time to use the steps. He jumped, falling so heavily that a stab of pain shot up from his left ankle. The pain had to be ignored for defeat was as close as a Dragoon's sword reach. His men followed him, grunting as they dropped to the flagstones.

Sharpe dragged the sacks north. He could see the horsemen to his left and he knew he had only seconds to spread the vicious spikes across the gap beneath the bridge which led to the bishop's palace. 'That way! Wait for me!' he shouted at his Riflemen, then swung the first sack so that the caltrops clattered and fanned across the narrow space. 'Join me, Sergeant!' Sharpe shouted at Harper, but his voice was drowned by the shouts of the French and the scream of their war trumpets. He seized the second sack and shook it loose. The metal spikes rolled and fell, scattering to block the narrow passage.

Harper had disappeared. Sharpe turned and ran after his men. The bells were clanging overhead. A trumpet was shrieking its defiance at the sky. He did not know if the Sergeant was safe, or whether he had blocked the entrance to the plaza at the cathedral's southern flank.

'Form line! Two ranks!' Sharpe shouted at his desk. Beyond them, in a tumble of panic, men fled from the cathedral's western transept.

The first horse pierced itself on a spike. The iron went into the frog of its hoof, and then more horses came. They reared, screamed, and lunged in desperation from the pain. Men fell from saddles. A horse, made frantic with agony, bolted back across the plaza. Another reared so high that it toppled backwards and its rider shouted as he fell under the horse's collapsing body.

'Hold your fire!' The Riflemen had formed a line fifteen yards short of the caltrops. It was a race now. The French infantry would be climbing the western steps to flood into the cathedral. It would take at least a minute for them to reach the door from the transept and erupt behind Sharpe's back. Some of them, seeing the agony of the horses, had come to kick the iron spikes away. They were led by a Sergeant. 'Hagman?' Sharpe said. 'Kill that bastard!'

'Sir.' Hagman knelt, aimed, and fired. The Sergeant somersaulted backwards in a jet of blood from his chest. The infantry noticed the Riflemen for the first time. 'Fire!' Sharpe shouted.

The volley was small, but it drove more chaos and pain into the narrow space. 'Reload!' There was no point in shouting at the greenjackets to hurry.

They knew as well as Sharpe how fragile was the balance between survival and death in this darkening city, and to shout them to speed would merely fluster them.

Sharpe turned. The last of Vivar's congregation was running down the steps. A Spanish officer carried the gonfalon that had been hastily drawn into shining loops. Two priests gathered up their skirts and ran eastwards. Louisa appeared on the steps and Sharpe saw two Cazadores bring her a horse. Vivar pulled himself into his own saddle and drew his sword. 'They're in the cathedral!' he shouted at Sharpe.

'Steady, lads. Fix swords!' As the bayonets were drawn, Sharpe looked around for Harper, but the Irishman was still nowhere to be seen. There were screams within the city. Trumpets were shrill in the evening air. It would be cold tonight. A frost would silver the flagstones where the French would take their revenge for the insults of this day.

'Steady now, lads!' The caltrops had delayed the enemy and his men were reloaded, but a mass of mounted Frenchmen still waited beyond the spikes that were being frantically cleared by infantry. Carbine bullets cracked above the Riflemen, but the Dragoons fired from the saddle and aimed too hurriedly. Sharpe knew he only had seconds. He cupped his hands. 'Sergeant! Sergeant Harper!'

'Retire, Lieutenant!' Vivar shouted at Sharpe.

'Sergeant Harper!'

'Bastard!' The voice came from the top of the steps that led into the southern transept. Sharpe whipped round. After distributing his caltrops, Harper must have known he could not reach Sharpe by running across the cathedral's western front. Instead he had taken the short cut through the cathedral and now appeared with

327

a French officer in his left hand. 'Bastard!' The Irishman was in a fury. 'He tried to kill me, the bastard!' He kicked the Frenchman, hit him, then turned and flung the man back into the cathedral's darkness. Vivar, seeing more shapes beyond the doors, fired a pistol into the transept.

'Sir!' Hagman warned that the last caltrops were being cleared.

'Present!' Sharpe shouted. 'I thought I'd lost you!' he called out to Harper.

'Bugger tried to stick a sword into me! In a church, God damn it! A cathedral. Can you credit it, sir?'

'Jesus Christ! I thought I'd lost you!' Sharpe's relief at Harper's survival was heartfelt.

'Sir!' Hagman warned again.

Dragoons and infantry were mixed together in the charge that was funnelled into the narrow space beneath the bridge. Swords were lifted, men shouted their war cry, and the French spurred to vengeance. 'Fire!' Sharpe called.

The volley flayed into the narrow space, tumbling horses in blood and pain. A fallen sword clanged and scraped across the stone. The horsemen who followed hacked with their swords to clear a passage through the wounded and dying. Infantry appeared at the top of the cathedral's southern steps.

'Run!' Sharpe bellowed.

Then was the chaos of flight. The Riflemen sprinted across the plaza to the dubious refuge of a narrow street. Louisa was gone ahead and Vivar, surrounded by a knot of his scarlet-coated elite, shouted at Sharpe to follow her. The Cazadores would stay to meet the French attack.

The Riflemen ran. The retreat from the city had become a mad scramble in the dusk, a plunge downhill through the tight medieval streets. Sharpe led his men into a small plaza decorated with a well and a stone cross. The exits from the plaza were jammed with refugees and he halted his men, formed them into ranks, and allowed the rear rank to tap load their rifles. The men poured in powder, spat the bullet after, then hammered the rifle butt on the ground in the hope that the impact would jar the bullet down. 'Present!'

The rifles, their muzzles weighted with sword bayonets, came up. They could not fire yet, for their aim was blocked by the handful of Cazadores who tried to delay the French Dragoons. Swords clashed in the street with a sound like cracked bells. A Spaniard, blood streaming from his face, spurred away from the fight. A Dragoon screamed as his belly was ripped with a sword.

'Major!' Sharpe shouted to Vivar that the rifles were ready.

Vivar slashed at a Frenchman, then turned away from the riposte. 'Go! Lieutenant! Go!'

'Major!'

A Cazador went down under a French blade. Vivar lunged to wound the Frenchman. It seemed to Sharpe that the Spaniard must be overwhelmed when suddenly a rush of volunteers in their brown tunics erupted behind the Dragoons and attacked them with knives, hammers, muskets, and swords. Vivar wrenched his horse around and shouted at his men to retreat.

Sharpe had backed his own Riflemen to the eastern edge of the small plaza and now he split them to let the Spaniards through. The volunteers did not want to retreat but Vivar beat them back with the edge of his sabre. Sharpe waited till the plaza was clear and the first enemy appeared at its far side. 'Rear rank! Fire!'

The volley was feeble, but it checked the French rush.

'Back!' Sharpe drew his sword, knowing he had cut it too fine.

The Riflemen followed Vivar into the next street. It was darker now as the day slipped towards a winter's night. Muskets fired from the windows above Sharpe, but the small volley could not prevent the French from flooding into the narrow street.

'Behind you!' Harper called.

Sharpe turned. He screamed his challenge and swung the heavy blade at a horse's face. The beast swerved, the pig-tailed Dragoon chopped down, but Sharpe had parried quickly and the two swords clanged together. Harper lunged with his bayonet to the horse's chest and the animal reared, blocking the street, and Sharpe slashed at one of its fetlocks. His sword must have broken bone for, as the horse came down, it collapsed. The Dragoon tried to chop at Sharpe as he fell, but the Rifleman's sword was hissing up, driven with all his strength, and the steel sliced into the cavalryman's neck. Blood spurted in a sudden spray that spattered from the gutter to ten feet high on the whitewashed wall of the alley. The broken-legged and screaming horse blocked the street. 'Run!' Sharpe shouted.

The Riflemen ran to the next corner where Vivar waited for them. 'That way!' He pointed to the left, then spurred in the other direction with his handful of Cazadores.

The Riflemen ran past a church, rounded a corner, and found themselves at the top of a steep flight of steps leading to a street that ran behind a stretch of medieval city wall. Vivar must have known the steps would offer safety from the Dragoons' pursuit, and had sent them to find refuge while he stayed behind to check the French fury.

Sharpe ran down the steps, then led his men along

the street. He had no idea if Vivar was safe, nor if Louisa had escaped, nor even if the gonfalon had survived the turmoil in the narrow streets. All he could do was take the salvation Vivar had offered. 'That bastard was a clever bugger!' Sharpe said to Harper. 'Inside the city all the time! Christ, he must have been laughing at us!' Doubtless, after Louisa had seen the Frenchmen parade in the plaza, de l'Eclin and most of his men had simply returned to the rear of the palace while a few hundred of the Dragoons had ridden south. It was clever, and it had led to this shambles. There was no honour in it, none, for the French had broken the truce, but Sharpe had seen what little honour there was in this bitter war between Spain and France.

'Fighting in a bloody cathedral!' Harper was still indignant.

'You did for him, anyway.'

'For him! I did for three of the bastards. Three bastards who won't fight in a cathedral again.'

Sharpe could not help but laugh. He had reached a break in the city wall which opened into empty countryside. The ground fell steeply there, leading to a stream that was a slash of silver in the gathering dusk. Refugees were fleeing across the stream, then climbing towards the hills and safety. There were no Frenchmen in sight. Sharpe presumed that the enemy were still embroiled in the streets where Vivar fought his hopeless delaying action. 'Load,' he ordered.

The men stopped and began to load their rifles. Harper, evidently recovered from his indignation at French impiety, checked with his ramrod halfway down the barrel. He began to laugh.

'Share the joke, Sergeant?' Sharpe said.

'Have you seen yourself, sir?'

The men also began to laugh. Sharpe looked down

and realized that his trousers, torn already, had ripped clean off his right thigh. He tore at the rotten scraps of cloth until his right leg was virtually naked. 'So? You think we can't beat the bastards half-dressed?'

'They'll run away in fright if they see you, sir,' Gataker said.

'All right, lads.' Sharpe sensed from their laughter that the men knew they were safe. They had escaped the French, the battle was over, and all they needed to do was cross the small valley and climb into the hills. He looked back once, hoping to see Vivar, but the street was empty. Screams, shouts, shots, and the clangour of steel told of the battles which still filled the inner city, but the Riflemen had slipped through the chaos to this safety. Nor was there any merit in returning to the fight. The duty of every man now was to escape. 'Straight across the valley, lads! We'll stop on the far ridge!'

The greenjackets left the cover of the wall, walking down through the rough, steep pasture which led to the boggy stream where, only this morning, Sharpe had neglected to placate the water spirits. In front of them, and scattered thick throughout the valley, was a mass of refugees. Some were civilians, some wore the ragged brown tunic of Vivar's volunteers, and a few were Cazadores who had become separated from their squadrons. There was still no sign of Vivar, nor of Louisa, nor of the gonfalon. Two monks, their robes clutched high, waded the stream.

'Shall we wait, sir?' Harper, anxious for Major Vivar's safety, wanted to stay by the stream.

'On the far bank,' Sharpe said. 'We can give covering fire from there.'

Then a trumpet called from the south, and Sharpe turned to find that it was all over. The adventure, the hopes, all the impossible dreams that had come so very close to triumph, were done.

Because, like gold heated to incandescence, the helmets of the enemy flared in the dying sun. Because three hundred Frenchmen had ridden around the city, Sharpe was trapped, and the day of miracles was done.

CHAPTER 18

The Dragoons, who had menaced the west of the city, had ridden around its southern margins to block the eastern escape route. Now they filled the valley to the south where their helmets glowed bright in the day's last light. They were led by the horseman who wore de l'Eclin's red pelisse, but who carried a sabre in his right hand.

The refugees began to run, but the boggy ground made their panicked flight clumsy and slow. Most tried to cross the stream, some went north, while a few ran towards the dubious safety of Sharpe's Riflemen.

'Sir?' Harper asked.

But there was nothing helpful that Sharpe could say in answer. It was over. No safety lay in the tumult which still echoed within the city, nor was there time to cross the stream or retreat northwards. The Rifles were in open ground, trapped by cavalry, and Sharpe must form a rally square and fight the bastards to the end. A soldier might be beaten, but he never grovelled. He would take as many of the triumphant bastards as he could and, in years to come, when French soldiers crouched by camp fires in some remote land, a few would shudder to remember a fight in a northern Spanish valley. 'Form up! Three ranks!' Sharpe would fire one volley, then contract into the square. The hooves would thunder past, the blades slash and glitter, and slowly his men would be cut down.

Sharpe cut at a weed patch with his sword. 'I'm not going to surrender, Sergeant.'

'Never thought you would, sir.'

'But once we're broken, the men can give up.'

'Not if I'm watching them, sir.'

Sharpe grinned at the big Irishman. 'Thank you for everything.'

'I still say you punch harder than any man I've ever known.'

'I'd forgotten that.' Sharpe laughed. He saw that some of the dismounted Cazadores and volunteers had run to form crude extensions of his three ranks. He wished they had not come, for their clumsiness would only make his final stand more vulnerable, but he would not turn them away. He slashed his sword left and right as though practising for the last moments. The French Dragoons had checked their slow, menacing advance. Their front rank stood motionless a quarter-mile away. It looked a long distance, but Sharpe knew with what cruel speed cavalry could cover the ground when their trumpeter hurled them forward.

He turned his back on the enemy and looked at his men. 'What we should have done, lads, is gone north.'

There was a moment's silence, then the greenjackets remembered the argument that had driven Harper to try and kill Sharpe. They laughed.

'But tonight,' Sharpe said, 'you have my permission to get drunk. And in case I don't have another chance to tell you, you're the best damned troops I've ever fought with.'

The men recognized the apology for what it was, and cheered. Sharpe thought what a long time it had taken him to earn that cheer, then turned away from the Riflemen so they would not see his pleasure and embarrassment.

He turned in time to see a knot of horsemen ride from the city. One of them was the Count of Mouromorto, distinctive in his long black coat and tall white boots. Another, in a red dolman jacket and with hair as gold as the Dragoons' helmets, rode a big black horse. The waiting French Dragoons cheered as Colonel de l'Eclin took his pelisse and colback from the man who had worn them. The Count rode to the rear squadron, the French reserve, while the chasseur took his proper place at the very front of the charge. Sharpe watched as he adjusted the scarlet pelisse on his shoulder, as he crammed the big fur colback on his head, and as he drew the sabre with his left hand. Sharpe prayed that he would see de l'Eclin dead before he himself went down under the hooves and blades of the enemy.

'Lieutenant!'

Sharpe turned to see Louisa ride up to the rear of his men. 'Go!' He pointed eastwards to where there might be safety. Her horse would give her a speed that was denied to the refugees on foot. 'Ride!'

'Where's Don Blas?'

'I don't know! Now go!'

'I'm staying!'

'Sir!' Harper shouted the warning.

Sharpe turned back. Colonel de l'Eclin's sabre was raised to start the French advance. There was sodden ground to the right of the Dragoons, and a steep slope to their left, so the charge would be constricted into a channel of firm ground that was about a hundred paces across. A few muskets flickered flame beyond the stream, but the range was too long and the flank Dragoons ignored it.

Colonel de l'Eclin's sabre dropped, and the trumpeter sounded the advance. The leading squadron walked forward. When they had gone fifty yards, Sharpe knew, the second French line would start their slow advance. The third line would stay another fifty yards behind. This was the classic cavalry attack, leaving enough space between the lines so that a fallen horse in the front rank did not trip and bring down the horses behind. It was slow at first, but very menacing.

'Front rank, kneel!' Sharpe said calmly.

The Dragoons walked their horses, for they wanted to keep their dressing tight. They would accelerate soon, but Sharpe knew they would not spur into a gallop until just seconds before the charge crashed home. Musket shots and screams sounded from the city, evidence that Spaniard still fought Frenchmen in the darkening streets, but that battle was no longer Sharpe's concern.

Colonel de l'Eclin raised the sabre in his left hand and the first squadron went into the trot. The trumpet confirmed the order. Sharpe could hear the cavalry now. He could hear the jingle of curb chains, the slap of saddle flaps, and the thump of hooves. A guidon reared above the front rank.

'Steady, lads, steady.' There was nothing else Sharpe could say. He commanded a ragged line of men who would resist for an instant, then be ridden over by the big horses. 'Are you still there, Miss Louisa?'

'Yes!' Louisa's nervous voice came from behind the ranks of Riflemen.

'Then, if you'll forgive me, bugger off!'

His men laughed. Sharpe could see the Dragoon's pigtails bouncing beneath the darkening helmets. 'Are you still there, Miss Louisa?'

'Yes!' This time there was defiance in her voice.

'It isn't gentle, Miss Louisa! They'll hack about like bloody butchers! They may not even notice you're a girl till they've sliced half your face away. Now bugger off! You're too pretty to be killed by these bastards!'

'I'm staying!'

Colonel de l'Eclin raised his sabre again. Sharpe could hear the creak of saddles now. 'Hagman? That cheating bastard is yours.'

'Sir!'

Sharpe forgot Louisa. He crammed himself between two of his front-rank men and held his sword high. 'Wait for my word! I'm not going to fire till the bastards are breathing down our necks! But when they come we're going to make these sons of whores wish they hadn't been bloody born!' The approaching horses tossed their heads nervously. They knew what was coming, and Sharpe allowed himself a moment's pity for the butchery that he must inflict. 'Aim at the horses!' he reminded his men. 'Forget the riders, kill the horses!'

'For what we are about to receive,' Harper said.

Riflemen licked powder-gritted lips. They nervously checked that the rifle pans were primed and the flints well seated in the leather-lined dogheads. Their mouths were dry and their stomachs tender. The vibration of the trotting horses was palpable in the soil, like the passing of great guns on a nearby road. Or, Sharpe thought, like the tremor of thunder on a sultry day that presaged the stab of lightning.

Colonel de l'Eclin lowered his curved blade in the signal for his men to go into the canter. In a few seconds, Sharpe knew, the trumpet would call for the gallop and the big horses would surge forward. He took a breath, knowing he must judge the moment for this one volley to exquisite perfection.

Then the lightning struck.

*   *   *

338

There were only just over fifty men, but they were Vivar's elite company, the crimson-coated Cazadores, who burst from the city to charge downhill. It was a tired squadron, wearied by a night and day of fighting, but above them, like a ripple of glory in the dark sky, flew the gonfalon of Santiago Matamoros. The scarlet cross was bright as blood.

'Santiago!' Vivar led them. Vivar spurred them on. Vivar screamed the war cry that could snatch a miracle from defeat. 'Santiago!'

The slope gave the Cazadores's charge speed, while the banner gave them the courage of martyrs. They struck the edge of the first French line like a thunderbolt and the swords carved bloody ruin into the Dragoons. De l'Eclin was shouting, turning, trying to realign his men, but the banner of the saint was driving deep into the French squadron. The gonfalon's long tail was already flecked with an enemy's blood.

'Charge!' Sharpe was running. 'Charge!'

The second French squadron spurred forward, but Vivar had foreseen it and swerved right to take his men into their centre. Behind him was a chaos of milling horses. Cavalry hacked at cavalry.

'Halt!' Sharpe held both arms out to bar his men's mad rush. 'Steady, lads! One volley. Aim left! Aim at the horses! Fire!'

The Riflemen fired at the untouched horsemen on the right of the French charge. Horses fell screaming to the mud. Dragoons kicked boots from stirrups and rolled away from their dying beasts. 'Now kill the bastards!' Sharpe screamed the incantation as he ran. 'Kill! Kill!'

A rabble of men ran to the broken French line. There were Riflemen, Cazadores, and country men who had left their homes to carry war against an invader.

Dragoons hacked down with long swords, but the rabble surrounded them and slashed at horses and clawed men from their saddles. This was not how an army fought, but how an untutored people took terror to an enemy.

Colonel de l'Eclin swivelled his horse to keep the rabble at bay. His sabre hissed to kill a Cazador, lunged to drive a Spaniard back, and sliced to parry a Rifleman's sword-bayonet. The Dragoons were being driven to the boggy ground where the horses slithered and slipped. A trumpeter was dragged from his grey horse and savaged with knives. Knots of Frenchmen tried to hack through the mob. Sharpe used both hands to hack down at a horse's neck, then swung back to send its rider clean from the saddle. A woman from the city sawed with a knife at the fallen Frenchman's neck. Fugitives were running back from the stream's eastern bank, coming to join a slaughter.

A trumpet drove the third French squadron into the chaos. The field was bloody, but still the white gonfalon floated high where Blas Vivar drove his crimson elite like a blade into the enemy. A Spanish Sergeant held the great banner that had been hung from a cross-staff on a pole. He waved it so that the silk made a serpentine challenge in the dusk.

The Count of Mouromorto saw the challenge and despised it. That streamer of silk was everything he hated in Spain; it stood for the old ways, for the domination of church over ideas, for the tyranny of a God he had rejected, and so the Count raked back his spurs and drove his horse into the men who guarded the gonfalon.

'He's mine!' Vivar yelled again and again. 'Mine! Mine!'

The brothers' swords met, scraped, disengaged.

Vivar's horse turned into the enemy as it was trained to, and Vivar lunged. The Count parried. A Cazador rode to take him in the rear, but Vivar shouted at the man to stay clear. 'He's mine!'

The Count gave two quick hard blows that would have driven a weaker man from the saddle. Vivar parried both, back-cut, and turned the cut into a lunge that drew blood from his brother's thigh. The blood dripped onto the white boots.

The Count touched his horse with a spur; it went sideways, then, to another touch, lunged back. Mouromorto snarled, knowing that this battle was won as his long sword lunged at his brother.

But Vivar leaned back in the saddle, right back, so that his brother's blade hissed past him and could not be brought back fast enough as he straightened and speared his own sword forward. The steel juddered into Mouromorto's belly. Their eyes met, and Vivar twisted the blade. He felt pity, and knew he could not afford pity. 'Traitor!' He twisted the blade again, then raised his boot to push the horse away and disengage his long sword. The steel shuddered free, blood gushed onto the Count's pommel, and his scream was an agony that died as he fell onto the blood-soaked mud.

'Santiago!' Vivar shouted in triumph, and the shout was carried across the small valley as the Cazadores rallied to the banner of the dead saint and raised their swords against the third French squadron.

The Riflemen were hunting among the remnants of the first two squadrons. Dragoons were turning their horses to flee, knowing they had been beaten by the savagery of the attack. A Cazador's sword opened the throat of the French standard bearer, and the Spaniard seized the enemy guidon and raised it high in celebration of victory. Colonel de l'Eclin saw the capture of the small flag and knew that he was beaten; beaten by the great white gonfalon of Matamoros.

'Back!' The chasseur knew when a fight was hopeless, and knew when it was better to save a handful of men who could fight again.

'No!' Sharpe saw the Colonel order the retreat, and he ran towards the Frenchman. 'No!' His ankle still hurt from his jump from the cathedral platform, the pain made his run ungainly and the soggy ground half tripped him, but he forced himself on. He outstripped his Riflemen and still shouted in frustrated anger. 'You bastard! No!'

De l'Eclin heard the insult. He turned, saw Sharpe was isolated from the greenjacketed men and, as any cavalry officer would, he accepted the challenge. He rode at Sharpe, remembering when he had fought the Rifleman before that he had used the simple ruse of switching his sabre from right to left hand. That stratagem could not be repeated, instead the Colonel would rowel his horse at the last moment so that the black stallion surged into a killing speed that would put all its momentum behind his sabre stroke. Sharpe waited with his sword ready to swing at the horse's mouth. Someone shouted at him to jump aside, but the Rifleman held his ground as the big black horse bore down on him. De l'Eclin was holding his sabre so that its point would spear into Sharpe's ribs, but in the very last second, just as the spurred horse surged for the kill, the Frenchman changed his stroke. He did it with the quickness of a snake striking, raising and turning the blade so that it would slash down onto Sharpe's bare head. De l'Eclin shouted in triumph as his sabre came down and as the Rifleman, whose sword had missed his horse, crumpled beneath that stroke.

But Sharpe had not cut at de l'Eclin's horse. Instead, with a speed to match the chasseur's own, he had raised the strong blade above his head and held it there like a quarterstaff to take the sabre's impact. That impact drove Sharpe down, almost to his knees, but not before his right hand released the sword's hilt and snatched for the chasseur's sword arm. Sharpe's sword thumped on his own shoulder, driven by the deflected sabre-blade, but his fingers had seized de l'Eclin's wrist strap. He released the sword blade from his left hand and hooked his fingers about the Frenchman's wrist.

It took de l'Eclin a second to realize what had happened. Sharpe was clinging on like a hound that had sunk its teeth into a boar's neck. He was being dragged along the boggy ground. The horse twisted and tried to bite the Rifleman. The chasseur hammered at him with his free hand, but Sharpe hung on, tugged, and tried to find a purchase on the soggy ground. His naked right leg was smeared with mud and blood. The horse tried to shake him loose, just as Sharpe tried to drag the Frenchman out of the saddle. The sabre's wrist strap was cutting like wire into his fingers.

De l'Eclin tried to unholster a pistol with his right hand. Harper and a group of greenjackets ran to help. 'Leave him! Don't touch him!' Sharpe shouted.

'Bugger him!' Harper slammed his rifle butt at the black horse's mouth and it reared so that de l'Eclin lost his balance and, with Sharpe's weight pulling him backwards, fell from the saddle.

Sword-bayonets rose to slash down at the Frenchman. 'No!' Sharpe screamed desperately. 'No! No!' He had fallen with de l'Eclin and, thumping onto the ground, had lost his grip on his wrist. The Frenchman twisted away from Sharpe, staggered to his feet, and slashed his sabre at the Riflemen who surrounded him.

Sharpe's sword was lost. De l'Eclin glanced to find his horse, then lunged to kill Sharpe.

Harper fired his rifle.

'No!' Sharpe's protest was drowned by the hammer of the gun's report.

The bullet took de l'Eclin clean in the mouth. His head jerked back as though yanked by an invisible string. The Frenchman fell, the blood fountaining up into the darkening sky, then his body flopped onto the mud, jerked once more like a newly landed fish, and was still.

'No?' Harper said indignantly. 'The bastard was going to fillet you!'

'It's all right.' Sharpe was flexing the fingers of his right hand. 'It's all right. I just didn't want a hole in his overalls.' He looked at the dead man's leather-reinforced overalls and tall, beautifully made boots. They were items of great value, and now they were Sharpe's. 'All right, lads. Get his bloody trousers off, and his boots.' The Riflemen stared at Sharpe as though he was mad. 'Get his bloody trousers off! I want them. And his boots! Why do you think we came here? Hurry!'

Sharpe, though Louisa and a dozen other women watched, stripped off his old boots and trousers where he stood. The last of the light was draining from the sky. The remnants of Dragoons had fled. The wounded moaned and scrabbled at the damp grass, while the victors moved among the dead in search of plunder. One of the Riflemen offered Sharpe the glorious pelisse, but he declined it. He did not need such frippery, but he had desperately wanted the red-striped overalls which fitted him as though they had been tailored just for him. And with the overalls came the most precious of all things to any infantryman: good boots. Tall boots

344

of good leather that could march across a country, boots to resist rain, snow, and spirit-haunted streams, good boots that fitted Sharpe as if the cobbler had known this Rifleman would one day need such luxuries. Sharpe prised away the razor-edged spurs, tugged the boots up his calves, then stamped his heels in satisfaction. He buttoned his green jacket and strapped on his sword again. He smiled. An old flag, made new, flaunted a miracle of victory, a red pelisse lay in the mud, and Sharpe had found himself some boots and trousers.

The old gonfalon, Louisa told Sharpe, was sewn into the new. She had done the work in secret, in the high fortress, before she had left Santiago de Compostela. It had been Major Vivar's idea, and the task had brought the Spaniard close to the English girl.

'The Sergeant's stripes,' she said, 'are made from the same silk.'

Sharpe looked at Harper who walked ahead with the Riflemen. 'Don't tell him, for God's sake, or he'll think he's a miracle worker.'

'You're all miracle workers,' Louisa said warmly.

'We're just Rifles.'

Louisa laughed at the modesty which betrayed such a monstrous pride. 'But the gonfalon worked a miracle,' she said chidingly. 'It wasn't such nonsense, was it?'

'It wasn't nonsense,' Sharpe confessed. He walked beside her horse, ahead of Major Vivar and his Spaniards. 'What happens to the gonfalon now?'

'It goes to Seville or Cadiz; wherever it will be safest. And one day it will be returned to a Spanish King in Madrid.' Already, in the small villages and towns through which the Riflemen marched, the story of the gonfalon was being told. The news raced like a fire in parched grass; telling of a French defeat and a Spanish victory, and of a saint keeping an ancient promise to defend his people.

'And where do you go now?' Sharpe asked Louisa.

'I go where Don Blas goes, which is wherever there are Frenchmen to be killed.'

'Not Godalming?'

She laughed. 'I do hope not.'

'And you'll be a Countess,' Sharpe said in wonderment.

'I think that's better than being Mrs Bufford, though it's uncommonly nasty of me to say so. And my aunt will never forgive me for becoming a Catholic, so you see some good has come from all this.'

Sharpe smiled. They had come south, and now they must part. The French were left behind, the snow had melted, and they had come to a shallow valley above which the February wind blew cold. They halted at the valley's rim. The far crest was in Portugal, and on that foreign skyline Sharpe could see a group of blue-uniformed men. Those men watched the strangers who had come from the Spanish hills.

Blas Vivar, Count of Mouromorto, dismounted. He thanked the Riflemen one by one, ending with Sharpe whom, to Sharpe's acute embarrassment, he embraced. 'Are you sure you won't stay, Lieutenant?'

'I'm tempted, sir, but,' Sharpe shrugged.

'You wish to show off your new trousers and boots to the British army. I hope they let you keep them.'

'They won't if I'm sent back to Britain.'

'Which I fear you will be,' Vivar said. 'While we are left to fight the French. But one day, Lieutenant, when the last Frenchman is dead, you will come back to Spain and celebrate with the Count and Countess of Mouromorto.'

'I shall, sir.'

'And I doubt you will still be a Lieutenant?'

'I imagine I will, sir.' Sharpe looked up at Louisa, and he saw a happiness in her that he could not wish away. He smiled and touched his pouch. 'I have your letter.' She had written to her aunt and uncle, telling them they had lost her to the church of Rome and to a Spanish soldier. Sharpe looked back at Vivar. 'Thank you, sir.'

Vivar smiled. 'You are an insubordinate bastard, a heathen, and an Englishman. But also my friend. Remember that.'

'Yes, sir.'

Then there was nothing more to say, and the Riflemen filed down the hill towards the stream that was the border with Portugal. Blas Vivar watched as the greenjackets splashed through the water and began to climb the further slope.

One of the men waiting on the Portuguese crest was impatient to discover who the strangers were. He scrambled downhill towards the Riflemen, and Sharpe saw that the man was a British officer; a middle-aged Captain wearing the blue coat of the Royal Engineers. Sharpe's heart sank. He was coming back to the strict hierarchy of an army that did not believe ex-Sergeants, made into officers, should lead fighting troops. He was tempted to turn, flee back across the stream, and take his freedom with Blas Vivar, but the British Captain shouted a question down the hillside and the old constraints of discipline made Sharpe answer it. 'Sharpe, sir. Rifles.'

'Hogan, Engineers. From the Lisbon garrison.' Hogan scrambled down the last few feet. 'Where have you come from?'

'We got separated from Moore's army, sir.'

'You did well to get away!' Hogan's admiration

seemed genuine, and was spoken in an Irish accent. 'Any French behind you?'

'We haven't seen any in a week, sir. They're having a hell of a time from the Spanish people.'

'Good! Splendid! Well, come on, man! We've got a war to fight!'

Sharpe did not move. 'You mean we're not running away, sir?'

'Running away?' Hogan seemed appalled by the question. 'Of course we're not running away. The idea is to make the French run away. They're sending Wellesley back here. He's a pompous bastard, but he knows how to fight. Of course we're not running away!'

'We're staying here?'

'Of course we're staying! What do you think I'm doing? Mapping a country we intend to abandon? Good God, man, we're going to stay and fight!' Hogan had an ebullient energy that reminded Sharpe of Blas Vivar. 'If the bastard politicians in London don't lose their nerve we'll run the bloody French clear back to Paris!'

Sharpe turned to stare at Louisa. For a moment he was tempted to shout the good news, then he shrugged it off. She would learn soon enough, and it could change nothing. He laughed.

Hogan led the Riflemen back up the hill. 'I suppose your Battalion went back to England?'

'I don't know, sir.'

'If it went to Corunna or Vigo, it did. But I don't imagine you'll join them.'

'No, sir?'

'We need all the Rifles we can get. If I know Wellesley he'll want you to stay on. It won't be official, of course, but we'll find some cranny to hide you in. Does that worry you?'

'No, sir.' Sharpe felt a burst of hope that perhaps he

348

would not be doomed to a Quartermaster's drudgery again, but could stay and fight. 'I want to stay, sir.'

'Good man!' Hogan stopped at the hilltop and watched the Spaniards ride away. 'Helped you escape, did they?'

'Yes, sir. And they took a city from the French, not for long, but long enough.'

Hogan looked sharply at the Rifleman. 'Santiago?'

'Yes, sir.' Sharpe sounded defensive. 'I wasn't sure we should help them, sir, but, well . . .' He shrugged, too tired to explain everything.

'Good God, man! We heard about it! That was you?' It was plain that this Captain of Engineers would make no protest at Sharpe's adventure. On the contrary, Hogan was clearly delighted. 'You must tell me the story. I like a good story. Now! I suppose your lads would like a meal?'

'They'd prefer some rum, sir.'

Hogan laughed. 'That, too.' He watched as the Riflemen walked past him. The greenjackets were ragged and dirty, but they grinned at the two officers as they passed, and Hogan noted that though these men might lack regulation shoes, and though some had French greatcoats rolled on French packs, and though they were unshaven, unwashed, and unkempt, they all had their weapons, and those weapons were in perfect condition. 'Not many escaped,' Hogan said.

'Sir?'

'Of the men who were cut off from Moore's retreat,' Hogan explained. 'Most just gave up, you see.'

'It was cold,' Sharpe said, 'very cold. But I was lucky in my Sergeant. The big fellow there. He's an Irishman.'

'The best are,' Hogan said happily. 'But they all look like good lads.'

'They are, sir.' Sharpe raised his voice so every tired

man could hear the extravagant praise. 'They're drunken sods, sir, but they're the best soldiers in the world. The very best.' And he meant it. They were the elite, the damned, the Rifles. They were the soldiers in green.

They were Sharpe's Rifles.

HISTORICAL NOTE

The retreat to Corunna was one of the most gruelling exploits ever forced onto a British army. The miracle of the retreat was that so many men survived to turn and repel a French attack outside the port. Sir John Moore died in the battle, but his victory gained enough time to let the surviving troops embark on the ships sent to save them.

The French had succeeded in driving Britain's army, all but for the small Lisbon garrison, from the Peninsula. It was heralded in Paris as a victory, which it was, though no one seemed to notice that the campaign had drawn French troops away from their primary task which was to complete the invasion of Spain and Portugal. That invasion was never completed. Yet, in February 1809, few people could have foreseen that failure, and only a handful believed that Britain, after the defeat of Moore's campaign, should keep a military presence in the Peninsula.

Yet, in the spring of 1809 Sir Arthur Wellesley, one day to be known as the Duke of Wellington, took command of the Lisbon garrison that was slowly, even grudgingly, expanded into the army that was to win a string of remarkable victories which would end with the invasion of France itself. Those victories form the framework of the Richard Sharpe books, which have already taken Sharpe and Harper into southern France.

This, then, is an early story, told against the background of the brutal French occupation of Galicia. That much of the book is accurate. The French did capture Santiago de Compostela, and did sack its cathedral, and did fight vicious battles against the growing resistance in the Galician hills. The rest, alas, is fiction. The scholars even tell us now that the romantic derivation of Compostela from the Latin *campus stellae*, 'field of the star', is also a fiction. They say the name truly derives from the Latin word for a cemetery. It is often wise to ignore scholars.

Marshal Soult was supposed to conquer all of Portugal before the end of February 1809. Racked by supply problems and tormented by partisans, he could only reach as far as Oporto on the northern bank of the Douro river, in northern Portugal, from which defence line he was to be ejected by Sir Arthur Wellesley in May. Then, having driven the French from Portugal, Wellesley turned east into Spain to gain the first of his Spanish victories, Talavera. Other British victories would follow, some astonishing in their brilliance, but those victories obscured (at least to the British) that far more Frenchmen died at the hands of the Spanish people than in battle against the British. The Spaniards were overwhelmingly partisans who fought the *guerrilla*, the 'little war'. Those *guerrilleros* fought *La Guerra de la Independencia* as the Spanish call the Peninsular War, and some of their enemies were indeed *anfrancesados*.

Sharpe and Harper, though, are now bound for Talavera. From Talavera to France is a long way, but that elite of the British army, the greenjacketed Rifleman, marched every step of the way, and when it became necessary, he foot-slogged from Waterloo into Paris itself. Sharpe and Harper have yet to complete either journey, so they will march again.